NO ORDINARY ANGEL

By C.C. Guice

The First Born Saga

Book Two

This is a work of fiction. Names, characters, places, and incidents either are the product of the author's imagination or are used fictitiously. Any resemblance to actual persons, living or dead, events, or locales is entirely coincidental.

Copyright © 2008 by C.C. Guice

Cover art by Benjamin Ezra Cremer
ISBN 978-0-578-00238-5

Other Available Titles

By C.C. Guice

BEING WERE

The First Born Saga

Book One

What Dreams Remember

To those who dreamed with me

To those who believed in me

Thank you for helping me see what you see

~*Prologue*~

In the beginning, that which is and had always been, looked upon the vast void that was, and was not pleased; so it was that the spark of all things, which are and were, was created. Of this spark also rose up the First Father and the First Mother, and from them came that which we are.

Now the First Father and the First Mother came to displease that which had created them, and they were cast down. We that had become of them, however, had not displeased, and were not, therefore, cast down. . . . We remained as we were: in the image of our Creator.

Now that which had created all things, loved all things, and was displeased also that they had fallen from grace, and sought to provide for them a way to redeem themselves.

So it was that we that had become of the First Father and the First Mother became absorbed, viewing this strange punishment the Creator had set down that is being human and those attempts that were made to return to His divine grace. Hence in our fascination we did not yet question what we were. . . .

Many an age passed and we began to wonder at ourselves. Being neither limitless as that which had created us, nor so limited as humanity which passed constantly before us.

We called to that which was and had always been, asking of Him, "What then shall we be?" Yet we heard no answer. So it was that we remained what we were. . .neither Creator nor human, neither angel nor devil, neither animal nor plant, but things ever changing, ever learning. . . and ever listening for an answer...

And when, after time unnumbered, there still came to our hearing no answer, we moved in our discontent out into the world, seeking to find a place in humanity. To capture some portion of the Creator's vision as the humans had done....

No Ordinary Angel

Part 1

~1~

Discovering Angels

Angel!

Now, after five hundred years of searching, I had finally discovered where she was. I would have her back at any cost.

I *will* have my Angel back!

I had no other thought than this as I threw off all the energies which gave me my form and flew up and up, leaving the earth behind me. The world became to me only an awareness of a great mass of energy swirling in the distance below me. After all of my long years of holding on to her as one of my only reasons, an anchor to keep me from doing just this very thing when the sheer dust of my years sought to overwhelm me, I too was now ascending. Yet this was no ordinary ascension into the Empyrean. I was not intent on escaping the earth and the constant barrage of joy and pain, hope and sorrow, it offered the living. I was intent on retrieving another, and bringing her back to it with me.

I had within me a consuming need to find my Angel, she that had been so many things to me: my pupil, my friend, my love waiting to be loved. It was that force of will which drove me upward, far away from all I knew and the security of its being; from all I was sure of, into what I could only dream.

I had gone howling blindly upward as my soul screamed its want of her. I had been so consumed by my desire to find her that I drove my soul, like a blade, deep into the soul of another. I had not even been aware that I had come near to it. Now I was deeply submerged within a soul as familiar to me as my own, and I could find no thought or word to describe the feeling of it.

Except, "Master?"

Then suddenly all the old wounds, the anger, the loneliness, salted by him having abandoned me so very long ago, were torn open afresh. Every half remembered pain or hurt delivered to me, by every question he had ever left me without an answer for, came back like torturous ghosts floating up unbidden out of their graves. From deep within me, it all reawakened and returned to me; every deeply buried memory come back now to haunt me and move my tongue to angry condemnation.

But then, that is a later part of this tale...

For now I will say only that it was he, whom I had once called Master, who told me my Angel was indeed there. It was he who calmed and comforted me, slowing me in my mad flight and showing me the first of many ironies. It was he that then set me back on my path to finding her.

I had swept out my inner vision then, eager to find my Angel. My soul had slid, silently, calmly then, out across the quiet plain of the Empyrean and I knew it for what it truly was. This was more than a mere resting place for the tired souls, those like my Angel and my Teacher, which had not truly died, but rather, chosen not to live anymore. It was indeed a place of refuge for those that sought such escape from the pain of living lifetime after lifetime without relief from the living itself that this plane offered.

There was more though, much more, there were those there who seemed completely unaware they were existing at all, those who slept within their souls and knew not a single thought. I knew the truth then, Angel had been right in what she had written and left for us to find. Her journal had delivered us unquestionable truth. Here were Changelings who had ascended for no other reason than they had believed they were dying. Here, sleeping in the Empyrean, were the Druids and Werewolves and lord-only-knew-what-else of old. All those Changelings who had not known what they were, who had changed throughout their lifetimes, constantly revitalizing their energies, but had created for themselves bodies that would age and die or were vulnerable to things they would not naturally have been, slept here. These had come to this plane for no other reason than they had believed it was their time to die.

I cringed in my soul as I thought of all these unfortunate, uninformed Changeling souls, who had been told they would die when their heads were severed or they were ran through with silver. Those who had left off their lives as Werewolves, or other such "cursed" creatures and ascended to this place, simply because they had believed it was the way of things. A good many of those I passed had most likely never known what they really were or could truly do. They had more likely lived out tortured existences as "cursed beings" much as my friend Baylor had for far too long. I prayed then that he was learning the right of things even now, by reading Angel's journal while I was here looking for her.

Suddenly I felt the familiar feel of her soul and immediately I knew yet another truth. Then, better than I could have ever hoped to when disguised in the flesh, I recognized her for who she was. I felt my Master's words course through me again and knew their truth. No ordinary Angel this one. I knew the feel of that soul, had always known it. I had longed for the closeness of it nearly every second of my very long life, and for that eternal moment both our souls had remembered that and more.

God what a blind fool I felt then.

Angel!

There, before me, floated two Yelms, now, for once, peacefully shared by a single soul. Two wills who once fought within my Angel for control of her mind. Had she not written of her "mean, English accented, inner monologue," had it not quite often been of a different mindset than she had, at least consciously? She had written of it beginning to escape the

7

normal confines of her head upon meeting me, and it had grown in strength throughout our time together. Angel had spoken of having two different thought processes running simultaneously at times, especially when around me. Now I understood why.

I also understood suddenly, how it was that she had enough force of will to steel the Yelm of another. I knew now why she had so often thought of herself as "the goddess of my painting" and the "mean little English voice" had condemned my stupidity and hinted at being willing to reveal more than just the cause of Baylor's curse when she was ready.

There, before me, floating peacefully were two Yelms, for one soul.

A soul I had once called Seraphim.

Under normal circumstances, when searching for another soul, I would have had a care not to make contact with it until I had discerned whether it was of a nature akin to my own. It is a wariness I had practiced long and always told my pupils to practice. I had managed to avoid all the others who inhabited this place, but it seemed almost as though I had been being pulled unconsciously toward this soul without my having known it. These may be useless excuses but I tell you these were most definitely not normal circumstances.

Nothing about anything between the two of us had ever been normal, if there is such a state. The sudden brushing of ones soul with another could have had frighteningly different effects, I warn you, especially when the other soul has no warning such a thing can and is about to occur. Even calmed after conversing with my Master, I was still desperate to finally find her, touch her. I had not taken the proper precautions, I admit.

We were blessed though, I guess we had always been blessed and had just never realized how much. I thank the Creator that it did not go as dreadfully wrong as it could have.

I had found her though and the manner in which I had done it was quickly forgotten as I flew toward her, with more force of will than I had ever known could exist within one soul, and thankfully she did not retreat from me. She did not fear or take flight from me, or try to withdraw in any manner. It seemed to me then as though I was divinely forgiven of any and everything I had ever done wrong, or even thought to; better spoken, I felt I had never even been blamed.

When we touched I felt no fear or condemnation in her, only an all-encompassing acceptance and forgiveness that felt divine. We were one, and it felt right and natural, familiar in a way I haven't the language to convey to you. But I knew, Angel knew, it had not been the first time our souls had touched and taken part in that incredibly comforting knowledge, nor could it be the last.

Memories had served us two Changeling well this time; rather than leading us down separate roads to private despair, they had led us to the final recognition of each other.

Suddenly I had to have her with me once more, in the flesh, and in my arms. I had to feel her loving me again as I did her. I had to get her back into the world, so she might hear with her own ears from my own lips all I had longed all these years to tell her.

I submerged myself within her. She wrapped her soul around mine. We had collided in an explosion of raw emotions and rather than spinning out and away it seemed the universe that was we two began to condense. No name could I have given those emotions, had my Master asked me then. There was in me a feeling like I have never known. A surge of love so deep it was like a tidal wave, washing away over two millennia of hurt and loss and loneliness. With it came a will between us both, to have flesh again, to hold each other, to talk about all things new and old that we longed for the other to know.

Suddenly I felt the energy which is balled together as the earth, close to me, coming up so swiftly beneath us I barely had time to acknowledge it. I felt her soul one with mine, and it consumed my awareness. I did not care then if we were become a falling star destined to collide with the earth and go up in flames or not. For in that moment we were so closely melded together none could have told us apart, we were truly one and the being together, feeling that love, was Heaven, there is no other word.

Then we were flesh and bone again and in each other's arms, in our house on Elm Street. I know not whether it was my will or hers or both combined, only that we had won. The laws of the universe had bowed once more to the will of a Changeling. It had taken us home and given us form.

There were no words at first. As I just held on to her and kissed her all over her beautiful face, holding her wonderful little head in my hands that it might never be lost to me again. I worshiped every remembered contour as it had appeared and molded so perfectly into my hands

It was sometime later, when the kisses had turned softer and quite a bit more intense and I had slid my arms down her back, pulling her body even closer to mine, that I realized we were not alone.

I heard Baylor's, "Ahem!" as he politely cleared his throat.

I came to myself and took notice of my surroundings, and so did Angel. It was the most beautiful sound I have ever heard when she began to laugh. It always has been. I looked around myself in amazement, still not releasing her from my arms. I was afraid still, I believe, that she would disappear again. Again that is probably a useless excuse.

Baylor stood a few feet from us, his huge form dominating the empty dining room. His flaming red hair and beard looking impeccably unkempt as ever, he still wore the odd collection of random braids and leather thongs tied up in it, as he had since the day I met him, nearly two thousand years before in the Highlands of Scotland. His deeply blue eyes smiled their joy at my having returned as promised.

"Wow! How long was I gone?" I asked.

I could smell fresh coats of paint and lacquer. The walls and floor had been repaired. I spun again with Angel still grasped close to me, to see that all of the house within my view had been repainted and the floors redone. I spun with her again, and saw the holes I had made in the floor and walls had been fixed. Some few odd furnishings had been placed in the living room, but I didn't care. She was in my arms and that was what mattered.

Angel was laughing all the harder now and it dawned on me that I had swung her back and forth in my arms as I viewed the transformations to our new home. It felt so good to hold her and hear her laughter again that I forgot myself once more and just stared at her beautiful little face. I was just lowering my head to kiss her again when I was again interrupted.

"Ahem," I heard for the second time, as Baylor tried once more to get my attention, only not as politely as the first attempt. "I missed the lass too, ya stingy bastard."

So it wasn't only my return that had his eyes shining. He had given up any attempt at tactfully standing with his back to the foyer awaiting his turn as I continued to hoard her. Finally I released her, remembering myself with a laugh, and she ran into his arms. He swept her up into a great bear-like hug and swung her around the still empty space that would someday be a dining hall again, much as I had just been doing.

"Gods, I missed you, Lass," he said finally. "You gave us quite the long goose-chase."

He had slipped thoughtlessly back into his old Scottish brogue, giving her a final squeeze and setting her back down to her feet. I knew from having read so much of her soul through her journal, that hearing such a thing had done her heart no end of good just then.

I looked at her fully then, now at that short distance from me, taking in my first real view of her in nearly five hundred years. As her feet came back down to the wooden planks of the floor, I saw that she was barefooted, as ever, and my heart jumped a little. I felt a fresh surge of love for her sweep through me again and it felt like a lump of it was condensing heavily in my chest and throat.

She looked up then at Baylor, absolute excitement evident all over her beautiful face. "I have the best of news for you," she said happily. "I have longed to tell you forever..."

"I know, Lass, I read your journal," he said, smiling.

Then he changed before us, becoming a huge black Great Dane, perfect down to the whip-like tail and the drool hanging from his too loose jowls. We both stared in amazement as he sat down there in the empty room, tail sweeping happily back and forth across the bare wood floors, and barked

11

at us as if demanding dinner. The rich depth of the sound was only further heightened as it echoed around the unfurnished space.

"Oh, hell!" was all I could manage in my shock as I jumped at the unexpected noise.

It was Angel who found her voice first and said it right for both of us.

"I had always hoped I was right, but I wasn't positive till now. This is wonderful!" she said, happily clapping her hands.

She was reminding me of a happy little girl that had just been introduced to her new-found favorite pet, and I could not help but laugh out loud when she furthered that train of thought by bouncing forward with a mischievous grin and patting him on his massive head.

"Good boy!" she laughed, then she threw her arms around his neck and looked up at me, batting her black lashes and feigning innocence into her playful query. "Can we keep him?"

"Yes, but how..," I stumbled.

My words, when they had finally come, died off, I could find no way to finish my still swirling thoughts. It dawned on me it had sounded like I was telling her she could keep him when really I had meant, "Yes it is wonderful he is a Changeling, but how did he get other forms down so fast?" And suddenly I was laughing too.

It seemed too much was happening too fast and I could not keep up with any of it. I had prayed she had been right and that this would be exactly what I would return to, and yet the actuality of it had thrown me for quite the loop. I had known this huge beast of a man for more lifetimes than I could count right then and never seen him change into anything but a Werewolf. As a matter of fact, I had never even seen him change of his own volition. Yet there he was, of his own free will, or better yet because of that free will, sitting before me in another form.

I stared at him in awe as though I had never seen such a thing before and had not even known it was possible. Then Baylor shook his massive Great Dane head, sending its huge un-cropped ears flapping loudly and drool flying everywhere. Again the sound of Angel's laughter let loose and made mine all the more heartfelt and happy. Baylor too reformed before us and joined in, no longer able to keep himself from displaying his mirth in that very human manner.

"Well, our Angel writes a pretty good Changing for Dummies book," he said, still laughing. "I couldn't rightly mess it up this time." He tried hard to sober but a huge grin split his face all over again as he reached forward to wipe a spot of drool from my t-shirt, and he burst out laughing again.

"This is wonderful!" Angel repeated, and then she added jokingly, "I should publish."

"Actually that's not a bad idea," Baylor said thoughtfully. "Save me having to kill any more Changelings that think they're Werewolves." He wiped his hand carelessly off on his own jeans, ridding it of the drool, then looked up at her again. "If others could fix themselves, like I did, it would save a lot of them from me."

Angel again laughed, not taking him seriously and again I fell in love with the sound. We all stood there then, just looking at each other, alternating between laughter and hugs as some memory or other tickled us. I was reminded of the old times when we had laughed always, telling each other tales to entertain, and constantly caught up in some jest. We had filled our home that was a cave, in the Highlands of Scotland, with such happy sounds endlessly. It might have only been a few weeks that we had been together there but we had fit a lifetime of the good kind of memories into them. I looked about at this, our new home, and was again reminded of my earlier and still unanswered question.

"How long was I gone?" I asked again.

"Four or five days," Baylor replied, smiling. "I might have lost one reading but I figured I'd get a head start getting the place fixed up before the two of you returned. I found it an impossible mess with nary a thing in the cupboards and not a single soft place to sit."

"That long? How'd you know for sure I'd make it back?" I asked him.

Not really thinking, I reached out and pulled Angel back into my arms and she came just as thoughtlessly against me. Her back was pressed into my chest, as I rested my chin on top of her head, waiting for his response. Baylor smiled then, looking at the two of us, and I realized what I had done, that I had done it without thought. I knew then exactly what she had meant by the strange level of comfort she drew from my presence. I had to admit now I had felt it too at times, though I had not admitted it to myself back then. Now when I felt it I had unconsciously reached out to take more of it, no longer denying myself the pleasure of it as I had back then, having finally realized that it was right, that I could and should love her.

"Hey," Baylor finally replied, "you gave your word."

He was still smiling at us and there was something odd in his look. Something I had never seen before was alive in his deep blue eyes. I had known him for nearly two millennia now and never had I noted such a look. It seemed a mixture of so many things, I tried to separate and name them. Just as I might have had my Master been there, questioning me again, as he had so often throughout our years together, wanting that each emotion should have a name for him.

Envy?

Happiness?

Understanding?

Hope?

Hope! That was it! That was the difference. Wasn't it? In all our years together I had never seen this in his eyes. At least not like this. Oh, he had kept his faith alive all the time we had searched for Angel, but this, this was different.

"What? What is it, Baylor?" I whispered.

"You know I must ascend now," he replied.

The unwavering determination in his voice chilled me suddenly despite my bliss. I could fathom no reason he should have come to such a conclusion and it be capable of bringing such light to his face.

"But why?" I gasped. "Why would you leave us when we've just found our Angel after searching so long? And you've become a Changeling now, well and truly! You are not a Werewolf any more and Angel is here now..."

My voice faltered, I felt like I was actually going to cry like a child! I searched my mind for any reason why he would want to leave us now, adding, "We are a family again, Piper and the twins will be here soon..."

I was heart-broken.

I could not understand. All my overwhelming joy at finally having found Angel was suddenly overshadowed by Baylor's unexpected announcement. I just couldn't grasp it. He was no longer cursed, we were all together again after five hundred years of waiting and searching, and now, out of nowhere, he was going to leave us. What about all the happy meals and reunion parties we had planned together?

Worse yet, somehow, his look, his happy shining eyes, said I should be happy about it.

"That's just it, Demon! You have found her and brought her back, safe into your arms," he said, smiling at me.

He was acting like I should be happy he was going to do this, as though I should have seen this coming and been prepared to bid him a pleasant farewell.

"Now I will go and find my Edana and I will tell her as Angel told me," he said.

"But," I began, but he never let me finish.

"Until we swear again," he said, and then he was gone.

~2~

Stories Later

"But," I had begun again.

I was thinking to finish my sentence whether he was there to hear it or not. Angel began laughing anew and I was confused by her mirth.

"What is so funny?" I asked her.

"He does no better with 'buts' than you," Angel said, still laughing. "You are two of a kind. Just as stubborn and strong willed as I, it must run in our family."

Angel turned within my arms, tilting her head up to better look me in the eye. I suppose she saw some worry still there for she slipped her arms around me and squeezed me then.

"He will be fine!" she said with compete faith clearly evident in her voice. "He is Baylor, he will be all right!"

I forgot completely whatever I had intended to say then, realizing she was right. She had to be right for I could not allow myself to conceive of the possibilities if she were not. Her mouth was suddenly far more interesting than thinking of how I might have to try to go and retrieve him as well, and whether or not I could succeed again. Her lips hovered just inches below mine, full and inviting as she smiled the confidence in her statements up at me. I began to sink toward them and no other thoughts could have surfaced then had they wanted to.

"How did you find me?" she asked.

I pulled back slowly, both mentally and physically, to better focus upon her whole face. I found myself having to concentrate very hard on the fact she had just asked me a question. My thoughts, I must admit, had been quite a bit elsewhere. I still had not really looked away from her inviting lips when my brain finally managed to come up with what I felt was a perfectly acceptable and appropriate answer given my current state of mind.

"I've only just found you and already you want stories?" I asked grinning.

"Of course! I want to know what took you so long," she replied, just as amused.

"A tale is it? You'll have to earn it then," I joked, pulling her in even tighter and kissing the tip of her nose.

"Well, I would hope so!" she said laughing as well, having read my mind. Then turning a good bit more serious she questioned again, "What took you so long?"

Okay, so I wasn't joking.

I swept her up into my arms and carried her into the living room, to find if Baylor had chosen comfortable seating for our new home. We were still laughing when I laid her down on the only available couch, but we both sobered quickly as we found not only the comfort of a well-chosen piece of furniture.

We awoke near dark that evening, having spent the entire day discovering things other than how I had come to find her, falling in and out of peaceful sleep whenever it came to claim us. Angel tilted her head up as it lay on my shoulder, and kissed me on my chin. Then she got up, walking through the house to the kitchen, not bothering to clothe herself. I knew then, if I hadn't already, that life was a marvel when one knew love, and I most definitely knew love.

Angel returned with a bottle of wine and two glasses. Baylor had obviously purchased some essential items for the kitchen as well. He had been a very busy man while I had been gone searching for her.

17

She put her hand over the cork, seeming to think little of what she was doing, and it worked itself out, flying the short distance into her palm by simple obedience to her will. I watched in amazement as she proved once more that mayhap nothing was truly impossible for such as we, unless we ourselves made it impossible with our disbelief. Then pouring us each a glass, she offered one to me. I sat up and accepted it, raising it in salute.

"To no ordinary angel," I said.

"And no common demon," she replied.

She smiled at our shared memory, reminding me of the first time we had met, after I changed her on the banks of a stream in Scotland and she had pronounced my name wrong on purpose. Saying it like demon instead of the proper pronunciation more like Day-moan, the "d" being more a "th." I clarify this now for those of you who do not know us already through her. Thinking back to those times I was suddenly aware of how stupid I had been and all the years I had wasted.

"I should have known back then," I said aloud. "That you were Seraphim come again..."

I recalled my Master's words and again wondered why had I not seen this. Why had it been so difficult to realize she had been known to me by more than one name? We had traveled in the same circle in more than one lifetime. My Angel was Seraphim, she was Angelica, she was my Love. By either name, in either life, I had known and loved her deeply.

A part of Angel had always known and fought to understand it, but it seemed she did not blame either of us for not having realized it before. In that moment, when our souls had made their sudden wonderfully shocking contact in the Empyrean, it seemed that not only had she too known of a certainty who she was and had been, but also who I was and that I loved her.

I was speechless, as my mind whirled in the relentless riptide, swimming blindly through the flood of remembrances and grasping to make sense of each of them. I remembered how I had heard her soul calling out not just for change itself, as she had lain beaten and dying on the banks of a stream, but how it had somehow seemed to call specifically for me. I remembered the oddity of having heard it, knowing I should not have because of how far away she had been. I recalled how amazed I had been when I had finally made it there, that she had resisted the pull of the light for that long. I recalled then vividly what it had been like to be bared in my soul, standing in the shadows behind her as she had stared sightless at the light, wondering what it was that I would say to this beautiful soul to convince it to remain on earth with me.

How many times after that, when she had accepted me and I had taken her under my wing and begun to teach her of Changelings, had I fought back the urge to be with her as more than her teacher, to kiss her? How often had I told myself no and yet sat in wonder of her strange way of bringing comfort not only to others but to me, to my very soul? How often in her writing had she spoken with confusion of my soul being a familiar thing, imagined herself so often as Seraphim in my painting? How many times had her subconscious mind hinted to her of her past, seeming to have repeatedly tried to tell her who she had been.

We had both been deaf, dumb and blind.

I wondered why it was that I, of all people, had not known it was so.

I had let my loyalty to a lover's memory blind me to the fact I was denying that same lover, my love, when she had come back for it. The scope and irony of it astounded me and again my purpose called to me: to love, to love *her*.

I would show her I loved her now as I had loved her then, when she was Seraphim. She had been right in what she wrote, she had been born to love me just as I had been, always, for her. I would make it up to her for having been such a fool. We had lost a lot of time but not any more, we would be together now, always.

I squeezed her tightly.

She seemed to know instantly what I had been thinking, for she smiled sweetly, "We both missed many obvious things back then. How many arguments did I have with myself as my subconscious hinted at having deeper secrets to tell me when I was ready. That we have loved in more than one lifetime seems the least of our oversights now. It does not matter anymore though, none of it does. We are together and safe, that is what counts. Soon Baylor will return and we will make up for all of it."

"Aye, together," I said.

She leaned back against me and we drank our wine quietly for a time.

"Not coffee, then?" I asked her, recalling she had mentioned developing a great love for that drink in the journal she had left us.

"Not now," she laughed. "Now is a time for wine."

I could not have agreed more. I had developed a definite appreciation for coffee as well but I was enjoying my wine then and my love of coffee is another thing that comes later on in this story. So I ran my free hand through her long black hair, idly enjoying the feel of its silky length, as it slid between my fingers. For I knew it would not be long before she would demand her tales from me. It took her longer than I thought it would, though. It seemed Angel, too, was simply enjoying the comfortable silence and wine.

"Well?" she said.

Okay, maybe not, just biding her time, she had obviously learned a little patience somewhere along the line. I laughed as she tilted her head up to me again, expectantly awaiting her answer. So, kissing her on her forehead, I decided I would give in, but only after I had had a little more fun.

"Well, what?" I said, feigning ignorance.

"Ugh! You said..," she griped, and swatted my bare thigh with the back of her hand.

"Okay, okay, just kidding! Where's your sense of humor?" I laughed.

"If it was up your butt you'd know!" she replied smartly.

Her eyes flew wide as she turned then to fully face me, apparently very surprised this had come out of her mouth. I was just as shocked as she appeared to be and we both started laughing at the same time.

"Sorry," she said finally gaining some control. "I guess I should warn you. I lived in this college town for far too long, with too many drunken students frequenting my hearing. Now when Seraphim's decidedly sarcastic, English-accented input, which I used to call my inner monologue, escapes its proper confines, it will probably tend to be quite shocking."

"And amusing as well," I said, still laughing, effectively letting her know I had not been offended and no apology had been necessary. "Just don't listen if it tries to convince you to go all hellcat and start killing priests again and the three of us will all get along just fine."

"Oh yeah, I did write about that, didn't I?" she said sobering.

"Aye," I said tweaking her nose. "But I don't blame you for it and I bet Baylor loved it. You know how he loves a good tale of vengeance."

I was momentarily worried she would grow pensive, having been reminded of her worst moments, but she shocked me yet again by kissing me soundly on the lips and then rolling onto her back again, snuggling close. Thus pressed up against me with her head nestled into my shoulder again, she seemed to simply set it aside and lose herself in the present and the more comfortable things it offered.

"You reminding me of your inner monologue reminds me of something," I said remembering, "You know I had thought often how it was that you were able to yank that other Changeling's Yelm from it. I wonder still if it might have something to do with that. Though you are the same soul, you spoke of often having two totally separate thought processes going when around me. One, your own, and the other, your inner monologue, which we know now is the part of you that remembered being Seraphim. It provided an alternate train of thought: older, wiser, more capable of seeing to the heart and truth of things, unhampered by reality and what you saw or were raised to think. That part of you seen beyond and offered a different view of things. I wonder if somehow that side of you took that Yelm for its own, making you stronger, it stronger, strong enough to eventually make it clear to all of us who you were and are."

"It is possible, I suppose. It has seemed, at times, that I have had two separate wills at work within me," Angel conceded thoughtfully, "but we may never know."

At this she did grow pensive and I wondered why. "What is it, my Love?" I asked her.

"It is just that I have this strange feeling in me," Angel tried to explain, "a wonder that is so irrational and useless…"

She trailed off and I was forced to prompt her further. "No feeling is useless My Love."

"My Love," she repeated, "That is just it, am I your love? Would you love me, like this, like you are now, had you not known I was Seraphim come again?"

Ahh, now this was indeed a strange dilemma. She was jealous of herself? I recalled some of the conversations she had written of having with herself, part of her telling her I would not love her because she was not Seraphim, even though she was. Conversations in which she seemed to be cruel and self-effacing, like the Seraphim part of her were angry with her for some reason I could not fathom.

"Angel," I tried, "I loved you more than anything when you lived as Seraphim and for nearly two thousand years I mourned your loss. When finally I came upon you again I was still so caught up in that mourning that I couldn't see past it to see it was you. But when I ascended to retrieve you, I went for you, for Angel. That you had been Seraphim all along was a thing I learned only after I was already there for you."

"So you did not yet know I was Seraphim when you risked an ascension to retrieve me?" she asked softly.

"No," I replied honestly, "I did not."

She nuzzled further into my shoulder and sighed and I hoped I had made myself clear enough to appease her. I had no idea if this was over or would continue to haunt her, but for now she seemed content. I was confused by why it should even matter, but a woman's mind is often confusing. Apparently it did matter, though, so I fervently hoped I had given the right response. We lay there for a while, just sipping our wine and listening to each other breathe.

"So how did you find me?" she said.

I took pity on her, as I knew how insatiable her curiosity was, and this was a better thing I thought for her to want to talk about. Actually, truth be known, I took pity on myself, giving her the answers she sought before she tortured them from me. I had not forgotten how lethal she could be with a brush when she wanted a tale and now she had discovered the added leverage of having learned she could conjure one without having to even get up.

"Well, let's see," I began. "Where should I start?"

"Start with what happened when you went to see the Elders. I have often wondered what you learned," she said.

"Ahh, yes, the Elders! Well, I went first to find Santon, thinking of all of them I would find the most honesty from him," I began. "As Piper had told me though, he had no better ideas as to how Edsel had come to disappear than we had. His only thought was as ours had been, that it had been a forced ascension, but again the two of us had met the same problem with this theory as when it had originally formed in the garden. We could not see a forced ascension having been even been possible without both Edsel and himself having been part in the joint will it would have taken to force such a one from our plane into the Empyrean.

"So I had gone to see Kynan and the other Elders, thinking perhaps we had all been looking at it the wrong way. I was slowly coming to see that with Santon's obviously wholehearted belief in forced ascension and Edsel's otherwise unexplainable disappearance, I had to consider it more fully as a true possibility if not a probability. If this was the case then I had to also consider that maybe Lachlan, Cathmore and Kynan were not as alone as we had thought. They may have found others to assist them in the deed, leaving Santon out of the knowing of it and eliminating Edsel, thus effectively reforming the Council to better serve their wishes."

"But," Angel interrupted, patting my thigh again, only gently this time, "the force I felt was not one I had felt in Rome before." She paused for a moment then continued, "Although I seemed to recall something important about those I did feel there when I was in the Empyrean. Just when we knew

I had been Seraphim, right before we collided but I can not recall what that was just now." She furrowed her brow a little as if this bothered her, but finally all she could come up with was, "It's like a dream, you know, the images are fading too quickly and the memories themselves are not so much memories as feelings now. Love is overwhelming throughout but there is fear as well." She grimaced sadly then quickly added, "Anyway, remember? I wrote about some of this for you. The force that attacked me wasn't like any I had come up against before or since, friend or foe, yes that was it and the fear, don't forget the fear..."

"Yes, I remember what you wrote, and I will come to that. Who is telling this story?" I chided.

"Sorry," she replied, instantly contrite.

"Good, you should be," I said laughing. "Now as I was saying before you gave me your 'but'," I continued, smacking her hip playfully. "I was thinking it was possible they had found others to assist them in sending Edsel to a premature ascension. I was still quite sure at that time that our werewolf friend Baylor had been the target of the attacks on our journey to Rome, so this assumption was lending credence to this new belief by providing a motive.

"You see, I thought if they were still upset that the werewolf issue had not been handled as they had thought best, and were still further frustrated by my 'insubordination' of a hundred years before, then they would have had to do away with the only solid voice among them that had stood in constant defense of me and my actions, or lack thereof, as the view might be, on that issue. Only then would they have been able to take what steps they had felt to be appropriate from the beginning to handle it more quickly and decisively.

So I had gone to Lachlan's villa thinking to confront him with these things. I was fully prepared to thrash the truth from all of them concerning both Edsel and Baylor, if that is what it took, and working myself up into a rage in preparation to do so. Only I found all of them worked up as well but for a different reason than expected. All three of them were there, deeply submerged in a confused and heated debate about the same thing. Each one equally very upset and frightened wondering what had happened to Edsel, and if one of them would be next.

I had been met at the door by a very worried looking Kynan and he had drawn me in quickly and hugged me like we were still the best of friends and had never grown apart over the years. If this had not been enough to convince me of their innocence, having the other two swiftly join him to clasp my hands and pat my shoulders surely did. They began instantly offering me refreshments and a comfortable chair hoping I might have answers for them. They were effectively letting me know I had been quite forgiven for walking out on them in the manner I had some one hundred years before.

"Demosthenes, you have heard? What do you know?" Lachlan's excited question came instantly on the heels of handing me my first glass of wine.

"From the looks of things no more than you," I had said.

"Then you have never seen or heard of such a thing?" Cathmore asked.

We had all ended up taking chairs around a large table on which books and random sheets of paper were strewn in apparent disarray. I began glancing briefly at each of these as I sipped my wine and found them to be the Council's histories. One caught my eye almost immediately as it appeared to be a large book recording all of the events that had not as yet been explainable to them. Baring a single word in the old Hebrew, written at the top of both displayed pages as it lay open and easily read: 'unknown.' I pointed at this as I answered him.

"Nay, have you?" I said.

Lachlan was the one to reply, saying, "I have gone over that book more times than I can remember, referencing any event among the Blessed that sounded even remotely similar to what we know of what befell Edsel. I can find no answer there, it is useless."

"The one that suggested we begin the Council in the first place also suggested we keep such records," Lachlan continued, pointing at various volumes around the table as he did. "Who was blessed and when, where they were from and how they might be found, even that record of all unexplainable events was his idea. Yet none of it does us any good now. I have tried to create a list of any of those we have recorded here." At this point he lifted one of the books he'd pointed at earlier in example and I assumed it to be the record of all that had been blessed, then he continued, "I have searched for any that might have cause to come together to do this deed, trying to destroy the order we have created by our existence, but..." he trailed off.

I realized they were, well and truly, as lost as I, and had no hidden knowledge of any of these recent events. Yet there was still the matter of Baylor that I wanted badly to clarify. I worded it as politely as I could so as to cause no further stir among us. I had calmed enough by then to at least have the presence of mind to realize this was a time when we had a mutual need for easy communication.

"So then it was not by any of your command, that I and mine were met with violent opposition on our journey here?" I asked.

"What happened?" Kynan's instant worry answered me better than any of them knew.

"We were attacked three times, by those with evil intent within their souls on our journey here in an attempt to kill the werewolf, Baylor," I said, but even as I said it I began doubting my own words.

Suddenly I recalled when you had said it had appeared to be after one of us and Baylor had only been in the way.

So I added, "Or at least I thought they wanted Baylor's death. But then I was assuming that with Edsel missing, you had all decided to retract your decision to leave the matter of the werewolves in his hands and mine."

"Nay," Kynan said in quick defense. "We have not even considered such old matters. Our minds have been only on finding what is become of Edsel. What time have we to debate such old things with these new ones pressing us so desperately on all sides?"

My old friend seemed to be speaking the truth and I thought about his words for a long time in silence. Finding I did believe him, the only course left to me then was to speak frankly to them of all my thoughts.

"If you had not to do with Edsel's disappearance, and did not send others to destroy Baylor, then it seems I must reconsider every aspect of this. What, think you, happened to Edsel?" I asked then.

"If not for the fact I can compile no list of those sufficiently powerful to have accomplished it, only Piper, yourself and mayhap one or two others were even considerable for such a list," Lachlan replied, taking no insult at my earlier assumptions, and being equally frank about what his own had been. "I would have said it was a forced ascension. His energy is quite randomly left behind. As it is, though, I can only think some powerful harm was done him, forcing him to disperse his energies quickly to flee, and he has not as yet been able to fully recover."

"But," Cathmore added, "we can think of no way in which such a terrible damage could have been done him. As the twins had told Santon, you taught them the art of awareness and they told him they are quite sure none came to the villa. Santon shared all he knows with us and still we can think of nothing that would take one as old and powerful as Edsel so long to recover from."

Cathmore made it clear to me in that manner that they had discovered what I had taught the twins, without their approval. Making it equally clear he held no grudge because of it, by making no further comment about it, or asking what else I may have taught them. I believe this was wholly due to our more pressing dilemma, and had nothing to do with signaling a change in their prior stance on such things.

I thought then of you and how you had stolen the Yelm of the Changeling that had attacked us on our journey here and how it might have been possible the same thing had befallen Edsel. Yet I found myself dismissing this theory as quickly as I formulated it. I think this was due not only to the fact that the twins had sensed no one at the villa, as I had already been told, but also because I could not bring myself to believe Edsel had been so permanently lost to us.

27

The hour had grown late as we spoke, and my mind was not working as quickly as it might have had we had proper rest on the last leg of our journey. I knew the brief stop in the olive grove had not been sufficient to revitalize my wits, as it barely occurred to me now to ask a quite obvious question.

"Are you not the original Council? I mean, Edsel, Santon and yourselves?" I asked. "You mentioned one who suggested the Council be invented in the first place; who and where is that one?"

They looked at each other very perplexed, I think all of them realizing at the same time the value of my question. They seemed also to suddenly recognize their own lack of vision, in not having asked it of themselves.

"Nay," Kynan replied, being first to find his voice. "I was voted onto the Council to replace another. That one, having left a letter telling the others of his intent to ascend a short time after the Council was set. Lachlan brought me up before the others feeling I would be a good replacement because I had been quite some time in his tutelage. It was decided I should take that ascended one's place; he had actually been the original one, not I. Two others also ascended in those early years but were never replaced by any other. The Council was originally seven now it is but four," he ended sadly.

"The one you replaced suggested the Council be formed?" I asked.

"I do not know. I do not think so," Kynan said.

Kynan looked then to Lachlan, waiting for that one to answer me. I did as well, trying very hard at patience. It was good for my heart to see my old friend appearing to take a more active role in his seat in the Council, speaking up of his own volition as he had when we were mortal friends, rather than being the puppet of Lachlan he had been appearing to become. It had broke my heart back then and put much distance between us, when I had first noted that unappealing tendency within him to be so easily led by Lachlan, some five hundred years before. I smiled slightly at my old friend, as memories of us standing up in the Senate and speaking our minds ran through my head distracting me momentarily. Then I looked back to

Lachlan, impatience growing, as he was pushing the books and sheets of paper around in front of him, still looking perplexed.

"The one that suggested we keep these records?" Lachlan said.

"Yes. What of him?" I asked, growing perplexed myself at his odd behavior.

"I do not remember," he said finally. "It seems he joined a conversation we had gathered in a tavern to have. We were all greatly disturbed by all that was occurring, with the rapid growth in numbers of unworthy being blessed. We were trying to discover a way that we might help to fix it. We knew he was a Blessed One but I don't recall any of us having asked his name, we were all quite predictably preoccupied. He had simply come and sat with us at our table and threw in his ideas with ours. They had all seemed good ones so we had adopted them, but..."

He trailed off again and I was thoroughly confused. I could not see any of them, as I knew them, having so readily accepted such advice without a thousand questions having been asked, and months and months of discussion.

"You mean to tell me some random Changeling in a tavern set up the Council as I know it?" I asked, aghast.

"Nay," Cathmore said defensively. "We debated all his suggestions thoroughly and they seemed good ones. He suggested to us how we might solve the problem of all the vile ones being created, by establishing a structure of those allowed to bless others, and taking a vote before it be done. He told us how it might be possible by combining our will to force such evil creations to leave this world; that they not be able to create any more unworthy ones. His suggestions were all good ones, correct? We were able to form this Council and it has fulfilled its purpose well..," he too trailed off.

I was speechless. They had built themselves up around the suggestions of some unknown Changeling. Thank God it had at least been a Changeling. At least they had taken this advisement from one of our own. How could they have built their entire system upon the words of one they didn't even have a name for, a complete stranger to them? I was aghast.

"You mean you have no name for this Changeling? No idea how you might find him again?" I asked, still in shock. "Who was he that you allowed him to sit in such council with you? Why would you accept him so readily?"

"He was a Blessed One," Lachlan said now as he took up the defense of their decisions. "We were desperately trying to find a solution for an extremely difficult problem. He had quite acceptable ideas as to how to solve it. He seemed to have no evil in him and none of his suggestions seemed to have vile ends. He seemed a helpful soul with good intentions and ideas when we were desperately in need of both."

It seemed terribly useless suddenly for me to try to make them see how odd this had been, considering it had been over fifteen hundred years before. They had quite obviously changed their ways and were no longer so open to strangers' input as they had been then, for better or worse. What mattered now was that they had led me to another idea of how to find the answers I sought.

"This one that advised you, do you know where he was from, at least, where he might be found again? I think we should speak to him," I said excitedly, setting my irritation aside for the moment.

"Nay, we never saw him again," was Lachlan's unexpected reply.

Now it was all becoming entirely too irrational, and I was getting very upset.

"So not only did you base the Council's formation, and apparently entire foundation, on this stranger Changeling's idea of how it should be formed to work best. You also took his suggestion for recording such things as names, dates of blessings and probable locations for the finding of all Changelings, and yet did not record this information regarding the very one who told you such record should be kept? What on God's great green earth were you thinking?"

I had raised my voice to an awesome pitch now and they all seemed to want to shrink into the fabric of their seat cushions. As my tirade had only just begun, I stood and started pacing angrily, thinking suddenly of all else I wanted to yell at them while I was at it.

"Now not only have you no way of contacting this one should you have further questions for him, as I do. Oh, I really, truly do, and you should too! Fools, all of you, fools! You neglected to realize he was giving you the most powerful idea Changelings had ever been given." I was ranting now, pacing angrily.

"He told you about forcing an ascension!" I said, turning to slam my hands on the table. "He suggested to you the only known way to rid this world of a Changeling and you let him slip away!" I chose at that point not to mention what you had accidentally discovered, that stealing the Yelm accomplished the same goal. I merely chose to berate them further. "You have apparently lost him, and his obvious wealth of knowledge, quite possibly forever, to the great wide world."

I continued now looking both Lachlan and Cathmore each in turn in the eye as I spoke.

"Now whether he had prior knowledge of such things, being older and wiser than any of us by far, or an extremely genius mind, in either case you were all idiots!" I gritted out. "Do you have any idea what you have done? Think about it!"

I slammed myself back into my seat, thinking about it all as well, the sheer immensity of all of it making me want to yell at them all the more. They had quite probably run across the wisest, possibly due to being the oldest, Changeling to have ever lived and let him slip away. I may not have always approved of their methods but they had worked thus far. The Council had been formed and its goals accomplished swiftly and powerfully. I was appalled to think it had all been due to the extraordinary mind of a single exceptional Changeling, slipping suggestions to them over drinks, in a tavern somewhere, and they hadn't even thought to learn his name. It was Lachlan that broke the brooding silence that had fallen over all of us.

"He did not feel old and powerful," he said, only somewhat defensively.

I think more likely he was trying to excuse it to himself; what he was realizing with the rest of us. They had made a grievous mistake in letting one

31

such as that one be lost to them. I used the twins' trick then, appearing before them as a simpleton and projecting for them the mind and aura of one as well, effectively disguising all my power and making myself for all intents and purposes into a half-wit.

"Then I am the idiot?" I asked.

I pushed myself to my feet then, confident I had made my point. I resumed my own form and bowed to each of them in turn, only without the rudeness I had exuded the last time I had left them. I was frustrated, angry and tired, I had bid them all an exasperated good night and told them I would return if I found any new information to share with them. Once out the door I added that I would be eagerly awaiting the same courtesy from them at the villa with the twins, should they find or remember anything else.

I was still very upset by all these new revelations, running over everything I had learned repeatedly within my now aching head. I had been effectively forced to rethink everything I had thought I knew, not only of the Council itself, but of the reasons for the recent attacks and Edsel's disappearance. It was all incredibly confusing and I chose to walk back, allowing myself this time alone to try and organize my thoughts into something I might derive answers from. Knowing the others would need me to have made some sense of it that I might share with them, I trudged slowly up the cobbled path toward the villa. Yet I was no closer to solving my original problem, and only finding new ones at every turn of a corner in my mind, when I arrived.

~3~

Another Angel Lost

When I arrived it was very late, or rather early, and I was surprised to find Baylor, Piper, Adonia and Adreal all still awake and in the garden talking. You, I was told, had been shown to a bed already, being near to "crumbling". At least that is how Adonia had put it with her ever present flair for drama. I told them all that I was in need of a bed myself. I could see they had all waited up hoping I would return with answers, but knowing I still had none for them, I had pleaded a desperate need of rest.

I had wanted wholeheartedly to be able to return and instantly solve all of our problems, but since this had proved not to be possible, I now simply wanted to rest. I was hoping after a good night's sleep, I might be able to better collate all I had learned, somehow making better sense of things in the morning. I knew it to be unfair of me, but I went off to the room that had once been mine many, many years before, telling myself I would make their having waited up for me up to them later, by figuring it all out tomorrow.

I finally surrendered myself to mental exhaustion and floated happily into the nothingness of a dreamless sleep. I had slept late and been rudely wakened by Baylor, shouting frantically, his voice echoing desperately throughout the house. It had taken me a moment to figure out what he was saying, but I had instantly been frightened by the way in which he was saying it. It was a single word yelled repeatedly.

"Angel!" he yelled out again.

Then my door had slammed open, banging loudly against the wall behind it and vibrating violently as Baylor stood there red-faced and huffing.

"Angel is gone!" he had said.

I sat up instantly, confusion and fear settling in my bones upon seeing his face and stance. I was trying fiercely to wipe the sleep from my brain as well as my eyes but I could not. It refused to make sense to me.

"Gone? What do you mean, gone?" I asked.

"Gone! As in not here!" he had replied frantically.

I had known Baylor a very long time and knew he was not one to panic over just anything. I threw off my covers, instantly awake, and ran out behind him into the common room. There I had found Piper and the twins filling the doorway to another bedchamber. I raced across the room to them. Their stances too were causing my skin to want to crawl off of me, making small bumps race up my arms and my heart, suddenly stopped its frantic beating.

"What? What is it?" I yelled.

But I knew.

I ran frantic into the room where you had slept. You were gone. I could feel all that had been you all over the place, but you were gone. I cannot begin to tell you what had clawed through my guts up to the surface then. I had felt it only one time before in all my many years. I could not have described it then and still cannot.

I had lost a second Angel.

I went blind. I went deaf. I lost all concept of control. I was howling rage at anything that came into my path. I began pulling the sheets from the bed, shredding them and screaming; I know I must have been screaming, for my throat and lungs burned but neither as badly as my soul. Then I sent the whole bed itself crashing over and threw the small table that sat beside it into the wall, watching in a sort of slow motion as it shattered in so many pieces. I broke the small chair over the vanity, then broke the vanity as well. Tossing the bureau onto its side, I kicked it uselessly for I do not know how long. I raged about the room wailing and screaming like a rabid and wounded animal, and at that point I confess I was not much more.

Slowly, very slowly, I took notice of my surroundings, hearing suddenly the distraught crying of Adonia and Adreal's feeble attempts to comfort her, the desperate pleas of Piper to get a grasp upon myself and Baylor. Baylor, over and over again, was begging the gods to give you back, pleading for a bargain, his soul for yours. Big strong solid Baylor, finally reduced to tears. A thing I had not witnessed in countless years and never like this: Baylor, broken and sobbing. Crying, repeatedly, "No, no, not the little Angel."

I was seeing suddenly all the broken pieces that felt still of you. I knew then they could not even come near to how many pieces I was broken into, and the feeling of having you near me in truth. I sunk to the floor and sobbed too then, for I had been a fool. I had been given a second chance and I had pushed it away. I had patted your cheek, like you were a naive child, and pushed you away. I could hear your voice, echoing in my head. "What will happen to me if you are gone?" I could not escape it. Over and over it came hauntingly back to me, and the response. The response I had given you was beyond my heart's ability to accept. Your voice in my head kept dragging me back to the edge. It was Piper who pulled me back. I felt his sure grip on my shoulder trying to still my shaking form, his voice, come to drown yours.

"We will find her," he said. "But you must first gather your wits. You are frightening Adonia and Adreal beyond what you know, and we need you to be strong and present-minded. We need you to be able to help us to solve this."

I looked up then, suddenly seeing the that twins were huddled together shaking and crying. Baylor had lost absolutely all color and was standing, still as death, staring blindly at nothing. Piper's words sunk in then. I could not disintegrate now, I had to be strong. I had to keep us all strong. I had to keep us all safe and figure out what was happening to us before more of us disappeared. I had to solve this riddle and bring you back.

I stood and walked to Baylor, standing directly in front of him, but he did not focus on me when I called his name. I could hear Piper calming and quieting the twins behind me but my attention was more focused upon my friend and I didn't bother to make out his now indecipherable words. I called Baylor's name again. Again I got no response. Finally I took my chances with the pain. I reached up and smacked him across the face.

He came alive instantly, grabbing me by my shoulders and hauling me up, hurling me across the room like I weighed nothing. He came at me, launching himself toward me, a vicious animal wearing my oldest friend's skin. He landed on my chest, grabbing me by the shoulders again and yanking me violently up off the floor, only to slam me even more violently back down. Repeatedly he bashed me into the hard stone floor until it seemed he would slam my soul right out of me.

Then suddenly he started sobbing again, and slowly it became not so much slamming me as lifting and dropping me, as his wailing became more intelligible as words.

"She begged you not to leave her! I couldn't protect her! I could not..," he cried. "I don't even know what happened! How could I protect her? Protect her from what? Why did you leave?"

I couldn't tell what enraged him more, that I had left, that he hadn't been able to stop it, that you were gone and he felt useless. Any one reason was sufficient and I understood them all. I understood his guilt and rage. I understood my own. I was crying again as well, but I was fighting to maintain a grasp on that deep-down knowledge inside me that none of it would do us any good now.

"We will find her," I cried, repeating Piper.

I had to believe it. Baylor had to believe it. We all had to believe it or we would all fall completely apart. I had to remember the twins as well. Edsel was missing in presumably the same manner, and we all had to believe you both could both be retrieved and brought safely back to us. Baylor managed to gain control of himself and got slowly back to his feet. After a moment of slow purposeful breathing, he closed his eyes and exhaled long, then he reached down and lifted me up.

Neither of us made comment, or apologized. It was done.

We walked silently from the room. I limped slowly to Adreal and took him under my arm, leading him as I went. I did not bother to repair my body; in some perverse manner it seemed an appropriate state of being. It seemed I deserved to be in pain. Piper followed with Adonia, and Baylor slowly led the way. It seemed without thought we all ended up back in the garden, as all Changelings seem to. Piper left us briefly, returning with wine, and we all drank deeply, calming ourselves, losing ourselves for a while. Then again it was Piper that put us back on the path.

"What did you learn from the Elders?" he had asked simply.

"That they are all idiots!" I had answered, not looking up.

"Yes, well, we all knew that," he said. "Did you learn anything useful?"

"Yes," I said.

"What?" Piper asked.

I was momentarily angry he would continue his questioning of me, when I so obviously did not wish to speak right now. Yet I realized he too was only trying in his own way to make things right by trying to solve the problem the only way he could, by asking questions and trying to come up with solutions. He too missed Edsel. He too had quite obviously come to adore you as we all had. It was wrong of me to hold it against him that he should disturb my pain trying to fix his own, when our pain was based in the same thing.

"That they, at one time, had access to question one that could have quite probably solved this entire problem for us." I said finally.

"What do you mean?" Piper asked.

"Did you know that the Council was formed and almost entirely based on the suggestions of one Changeling?" I said.

"No. How so?" Piper asked.

Piper and the twins were very interested now, as I had been. I looked to see if Baylor was paying our conversation any heed, but he seemed far more interested in his wine and the grass. Plucking blades at random, examining them, then tossing them away as though they displeased him, he drank deeply. So I left him to them, wishing in some recess of my mind that I could escape into silence and pain as well, as I too drank deeply and then tried to better explain.

"It seems that an either very old and wise Changeling, or an extreme genius of a young one, joined a conversation seven of them were having, "I said. "They had been gathered, trying between them as a small group of friends, to figure out some way in which to solve the problem of the growing population of the unworthy. Not Kynan though, Kynan replaced another of the original seven that had later ascended. This Changling I speak of had invited himself to their table; joining without there questioning of it, if you can believe that, Cathmore, Lachlan, Edsel, Santon and three others I don't even know as they too have ascended; in what we know now was the creation of the foundations of the Council. He even told them how they could solve all these problems, including, I might add, giving them the idea for forced ascension, and then disappeared completely."

"We must find him!" Piper said, as excited as I had been.

"My thoughts exactly," I told him. "Only the idiots never got his name, let alone any ideas as to how to find him."

"What?" Piper said, aghast as well.

"Exactly!" I said.

I took another long draught of my wine. Piper and the twins sat open-mouthed, absorbing the import of all I had just told them. I had no idea Baylor had even been paying attention, let alone taken important notice of something I had missed completely, until he made his unexpected suggestion.

"Let's just kill the rest of them now," Baylor said.

"What?" I said, shocked.

"Why not?" Baylor demanded far too seriously. "They want me dead. They are useless, antiquated law inventors that can't even invent laws by themselves. They sat on their backsides and failed in their protective duty, having set themselves up in that capacity." He continued, still sounding frighteningly serious, "They can't keep their own safe, let alone ours. Let's just kill them all; if not us, then obviously something else eventually. I'd prefer I had the pleasure."

"What?" I repeated stupidly, still shocked at his suggestion.

"Think about it! Everything you've told me of Changelings makes me think it is probably pretty rare they choose to ascend, correct? It's an insatiable longing for life that keeps them here, makes them Changelings in the first place. Am I right?" he looked at me squarely, and I nodded. "Especially, I would think, when they're on top of the world. As they all must have been, having solved all these problems you speak of, and set themselves up as a supreme Council over all the rest of the Blessed. Yet as soon as this is done, they start ascending one by one."

He gave a short laugh, adding with the same biting sarcasm as before, "Don't tell me you think it was by choice, or I will call you all fools as well. Do you not find it the slightest bit odd that their number was originally seven and now they have all but three ascended, choice or no? That the one that started it all disappeared without a trace and now they are too."

We all sat dumbfounded for a long time, as all of this began to settle in our minds. Most of it started to try and make sense then. The Council was being slowly eliminated. What if something was hunting and destroying them one by one? I began to wonder about what you had said. How you had said the one you felt was not like me. I began to think, what if you had meant not only not good like me, but not a Changeling at all. What if there existed some other entity that was destroying Changelings from their foundations up. But why you? Why would one such as that have chosen to destroy you rather than Piper or myself? Why not an older one with more to pass on to other new Changelings, that could refortify our numbers with our wisdom?

"But why Angel?" I said aloud.

"Why Angel?" Baylor repeated. "Because the lass was too smart for her own good, or too strong. Either way, she figured out a way to kill a Changeling. If you have a group of evil Changelings running about trying to eliminate order by eliminating those who bring it, then they encounter one who, on her own, destroyed one of their number, they are going to want her gone quickly before she can teach others to do the same. I would, anyway."

"A group of evil Changelings?" I repeated thoughtfully.

Was it possible a kind of Anti-Council had been formed somewhere? Was a kind of quiet war being waged right under my nose? Could that have been why my Master had so insisted I know about how to disguise and defend myself? Why he had been so insistent I learn so much? Had he known of such a group and been preparing me should I come up against them? Could it even be that all I had taught the twins had brought Edsel under their scrutiny?

I began to voice all these ideas to them and more, talking about all the new possibilities. We came to think that Baylor had been correct and that you, with your unintentional discovery, had posed a threat to some plan this evil group had been quietly working on. We ran with this idea, for it was all we had that made any sense. This line of thought brought us all around to the fact that not only Santon had known of the things I had taught the twins, but Edsel had as well. He had not disapproved so much as begun to think it wouldn't be such a bad idea for more of us to know such things, and if he had been contemplating making such things common knowledge then he would have made himself a threat and likely a target as well.

Perhaps these other Changelings had somehow found a way to destroy us as well and were systematically doing so. This posed the same question, though. How? Had it indeed been a forced ascension by an Anti-Council or was it something else? I recalled the conversation with the Elders the night before and wondered if some powerful harm could have been done that would force a long-term dispersion, if not ascension.

I wanted desperately to believe this had been the case, that you and Edsel both had merely been forced to disperse and flee. Perhaps the damage had been so great it would take a long time to recover from, but that recovery would happen, it had to happen. I needed to believe that neither of you had been forced to actually ascend because none had ever been able to return from that that, as far as I knew. I could not think of your absence as a permanent thing. I needed to be able to think you would both recover somehow, someway, and return to us. I also had to admit I needed you to return to me on a deeper level.

I could not have lost two Angels in one long, lonely lifetime. I was not able to accept I had squandered my second chance at love by being stubbornly loyal to a lover two thousand years gone. I began to think of all the times I had wanted to kiss you, and denied myself that pleasure. It might have been the amount I had drunk by then, but it all began to congeal into one big, hard lump at the base of my throat, seeming to want to choke the air from my lungs and push my heart out my open mouth. I think I hated myself for a while then. Sitting in silence and berating myself not only for my lack of vision in all we had just figured out, but also my lack of vision when it had come to you.

I stood then, suddenly needing to be doing something about all of it, needing to be looking for you actively. I felt suddenly dizzy with this action, as though the world had decided to spin just as quickly as my thoughts in a belated effort to keep up with my mind. I sent out my inner sight throughout the city, trying to ignore this new nauseating state of things, hoping I might come across your wounded soul and assist you in some manner in recovering yourself. Determining within myself that you had only been forced to flee and I would find you trying desperately to call up a new form somewhere.

I know now from reading your journal, the reason I found no sign of you was that you had no concept then of your own existence, let alone knowledge of yourself as a Changeling. Just as when I had not been able to recognize Baylor as a Changeling because he had not known what he was and did not then project himself as one, I could not recognize you then either.

I did, however, feel some sense of something familiar and comforting out toward the Trajan baths, and I felt a strange desire to go there. I know now this was probably my soul recognizing yours on some deeper level not understood by me at the time. Then, though, I mistook it for my mind recognizing a place it had found pleasure, a place where I had spent so much pleasant time with the twins, and found so much joy. I simply thought that my mind had wanted to return there to find that same sense of peace. This I denied myself, telling myself to concentrate on finding you and, therefore, ironically, I missed you.

I'll convince myself it was the wine that made me so stupid, made me miss such a thing, even though there were many such ironies I would recognize later while reading your words. Ironies that would make me squirm and want to scream at your writings that we had been so close. So often, we came so very close to finding each other before now.

But, I digress, love. I had noted then that there were those in the city my soul had not cared for, as you wrote you had. This reminded me that we had quite probably discovered the truth through our discussion and were likely facing some sort of Anti-Council bent on destroying order through destroying those who created, enforced and taught it.

I made mention of this to Piper and the twins, and they stood with me and scanned the city as well. All four of us came to the same conclusion. There were at least three of these ones here. Ones our souls withdrew from, feeling quite uncomfortable. They were exuding waves of foulness and vile purpose. Who would change such beings? These were far worse than those three that had hounded our heels from Scotland. We began then to discuss what to do from there.

"What will we do?" Adonia said worriedly. "We cannot simply sit here waiting for another of us to disappear."

"Yes," Piper said. "We must figure out how they are doing this to us, what they have done to Edsel and Angel."

I was wholeheartedly agreeing with Piper's statement when Baylor spoke up from the carpeting of grass behind me.

"So let's go hunting," he said. "Let's catch ourselves an evil Changeling and make it tell us what they've done to our Angel."

"Though that is an excellent idea in theory," I said, "it is not really so simple to capture a Changeling."

"I realize that," he replied, astounding me with his insight and how much he had paid attention, not just now but always. "So you locate one of the ones we have already battled twice on our journey here. They will not be so willing to give up their forms and flee us now. You direct me to it on the next full moon and we will have our answers. I will find out what they have done to her."

His determination and confidence gave me hope as I realized it just might work. They might not have any idea you were the only one who knew how to kill them and if we could convince them we had this knowledge as well and would use it, they just might tell us what we needed to know.

"It just might work," I said hopefully. "One of us needs to go and gather the Elders here, they also need to know what we have discovered and what we are thinking. We need to make them aware of the ones we sense here now and it is better we are all prepared and made stronger as a group."

Adonia and Piper volunteered to go gather the remaining Council members together while Adreal and I set to trying to scan if any of those in Rome itself was one of the ones to have attacked us when we first came to France. I made no mention of how much Adonia and Piper seemed to find every possible reason to be in close proximity. I knew the why of it and, though I knew the Council would never approve, I myself would not be the cause of any further discouragement, by making it known how obvious their feelings for each other were. I knew of their feelings, had for quite some time, and could only hope they would find a way to overcome all those that opposed them, just as I hoped I would someday find you and have the same opportunities to pursue something deeper with you.

Adreal and I had no luck by the time his sister and Piper had returned with the others. Soon we were all gathered in the garden and had put the search off for the moment. My attention seemed to be needed fully by present company. I was still more than a little bit wary, for this was the first time I had allowed any of the Council to be anywhere near to Baylor. It seemed though that none of them cared, though I continued to watch everyone closely. Baylor, thankfully, showed no further inclination to kill them, although I noted that at some point he had retrieved his sword, Bane, from his room, and it lay behind him in the grass, at the ready should he need it.

I introduced each of them to him and they were all very polite, seeming more intent on his size and hair color than the fact he was a Werewolf, in the flesh, before them. He nodded politely and accepted their stares, and this gave me heart as we all began searching for solutions to all our problems. Though I stayed ever alert to their every move, and his, should it appear any of them might change their mind, nothing happened to change my level of comfort or discomfort with the situation. We spoke openly throughout the day, sharing all we had come to know.

By the evening, Baylor's suggestion of trying to capture one of the ones we had already damaged once or twice, and who may have witnessed their comrade's death or heard of it, seemed our best course. Though I had not found such a one in Rome itself, we did not give up the idea. We decided then to broaden our search, going out from Rome in all directions, not only to find one of those two vile creatures we had encountered before, but to search more thoroughly for you and Edsel as well. All of us had come to the same hopeful conclusion, that you both had merely been grievously wounded and were at this very moment somewhere recovering yourselves, and we decided to begin to sweep further afield.

Then it was decided Piper and the twins would stay there in Rome, continuing to scan should Edsel or you return. Santon and Cathmore would begin searching toward the west, heading toward the Pantheon then sweeping back south. Lachlan and Kynan would head to the east, passing the Trajan baths then sweep south, meeting up with the others and returning on the southern road. Baylor and I would take to the northern road, sweeping broadly to both the east and west and in a zigzagging pattern retracing the route toward home. We would scan as far as each of us could within a week, and meet back here at the end of it, to inform each other of whatever we might have found or sensed.

As Baylor and I searched, it became more set within us that you had merely been forced to disperse, once again all other possibilities proving unacceptable for us to think about. We did not mention the episode of him near beating me from my body. Neither of us was wasting any more time placing blame on the other for your loss; we simply concentrated on making it right by recovering you. I think the mere fact we had begun actively searching for you and those who had done you harm made it possible for us to think of taking our wrath out upon one of the evil ones when we found them. Yet no relief came from either our anger or our loss.

We searched slowly and thoroughly, well past the olive grove where we had made our final camp on the journey there, and I was heart broken anew when I came to that place, for I could still feel a small part of you there. I again began berating myself, for it seemed there would be no end of remembering lost chances for me. How innocently you would curl up to me to sleep, not knowing what damage it did me. How hard I fought the desire within me to do far more than lay there and try to sleep.

I had constantly reminded myself how I had been created for one. Known somehow deep within me that my soul had been made for my Seraphim's, that what I felt was merely an attraction to a very beautiful young woman and I should push it away. I would look to my painting of her often to strengthen that resolve. So would I waver now in my belief that someday the gods would repay my loyalty to her and return her to me? Yes, I would. I had and was. Even before finding out that you both were one and the same, that I had indeed been rewarded, I wavered back then as I had so frequently before.

I knew, even then, that I had been given the opportunity to find love again. I had slowly begun realizing that, even if they would not see fit to return my Seraphim to me, they had given me another Angel. They had even seen to it that you received the proper name, mayhap a sign for me as to their blessing. I had been blind. I had heard your call from halfway across Scotland. My soul had been drawn to yours, as surely as if an unseen hand had reached out from it and pulled me in, and still I had been blind; told myself you were merely extremely strong willed, an extraordinary young woman and a wonderful pupil and friend, but that it should and would be no more. It was, though.

I thought then how I had to find you, had to make you love me, take that chance and make the very best of the opportunity provided to me. I loved you, right or wrong. All loyalties aside, I had been given no choice by my heart, and realizing all of this, while knowing you too had been lost to me no matter how I tried to tell myself it was only temporary, destroyed me. I scanned brokenly, wounded in my soul but always faithful, faithful and hopeful to the last, that on the next sweep of my inner vision I would find you, go to you and help you to heal. Then you would forgive me for having treated you as a child and pushing you away.

You would forgive my blindness and love me in return.

~4~

Back Home

Come the end of the week, Baylor and I had still found no sign of you or the vile creatures we sought. We returned to the villa heavy-hearted, yet hoping the others might have had better luck. We arrived at dusk and were in the garden drinking more than was necessary to quench our thirst with the also disappointed Piper and the twins as the others also began to arrive, each with the same disappointed looks and no better news than we had. We all then sat and got well into our cups trying to wash the pain and disappointment from our mouths. I say that, but really I think we were just trying to drink ourselves into a more comforting oblivion.

"What if she just went home?" Baylor slurred sometime near midnight.

"Huh?" I managed, jerking back to the present.

"What if the lass just went home? She must have been frightened and confused. You say being incorporeal is sometimes confusing," he said, albeit a little drunkenly. "What if she lost her way and was simply drawn somehow to the place her soul remembered as safe and happy?"

He might have been too far into his cups, hell, we might all have been, but it made perfect sense then. Suddenly I had new hope and latched onto it like it was life itself.

"Yes!" I said.

I looked blurry-eyed first at him then all the others to see if they were following and agreeing with his theory. Looking back now, this scene must have been an event to mark in history. Four Elders of the Council were drunkenly trying to focus on the words of a Werewolf who was just as drunk, drawing themselves up not only to better look him in the eye, but to see if they could gather from his words the same hope my tone said I had.

"You say their souls might have sought comfort at a place they had found it before?" Lachlan finally managed to grasp his words. "Mayhap Edsel would have returned to Antioch then. That is were he grew up, he was happy there, no?'

He turned to Cathmore in an exaggerated jerking motion, as though his head weighed too much and was improperly balanced on his shoulders. Awkwardly checking to see if that one agreed with him, he ended up working again to still the garden and refocus his vision on this new target.

"Antioch? Yes, he was from there, but happy? Nay, seems I recall he moved here to escape the pain of memories it brought him," Cathmore said, finally realizing he was being asked a question.

"No, not so," I said. "It was I who moved here to escape painful memories, only from Athens."

I whirled back to face him, having no cause other than my own drunkenness to argue the point so loudly, also having no idea the havoc I would start among them once again. I was shocked when Cathmore raised an accusing finger at me, pushing himself unsteadily to his feet.

"You are not the only one to have painful remembrances. We all have to escape the ravages of time and a too long memory sometimes. We feel pain too," he fairly shouted at me. "You young jackanapes think you have the exclusive on such things because we appear strong and heartless in our quest to do our self-appointed tasks, constantly protecting and teaching the young ones. And you," he said, spinning to face the twins who were ever unrepentant in their mockery.

They were as dangerously close to falling over themselves in a fit of laughter at his slurring and swaying as he was to falling over just trying to stand up. I suppose none of us had ever seen the Elders so out of character, stumbling around the garden like they had never met a bottle of wine before tonight.

"You two," he continued, once he had steadied himself and focused upon them again. "Of all those we have Blessed over the years, nurturing and caring and teaching you, you make constant mockery of us, constantly chirping through your lessons and, and…and…"

"Teaching?" Adreal said, suddenly not finding it all so amusing anymore.

I was surprised that it was Adreal to confront him, for usually bravery had been Adonia's hunting ground, and taking the blame for the trouble she caused by it had always been his.

"We learned more in one short night from Demon than in centuries listening to your useless prattling," he said, standing now as well. He shocked me still further as he continued, "What do you really know that you could teach us, that he has not already?"

He flung his arm out to indicate me by trying to point in my direction, effectively spilling off the liquid courage in the cup that hand held. Allowing it to seep unnoticed into the grassy floor of the garden, he continued, undeterred. It seemed having finally spoken up, he had found a liking for it.

"What do you teach? What some other unknown Changeling told you to teach? Someone else's ideas of what we should be allowed to know and learn?" he said. "Nay, I will take my lessons from one who learned them first hand and cares more for the actual learning of things that will help us in this life, than the ceremony of attending one of your long-winded classes, in which we have wasted much time, and derived nothing."

He stopped for a moment, raising his glass to his lips. I suppose he meant to take a drink, but finding the glass empty seemed to jerk him back to reality. Not only the reality of what he had done, but I think also of why he had done it. He looked quickly to his sister as if to apologize for having just gotten them both into a lot of trouble, when she surprised me as well. I must admit I don't know whether I was more amused or shocked, but either way I thought my eyes could have gotten no wider. It would appear, having found her brother was willing to start this, she was more than willing to be the one to finish it.

"Adreal is right!" she said, standing up and steadying herself against him. "I am sick to death of all of it. We sit here, in this, our home, bowing to your wishes and rules and the precious Code. Well, yes, some of it is good and I see value in it as would any being possessed of common sense, but the rest can go to Hades. I am done. *We* are done," she declared, smiling at her twin. "You may treat us as equals and we will solve this together, or you may say goodbye to any further compliance from either Adreal or myself."

She had patted her brother on the back then, as if to congratulate him, and whirled as though she would stomp from the garden to further make her point. Suddenly she whirled back. The shocked surprise on all of our faces could have far outdone the scene I had created over a hundred years before, for none of us could have found words then, as she instead stomped back to Piper, putting her hand out to him while facing and addressing the Elders again. Piper slowly raised his hand up to hers, a look of amazed bewilderment plastered to his paling visage. He put his hand slowly into hers, as if he was afraid it would develop teeth and bite him.

"And, furthermore," she said. "I love this man."

I thought I was as close then to popping my eyes clean out as Piper suddenly appeared to be.

"I do not care if the high and mighty Council," she continued, dragging Piper to his feet, "that is, you high and mighty drunken four, approve. I am old enough to make this decision for myself and I could not give a fig if you like it or no. It is done, I have chosen Piper, and he will be my mate for the rest of my life."

I thought for sure poor Piper's legs were going to buckle beneath him, as his face quickly registered more emotions then than it seemed his body could handle. She dragged him by his hand from the garden and into the house, pulling his extremely shocked and near useless form behind her as she went. You could have easily cut the silence that descended, as her bedchamber door slammed shut, with a dull, rusted blade. A fly on the wall of the interior of that chamber would have gotten an ear and an eye full.

We all sat there, mouths wide open, none of us able to formulate a word, until Baylor started to chuckle. Then he started to laugh outright, full-bellied and painful sounding, sitting on the grassy floor behind me. I thought it would disintegrate into crying if he were not to get control soon. So I intervened, interrupting him as best I could by swatting stupidly, and of course missing, at his leg as it flew into the air beside me. He rolled onto his back, holding his belly and kicking his legs into the air, and I could not stay focused on either one of his legs long enough to smack it and get his attention.

"What?" I said, trying a third time and missing again. "What is so damned amusing?"

"Adonia! What a smart little woman," he gasped. "She is far more intelligent than all of us!"

He sat up wiping a tear from his eye, and I still do not know if it was from his laughter or from thinking about what he said next.

"She's decided to be with the one she loves while she can, consequence, convention, right or wrong be damned! Smart, brave girl! Nothing else matters when all is said and done. Did you live well? Did you love better? If you can't say yes to those, then why bother?"

He quieted then, lying back again, and staring blankly up at the stars. With one hand behind his head to hold it elevated, he began silently sipping his wine. I too sat dumbfounded, not only by the scene the twins had created but by Baylor's words. The Elders sat just as still as Adreal, all of us lost within our own thoughts again. I cannot imagine what each of them had been thinking or how they were coming to terms with all of it. I only know what I myself thought.

I wanted to die. I wanted to crawl into a deep dark hole in the earth and pull the world down over me. I wanted to cease then to exist, end the hurting, the realizing. I wanted to end it all, especially the cowardice, the cowardice I now recognized within myself, that had been more prevalent than loyalty in all my years of faithfulness to a memory. I felt then that it was the stronger cause for my denial of my feelings for you. I had been afraid to feel this again, this emptiness that was sucking me into itself.

I wanted for the first time in my great long life to give up. I think I even might have then, unable to convince myself I could say yes to both of Baylor's questions. Then he asked another one. Suddenly pushing himself up to his feet and stretching his arms above his head, he looked down at me from his great height and I was somehow reminded of my Master demanding I quit dilly-dallying with my broodings, and be about my life.

"Are you coming?" he asked.

"Coming where?" I repeated stupidly.

"I'm going home to see if our Angel has returned there," he explained. "Are you coming?"

Instantly I was up and on my feet, holding on to him to steady my whirling world, as it began to spin too quickly with my rapid movement. He had grabbed my elbow then, laughing softly at me.

"We will find her," he said.

It seemed we would be forever passing this promise around amongst us to strengthen whichever of us needed it. I had needed it then and he seemed to know it, whispering it in my ear as he led me from the garden.

"Tell your sister to go easy on Piper, he's an old man," he called back over his shoulder, almost laughing again, to a still quite obviously bemused Adreal. "We will be back soon, so go easy on them!" he added then to the Elders in a more serious tone I recognized all too well as meaning there would be painful hell to pay did they not heed his warning.

I was sure they would, the twins and Piper were not allies to be estranging themselves from over a matter so acceptably noble as love. I did not think they would risk losing all of our support and incurring our wrath, merely to uphold some standard of behavior I knew now that they had probably not even thought up themselves. Unbelievable as it may sound, I had to leave this matter to the twins in any case, for they had proven themselves to be capable of taking care of things on their own. I had to find you; finding you and caring for you, protecting you from then on, seeing to it that no harm came to you ever again had become my priority now.

Baylor led me stumbling at his side through the darkened streets of Rome. Too much in a hurry to be home and find you to care, I was near dead drunk and he was nearly carrying me. He held me up by my elbow, walking at my side until we had reached the outskirts of the city, somehow finding his way without my help as I was quite useless then. I sobered to a slight buzzing in my head by the time we had taken to the northern road again, walking on my own, becoming more capable of coherent questions and answers.

"She'll be there, right?" I asked.

I'm not sure why I had asked him, perhaps I simply needed the extra push his answer would bring, my own hopeful heart not seeming sufficient for the moment.

"Aye," he said. "She is a strong lass, you know that, whatever was done she would have survived it. She is probably just badly confused. If as you say she was done some extreme damage which sent her energies flying, then she most likely has become lost a little in her mind as well. When she comes to herself both mentally and physically, she will most likely go back to the relative safety of home. If she is not there when we get there, she will go there soon."

"Aye," I said simply.

I believed as he had then, that whether you were there when we got there or not, you would eventually come home. We would be there when you arrived and all would be made well. You would be with us again, with me again. So I walked quietly at his side, holding this hope to myself, until mid-afternoon. By then he had found us a secluded grouping of trees off to the left of the road, where we made camp to rest and recover from our drinking.

I awoke sometime after dark to the smell of Baylor's cooking. It was awful. Well, not really, his cooking has never truly been awful but the smell of anything would have been awful then. He offered me a wine sack when he saw that I had opened my eyes, and my head had pounded a resounding "No!" I put my hands to my temples and he had started laughing at me.

"Water then?" he asked.

"Aye," I grumbled.

He tossed another sack toward me and I fumbled to catch it. Missing clumsily, it landed with a thump on my belly, causing instantaneous nausea and a renewed pounding in my head. I looked daggers at him and this had only renewed his laughter at me.

"What's the matter, old man?" he laughed. "Can't handle your wine like you used to?"

"You may want to stop your tongue," I growled, "before I remove its nuisance from your mouth."

He of course made it a point to ignore my threat. He began "la la la-ing" while he eyed my prostrate form with amusement, and finished preparing his breakfast. I lay there a moment more before realizing I didn't have to deal with any of it. I changed into a huge black wolf then and raced happily away for the tree line, effectively escaping the headache, and the annoying "la la las" Baylor insisted on singing. I came across a stream at one point and dove in as I was, swimming in a few circles, then racing back to our camp.

I ran up to him. Stopping close to his relaxed and eating form, I shook off as much of the water my coat had retained as possible. Then I began sidestepping quickly away as he set his plate aside and got to his feet. He came stalking toward me and I would easily dance away whenever he got too close. Any one observing us would have thought it extremely strange, I'm sure, a giant of a Highlander, stalking a huge black wolf, hollering profanities at it all the while.

"You must sleep sometime!" he yelled, finally giving up and returning to his food.

I could not resist it. It was far too tempting. I raced ahead of him, beating him easily back to his unguarded plate. Hurriedly I ate all of it down before he could make it back to me. I did not feel too bad about this, for I knew there was more near the fire, left there as it had been prepared for me. It was only that his was so much more tempting than my own, for some strange reason. I looked up as he came racing at me, sliding to a stop beside me. I licked my jowls appreciatively, looking up at him.

"You, you, ass... no good waste of fur!" he stuttered and stammered, trying to figure not only why I had done this but what to say or do about it. "What, why...yours is right there!" he pointed. "I had mine seasoned perfectly. You lout!"

I could take no more. It was far too amusing to contain my mirth any longer. I stood then, taking my own form, and laughing I began walking slowly back to the place where I had been laying when he had tossed the water to me, leaving him still dumbfounded and open-mouthed, staring at me. Bending over, I retrieved the sack and began uncorking it to take a drink.

"La la la, lala, la, la la!" I sang, looking back over my shoulder at him, as I sat down.

He was the one staring daggers now, while he removed once more his small sack of seasonings from his belt and began the task of bringing my food to the same perfection he had achieved with his own. I merely sat, alternately laughing and rubbing my belly and drinking my water, still singing my own "la la las." Eventually he started to laugh as well, and it was in relatively high spirits that we took to the main road again.

We traveled slowly, not wanting to risk missing you if you were still somewhere along the way. We took to traveling mostly during the cooler nighttime hours and resting in the heat of the day. Thus it was that even though my repeated scanning for you turned up nothing, we managed to keep our spirits high, whether by having constant jest at one another's expense or by reminding ourselves you would either be home when we arrived or soon thereafter.

It got us through.

It took us nearly eight months to make our slow progress from Rome back to our home in the Scottish Highlands, for we were further slowed by the harsh onslaught of winter, but as we approached our destination a sense of excitement began to grow in us. Not only due to our newly achieved close proximity to where we felt we would find you, but also in Baylor at having come back home. He had, over the course of the last few cycles of the full moon, become increasingly foul-tempered. As during one of these cycles, the last one before we arrived, we had came upon two Werewolves together.

We were crossing through the beautiful countryside surrounding Edinburgh and I had been scanning for you or one of the foul others again. Baylor was already in his Werewolf form, walking silently, nose in the wind. He had increasingly been feeling he was not doing all that he should be. By not having been here and hunting those others of his kind he knew to have been roaming freely in his absence, he felt he had been failing in his duty. I think to some extent he felt this all to be yet another punishment for having left his people once more to the mercies of those beasts he felt responsible for destroying, and it seemed to me he was hunting all the harder now trying to make up for the lost time.

I had realized long ago, that he was not at all as aware of things as a regular Changeling when he changed his form. I knew to stay quiet and out of his way, for it seemed at times he might not fully remember who I was, let alone who he himself was. He had in mind a single purpose: find others of his kind, kill them, and not do harm to his fellow man. Which had all worked quite well for all these years, but then I had never tested it. Therefore I was very shocked when he put his arm out to stay my forward progress through the darkened field we had been crossing.

He dropped low to the ground then and I crouched beside him as if on some silent command. He sniffed the air ahead of us and his eyes widened in an almost human gesture of surprise. I was very much in wonder of this when I saw two other Werewolves rise up from the field not thirty meters ahead of us. They were hard at work, pulling apart a human body, tugging back and forth between the two of them and, almost cordially it seemed, sharing it. They were working to divide it and not fighting over it. I was shocked. They were working together, they were sharing a meal. I was disgusted.

Baylor stood and howled in rage, racing across the space that was separating us from them with extraordinary speed. I could only think he had been outraged at what they doing: feasting on a human being, dividing it between them like they were sharing a pheasant. The larger of the two, a male, immediately dropped his portion and ran to meet Baylor; while the smaller, a female, merely looked up and continued chewing on her human morsel a moment more, before slowly putting it aside to join her mate in the battle.

I was deeply shocked not only by the sight of what it was they feasted on, but also the fact they had been working together and were quite probably a mated pair. Could such a thing be, a mated pair of Werewolves? My gods, the possibilities were horrifying! It therefore took me a bit too long to react, and Baylor had howled out twice in pain by the time I realized he was outnumbered and might be in need of my help. The female was on his back, apparently trying to tear his ears off or perhaps his head off by his ears, but he had his hands full with the male.

I suddenly realized I had never battled a Werewolf before. The extermination of such beasts had always been Baylor's domain. Yet I was running across the field to help him and had no idea how I would do it. What I would do when I got there? I had Bane strapped to my back, but didn't I need silver? How could I sever their heads when they were in such proximity to my friend?

That was when I recalled your hellcat form. How you had invented a creature capable, with claws and fangs to defend and inflict much damage, but not provided it any instinct but your own, to protect those you love. All of this went through my head with lightning clarity, and it was as a Werewolf myself that I appeared when I reached his side. Not a true Werewolf but in one's form, with my mind and instincts my own.

I tore the bitch from off his back, ruthlessly hurling her away. She leaped back to her feet, coming back at me, snapping and growling her rage. She launched herself into the air at me and it was suddenly difficult for me to focus. I was overwhelmed, for knowing then that I was fighting what was in truth a woman who most likely didn't know what she was doing, with full intent to kill her, was very disturbing. I was saved from this, however, for even as we collided, she turned her head and attentions toward Baylor.

He let out a long low mournful howl that I knew well. Then he raised her mate's dismembered head into the air and she howled out then, seeing this. She was off of me instantly, attacking Baylor again with renewed ferocity, clawing her way up his back as if seeking a height at which she might retrieve her mate's head from his hands, and do as much pain to his killer in the process. Baylor's clawed hands were still raising it high into the air, seeming to be offering it up to the moon. I then had no more cause to worry about the right or wrong of doing harm to a female, Werewolf or not.

Baylor dropped the other's head and, reaching behind himself, took her by her ears, twisting and pulling forward. He slung her off of his back and over his head, slamming her to the ground before him. Still he did not release her head, though her neck was twisted at an outrageously impossible angle. I knew that it had to be broken but still she growled her defiance, showing him all of her numerous and very sharp teeth. He then put his foot on her hip, effectively pinning her body to the earth, as he twisted and pulled her head from it.

I lay where the force of her collision with me had put me, on my back in the grass. Now I watched from this perspective in awe, as he held this one's head also up to the moon, letting loose that terrible heartbreaking howl again. Then he turned back and took notice of me.

Suddenly I was very afraid, for he seemed not at all to know me. The look in his eyes was foreign and feral, terrifying to me. He reached down and hauled me to my feet, grabbing me by my head as I had seen him do all too often. Instantly I became myself so that I might have a mouth capable of forming words, for I had in me a near paralyzing need to make him know me.

"Baylor!" It was all I could think of.

He dropped me instantaneously, stumbling backwards away from me, as though I had caught on fire in his hands. I recovered myself and looked on in horror as he threw back his head again, howling a whole new depth of rage and pain at the moon. It was a sound I will forever recall and associate with eternal torment, like hell's own voice had been let loose from his lungs. It began like the wind, low and keening, sounding something close to screaming, but a duller roar, a rarer, aching sore, the sound of true breaking. It was something so far beyond anything I had ever heard before, that it tore out my heart to hear it.

He raised his hands to his own head then, seeming to want to either block out the sound of his own torment or to pull his own head free as he had so many other's before, releasing himself forever from the torturous confines of living within it. I was horrified and heart-broken as I saw his muscles flex, and realized with excruciating clarity, it was the latter. My dearest friend sought to end his own life.

"Baylor! No!" I yelled, with all the force of will I could muster.

I was on my feet in an instant. Grabbing his hands in my own trying with all my might to force them down, willing myself to have the strength to prevent this, demanding that the gods not allow this one to leave me as well. He was incredibly strong and he told no lie, his arms did not grow tired. I was forced repeatedly to recreate my own weakening being, to keep his strong arms from doing their owner's intent. I struggled with him for what seemed an eternity, trying to break through to him with either words or force, but it seemed nothing would make him hear me.

Dawn came finally, almost unexpectedly and far too slowly, crawling its way up to the horizon like the wounded things it came to observe. We collapsed to the ground, breaking down and crying like children, both of us. I must admit it was a very unmanly display to say the least.

"I tried to kill you!" Baylor said finally. "Why wouldn't you let me go!"

"I'm not so easy to kill, you fool," I said, somewhere now between hysterical laughter and more tears. "And I should have known better than to look anything like a Werewolf anywhere near you. It was my fault, not yours."

Then suddenly I punched him, hard, square in the jaw, not even realizing at first that I would do it. His head flew back from the force of the blow, then came slowly forward as I shook my hand out, repairing it quickly. Damn, he had a hard jaw! He rubbed this part of his face slowly, looking hard at me, trying, to decide if he should punch me back. The morning was cold and the dew seeping through my clothing chilled me and made me shiver. At least that is what I will say till the end of time, though one might have thought the look he was giving me just then was frightening enough to have quite easily been the true cause.

"Don't you ever think to do such a thing ever again," I said, deciding to be very angry again. "You are not allowed to give up on me. If I am not allowed to die, then neither are you. We are in this together forever, you and I, and we have a mission. We must find Angel."

~5~

Broken Home

We said no more about that incident in the field outside Edinburgh, merely quietly continuing on our way home. We put that event in the same casket as the one that held what had taken place in the room that had been yours in the villa in Rome. These memories were not to be dug up and danced with too often, they had happened so we buried them, but we did not chose to leave flowers for them regularly. It was vital to me that I have these memories for the things that they taught me, but also vital that I had learned how to put them away so that they could not wound me on a daily basis. I think Baylor did much the same, whether he recognized it or not, because he seemed no more willing than I to make mention of such things after they were done.

As we came closer to our destination, with still no sign of you, we managed somehow to become more convinced you would already be there waiting for us. We had no other option, really, for we could not believe you had been destroyed completely, as I have said, and this drove us onward. We began to dream aloud of what we would do when you were back with us, Baylor planning out an elaborate menu for a reunion feast and I contemplating other things I had not considered in a very, very long time.

The heather had long since gone from yellow to blue as we came to the foot of our mountain, and somehow I used even that to encourage me you would be there. As though because the heather had time to change, you would have too, you would have fixed yourself and returned by now.

Baylor and I broke into a run, chasing each other up the mountain's side, alternating the lead. There was in us both then a great sense of joy, and although we quickly wore ourselves out having to slow down to better pick our way up the increasingly difficult track, our spirits were higher now than they had been in months. We had encountered no other Werewolves the last two days of that final cycle before arriving here. So it had been only our reuniting with you, that filled our minds. We made a quick stop to drink at our stream, but not even its beauty and serenity could keep us overlong.

"Gavannon's bones, I cannot wait to hug the lass and tell her how I've missed her!" Baylor said excitedly, coming up to drink from the stream beside me.

"Aye! And how much I love her!" I said, without thinking.

I dropped the water I had just scooped up, letting it escape from my palms, as Baylor too froze in mid-drink and slowly looked at me. I had never admitted it aloud before and it had felt oddly right to do so. Baylor quietly looked back to the water and lifted another draught to his lips, saying nothing, but I saw his lips twitch and I knew he found it amusing. I sat in quiet awe for a moment then suddenly splashed a handful of water into his face.

"I love her!" I repeated excitedly, as he sputtered and looked at me like I'd lost my wits completely. "I love her, I do!" I splashed him happily again, saying, "You hear me?"

"Aye! I know," he replied.

"How did you know?" I asked, grinning like an idiot.

"Well, any fool could have seen it," he said, sarcastically. "Even had they water in their eyes as I do now, many thanks to you for that. I'm not as stupid as you are, obviously! And even with water in my ears as well, I hear. You've announced it three times in the time it took me to get a drink."

He smiled happily at me then, mirroring I suppose the look on my face. Then he put his hand on my back, patting it as if in congratulations. I was very happy then to be with my friend in this moment of revelation and acceptance, for him to be there to understand my joy, to be so near to finding you now. I was just enjoying a deep feeling of camaraderie when suddenly he pushed me hard, shoving me head first into the stream.

"I owed you that!" he yelled, as he ran off up the path to the plateau, laughing uproariously.

I came up sputtering and laughing, chasing him up the mountainside. We crossed the plateau at a dead run, slapping and swerving into each other, vying to be the first to the door. I had not scanned while at the stream, because I did not want to know what I feared I already knew. I could not at that time bear the disappointment were I not to sense you there. So I had avoided the probable disillusionment as long as I possibly could. I had not even allowed myself the use of the word 'probable', when combined with 'disillusionment', for that matter.

So we raced happily inside, pushing and shoving like starving children vying for the first slice of pie, only to find you were not there. Quite obviously no one had been in better than a year. Yet we were prepared for this, were we not? We still had hope, for we had convinced ourselves if you were not here now, you would be soon. Yes, we were very disappointed, but we made the best of it. Disillusionment was still not probable and we had figured out how to keep it postponed.

Baylor set about dusting and cleaning the place while I went and hunted some game. We made a simple meal, as we had so often of late, eating in silence, expecting you any time. This proved to become a new habit for us, although I went to the nearer villages to purchase supplies for slightly better meals. Our meals remained simple, as though Baylor wanted his celebratory return feast to be made all the better by our lesser meals then. So we waited and waited, and waited some more, and still you did not come back to us.

Baylor became restless and moody again, as well as, I suppose I must admit, I did. By the third month of waiting for your return, I was becoming very desperate, with certain hopeless words trying to wiggle their way into my subconscious mind and Baylor quickly became downright impossible to live with. Combine all of that with the fact he had found four Werewolves in the last two days, and you had a disaster in the making.

He left me to do his final night of hunting for that cycle, saying not a word in parting and slamming the door behind him as he left. I was already been in a foul mood and this had done nothing to help it. I sat looking at the poor fare he had left calling it dinner, and felt even more disgusted. I shoved the food away, wondering when it was that such had become an acceptable quality of life. Had we not lived like this for hundreds of years before you came to us? Had we not been satisfied with our lot at least to the extent of finding the energy to hunt up and cook a decent meal?

I found myself thinking to soothe my mood and perhaps come to better terms with how things stood somehow. Hence, I decided to take a nice long dip in the bath. I was hoping that a return of the small pleasures I had subsisted on for so long, before becoming accustomed to the larger ones provided by your company, would content me again as they had back then, back before either Baylor or I had realized how much better things could be.

This had been a mistake, a terrible mistake, for once I entered that chamber I was assailed with memories of you. I saw you with your soft white cotton shift conforming so perfectly to your body, wet and see-through, and you too innocent to know the damage that even your innocence had done to me. You had put your hand in mine, allowing me to draw you forth from this very pool I now stood before, with no idea how close you would come to breaking me. I stood at the edge of that pool recalling it all so vividly. I thought then how I couldn't change it. I was change and yet I could change nothing. I thought then how I couldn't reach into the past and pull your wet, innocent form to myself.

I flew into another rage then. I became so incredibly angry, incensed by the unfairness of the Fates. I lost control completely. I couldn't have cared less then about anything. I ran back into the main chamber, suddenly offended that all of it should appear so perfect and well-kept, when our actual lives had truly been thrown into such complete disarray. I was deeply disgusted by all the apparent comforts it offered, without actually offering anything nearing comfort at all. I had known true comfort once; it had been beautiful and innocent and I had patted its cheek and pushed it away.

I broke chairs over other chairs then, throwing some clear across the length of the large room. I tossed random tables over and ripped through Baylor's cupboards, slinging their contents as if they truly offended me. I broke so many things then, caring not how hard they had been to find and transport there or how far I had gone to find them. I knew I had gone quite far to find you as well, and you had been far finer than all of it combined. I wanted, I suppose, for all these things to better reflect for me the true state of my life. I was lashing out, releasing my rage on anything in my path, and the more beautiful the object, the more it suffered, because it seemed to compete with and then fall far short of being you.

Baylor came home as I was doing all of this damage, running forward quickly to grab me and stop me. He said later that I had lost myself, gone completely beyond any normal sense of mere random destruction. I could not even hear him as he entered and called to me to stop. I didn't even know he was there. He had returned to find me standing upon a broken chair, a knife in my hand. I had been screaming my outrage before my painting of Seraphim. He told me later that none of my words had made any sense, he had only known I would regret it later, if I had done it harm.

He ran at me when I would not acknowledge him, knocking both of us to the ground beneath that painting. We wrestled then, only not in play, and I dangerously armed with a knife and not my wits. Baylor managed somehow, to avoid being skewered, for I do not recall being present enough of mind to have purposely avoided doing him that damage. Finally he pinned my armed hand to the floor beneath his knee and backhanded me hard enough across the face to bring me slowly back to reality.

It was a harsh reality to have to return to.

"She is not coming," I raged. "She has been forced to ascend!"

"Nay, Edsel mayhap, but not our Angel!" he yelled back.

"Why?" I cried.

Now I do not really know why I asked him that, whether it was I expected him to explain to me again why you had been harmed, or if I had wanted to know why he felt Edsel had been forced to ascend and not you. I only know that his answer went quite far in replenishing my failing faith.

"You said the Yelm is the anchor, and she has two," he said determinedly. "She is well-rooted here; it may take her awhile to find herself, then mayhap even longer to find her way home. She will come though, she will come home!"

He was so sure, his confidence so solid, I had agreed with him again. Baylor thus further fortified me yet again, and our belief you would return was not allowed to fade from view. Though we did not know when or how long it would take, we had once again found the faith to believe it would happen someday. I took heart again that I would have the opportunity to fix my mistakes. Baylor had demanded I do so, for he would not allow me to steal his carefully guarded faith with my poor outlook and foul temperament. I don't believe he would have let me up had I not been reassured and shown it.

"She may be out there somewhere looking for us now," I said then.

"Aye! That's the spirit," Baylor replied, lifting his knee and letting my arm free so I could rise.

"We should return to Rome," I said hopefully, "looking hard for her the whole way back. She may be in need of some help we could give her, somewhere between here and there."

"Aye!" he replied. "I will go with you as well, but first I must destroy this new crop of Werewolves that sprang up in my absence. They have been nearly everywhere I have looked lately and seem to have no limit to their numbers, no matter how many of them I kill each cycle."

"I will help you to do it, then," I said.

So I did. We went out on the following three cycles and destroyed as many as we could find, hoping we could slow their progress back to a crawl, that we might take our leave from here again and they not be able to overtake his homeland. I became quite good at it actually, finding they made a much better target for my rage than expensive and rare pieces of art or furniture. Baylor would point me in the right direction for the finding of one and it, rather than some unique vase I would never be able to replace, would suffer my wrath. We had destroyed enough, in this way, that at the end of the third cycle, Baylor felt ready to return with me to Rome.

He made no comment about all of the things I had destroyed; like so many other things of late, we left them completely uncommented upon. Even his precious dishes, though I know he had loved them, were not cause enough for him to bring the matter up. As a matter of fact we never even bothered to clean these things or set anything to right. We merely walked around these items, somehow comfortable with their state of disrepair, leaving them where they had fallen as though this suited our new lives far better than being surrounded with beautiful things.

The incident that had caused this new state of disrepair went quietly into the casket with the other memories we refused to confront and conveniently ignored. This large wooden box of those memories that showed me life's many injustices and my own inability to deal with them was swiftly growing full, and that realization too was a thing I shoved into it. There was never any comment made as to just how full that casket was getting to be.

So when after we felt we had done what would be sufficient to keep the Werewolves at bay, we simply left again. Leaving the house in its new state of permanent disarray, we took to the road, traveling back and forth between the Highlands of Scotland and the streets of Rome repeatedly for many, many years once we even went to Athens on the outside chance you might have thought I would return to the place of my birth for some reason. However, we neither found sign of you there or any opportunity to question one of the foul breed.

We kept to this new kind of pattern for a very long time. We would stay in Rome for a period of time then return to Scotland to see if you had made it back there. Each time we returned home we took down the numbers of Werewolves that emerged in our absences. These absences eventually became longer, the trips between slower. Occasionally Adreal would join us,

leaving Piper and Adonia and those of the Council that still remained in
Rome to wait for you. Adonia and Piper also came along quite often, leaving
Santon to remain at the villa should you or Edsel return. The searching
slowly began to feel more and more heartbreakingly futile. Yet we traveled
endlessly, looking always for you. We continued to divide our time between
one place and the other, hoping against hope the next time we arrived at one,
you would be there waiting for us.

It must have been near to the forty years your journal told me it took
you to recover yourself that we came to our new decision and formed our new
plan. Most likely, it was just as you were about to gather enough energy to
you to be able to come in search of us, when we broke in our pattern. We had
been once more in Rome, all of us sitting, as was our habit, in the garden,
passing the wine around and trying desperately to instill hope in one another.

"Forty years is a long time. Do you think..," Adonia began, but
trailed off quietly, looking off toward the setting sun.

"No, I do not," I interrupted her wandering thoughts, maybe a bit
too harshly. "We will find them, both of them, I just think we are doing
something wrong in our searching."

"But what could we possibly do differently?" Piper asked, putting
his arm almost defensively around Adonia, to comfort and protect her
against my tone.

"I think Edsel is quite possibly gone, well and truly gone, but not
Angel," Adreal spoke up, swallowing hard. "I mean, we must be frank about
this. Angel had the advantage of a second Yelm to anchor her, as Baylor has
pointed out more than once, and still she hasn't recovered enough from
whatever has occurred to be found or find us. Edsel must have suffered far
worse."

"Nay, brother," Adonia said, sounding heartbroken yet unsure of
her own words. "They will both be found. Demon is right, we must just be
searching in the wrong manner."

"Or the wrong place!" Baylor said, suddenly coming alive with
renewed excitement.

"What?" I asked. "What are you thinking?"

"We are fools! We told her we would be going to Egypt," Baylor said, sounding torn between anger at himself and joy at his own realization.

We all stared at him stupidly, not understanding what he was talking about. Piper and I had forgotten the conversation, and the twins had never heard it. I realized instantly, with renewed hope, just how truly right he probably was when he continued. We were fools, no better than the Elders in our shortsightedness.

"Talking about her having two Yelms again reminded me," Baylor said. "How many times have I said it and not reconsidered the way in which it came to be or the conversation that followed?"

"What?" I asked, very confused yet dying to be given some of the new hope his tone said he had.

"When you were all talking about how she might have done it, how she might have stolen the Yelm, back at the sight of the fight in which it occurred. Remember?" Baylor asked. "You had made comment to all of us about how little you truly knew, how you needed to seek the council of one older and wiser. You had told all of us that if you found no answer as to the cause of Edsel's disappearance here, you would go to Egypt to find the old one Lachlan had spoken of."

"What if," he continued excitedly, "she came to herself and scanned Rome for you? She could not have scanned for me, as you say, even you cannot scan for me, I am not like the rest of you. But what if she scanned for you and could not find you? What if we had all been off in Scotland and just missed each other or even that time we all went to Athens? So when, or if, she found us not to be here, she might have thought we had gone on to Egypt, as we said we would, to find the answers which would have become even more important after she had also disappeared."

We all sat speechless for a time. All of us were trying desperately to absorb the import of his words. It seemed he had become for me an endless source of hope.

"You think she would remember that part of the conversation?"

69

Piper asked. "It was a highly trying time and we were all confused. She may have forgotten it."

"And then again she might have remembered. It's a thought, if nothing else. It's worth a try!" Baylor said. "Better than sitting here, doing nothing more than drinking ourselves into oblivion."

"And finding an older, wiser one to question is still a very good idea, mayhap we might even locate the one that had all the ideas for the Council in the first place," I added. "Of all the Changelings I have ever heard of, it would seem that that one would be the one to ask what might have come of them. I just don't know if I want to give up searching here."

"Then we will return one last time to Scotland," Baylor said, surprising me he would be willing to leave his Scotland for such an extended period of time as a trip to Egypt would take. "If we find no sign again we will go then to Egypt. If no other good comes of choosing to take a new track, at least we will be able to say we tried it. Who knows? We may find this old one and at the very least he may have knowledge of a new method for continuing our search."

"You are right!" I said. "We will go one last time to the Highlands. Then once more through here and off to Egypt, for if nothing else we have delayed a very long time in our search for answers, and can afford to no longer. We should have been seeking answers as well as Angel. We must discover how this is being done, so that we may prevent it from happening again to another of us."

"Yes, and it seems the evil ones have stayed well away from us and we will find no answers from them," Baylor lamented. "So we can take care of what new Werewolves we find while home, and the new crop that springs up while we are away will only serve to put me back in practice when we return."

"If you find no old one in Egypt, you might try again to find the one that blessed Piper," Santon said unexpectedly, breaking his perpetual silence.

As Santon was the only one of the Elders to join us this time and in general usually always silent, we all turned quizzically toward him. We were all not only surprised at his suddenly joining our conversation, but at the oddity of his suggestion, especially when we had just been discussing Werewolves. It had just seemed so odd it took all by complete surprise.

"Why?" Piper asked. "I have heard nothing of her in nearly fifteen hundred years. Why would we detour now to begin again to search for her?"

"You are of an age with Demosthenes, correct?" Santon said patiently.

"Well, yes," Piper replied, still confused. "I believe so."

"And the woman who blessed you was old and very wise already then, correct?" Santon continued, unfazed by the questioning looks from all of us.

"Yes, very," Piper replied, as understanding began to dawn on all of us.

"So then it follows that she would also be very, very, very old and wise by now, and mayhap also experienced with such things," Santon finished, and fell back into silence.

We all did, quietly considering these new options and revelations. The soft sounds and scents of the garden around us imbued a certain kind of calmness in our frantically working minds, giving what was actually a very exciting night of planning a strangely relaxed feeling. Once more a garden had proved a place of refuge for our kind. We finished our wine, while making, revising and re-revising our new plans, carefully considering everything we now knew and hoped still to learn. Trying to put these ideas into some working order, as to which new avenue we should be pursuing first, and which we felt would lead us somewhere.

We left the following morning, having decided on making one more trip to Scotland before heading to Egypt. If nothing came of the trip to Egypt, we would begin to search for Piper's creator. We would continue to look for any of the vile creations who had attacked us before but also we would try to locate the one who had helped to form the Council. Of course we were in no way sure how to go about the last, but at least we had recognized and reprioritized the need to figure it out. It was a plan, a new plan, and it renewed our spirits. We took to the northern road with a newly strengthened purpose, Adreal joining us, while Piper and Adonia would remain until we came back to begin the trek to Egypt, to be there waiting should one of you return.

We had a new course of action and with it the renewed faith we would get some positive result soon. Looking back now, I cannot help but think how terribly hard it must have been for you. It was almost unbearably difficult for us and we had each other for constant support. We at least had each other to constantly share our ideas back and forth, and lend credence and hope to those ideas if only by having had someone else to listen to them. You, on the other hand, only had the voice of Seraphim in your head and at times it was not entirely kind.

We traveled slowly again, taking our time that we might not miss you on this final trip for what we knew would be some time. These were most likely the very days you were slowly coming back to an awareness of yourself, as I have said. Considering all that I have read of what became of you back then, it must have been during this time, I can think of no other way it could have gone as it did. For it was also during this period of time that the house in Rome was left completely empty for the first time ever, while awaiting Edsel or your return.

Here is the tragic reason why, and another of our ironically near misses. You see, when Baylor, Adreal, and I had reached Calis, we had approached a vendor to ask which boat would depart for Dover soonest. Most likely this is the same one you approached, since you mentioned he had looked at you strangely. He probably thought I had lost my mind, asking him the same question twice within what was most likely the span of a few hours. After all, you were appearing to be me and as far as he knew he had already answered this question for me once.

The vendor had directed us to the same boat he would have directed you to, with the same Captain overseeing its loading. This Captain had informed us he did not have room for three, that we would have to see if another ship could accommodate us, perhaps one leaving later. This is most likely why this same Captain would have wanted to be sure you only sought passage for one, since you were me for all intents and purposes, and before I had asked for passage for three.

We had entered a tavern then, which you had declined to do, preferring to purchase your wine and sit on the pier in relative safety of solitude. We were so close then. If only you had not been so good with the trick of disguising your identity as a Changeling, I might have scanned and found you then. If only you had not been so afraid of announcing your presence to the great evil that had nearly destroyed you, *you* might have even scanned then and sensed us. You are here with me now though, and it is all in the past. No need to toy with the implements of torture, which are the 'what ifs' of ones life.

As I was saying, though, the reason the house was empty when you arrived was they had been given sudden and unavoidable reason to leave it. Piper and Adonia had been awoken from their afternoon nap by a pounding upon the door. Kynan had been there when they opened it, frantic with the worst news, we had all been dreading would someday come. He had gone to see Santon that afternoon with some question or other and Santon had been gone.

Santon had disappeared as well!

They had searched in a veritable frenzy throughout the entire city, revolving in ever widening arcs, scanning relentlessly. Probably somewhere far beyond your brief and freighted scans, leaving nothing to be found of us at the time you had finally arrived and scampered through the empty villa as a frightened rat. They had put off their search and quickly come to find the three of us, hoping to catch us before we left for Britannia. They had rushed into the tavern, Adonia very frightened and Piper extremely angry, gesturing we should follow them.

I had at first been overjoyed on seeing them, thinking you would appear directly behind them at any moment, for why else would they leave their posts in Rome? When you did not appear, however, I became frightened and upset as well, following them quickly out into the alley behind the tavern. The stench of refuse filled our noses, as we filled the skinny corridor created between the two buildings, and it seemed only appropriate for the news we were about to receive. Somehow I think I knew it, even before I was told. We gathered in a tight group awaiting the worst, Baylor at my side and Adreal going to stand beside his sister.

"Why have you left the villa, do the others know to be on the lookout for her?" I asked, confused and angry, but mostly afraid I would know the only other possible reason for them to have left already.

"Santon has gone missing as well!" Piper exclaimed. "We came quickly to tell you, as it can only be in the same manner as Edsel and Angel."

"We must discover what is becoming of us before we all disappear one by one!" Adonia added, near to tears. "I can bear to lose no more of you!"

"They are correct, Demon," Baylor said slowly, after a long silence. "We must be about finding answers. How many more fruitless trips to the Highlands, looking for her, will we make? We must find out how this was done, prevent it from happing again, and in the process mayhap discover a better way in which to recover her."

He had spoken gently, knowing how wrong this would feel to me, how much like giving up it would be, but also knowing I must hear it. He had suggested the trip to Egypt, which we had planned some forty years before. We had agreed to one last trip to the Highlands before making it, but now it seemed circumstances demanded we move forward faster. We were being picked off, so to speak, we needed to find another with hopefully more insight. I could also hope we might find you there, on the off chance you had remembered the conversation.

So, we had changed our course then, we had turned and headed for Egypt, unknowingly leaving you behind on the piers of Calis. You would board that ship, which hadn't had room for all of us, and head off in the opposite direction, to be lost to us all for more than another four centuries.

You had come back from the depths of madness only to be held at its razor edge as you spent the next three years searching everywhere between the Scottish Highlands and Rome, in the same fruitless manner we had for the forty years prior. You would find the mess of broken furniture I had made, where Baylor and I had unhappily lived in for years, allowing it to reflect our state of mind. You would find the place undusted and not cared for, for we had not cared in a very, very long time. You would take these things as signs we were lost to you, just as you had nearly been lost, and come close again to losing your mind.

You would find all you had come to know, to have been lost utterly and then seeking out what had been before, you would find your only tie to the mortal world was gone as well. Your mother had been torn from you, and you would fall off that razor edge again, dropping into it willingly, the pit of despair and insanity that you had so desperately fought your way up from mere years before. You would exact your own brand of justice, you would have your revenge; then you would have to escape it all, running away to the New World.

For this I do not blame you.

We would all have taken to a different path by then, and even when you recalled the conversation we had had, mentioning our intent to do so, it would be far too late to matter. Going to Egypt then would have done you no good. You would later have simply written it down as part of the content in the telling of a tale you felt we would never hear otherwise, a kind of footnote to the main part of the story you wanted us to know, but had missed for yourself the value of. By then it had been beyond mattering anyway, as I have said. You had been driven mad yet again and were mere days from your own chosen ascension.

~6~

About Love

So it was that in the year 1563, the year in which you returned to Scotland to find us, we five you were seeking were making our way down into Egypt. None of us felt safe to leave the others unattended or so far behind, so instead we left instruction with Lachlan, Kynan and Cathmore, that should any of our missing return, to come to us, bringing us word.

We all had mixed feelings about this endeavor, which was made obvious by the complete lack of conversation during the first part of the journey. For the most part I think we were all excited to be trying a new tack for finding not only answers but mayhap you as well. Although I believe there was also much remorse, for I know I at least felt in some manner that I had left you behind, abandoning you. I fought these feelings of guilt daily, and it seemed the others did as well, for we were nearing Greece before conversations began to flow more easily.

One such conversation I will share with you, for I know you had much the same question that it addressed, with never the heart to ask it of me. I cannot say now how it would have affected me then, but I am better off now to answer it for you. So I will tell you as I told Adreal, when that one's newly discovered bravery caused him to ask what you never had.

We were walking, as that is how we still traveled when in no big hurry and Baylor in our company, and Adreal was near to my left. He had been watching the progress of Piper and his twin sister as they moved, hands clasped together, with a look of growing perplexity upon his face. He stopped then, as we all had occasion to do more and more frequently lately, to remove yet another pebble from his sandal. After looking it over, as if it might answerer some question for him, he tossed it aside. Suddenly he turned to me quizzically.

"That is love?" Adreal asked me.

"What?" I was now as perplexed as he had appeared to be.

"That," he replied, jutting his chin to indicate his sister, making her slow progress at Piper's side.

"You mean are they in love?" I attempted to clarify.

"No," he replied. "I know they are *in* love. Adonia says she loves him. Piper says he loves her. I believe them, they are in love, but is that it?"

"Is what it?" I asked, thoroughly confused now.

"That!" he said, nodding his head toward them again. "That other world they seem to have unlimited access to. The one in which no matter the trials of the day or the hardships and pains it presents, they act as though life is wonderful simply because they are together. They smile stupidly at one another, like no threatening force lurks in the shadows waiting to steal another of us away."

"Yes," I said.

"They walk along hand in hand," he continued, "which seems an awkward way to walk, especially in this heat, and have not a care. It's like choosing to continue on with a pebble in your shoe as if its pain and hindrance is a good thing. If one stumbles the other is pulled off balance or slowed down. Yet they whisper and giggle and gaze into each other's eyes! They don't even notice. It's disgusting! What about what we are doing? What about why we are making this journey? Love seems to have addled their wits!"

I think it dawned on me that his tirade might be based at least somewhat in the fact he felt he was somehow slowly losing his lifelong companion. Mayhap he even felt he was losing his sister altogether, but for certain it seemed he had lost the pleasure of her constant company. I felt for him a little but not so much as I felt suddenly sorry for myself, for all his tirade had made me think of.

"Yes," I said again. "That is love, but it's not really such a horrible thing as all that."

"Have you ever been in love?" he asked slowly, almost as if he was afraid I would disappoint his image of me, by forcing him to envision me giggling.

"Yes, Adreal," I said softly. "It happens to the best of us."

"With whom?" he asked.

"Well, with Angel actually," I said, ignoring his surprised look. "I just hadn't allowed myself to see it. I was still focused upon the love I have for Seraphim."

"You are in love with two people?" Adreal asked. His shock and confusion was so comically obvious I almost laughed then, despite my sadness.

"It is a hard thing to explain," I said. "I will always love Seraphim, she was my first love, but she was stolen from me, and I must move on. I had fallen in love with Angel and just not allowed myself to face that truth, being too afraid of feeling such pain of loss again and simply feeling I would be betraying Seraphim in some manner by allowing myself to love another."

"Who was Seraphim?" he asked then.

"Seraphim had been my betrothed," I said, now almost needing to speak of such things, to get them off of me, out of me. "When I was still a mortal young man, growing up in Athens, she was the very moon in the night sky of my youth. Kynan, Sera and I were constantly together, from the beginning, having been born to the wealthy class that made up the Senate, and to parents that were also friends or at least happy co-conspirators. You see, our fathers had decided when Sera had been born a girl child, and not the longed for boy, that she would still serve, in that she would be raised and groomed as a perfect mate for Kynan. Of course I would still have a very acceptable match found for me, at some later date, as my father was not so well placed. It had been all very acceptable to every one.

To see that all things would go according to their plans our parents sought to keep us always together. We were even schooled together, seeing that Seraphim received an education worthy of what she was destined for. For the most part our parents had the right idea, for we were a tight trio, the best of friends. Oh, there were others of course, both male and female children either born or introduced into our father's plans, but we were the inseparable three. As we grew, though, it seemed Kynan paid her less attention, as a young woman leastwise. He seemed to continue to want to see her as merely another of the boys, or mayhap his knowledge of their betrothal made him feel there was no need to treat her any different, he had nothing to lose or prove which required he treat her special.

Then came the tumultuous times when Phillip of Macedonia was conquering all of the Persian Empire, there were power struggles and power shifts, but we three still had not a care. None of us knew what the future would bring but we would be in it together and it would be good, or so we thought. Kynan and I began joining our fathers and raising our voices up with theirs, taking our places in a society that was slowly loosing itself, trying desperately to maintain some semblance of order. Slowly we began to find our own voices, disagreeing occasionally not only with each other but with our own fathers, but where my arguments with my father seemed to be productive, Kynan's seemed to push him and his father apart. All in all, though, it still seemed a promising time, at least in my mind. Change meant that I might make a difference.

It was in this same period of time that I began to realize I had fallen madly in love with Sera and she with me. Kynan had been growing steadily more distant and subject to constant mood shifts, and this had left Sera and me alone more and more often. I think Kynan's changing temperament was due, for the most part, to his failing relationship with his father, and his father's now failing relations in the Senate. Of course Sera and I felt dreadfully guilty, he was our friend, she was his betrothed and now more than ever he needed our support, but it could not be helped. We tried to combat what we were feeling but it only grew stronger, our need for each other seemed to override all our better intentions. That is the way with love."

I had continued, finding that once I had started I didn't want to stop. Speaking of it after all these years seemed to eradicate some small portion of the pain.

"When Kynan's father had passed on suddenly, going to his reward, my family had continued undeterred in its rise to prominence," I said. "It seemed to happen so quickly, the changes just slid into place and the world seemed to be molding itself to suit me. With Kynan's family name no longer a thing to bow unquestionably to, Sera's father retracted the betrothal, based on some grounds I do not recall. None ever disputed this and Sera's subsequent new betrothal to me seemed the ultimate proof that the world would be mine. Kynan did not even seem the least upset; adding to this conviction, he even congratulated us, telling me it was meant. As I said, he had never shown much interest in her as a woman or their proposed marriage, and of course Sera and myself were extremely happy.

"But," I said, "I suppose the Fates changed their minds and decided we would not be allowed to have our utopia after all. For when I went to visit her at her villa one morning, I found her lying still and cold, her life's blood staining the pure whiteness of her robe. At first I could not grasp what I was seeing, no such thing would be possible, we were meant to be together. Had the Fates not smiled upon us and made our path clear that we might be together? Yet there my Seraphim lay, lifeless, in her family's garden.

I supposed later, when my mind began to try and wrap itself around all of it, that she had surprised a thief who was trying to exit. For there was a discarded bundle of valuable things belonging to her family on the grassy floor beside her. All these items I recognized as being from within her home. Things I had seen on tables and shelves as a backdrop in the beautiful view of her, while she had been alive and smiling or laughing, lay strewn about her lifeless form. They did not now seem right tossed about in this manner and her so still and quite. The one unrecognized thing was the thief's discarded dagger, still standing upright in the stillness of her abdomen, the only thing that seemed right, yet so very, very wrong.

"I was destroyed then, I would have destroyed the world as well. I would have broken it apart and put it together in a new manner, one in which we would be together again and no harm could come to her. It had failed me, the change was not good, every law I had helped to make, every change I had embraced, none of them had worked out as I had foreseen. My utopian dream had become a nightmare and I could wake from it no more than I could wake Sera. I had taken the dagger from her stomach to plunge into my own, thinking to go then into Hades and retrieve her with my own two hands, but that is when my Master came upon me.

He wouldn't let me, he taught me that some things could not be changed, but that I could be. He told me that I could, and would, someday make a difference, as would he, but that it would not be that day or in that way. He had said then that there must be reasons for everything even if we both were barely discovering them, and for now we would merely learn and observe and prepare for our moment, for we were change."

"I have kept that dagger always on my person, I still have it here," I said, patting the belted waist of my kilt. "I think, I thought back then, that I might come someday upon the owner, and give it back to him in my own violent manner. Yet it seems that was not to be the case and I merely carry it now out of habit and in remembrance. It reminds me everyday that there is reason for change and I must be ready when my time comes. I still hate thieves for that same reason though, they never steal mere possessions, they tend to steal parts of our lives. That one stole my Seraphim, and my willingness to love another."

I had caught myself then realizing I was heading completely off the subject. I was supposed to be explaining something about love so that my young friend would see it might not be such a bad thing. Yet I had seen myself doing to him much as I had done when conversing with you some forty years before, scaring him completely away from it. I feared he would come to the same conclusion I thought you had when you'd stared at me and told me you must not fall in love. I would not realize until I finally found and read your journal, many, many centuries later, just how badly I had misinterpreted that particular exchange of ours. I had to pause then momentarily to figure out how to repair it for Adreal.

"So yes, I have been in love," I tried. "Still am, such things never go away, the ways in which we deal with them and express them merely change. And yes it does make you do silly things, it can even overwhelm and destroy you if you let it. I have almost let it on more than one occasion. Had my Master not been there, I would have ended my own existence long ago. Had my love and loyalty to Sera not been so strong, I might have allowed myself to recognize my feelings for Angel long before it was too late. I might have done many things differently throughout my life had it not been for love, but we can only learn from these mistakes, we cannot go back and change them. I cannot even so readily dismiss them as mistakes, for without some of them other things that have been very good would not have happened."

"But then being in love only opens you up to pain!" he said, looking ahead again at his sister, appearing suddenly worried.

"Nay, it opens a whole new world of possibilities, not just painful ones," I told him then, seeing I was failing miserably, and had only made a mess again with yet another young mind. "I would not be here with you now as a Changeling, were it not for love of Seraphim. Had my loving memories of her not driven me from Athens once again I'd have never arrived at the baths the night the two of you came upon me. Therefore in turn I would have never gone to Scotland hunting Werewolves and befriended Baylor." I tried again, "Don't you see? You would not be so worried over your sister being in love, were it not for your love of her. We would not even be on this journey, having this conversation, if not for love. If we did not love each other and wish to keep all of us together, retrieving those we love now lost to us, we wouldn't be going in search of answers even now. Think of it like flying, and love is a good strong wind, it is merely whether you get it beneath your wings or allow it to press you down which might make it a painful thing."

He had gone quiet again then, as had I, both of us considering all I had said. It seemed I had given myself a little bit of wisdom as well, without even realizing I was doing it. I put my arm around his shoulder then, giving him a brief squeeze, giving him a kind of thank you, that he should lead me into a conversation that would do me such good. I wanted also to encourage him, as well as I had myself, that all things would work themselves out in the end.

"So when your Master made you," Adreal asked, "you had to go with him to learn from him, but did you first go and see your family? I mean did you get to say your farewells?"

I wasn't sure now what drove his questions, only that it seemed he wanted to know how I had dealt with my losses. Mayhap it was that he and Adonia had not been given the opportunity to say farewell to those they had loved and lost, such as their own parents or Edsel. Perhaps it was something else, but I merely answered him as best I could and hoped my answers brought him some measure of peace.

"Yes," I replied. "In a manner. I did not know then that it would be the last time I would speak with them as their son or I might have said more. I might have done it better. As it was I only told them that I had to leave for a time; that I was going to travel because I could not bear to be in her city without her. They had been supportive, wishing me only the best. My Sera had only been gone some few hours but they seemed to understand how it was too much for me to bear and my desperate need to escape it. I told them all, including Kynan, I would return to them in time, I swore it, but..."

"I know," Adreal said compassionately as I trailed off. "You never went back, did you? That is why it surprised you to see Kynan at our villa that first morning; you had not known he had been blessed, because you never returned."

"No, I had returned," I said, "it was just too late to be of much use. Too many changes, too many power struggles. My parents had been left without means and had aged beyond their years. It seemed they did not know me when I came to them, I do not know that they knew themselves. All

I could do was see that they were made comfortable for what remained of their time."

I paused for a moment, not really wanting to remember but doing so for him. So that he could see that loving them was not what pained me, but rather the losing of them whom I had loved so deeply. I wanted him to know that just because I had not said the words "I love you" before losing them didn't mean my parents hadn't known. These were things I myself had still not fully come to terms with, but I had at least known my parents had not held it against me that I had left them, they had wanted to see me happy because they had loved me too.

"My mother did tell me something once that gave me heart," I said, remembering her smiling up at me as though I were some beautiful stranger she was just getting to know. "'I have a son', she had said, 'he looked so much like you, he could be your father. You would have liked him. He was a good man, just like you.' I had asked her where he was just to better understand what it was she thought of me and she had told me he was on a journey to find himself and happiness. I had asked her then if it upset her that he was not there with her then and she had said, 'If he finds his peace, then I have mine.'"

"You see, I know they are happy, even though they are gone and I cannot ask them, because I am happy and that is all they ever wanted. If it is thoughts of your parents that haunt you now, or Edsel and Santon, you should know they would be pleased merely because you and Adonia are alive and happy."

He smiled then, seeming to accept my words and allow them to put him at some ease. We walked along another few moments in comfortable silence before he turned to me again, another look of query written plainly on his face. I tried to mentally prepare myself for what new memory he would ask me to dredge up and share with him but I could not have, even had he given me months rather than a second or two.

"But then, how is it you didn't know Kynan had been blessed?" Adreal asked. "He was your best friend, surely you returned to see him as well."

I was at a complete loss now as to what was driving his questions. It seemed he was no longer as concerned with love itself, having reconciled himself to feeling it, but more what it drove people to do. First he had seemed to want to know how I had handled the losing of those I loved, mayhap to see how he should react to the losing of those he loved. It might not have been the possibility of loosing Adonia that was concerning him at all, but the loss of all the others he could not now make good with. Now he seemed intent on understanding how I could have not made good with one I could have. Yet to help him understand I would have to look into even more coffins of the long departed times and view those buried memories I had long tried to spare myself.

"Every one deals with their emotions differently, Adreal," I said finally. "There is no wrong or right way to deal with pain and loss, especially when it is of someone we love, only ways that are less painful in the end to those involved. Love, be it for friends or family, even your lover, is a many faceted gem, one can view it a hundred times and it never appear exactly the same at any given moment, or even reflect the same light on a like situation as it did but a year before. Do you understand?"

I looked hard at him, knowing he did not fully comprehend but trying to see if I was helping at all. I continued eventually, finally realizing that whether or not I understood exactly why he asked the questions he did, that he wanted the answers nonetheless, and I had never been one to withhold from either of the twins any part of my knowledge did they but ask me for it. I could not now try to avoid answering his questions by hoping to cut to their roots, all I could do was tell him what had occurred as he had asked. Perhaps it would not be so bad to simply tell how I had done with it, and hope he could garner something useful of it.

"Yes, I did try to find Kynan when I returned, but he had completely disappeared, none had seen him since the last time they had seen me. I might have handled our parting better, I must admit, things might have been different then, we might have avoided some pain for the both of us. But..."

"Why? What happened?" Adreal had asked.

"Well, you see," I began, having a hard time with it at first, "when I had gone to tell him I was leaving he had taken it far differently than my parents had. Word had obviously already made it back to him of Sera's death, for I had found him drunk at his family's villa. His eyes had been bloodshot and swollen and I knew he had been drinking and crying for quite some time. I knew with a certainty that he had been told. But seeing him with his pain so evident, I was destroyed all the more.

He had flung open the door, drawn me into the foyer, and wrapped his arms around me sobbing. Crying almost unintelligibly how it wasn't right, how she shouldn't have died, that he never thought it would be that way. He had been barely understandable as he hiccupped and wiped his eyes, whimpering that it had not been meant, how none of it had been meant. Then sniveling and beginning to cry again all the harder, telling me he loved me and he was sorry. I had known then that he too had loved her, mayhap not as I had, but he had wished us all the happiness of love with much love of his own. I had known her death had broken him much as it had me and not known what to do about it.

I had been heartbroken then all the more, made to feel my pain all the harsher by the one there with me, sunk in it beside me, feeling it with me. He was right, none of it was meant, had I not thought the same? Had not we been meant for better things, had the Fates not smiled on us once for just a moment? I was afraid that he was going to crush me then, that he wouldn't ever loosen his grip on me physically or emotionally, that I would never be able to forget any of those moments, both beautiful and heartrending, because he would always be there to remind me. I had tried to pull away, not only from his rib-crushing grasp, but from the heartbreak he was making me face all the more.

I had to get away from all of it, to avoid for the moment the realization that she was really and truly gone. I had to escape it and to do so I had to escape him. I had finally broke free from his grasp and backed toward the door, telling him I would return, that it hurt too much now but that someday I would return to him. I told him he was still my most beloved friend and I would not forget him, that I only needed to be away for a time, to be quiet within my soul for a moment to heal. He had begun wailing all the harder, reaching out to me, sobbing about making it better together, begging me not to leave him too, that it could be fixed. Saying we could be all right if we could be together, sobbing he loved me and could not bear to lose me too.

I turned and ran then, blind in my own pain and tears, desperately seeking my Master and what peace his presence and teaching could give me, wanting to be away from all of it and quickly, unable then to feel any more of it. When I returned, as I told you, he had completely disappeared. I learned later when I saw him at your villa that it was because he too had been changed sometime shortly after I left. So I may have made it harder for Kynan by leaving him as I did, but I did so because it was the only way I knew how to do it for me. It all came out in the end, though, I suppose. He forgave me, or at least he never spoke of that parting with me again like he held it against me."

"Who blessed him?" Adreal asked suddenly.

This surprised me immensely because I had always assumed Lachlan had been the one, and felt that Adreal would have known that better than I. Yet suddenly I found myself recalling Kynan saying Lachlan had taken him into his tutelage, but not used their preferred word, blessed, in describing the process. I wondered if I could be wrong, if mayhap Lachlan had merely adopted him in a way and continued his training where another had left off. It seemed to fit the wording Kynan had used and yet I could not understand why or how such a thing would have happened. Finally I ended up simply letting it be known that I wasn't really sure.

"Lachlan, no?" I said looking quizzically at him.

"I don't think so, mayhap though," Adreal replied, equally confused now. "I had thought the one who made you must have made him too, being of a place and time together as Kynan and you were."

"Well..," I began.

I trailed off. Of course I was also hoping Adreal had learned something of use from my tale, that I had shown him things were not always black or white, sometimes they were grey and we lived with them. Yet I was wondering more so at myself and the fact I had never thought to question Kynan's change before now or find out for sure who had changed him. I soon put it from my mind, merely telling myself I would have to ask him when next I had the chance.

Adreal didn't ask any more questions, so I assumed he had found what he had been looking for in our conversation and left it at that. We simply went back to walking in silence and when I looked over at him he seemed contentedly lost in his own thoughts, so I left him to them. If he had anything else he wanted to know from me he would ask and I would answer as best I could, but for the time being I walked on in silence and set about putting my coffins back in the earth.

We took a route by which we might pass through Athens once more. This might have been a subconscious decision, but I am not sure. Having spoken then of Seraphim, my mind may have somehow guided our feet in the direction where memories of her still thrived, taking me back down streets we had wandered as young adults in love, and passed the villa she had called home. My mind threw out visions ahead of me, of her running laughingly ahead, daring me, that I would catch her up and kiss her.

Yet, this time I looked with different eyes, eyes that searched for sign of you. Those visions twisted themselves so that her face became yours, her laughter became your own, and you remained somehow too far ahead of me to be kissed, but in my heart. We all looked once more throughout that city, to see if you might have returned to my own home in search of me, knowing it was the place of my birth. As you know though, we found no sign of you there; such thoughts had never entered your mind. So we then found the necessary passage to Crete, and from Crete to the ports of Alexandria.

We had for the moment, it seemed, not so much forgotten the disappearances as put it to the rear of our minds, in deference to the search for the answers as to how to recover those that had disappeared. We continued scanning relentlessly for either you or Santon and Edsel, but found nothing at all. No lost loved one was to be found, just as there was no sign of those that had done them harm.

It seemed that those that would cause such harm to us as well, if given the opportunity, found themselves seriously lacking in any such course. We remained together and ever watchful and none dared to attack us as we traveled in such force. So it was we did not come into any further contact with those vile creatures that we felt had played part in this tragedy, and could not garner such answers as we sought from them. It appeared that they had withdrawn quite completely from the field, and we would indeed have to seek out the old one of Egypt for our answers.

I had often wanted to see this place, from which my Master had said he came, but had always been taken away from that goal by some matter or other. I had dreamed of a day when I would set foot in Egypt and be swallowed up by the masterful beauty my Teacher had described, but this day was not so glorious as my dreams had portrayed. I was not as happy as I might have been, had the circumstances of my visit there been better ones.

The beauty was there, I do not take that away from Egypt. The glorious golden miles of molten sands, rolling endlessly toward the horizon, could have taken one's breath away, had it not already been stolen as mine had been. It was indeed a place that felt of gods or at least professed to have known them first hand. I could feel the presence of the great pyramids long before mere mortal eyes could have told me where they stood. They felt good and kind and wise to me.

They felt like my Master.

I was greatly confused by this, for I knew my Master had ascended of his own accord more than fifteen hundred years ago. I knew now what old one's presence it was that had been felt by others of our kind over the years. I just couldn't figure why or how. Had he returned and not cared enough to have let me know? If he had returned, could others? Was he still here somewhere? If I could find him, would he have the answers I so desperately needed? Would he even allow me to find him considering he had made himself impossible to find by all the others who had search so many times before?

All these questions along with more became a veritable fount of conversation between all of us; where so recently there had been drought, now there was a flood of query and tentative thoughtful response. We began to try and refocus and redirect without becoming too hopeful that all would be solved by that one simple discovery, that of the one that had once instructed me.

~7~

Rajesh

It took us some time, but we managed to discover one of our own within the sprawling city. Now I have to give credit here for that idea to the twins, for I had been preparing to go about finding other accommodations for all of us, despite how difficult I knew that might be. They were the ones who thought to use their connections to the Council to some good, for once, seeking out one they knew of from Lachlan and Kynan's previous visits who would take us in. He willingly put us all up with the utmost show of the old world hospitality.

We were shown into his home with a great display of appreciation for our visit and found quickly he had actually been awaiting us. Not only had word of our imminent arrival gone ahead of us, but so had news of the recent occurrences which had necessitated it. Our host was distressed by what he had heard of the events taking place in our realm and eager for any new news, but politely left his questions until after we had all been cleaned up and were settled down to a wonderful meal.

His name was Rajesh. He was Arabic and had lived in Egypt for over four hundred years. He had done much, as you said in your journal that you had done, to maintain the same residence for all that time. He had even employed the same families for generations, but all of this comes later. For now I will tell you that you would have liked him for he loved to tell stories and seemed to never tire of them. He also held certain parts of the Code in as little regard as I found you did in the reading of your journal, but I found all of these things out over time, coming to realize that though he would assist the Counsel and their associates willingly and with unlimited grace, he would still do many things according to his own judgment and their approval was not a necessity to him.

He loved good food and fine wines and took his time with all things. He was a great lover of the finer things, such as a good cup of fine Arabic coffee and a long talk with good friends. You would have also considered him quite beautiful, knowing you, because he had skin a little darker than Piper's only without the aid of the sun, which I found he carefully shielded it from, and hair much like your own. He had been blessed with all the darkly handsome features those people are so often gifted with and a smile that showed them all off to their best. Even Adonia could not keep her eyes from wandering to him once in a while, and it is a well known thing she has never loved any other than Piper.

We had been led through his huge, beautiful mansion, the whole of which abounded with open archways, shutters thrown wide and sheer drapes allowing the cool morning breeze to make it seem to breathe. The whole of the place seemed a living thing, as inviting and pleased with our presence as its master.

We were led to our prepared rooms by an exceptionally quiet servant, and shown where to bathe. Later we all met up again, in another chamber which had also been quietly pointed out. We sat resting in this beautiful room and it was amazingly comfortable, I must say, strewn about with gloriously thick, intricately patterned rugs one on top of the other in seemingly disorderly layers. There were pillows of all sizes and shapes, made of more colors and textures even than the rugs, while somehow still managing to match, strewn everywhere, and plentiful wine in freestanding basins. Candles and incense burned randomly about the room, sending the most beautiful intermingling of scents wafting throughout. The entire chamber, with all the vivid color displayed in absolutely everything, combined with scent and endless comfort, to give it the feel of an overgrown indoor garden.

The questions we had been so recently considering, concerning my Teacher, were enough to keep us well entertained until our host would join us. We drank of the wine and took in the scented air, lounging in padded comfort. We were content for the moment to throw out the occasional conversational query and consider it slowly as we sipped. Yet we were soon approached by the same manservant with the eerily silent feet that had shown us about earlier. He mutely invited us to join his master elsewhere to dine, with nods and bows.

I think I was more impatient then for the true conversations to begin than our host. Rajesh seemed to have no end of patience. He appeared relaxed and incredibly content as we entered the hall and were shown to our seats. He seemed unbothered as his servants scurried about on silent feet, showing little need to hurry them so we might jump into the endless rounds of questions any one of the Elders would have. He remained silent, as did we all, as his servants delivered endless amounts of the most wonderful smelling covered platters, then placed a smaller covered platter before each of us. These larger ones were placed in the center of the table in a seemingly random procession that only made sense later.

Rajesh finally shooed them all but one away and proceeded to do the rest of the serving himself, showing us the first signs since that morning that he had indeed wanted desperately to speak to all of us. The single servant that had remained in the room was the same that had so silently invited us to this dining hall earlier, and he now backed to the door just as quietly with his eyes down, effectively placing himself at a discreet distance from his master and his guests but within the same chamber should he be needed. At the same time his presence was keeping the others from being able to reenter. This struck me as odd, considering the Council was quite strict on the matter of humans being allowed to know of us, and indeed I felt Rajesh would not want his servant to be able to overhear all that we were destined to discus. Yet I trusted that there were things I might not know and that our host was well aware of what he was doing and who could be trusted. It was not, nor had it ever been, my place to enforce the Council or its Codes and I was not going to change that now by confronting this intriguing new comrade about his allowing a servant to remain within earshot, so I left it be.

Soon the human presence was forgotten as Rajesh began lifting each covering from the platters one by one and dipping out a small amount onto his own plate before sending the platter around the table, suggesting a small portion of each be eaten with the bread that the smaller platters before each of us contained. He offered us brief descriptions of each dish as he dipped out his part and, though some of it sounded strange, to say the least, all of it was delicious. Of course because he had been there, in that area, for so very long my first question of him was to be the obvious one and I was having trouble not rudely blurting it out. Yet I schooled myself to patience, taking my lessons from our host, and simply enjoyed the food for the moment.

When we each had a full plate before us and the occasional 'ooh' and 'ahh' could be heard from all, it seemed only then that our gracious host felt it right to begin to question us, as though having done so well by us the whole afternoon, and evening as well, finally gave him the right to ask something of us in return. His manner was a sharp contrast to the way of Edsel and I approved. Thinking of Edsel then and my reasons for having met this intriguing man at all left my mood darker than mere moments before, and the wonderful food lost some small measure of its appeal. Then the wine made it to my end of the table and I filled my glass as Rajesh opened the floodgates of conversation.

"To new friends." Rajesh's rich voice and raised glass cut into and disrupted my settling brood.

"To new friends," we all said, raising our glasses then sipping to accept his invitation to friendship yet again.

Now that the silence had been broken it was destined to be a very long time before it would come again. The questions began flying from all of us in total disarray. We all seemed to forget our manners completely, talking around mouthfuls of food and over each other. Then suddenly we seemed to notice ourselves all at once and began with the 'go ahead' and 'no you first' and so on until finally we had established some sort of order in the conversation.

"Well, to be honest, I am eager to learn if you have ever met the old one that I can feel here, since you have lived here for so long," I said, accepting the invitation to go first since this question weighed heavily on me. "He was my Teacher and I long for his counsel now."

"Many apologies, my friend, but I must tell you as I have told all the others over the years," Rajesh replied sadly. "I myself searched for many centuries before realizing he would only be found if he wanted to be. I must say your Master stays very well hidden indeed, for none of us have ever seen him."

"I suppose I expected to hear no different, really," I admitted sadly. "He left me to ascend over fifteen hundred years ago now. It is only that it is very confusing to me to feel his presence so strongly after all these years. When first I did, I had hoped he had returned somehow and that he would find me here, but there must be some mistake. Surely he would not have returned and had such disregard for me as to not seek me out that I might know it."

"You still may find him, my friend. Because he chooses to remain apart from us does not mean he will not allow you to rediscover him," Rajesh said kindly. "It is not our part to question in what manner another chooses to exist. He obviously held you in higher regard than any other, to have made you over in order to keep you to himself rather than surrender you unto death. Do not be so quick to think of it as disregard, perhaps he merely awaits you coming in search of him, rather than the other way around."

I thought about what Rajesh was saying and it did make sense to me. Why should my Teacher, my Master, have to come in search of me? Should not I, as the loving and studious pupil, be the one to seek him out? Then another thing occurred to me which left me even more confused than the initial feeling of him being here in the first place.

"But then this presence I feel now is the same others have spoken of and sought throughout the ages?" I asked, trying to clarify. "It is not recently come?"

"Aye, the one we feel now has been felt by me here since the day of my rebirth. I have felt no other even nearing him in power, in all that time, and still he has never been seen by myself or any other I have had occasion to speak with," he said, now looking a bit confused as well.

"But if this presence here is the same others have sought out since the times following the birth of the Council, even before Nero, then there must be some mistake," I said. "My Master had already ascended by that time and surely his presence would have dissipated from here. He came to me in Athens in the years following the fall of Alexander the Great and we never returned to this place, though he told me he had come up from here. That would mean he had been absented from this, his homeland, for some three hundred years and still his presence was pulling Changeling seekers of knowledge from across the seas. That is not possible. "

"But this presence which surrounds us now is the only one of its kind I have ever encountered here, or anywhere for all of that. If you say that it is your Master then it must be, and he must have returned then and now somehow. You will find him one day, and mayhap he can explain what I cannot. If anyone can rediscover him, it will be his own reborn."

I could tell he didn't feel the complete conviction of his words because now we were both thoroughly and obviously confounded. Yet he had spoken to elevate my ever lowering spirits and I appreciated the fact he even cared enough to do so after having known me for such a short time. Once again I was forced to note his manners differed greatly from those of the Council as I knew it now. He had hoped to someday speak to my Master, as any other Changeling would, if only to learn what one so old might be able to tell. It was obvious that Rajesh's hopes might have been revived by having one of the old one's own to draw him out, but the possibility of its actually working was still far fetched and he seemed to know that.

If my Master had ascended and left me once, what would cause him to return to me now or even allow me to find him if he had remained unreachable by all others? It was a lot to think of oneself to believe I could draw him out when I could not convince him not to ascend in the first place. Quite probably his original reasons for ascension still plagued him and he would remain as far away as possible from emotions, and the attachments they forced one to create, even if he had returned. Thinking all of this only served to convince me further that he was avoiding me and would continue to do so, for had I not been the one to teach him of such things in the first place? Had I not been the one to learn how to better control my own emotions by teaching him how to let his go?

All my old wounds, the loneliness, the feelings of abandonment, all the losses of those I had loved, it all began to feel very heavy as though a boulder had come to rest within my stomach. I found I was following a dangerous path again, one that went the way of depression and would see me haunting the graveyard of sorrowful memories. I recognized this route almost instantly, and I knew it would fast become impossible to disengage myself from it were I to continue to allow myself to follow these kinds of ghosts to where they slept. I had more years of painful memories to lure me on than I could possibly risk turning upon me now.

I realized, as I had been blessed to realize over and over again, that I was not the only one suffering, and that is all that has ever saved me. Just knowing that I had no right to worsen the situation of others, by falling into self-pity's grimy grip, when I might be able to help them otherwise, brought me back up out of it. Right then I had a group of trusted friends that needed my assistance, before I had had a strange Teacher with a lot of questions, but always I had someone that needed my attention more than those haunting memories that only played at being friends. So I put my sorrows back in their graves where they should have been left resting and stored them back were they belonged, at the very back of a dusty vault where I kept all such memories that should have long been resting but still rose up sometimes to rewound me.

So I began listening again as the conversation turned from the 'what ifs' to the 'what to dos' all around me, and joined in as we all conceded we should not count on finding my Master to solve our dilemmas. Though I knew I would have to try, that my own heart would give me no quarter on that demand, I also knew we must find another means to solve this mystery by ourselves for when and if that proved to be impossible.

We gave our new friend Rajesh every bit of detail we knew at that moment and he interjected his views at every interval he felt inclined to. He seemed, however, more intent on hearing us out before making many comments. It was only when it came to the Yelm you had stolen and the consequent permanent death it had done the other Changeling that he became unable to merely listen. I realized then he had been lost sometime before that on many things concerning you.

"You mean this Angel you speak of stole the Yelm of another and sent it into the light?" Rajesh was astounded.

"Yes," I agreed, "in so many words I suppose that is exactly what she did."

"What manner of Angel is she that she had such a power to intervene in this manner?" he asked, confused now.

"A Changeling only," I clarified, realizing where our conversation had been confusing him. "I changed her myself, and Angel is merely the name given her by her mother, her sister I mean," I added, confusing him still further.

"But she was special," Baylor cut in. "You said yourself that you heard her soul calling out to you from further away than any should have been able to be heard, even by one as old as you."

"And she did things others do not do for the mere fact she never thought not to do them," Adonia added. "Her hellcat form was ingenious. Who else but Angel would have thought to invent and wear a half-form like a new gown and use only her own instincts?"

"Your points are well taken," Piper cut in then, addressing Baylor and Adonia like naughty children. "We will concede that Angel was not ordinary, but I think what we are trying to clarify with our friend Rajesh is that she was indeed only a Changeling and not an Angel in fact."

"And what we are trying to clarify," Adreal said with amusement in his sister's defense, "is that she was by no means ordinary in either case."

"Right then," Piper conceded, raising his glass to all of them as I tried not to grin, "all points taken in better light then."

"So this Angel, she is a Changeling who took half-forms, without either's instincts?" Rajesh was still spellbound, having missed, I think, the majority of the exchange and focusing only on that. "And stole from another that which makes it whole?"

Rather than sounding condemning as an Elder of the Council might have, he sounded only very intrigued. That is when I began to realize even more so that he was not only very different from them but very much like Piper and myself, that though we had all worked in coordination with the Council on many occasions we would not bow to them and their teachings blindly. Like all of us, it seemed, he too thought for himself, and if it could be proven that the Council was mistaken, then he too would be one to stand firm in his own reasoning, and leave the Council to deal with their own strictures and shortsightedness.

"What then does the Council say of these things?" Rajesh asked finally, as if reading my mind.

"They have nothing to say, not that I will hear. Most of the Code is not theirs to begin with, so I will brook no attempts on their part to enforce it, especially if it means the punishment of one I cherish and have taken under my wings." I said this more vehemently than was necessary given the company I was speaking to, but with regard to you my emotions were raw and I spoke without thought.

"You need not fear judgment from me," Rajesh quickly protested, "I am merely intrigued. This Angel seems quite the rare jewel, I am saddened I cannot speak with her myself and I can see why you are so desperate to find her."

"If you only knew," I had whispered, but then his look had said he did.

"What do you mean, though, 'is not theirs'?'" Rajesh had continued quickly, as though recognizing a tendency to brood within me that he did not want to encourage by a long silence. "If not the Council's Code, than whose?"

So he had averted my thoughts from the loss of you by leading me to relate our own recently acquired knowledge as best we could, each of us interjecting what we felt the other was destined to forget. He was supremely surprised, just as we all had been, to find its origins sprung from the mind of one as yet unnamed or locatable. More notable, though, was his reaction to my assertion that I felt it was another very old and very wise one. I was no longer able to think it merely a very intelligent one of equal years to those members of the Council it had met with.

"Then you believe this one was old enough and wise enough to not only have known what he suggested would work, but smart enough to disguise the full truth of his age and wisdom, so as to not alarm them or have them question him further on other things or his motives? Thus he was able to manipulate them, effectively setting them up to do his bidding, without having answered for himself to them at all?" Rajesh said almost too matter-of-factly, simplifying it so much better than I had as yet been able to.

"Yes, in essence, I think that is what I am saying," I admitted, realizing it was even as I said it.

"Then we must figure to what purpose," he said, "and whether or not he too has been done this same damage that has befallen the others, or is somehow behind the doing of it. Only by figuring out his motives might we learn if he is evil in nature or good, for you will know a tree by its fruit. From there we may decide our next course of action. If he is good then it is only a matter of searching for him, hoping he too has not vanished and acquiring more of the knowledge he seemed to have so liberally at his disposal. If he is evil we must begin to discover what part if any he has had in all of that which is now befalling our kind. We may indeed be facing an anti-Council as you have suggested, but what we have yet to consider is that the very one who started ours may be the master behind its counterpart that we do not as yet even know we need to fear."

Having it put into words just so ran a chill up all of our spines, leaving us to wonder just what exactly we were facing and if we were going to be able to figure it out in time, or if we were all destined to disappear one by one with the last one standing still asking, "What is going on?" There was a moment then when it seemed I should remember something you had said to me in the Highlands, a brief flicker at the corner of my mind, but it fled from my grasp as though looking toward it had sent it scurrying for cover.

We had talked the evening away, and between the hour having grown very late, or early rather, and the wine being constantly replenished by the ghostly silent manservant that Rajesh had allowed to remain, all of us had been yawning frequently as the sun began to make its presence known about the horizon. Rajesh suggested that we should all find our rest and join again with him later that afternoon, saying that a good nap and even better Arabic coffee thereafter would have us thinking more clearly on all the matters laid out before us.

Our host had then seen to it that each of us was shown to those exceptionally comfortable rooms we had used before. Bidding us enjoy our rest and pass the hotter part of the day in peace, he told us we would meet later in the room I had dubbed the indoor garden. I was very much frustrated by that fact that I knew I was forgetting something very important in regards to Rajesh's last statements to us, but I found myself falling into a deep, worried sleep before the answers would come to me. I found my dreams reflecting that worry and I caught myself analyzing them even as I had them.

I was dreaming that I was walking across the golden surface of the desert, the sand sucking at my sandals and burning my feet. I was hot and very uncomfortable but there was absolutely nothing I could do to change that. This made me feel unspeakably hopeless, for I was a creature of change, it was what I was and I didn't know how to be other than that anymore.

The pyramids ahead of me were trying to eclipse the setting sun, throwing over the entire world an amazing molten glow that did little to lessen the heat. Suddenly I could feel my Master at my side, his presence almost engulfing me, spreading peace like a blanket thrown over my shoulders to ward off the discomfort of the hopelessness, if not the actual heat. Yet I saw no prints forming where I knew his feet must be coming down invisibly beside mine.

I wanted desperately to speak to him but I told myself he would not be able to answer me, for if he had no feet then obviously he had no mouth. Still I felt compelled to speak my mind to him as though he were telling me he was listening and he would help me in what manner he could. So I tried then to form the questions, wondering which should come first, but I had become too parched and my mouth would not make the words for me. My tongue would not move from the roof of my mouth and I began to scan the horizon for any place where I might find a well from which to drink; wondering at the same time how my Teacher would drink if he would not make for himself a mouth even to speak with me.

Then suddenly I felt him slipping away from me, up and up he went, just as he had so long ago. I felt as completely alone as I had after his first ascension all over again, left with a thousand unanswerable questions running rampant and unchecked throughout my troubled mind. I wanted desperately to call him back but my voice had abandoned me completely and I needed water to coax it back.

I awoke with a start as a glass was pressed to my lips and I tasted water. I blinked, trying to figure who had brought this gift to me and how they had known I so desperately needed it. I recognized finally that the person holding it there for me was Rajesh's manservant, the one that had been allowed to remain in the hall as we dined and spoke the night before. Though I know my face must have revealed a million questions, his look was very plain and showed no answers to me. Even as I asked him how he had known I was searching for the water he had brought, I began to wonder if it was merely the fact he had been there with the water and I had felt his presence which had caused me to thirst for his offering in the first place. He made no move to respond to my query, merely placing the glass in my grasp and backing silently to the door, closing it quietly behind him as he left me alone with my now even more confused musings.

I sat there holding the water for a moment, almost forgetting how badly I had needed it while dreaming. Slowly I got to my feet and walked to one of the bedchamber's many open arches. I looked out on the desert, so much now as I had just been dreaming it, with the sun setting behind the tips of the pyramids just as they had been mere minutes before in my sleep. I was asking myself once more how it was that Rajesh's man would have known I needed water when he had not been in my dream. I wondered why it was that the scene of my dream and the one I was now looking out on had been so similar, even to the position of the sun.

I know it sounds like an insane line of reasoning, but it made me think for just a moment that perhaps it had not been a dream at all, that I had gone on a sleeping walk and my Master had joined me, if only to let me know that though I would not see him, he would help me in any manner he could. I drank down the remainder of my water and found I was mildly comforted by this line of reasoning. Though the manservant's presence there with the water I had just finished was still unexplainable, I felt strangely at ease with the rest.

I stood still, allowing the cooling breeze to further soothe me for a long time, thinking how easily one could fall in love with that view and understanding why my Master would choose to return to it to find peace. I sent out a silent thought to him giving him thanks for the dream and asking him to return to me again. I told him I was grateful for any gift of his presence but that to see his face and laugh and talk with him again would be the ultimate gift, if he would ever grant it to me. I tried to mean it when I told him I understood why he had left me in the first place, for even I at times had felt the burden of living to be too great, but in truth I did not forgive him. In truth I felt abandoned even more so at that moment than ever, left to the great wide world and all of its misery and mystery, with nary a clue or defense.

Oh, I knew that he had trained me far better than most, that among Changelings I had been equipped far beyond even those Council members that had been so long responsible for the training of others. He had assured himself that I was prepared to handle all he had thought I might encounter, but he had not prepared me for the one thing he himself had not been able to deal with either, the never-ending barrage of emotional tortures that comes from merely remaining a living, feeling being with emotions while all else fades around you. For that, no one can be prepared. I do no think it is a thing that was ever meant to be. Humans were not designed to live so long, I do not think. We were meant to live out one life at a time, to learn what we can and choose what we may. To survive longer we must learn to change. That is, after all, what we are equipped to do when we choose to remain.

So change is what I decided to do. I decided right then that I had to remember to think less of my losses and more of what I still had. I had to remember that if I could not focus my efforts and stay away from the despair I had been so constantly drawn to, especially of late, that I stood to gain nothing and quite likely lose even more. This is not to say that from that moment forward I no longer found myself falling into a pit of sadness when some bleak memory lured me to it, but only that I had finally decided I could not continue to live as I had been. I could not even call it living any more, really. I had lost so much due to my previous inability to accept it all, including you and what love you could have given me. How long could I hope to survive like that, and surviving is what it had been a lot of the time, the living had taken place in small sweet intervals and had been due to the presence of those friends I now needed to join with and find a way to save.

It was nearly the same realization I had made the night before at the dinner table and many other times before that, but the real difference was that I was not going to do it for someone else, I was changing my outlook for me. I was changing, period, because it was what I was, what I was meant to do, and because I wanted to do more than survive. I wanted to live, not just for them and for finding you, but because I wanted to. I wanted to, and it felt good to want life again. I went to join the others then in an uplifted state, finding they had been awaiting me for quite some time.

~8~

Dreams

Upon taking my place among them, I was immediately offered a small cup by the same man that had been at my side with the water when I had awakened. The liquid inside was very hot and smelled amazingly good, dark and rich, it invigorated me still further merely smelling it. We had gathered once more in the room of carpets and pillows and somehow this lent a feeling of comfort to the conversations going on, even though they were not the happiest of things to be discussing. As I took my first tentative sip of the delicious brew, Rajesh turned and posed a question to me, drawing me into what was obviously a polite argument between himself and the ever increasingly stubborn and outspoken twins.

"What purpose do you think this unknown Changeling had in helping to establish the Council as we know it?" Rajesh had asked.

I was having a hard time keeping my face straight, not only due to the temperature of the liquid I had just taken into my mouth but the mere fact of the changes making themselves so apparent in the twins. It amused me greatly that they no longer resorted to taking various animal forms and poking fun at their elders when they were in disagreement, but seemed to now enjoy arguing for the sake of itself and their own newfound bravery to do so. The fact that all had turned to face me, as if I had grown horns when I did not respond immediately, also went far toward making it very hard to swallow. Well, if they thought the newly horned demon was going to shed some light on this quandary they were mistaken, because what came out of my mouth only stirred the dark pot more.

"We are assuming then that he meant for it to be 'as we know it' and its formation a help to us?" I asked, finally managing to swallow. "I had considered that if he were evil in his intent, then the fact that the Council became what it is would be why he has decided to eliminate it one member at a time."

"As had we all," Adonia said, very self satisfied. "Had you been here with us, you would have realized we had ruled that out due to the fact if he had wanted to eliminate them and was the one doing so, by such a devastating means that we are still trying to uncover it, then he could have had done with the lot of them ages ago."

"Yes, if he is so powerful as to have accomplished being rid of them one by one so efficiently, right under our noses," Adreal added, "then why waste fifteen hundred years in the doing of it?"

"I would!" Baylor replied. "If I were your enemy I would want to remain an enigma as long as possible. To pick you off one by one without you even being on your guard because you had no knowledge you even had an enemy. I have found it is always easier to kill those who don't know I am coming."

"Exactly," I agreed. "What better way to hunt than never to be seen as the hunter, not to be thought of as a predator by your prey?"

"But why help them in the first place, then?" Adreal asked.

"Was it meant to be help?" I countered. "Or was it setting them up to thin the herd for him and then putting them on a path marked in his mind for a later leisurely hunt?"

"What if," I continued, thinking these things even as I said them, "he showed them only enough to do him the good of ridding the world of those he could not herd easily, and then turned the rest into sheep to be easily led to the slaughter as he would. I mean he led them to think it would be a better choice to leave the new ones in somewhat ignorant states, especially when it came to how to disguise what they were from the detection of another who might be looking. He even suggested keeping records which any might use to easily ascertain in what general location they might most likely be found. All he would have to do is sneak in unseen and undetected and take a peek at one of these record books the Council had kept so meticulously since he told them it was a good idea."

"But if they were keeping these meticulous records for him and he was making use of them as you suggest, then they were still serving a purpose." Rajesh asked then, "Why destroy them?"

My brain seemed to be working very fast now because I had almost seen this question forming in all their minds before it had been spoken aloud. I took another sip of my now cooling drink and looked at them over the rim of my cup.

"Only think," I said. "I had taught Adreal and Adonia all that the Council had withheld and Edsel came to know it but did nothing."

"No, he did do something," Adonia interjected. "He spoke with Santon about it and they were thinking to bring it before the rest of the Council, acknowledging that it might be a thing of value for all to learn."

"Then that is it!" I said triumphantly. "I know it now more than ever. It makes too much sense to be otherwise."

"Then they made themselves a liability to his plan by thinking to change the way all other Changelings were instructed," Rajesh said. "If they had managed to change what he had arranged to be a weakened new generation of us, then they would irreparably damage his designs."

"Yes," Baylor replied, "just as our Angel did when she accidentally discovered a way in which to stop his plan completely, by killing all those working in unison with him with the same sort of single decisive blow."

"Only one problem exists with this new theory, though," Piper said then. "Us!"

"What do you mean?" I was momentarily baffled.

"It has not come for you or me," Piper answer. "We have not been targeted, and we of all of them are the ones one would fear would teach others too much. We have always been equal yet separate from the Council, older and sometimes wiser than even it, and you especially have taught things our supposed enemy would not want others to know."

"We have been attacked," I said, trying to defend my theory, for it had seemed sound up to that moment. "They just have been unable to succeed in doing us whatever harm they have done the others."

"I don't think it has been tried," Piper countered again. "For some reason we have not yet been targeted by any but other Changelings. If it is this same old powerful Changeling the Council members met that is behind this and he can somehow force one to ascend, or destroy it outright, on his own, then why has he not dispensed with us yet? He has to know we exist and can teach others to be aware, and..," he trailed off, seeming irritated by his inability to put it all to rights in his own mind.

"We have remained together?" I asked then, wondering if I had been wrong and that this old one was not involved, at least not in the way I had been thinking. "We have not allowed for the opportunity to attack us because we have remained together, and together we are formidable."

"You may be correct," Piper had admitted. "But if he was brazen enough that he came into the very villa, with Edsel and the twins all three present and aware and was never even noted, it seems he could accomplish our demise as easily if he so wished. I don't know, I still think there should be more reason than that we have all been together. I mean, I left the twins by themselves when I went to Scotland to retrieve you. You and Baylor were alone often."

He had trailed off again and we all thought about things in silence for a time. The eerily quiet manservant, who seemed ever present, had kept stealthily refilling our little cups so that I could not have told you how many I had had already when he silently leaned forward to fill it once more. I was suddenly reminded that he had never answered me as to how he had come to be in my room earlier that afternoon and in possession of the water I had so desperately wanted in my sleep.

"What is your name?" I whispered to him as he started to lean back.

I know I startled him, for he nearly dropped the hot container he had just been using and made some small noise at the back of his throat which resembled a small dog whining to be let indoors in winter. He looked to Rajesh then, as if to be saved, and I too looked at his master, wondering if I had done something highly improper in addressing our host's servant directly.

"He is called Manji," Rajesh answered for the man.

"Thank you," I said, dipping my head slightly toward him. Then I turned again to Manji, saying, "You never answered me. How did you know about the water earlier this afternoon?"

His eyes showed me something like fear, and this was odd to me because I had no intentions of doing him ill, nor had I thought that I'd given the impression those intentions could change. He looked quickly from me to Rajesh again and I was about to apologize and ask Rajesh directly if it was frowned upon for me to speak to his servants or they to me. I was surprised when Rajesh spoke for him again.

"He cannot answer you," Rajesh said. "He took an oath upon becoming my personal servant that he would speak not one word of what he knows or learns by being in my presence or does in the service of me."

"But I am not asking him to divulge a personal secret concerning you. I merely wish to understand how he came to be in my room with water when I awoke," I said, still confused.

"You misunderstand the nature of the oath itself, it was never to speak and is thus never spoken," Rajesh said patiently. "He presented his tongue to me as an offering of loyalty and trust, his proof of worthiness just as his father before him and so on throughout the years. Thus he has no tongue now with which to speak. His family has served me for longer than most can trace their comings and goings in this world, and it has always been so."

"That is awful!" Adonia said, "Why would you ask such a thing of one that serves you so well?"

She had spoken hastily but I think we had all thought it, it was merely she that said it because, well, because she was Adonia, and Adonia seemed to be growing more and more outspoken as the days passed. Rajesh did not show any feelings, other than a mild amusement, at having been judged so sharply and quickly by a woman. One might have thought that it would have greatly upset a person of his lineage to have a woman speaking down to him at all, but he took it in stride and his answer only more astounded us.

"Again you have misunderstood, my friends," he said, smiling. "I do not require it, they do this of their own accord. I did not ask it of the first, I have never asked it of any of them and will not up to the last. If they choose to break or not the tradition set down by their forefathers, I will not begrudge them either choice. It is they that from the first have thought it a proper token to be offered to me before the entering of my personal service."

"You mean they chose to give up their tongues without you asking it? Why?" Adonia said, seeming even more aghast that a person would do such a thing by personal choice than she had been when thinking it had been something required by Rajesh.

"A very long time ago, I saved Manji's forbearer," Rajesh said slowly, as though not wishing to speak of it yet unable to stop himself. "He was in a position of impending doom and in the saving of him it was unavoidable that he learned what I was. All I asked him in repayment for his life was that he not ever speak a word about me or what I had been capable of doing. His answer to this request was to fall to his knees and cut out his own tongue placing it at my feet." Rajesh paused here, looking down, as though remembering the man at his feet somehow saddened him.

"He then followed me everywhere I went," he continued a moment later, speaking softly now, lost in the memory. "I could not shake him, he seemed to know my paths better than I. Soon he had effectively become my manservant, for he was ever there when I had even the smallest of needs. Before his death he brought his son to me and that one did the same. Making me the same oath his father had and in the same manner, keeping to it his

whole life through. It has been the way of their family now for many
generations. There is no requirement on my part that the tradition remain,
but neither do I require they change it if they do not wish to..."

He had gone suddenly quiet, looking out to the nearly extinguished
sun through the huge open archways that edged the entire great chamber.
Somehow I knew this to be one of those memories he too had had to learn not
to follow, and I decided not to press him further. Memories were such
treacherous things, especially to those with so many. I still had not received
the answer I had originally set about to get, and wasn't sure how to without
possibly worsening his now apparently somber mood. I was just about to
decide it wasn't all that important when Rajesh spoke up again.

"Somehow his line has always seemed to know things, see things, it is
what brought Manji's forefather to be in the position of needing to be saved
in the first place," he said. "Some men would ask what they are not willing to
hear of those too honest for their own good, you see? So when Manji went to
bring you to us and he had taken water with him, I had not thought to
wonder why. I simply figured he had known you would want it by whatever
means he and all those before him have always known such things."

"I have never understood it," he whispered, almost as though he
spoke of sacred things. "But it is again a thing I neither question nor desire to
change. We all have things about us others do not understand, it is what
makes us who and what we are. Some fear what they do not understand, but
I." He paused for a moment, then looked hard at me as though something
had just grown out of my forehead again. "Mayhap you and Piper have
something special about you that causes this other one we were speaking of
before to be weary of you? That keeps him from drawing near the others if
either of you is present?"

I had stared back at him stupidly for a moment then looked at Piper
probably much as Rajesh had just been looking at me. As though whatever it
was that might make us different would somehow manifest itself in a physical
manner and I would be able to see it. It was only when I gave up and took
another sip of my fine Arabic coffee that I noticed Rajesh's man was smiling

at me. Oh, not a huge smile, but a smile nonetheless, and I knew then if he could have spoken he would have told me he thought his master had the right of it. As it stood, though, I could only drink my bottomless cup of coffee, wondering how the one pouring it was so sure and how he might have come to know such a thing.

We spent the remainder of the evening, or at least until dinner was readied, in more idle conversation, exchanging stories and coming to know each other better. Energies started to run high as the stories brought us to almost giddy laughter, with the coffee beginning to have its own effect. I think we all had grown almost anxious, as if we felt a need to be moving about, because one after the other of us started to pace as we listened or spoke, until soon we were all milling about the room.

Somehow the evening had taken on a morbidly festive feeling that none of us seemed inclined to ruin with a return to the earlier topics. Even after dinner the mood had remained unnaturally light, at least in regards as to how heavy we were letting things weigh on us and we found ourselves in the actual garden, the one outdoors, as is so often the case with us, telling our tales like the old bards of Erin.

In the dark, with just a few torches placed here and there, it seemed we were the only creatures on earth; the world was smaller then and weighed far less upon our shoulders. I even allowed the feel of my Teacher's presence all around me to be a comfort to me, rather than a reminder of sad things. The twins began telling of their various escapades, which made us all laugh, especially when they began to relate for Rajesh the scene in the garden at their villa with the Council members swaying drunkenly about. They took turns with each Elder's form and tone while slurring wildly through rambling speeches that quite likely made more sense than a true recital might have, and crossing their eyes between exaggerated hiccups.

The evening passed in this more comforting manner quickly, and for a while I think we all remembered how to be happy in the moment rather than lost in a communization of them. We all eventually went to our rest with smiles and hugs, wishing each a good night, and somehow I knew it had been and could continue to be, that though some things had gone terribly wrong, together we could see that others went beautifully right.

I fell asleep late that night with thoughts of my Master and what he might have thought of all that was taking place, wondering if he was even aware of it and had any answers for me. It was strange to me to be so close to the feel of him, as though he were in my very room, and yet be so far from the actuality of being able to simply ask him even the most mundane of questions. My mind swam in such thoughts even as sleep came to me, and I believe that was the cause of the second dream.

I was floating out over green pastures which should have been dunes, feeling drawn somehow toward the pyramids that were not there before me. All my confused mind could see was a huge lake like a mirage before me and, in its center, elevated on an earthen pedestal, rested a huge statue of a lion with the head of a man, a man I felt I should know.

As I drew closer I felt my Master's presence growing stronger and stronger, as if it drew me to it by pure virtue of its being at all. The lush green expanse began to shrink as though time was flying forward without me, and soon there was not but a drying moat of mud where the life-giving lake had been, and lifeless dunes where once lush greenery had thrived and supported herds of livestock. Still my Master's aura remained constant and strong, the only survivor of this awful drought I had just born witness to.

I knew he would be there, even before I saw him as a concentrated form, before me. As I drew ever closer, this form came into view and I saw that he was not as any creature I had seen as a living thing, ever before. I recognized him by his aura, but the actuality of seeing him was so completely foreign that I can only describe it like I was witnessing the movements of a myth as it came to life, stepping from its prison on canvas and giving out commands one wouldn't dare disobey.

I was shocked beyond comprehension to see him that had told me it should not be so, doing as he himself said was wrong to do. There he was before and below me, as a god from a time long departed, sitting upon a litter surrounded by slaves bearing palms they waved unceasingly to cool him.

There was my Master mixing forms, relaxing regally in the body of a man with the head of a jackal. I could feel the power emanating form him like waves of heat sweeping out toward me, making me feel increasingly heavy, as if my very awareness was on the verge of being dragged from the air and placed prone on the ground at his feet.

I had always known my Master to be a very powerful Changeling, but this power he was exuding now was nearly overwhelming me, by sheer virtue of its awe inspiring incomprehensibility, and I felt small and inconsequential. In short, I felt I was in the presence of a god in truth.

He did not seem to take notice of me, only gazing ahead toward this lone pyramid that seemed to have risen before me just as quickly and incomprehensibly as he himself had. He stared at it as though he had asked a question of it and was patiently awaiting a response. It seemed after some time he grew disgusted with it, for he motioned for his attendants to leave him be and turned his back to it. Soon another was being constructed and he again came to gaze on it only to show no pleasure.

This scene was repeated once more so that the view I now saw as he too took it in was the one I had expected to see at first. Then he sat before the three pyramids quietly as the days and nights again spun before me until I lost any concept of how long I had hovered in his presence.

Then it seemed his answer came. Slowly I felt two others drawing close to us, powerful beyond my comprehension, the entire world seemed to hold its breath, awaiting their next request of it. They, too, took forms such as he had spoken against, things incomprehensible to humans that should not be made so shockingly aware of our abilities, and before me stood some of the oldest gods I had ever heard tale of.

Then he arose and put his hands out to them, and they threw off these forms and flew with him out over all of Egypt. Somehow I had been swept up in their powerful wake as I too was drawn along, over this place I thought I had known yet seemed so incredibly foreign to me in its present state. I was forced to reevaluate all I thought I had known of it.

As I was drawn along with him, I saw all those things that he had been wanting to show these others, not only these three great structures pointing ever upward but also great statues and pavilions. Wonderful complex centers of trade and worship, living and working, streets lined with life both green and gold. All of it seemed a treasure he was offering to share with them.

There were many places where the Nile herself had been diverted, making small reservoirs and lakes further beautifying this place he now showed them, as though displaying a prized sculpture they could not refuse to accept. They paused as he pointed out to them a great creation in which he obviously took much pride: the great lion with the head of a man posing regal and eternal in the center of its earthen bowl. He took this form then and posed in this position, and it seemed to please him all the more then when they smiled at his display.

Yet his face fell and the overall momentary feeling of joy fled as one then turned to the other and they began to float away from him. It seemed to me they were telling him that nothing had changed and he could not return things to the way they had been. Though I heard no voices, I knew these words in my soul as though it had ears of its own that heard what the body could not. He seemed to cry out to them that he had changed it all and it could be fixed in time. He seemed to call out to them not to leave him alone, but they would not return to him.

I watched with him as they drifted away and slowly I noticed they were followed by other souls just as mine had followed my Master. It became clear to me, as the feminine aura of the two leaving us got further and further away, that what had originally appeared to be just a single large and powerful soul was actually a great many bundled closely together, and the majority of them were weak. Only a few stood out as having any amount of power that would have held them separate from the others, which seemed to only amount to anything recognizable as power by being together.

The masculine one that had left with her also had a following soul hovering about him, just as I hovered about my Master, but this one seemed almost a wounded thing. It exuded sadness, a kind of incompleteness that left it feeling of a tortured and frightened thing. It was still a powerful creature by all means but it did not seem to know it, it seemed it followed as though it knew no better.

I knew somehow that I was there through my love and respect for my Teacher and his for me. I also knew that those with the woman followed more in a manner of those attached to their mother in mutual love and adoration. This one seemed to not even know it was attached to anything or even know it was existing in that moment at all. This soul seemed lost and out of place in my dream and I did not know how I knew such a thing. I didn't know how I was knowing and dreaming such things at all, but they were known nonetheless and a new enigma to me.

I felt my Master's pain and loneliness reverberate in my very soul, and I longed suddenly that he would take notice of me that he might know I had remained with him. I had not left him. I tried to swoop down before him that he would see me and I might somehow comfort him in these moments of intense hurt. I understood all these emotions for I had felt them in my time and named them for him ages before. Suddenly I was reminded of him having asked me what the name of this pain was and my having answered him as best I knew how. I thought then, how had I known what to tell him, when he was not to have left me with that feeling for at least another three hundred years after having asked the question?

Yet my mind refused to stay focused on such things, and I was soon following him again as he returned to one of the many temples he had shown the others that had just left him. Throwing off his form, he grew silent in his soul. Again the nights and days began spinning before my mind's eye, as they had while watching this place's awesome evolution, swirling far too quickly to be counted. Suddenly I somehow came to realize I would have to leave him soon. Something within me said I would have to become, so that he could find me, and I knew it was time to go and be born that I might live. Only then would he be able to take notice of me and only then would I be able to show him that he had never been truly left alone. It was the only way I could ever tell him what it was to feel abandoned, and tell him he had not been, even back then.

I did not know where these various realizations came from because it felt as though it were from a higher understanding than my own and not things I would have normally thought waking or sleeping. The manner in which my usual senses worked to ascertain a situation's meaning had been totally discarded in this dream. The thought processes which led me to the conclusions I had come to- not only the one that said it was time I go and be born but those about the other souls- were the same kind that led me to wake up and become aware. Yet they were separate and oddly different, like two different sides of the same coin leading to a single awareness of self as a whole. I know that sounds very strange and probably does not explain it at all, but I say it so that, at the very least, you will know just how strange it was to me to have felt them at all.

~9~

Manji

I adjusted my eyes to the brightness around me, having found I had awakened sometime near noon. My mind refused to process for a moment the light and heat filtering into the room, still I think trying to rest in the cool confines of the temple it had just departed in my dream, just as it refused to accept the lesser feel of him as it remained ever present about me, but not so powerful as it had been while sleeping.

I missed my Master now more than ever; I had just felt closer to him than I had from the moment of his ascension and it shook me anew to have that closeness taken away again. I refused to begrudge him, though. I would not allow myself to be made angry that I could not find him, if he was to be found he would be, and otherwise I would not allow it to hurt me anymore.

I got to my feet, strangely wanting to see the Sphinx as it stood now, needing to see it again, to see the face it wore with my real eyes. I wanted to view it as it sat now, nearly buried in the desert plain with nary a drop of water come near it for eons. Eons, I knew it had been eons, I knew the world I had just been part of was a world my Master had ruled as a god long before I had known him. I knew now his meaning when he had said he had come up from Egypt before time was even time. He had been a part of it all, a part of its very creation, when the Nile had run full and ready to tame and made a lush and beautiful oasis of this place.

I looked out upon this land as it stood and it was still beautiful, but now I had seen the beauty of which he had spoken so reverently. Now I knew what his mind's eye saw when he had gazed into some far away memory and he had seemed lost within it. I leaped onto the ledge of the nearest arch, squatting there for a silent moment considering what to do next and what to make of my dream. Then, leaping from the ledge, I threw off my form and flew out over the whole of it as I had in the dream. I realized, because of the dream, I could and should be much more aware of all things and capable of viewing them clearly, even in this state without my eyes. No longer did I merely feel about blindly with my spirit and guide myself with those feelings, but I could literally see it all laid out before me, baring itself to my very soul to be seen through its eyes, eyes I'd never thought to use.

I worked within my consciousness then to see those things I saw now, as they had looked mere minutes before while I had been sleeping, using the memory of my dream to guide me to where it was I wanted to go. I came finally upon the Sphinx itself, appearing now to be barely a short protrusion from its grave of sand, lacking now its great height of pedestal, which had held it above the great bed of a lake the Nile herself had once given it to rule. It amazed and drew me then, just as it had in the dream, for somehow it seemed alive, as if it had an aura all its own and that aura spoke of having been part of something amazing.

I came down before it, recalling clearly the way my Master had so proudly shown this amazing creation to those he had awaited. He had sat, recumbent, before this, his gift to them. I was saddened a little that I could not see it in truth, as they had, except for in my mind's eye. I squatted before it and took the form as he had, ignoring the slight feeling of guilt for doing something I had so often been instructed not to do. He had done it, and so would I, yet I was not seen in the doing of it as he had been.

Yet I did this in the manner you had made clear to me, Angel, not asking of it any instincts that might bring unforeseen danger, merely wearing it like a new outfit and remaining myself in my mind. I then did as he had done, posing before it on the desert floor, mirroring the stance it had held for so very long, and staring into its lifeless eyes. I knew that face, I knew those eyes; as surely as I wore it now, my Master had worn it for me on more than one occasion. That was why I had needed to see it, that was the nagging desire to view it with my real eyes and not from within a dream. Indeed he had been here and this had been made in his image.

I do not know how many hours passed as I stared into its large sightless eyes, wishing somehow they would show me something more of what they had witnessed in their countless years. I think I even spoke to it from within the confines of my mind, asking it as though I were asking him why it was that it was here. I wanted to understand not only why it was man had chosen to make such a creation for my Master, but also why he had made such a form of himself in the first place for them to witness. I wanted to understand why he had broken his own rules.

I could not see my Master, the great teacher and sometimes student that he had been to me, using his gift of change to make man do his bidding and serve him, yet it seemed he had taken the form of the gods they worshiped to do exactly that. Through his deception, in essence, he had led them to build his gifts to the other two which he had so wanted to return to him. I didn't know if somehow I had seen the face of the Sphinx, mayhap in a painting, and my mind had not registered it until I had relaxed into sleep, or if it had been just a strange coincidence, that having felt him here I had begun to dream of him, and this discovery was pure luck. It seemed so unlikely to me he would do such a thing, and yet I saw no other answer as I gazed into his visage carved onto the shoulders of that great beast. It seemed to me my dreams had been presenting more questions than answers, and I would make myself mad if I tried to analyze them for too long.

So I decided at last just to do with these unanswerable questions as I had with so much else, simply set them aside because I had more pressing mysteries to deal with. I returned to the house where I knew the others and our host would be awaiting me. Night had set in again already as I entered through the open window to find Manji standing before me with a slight smile on his face. I took his smile to mean he had been awaiting my return and was relieved to see I had finally done so.

"You have been waiting for me long, Manji?" I asked him.

His answer was a slight dipping of his head, and with one hand held across his belly he swept the other around, palm up, toward the door. He allowed his body to turn slightly in that direction, leaving him ready to follow me after I went out ahead of him. I went before him amazed once more at his gift for silence, and that my own unclad feet made more sound on the carved stone floors than his soft slipper-shod steps as he came along behind me.

I met the others in the indoor garden, I'm not sure what the proper term for that particular room was, but that is what we all came to call it. Once more Manji was the only servant that remained in the room with us to serve us our choice of coffee or wine. Once more we spent the early evening hours talking about all the various theories we had come up with to explain what we were up against. Once more we went back and forth and over and under, and still came to no real solid conclusions, only a few more good ideas and plausible explanations.

So it was quite a few hours before I thought to mention the dreams, for though they were much on my mind they seemed irrelevant to all that was going on then. The last two evenings, what visions they'd brought me and led me to believe about my Teacher, did not seem to matter to the current conversations. As a matter of fact I probably would not have thought to speak of them at all had it not been for something asked of the twins.

"Were there any other parts of the Code," Rajesh had asked, "that either Angel or you two had gone against?"

"What do you mean?" Adreal had asked, appearing instantly ready to defend his sister if it proved necessary.

"What I mean to say, my friend," Rajesh said, grinning patiently and showing his unspoken approval of Adreal's protective love for his sister, "is we know why Edsel and Santon were targeted, at least if we have concluded properly, but we do not know why you two were left. If we are indeed correct, then the two of you and Angel were the new undesirable generation.

You three had learned what this, as yet unnamed, evil entity had tried to prevent all future generations from learning and had eliminated Edsel and Santon for having no intention of stopping."

"You are looking for something that makes us special, like you think keeps Piper and Demon safe?" Adreal asked, lowering his proverbial hackles quickly. "I thought you felt we were made safe by being with them. There is no more powerful secret we could have uncovered or learned than the one Angel had, and it went after her immediately for having learned it rather than staying from her path."

"I did believe you were safe by being with them, but then I remembered Piper said he had left you to go warn Demon and Baylor in Scotland," he said thoughtfully. "So it would have seemed a prime time to attack you two, since you were now without the protection of both Edsel and Piper."

"In Scotland," I had repeated as though it were an answer from heaven. "The other night while we were eating you said something like there was a master behind it we did not as yet know we needed to fear. It had needled at me but I could not remember why." I said, now facing Rajesh, "Mere minutes before Piper arrived at our door in Scotland, I had to revive Angel from an attack of pure fear. She had tried to tell me that she had become afraid when we had left her and that the fear had seemed to take on a life of its own."

"I had thought at first that a Changeling bent on evil had come searching for Baylor," I continued. "And its searching soul had nearly contacted Angel and that had frightened her by feeling of ill intent, but I don't think so now. She had said it was not a Changeling like me, it was frightening and unfamiliar. I think she had meant it was beyond us, mayhap not a mere Changeling at all, and she had sensed it. Mayhap she had recognized something about it, that it wanted kept unknown and merely having been recognized at all made it also aware of her.'

"Do you think it could be not just that Edsel and Santon, even those that had been with the Council before, had allowed his plan to go awry by allowing new ones to learn but more so that they knew it at all?" I continued excitedly. "Somehow they might have been able to recognize it later and it could not allow that? I had thought out some of this before, we have talked about many possibilities, but now I think there is more to it by far. I think it has something to do with the fear itself. "

But I wasn't sure, it all seemed to be trying to form in my mind, but somehow it was all too hot still and could not as yet congeal. The others seemed to have become spellbound in considering all I had said, realizing the possibility were limitless. I felt I was missing some important ingredient which would turn these thoughts into something solid if I could only come up with it. I shook my head as if I could clear it, but to no avail, and eventually I had to simply finish with what I did know.

"But," I said then, sure of at least this last part, "Our unnamed entity was surely in Scotland then and that is why Adonia and Adreal remained safe in Rome with or without Piper. Not to mention that Angel had not yet learned how to take the Yelm and had not yet shared it with the twins. As a matter of fact, it was the very night she did share that knowledge that she disappeared. And there is something else," I added, suddenly thinking it. "My own Master broke the Code in many very grievous manners and none ever came hunting him. I know for a fact that, though he did indeed ascend, it was by his own choice. So there must be things we are missing that are important in figuring who it will target and why."

"What do you mean?"

I cannot tell you which of them had spoken, for they all seemed to have spoken at once. As a matter of fact I think all present asked, except of course Manji, although that one did seem to be interested as well. This surprised me a little because I had not seen him pay any special attention at all to any of our conversations before now. I could have been wrong, though, for he made no real movements, per se, it was just something in his face.

"Truly it was only a dream," I admitted, thinking their questions had been in regard to my last statements about my Master. "But somehow it was real, I know it, I have gone to the Sphinx to be sure. It is a sculpture of him, a tribute of some kind or monument to him, I think. Not only did he split forms but he allowed all to know it. He took the forms of the gods of these people eons ago and walked among them, he let them think he was their deity."

"He used his gifts as we are not to," I said slowly. "He used this to his own advantage so they would create for him things of beauty meant to induce two others of our kind to join him here. The people of this place worshiped and adored him, made sacrifices and offered him prayers. He broke all of the oldest rules."

I went on then to describe both dreams for them in detail and they all listened quietly. I was confused and so I spoke slowly and descriptively, trying to assure myself I would omit no detail that might shed light for others on things mayhap I had not been able to see. It was the reactions of both Rajesh and Manji that gave me the most heart, for their smiles seemed to say they were deriving from my words the answers I myself had been unable to. Suddenly I was almost unwilling to finish the telling, so anxious was I to know what it was they had begun thinking.

"I cannot tell you how long he did these things," I said, finishing up quickly. "But if those particular parts of the Code commanding against such things were also something this one we are searching for 'suggested,' then my Master too would have drawn his unwanted attention." I paused then, remembering it clearly and trying not to be judgmental. "Really, though, it was all very sad, he just didn't want to be alone, he wanted them to be with him. I think it was only that he was lonely and he didn't do it to be malicious." I paused for a moment then, thinking about all of it as a whole, then finished with, "It was truly the strangest kind of dream I can ever remember having had."

"What you are not considering," Rajesh said slowly and thoughtfully, choosing his words carefully, "is that quite likely whether this force we are facing had wanted to or not, it may not have been able to destroy your Master. It may even have been afraid to try. Your Master's presence here has been a power unlike most have ever known the touch of. It has

125

drawn others of us from all over the world. It inspires awe and sometimes even fear in Changelings of every aspect. I was very much intrigued to learn you knew the feel of this presence here as that of your Master when first you had told me."

"But the main thing you haven't considered, which is quite likely even more important, are the more obvious possibilities of your dream," he went on, now smiling again. "You have just told us, for all intents and purposes, you are the reborn of a god of old. You have told me what it is that makes you special. I would not dare to hunt the chosen son of the Almighty Amun Re."

"That is impossible," I said, aghast. "I told you he took the forms of the deities of old, not that he was one. He was a very, very old and powerful Changeling, yes, I will not contest the power felt here even now, but he was a Changeling only, we know this. I knew him and he was not a god. He could not have been."

But I was confused now, very confused. It seemed impossible, and yet if he was a god, it would be an explanation where now there was none. Yet I could not believe my Master had been a god in truth, he had had too many questions. I had taught him just as he had taught me, things a god surely would have known. Still I could not understand how it was that my Master had ascended so very long ago and yet his presence was still everywhere about me. He had to have returned, it was the only way it could be explained that seemed acceptable to me. Even Edsel, old as he had been, had faded completely from the villa within the first ten years following his disappearance.

Above all it made no sense how he had broken the oldest and most necessary of the Code, that of never allowing humans to know of us, and not been targeted. Or mayhap he had. Mayhap that is why he had prepared me in the manner he had and taught me the things it had been so important to him that I be made to know. Mayhap that was why he had repeatedly told me I should never split forms, thinking to prevent me from ever being targeted as well.

"And you, my friend?" Rajesh was now questioning Piper as my mind continued to refuse to work fast enough. "Might your maker have also been a goddess of old?"

"No," Piper replied. "My mother was more in the way of a Druid, if anything she was more a priestess or servant. She led others to worship the Creator of all things, never herself."

"Neither were gods," I said, finally regaining my wits and rejoining the conversation. "Only Changelings- old yes, wise yes, but gods, no."

I was still thinking these things when Rajesh said something else which gave me one of the greatest and most extraordinary pauses of my very long life.

"But what then makes a god, my friend?" Rajesh asked, smiling at me patiently as though I were a slow student. "Except that those who choose to pray to it, believe in it, give it a name and thus imbue it with the power of their own belief? I do not suggest your master was God, only that for all intents and purposes he was one to the people of this place. Mayhap you should not think that he took the forms of the deities of old to make himself be worshiped but that he invented those forms in the first place and was worshiped with or without that being the original intent."

"Still," I replied finally, when my voice and mind would work coherently for me again. "If the one hunting us is also very old and obviously wise, whether for good or bad be the wisdom, then it would know as I do Amun Re was a Changeling only, so why fear him and not other Changelings?"

"Again, my friend, you overlooked the obvious answer. You yourself gave it," he said, still smiling. "Mayhap it is the very fact of both its age and its wisdom which protect you. Mayhap this one is old enough to have known your Master and wise enough not to want to draw his attention or anger. What better way to bring down the wrath of any being, be it Changeling or god, than to threaten the existence of one they love?"

We all grew silent again for a long time, and I noticed Manji had a smile on his face, once more signaling his agreement with his master. If

Rajesh was right, and indeed I had no good argument to contend he was not, then we were looking for a Changeling equal to my Master at least in years. For it would have had to know of him and his power to have formulated the respect to remain far from me. As I thought these things, I noticed Manji nodding slightly with his eyes closed and smiling to himself and I wondered then if he had been following my very thoughts.

It seemed absurd, but the moment I thought it, we locked eyes. He seemed momentarily on the verge of frightened flight. His huge jet black eyes, unable to hide in their fringe of lashes, seemed ready to jump from his head. I do not think he had meant to look at me so directly. His head had always been slightly down whenever in our company, but it seemed my having thought of him directly had drawn him. Now our eyes were locked and he seemed deathly afraid of this. Yet when I thought then, that must be how he knew about the water, he amazed me deeply by bravely dipping his head signaling in the affirmative.

"By the gods! He reads thoughts," I said out loud in my amazement. "What?"

It seemed only Rajesh had not spoken out in surprise with the others. Instead he had merely turned to Manji and smiled softly as if to tell him it was alright and he was not about to be killed for this abnormality. Manji relaxed slightly under all of our scrutiny and Rajesh finally cut the confused silence that had descended.

"I told you all he had a way of knowing things," Rajesh said. "He does not use his gift to pry, only to help where he may. You have nothing to fear from him, and, Manji, you have nothing to fear from them," he added, turning first to Manji then back to the rest of us. "He has been only loyal in his service of me and will not be judged harshly for the manner in which he has been able to do it so well."

I was reminded sharply of the time I too had spoken up in the defense of another that was possessed of an oddity. Only then it had been I against the Council in defense of a Werewolf. I looked to Baylor then and he smiled his understanding to me as we both remembered the occasion well.

We then began to survey the reactions of the others, wondering how the twins would take this new information but having no real fear it would be with condemnation.

"Oh, but this is a wonder," Adonia said, being the first to find her voice again. "You were born with this ability?"

"How does it happen for you?" Adreal chimed in.

His voice caught up quickly with the twins and I was proud of them once more for their openness and accepting natures. Yet when suddenly they faced each other as if sharing some joke between them, I felt like laughing that I should have thought such a thing surprised them at all. Of all of us, they had always seemed connected on a deeper level, at least to some extent. Mayhap their interest stemmed from merely wondering how such things worked for others.

Piper kept his usual quiet at Adonia's side, smiling warmly at his love, apparently enjoying as ever her inquisitive nature. Manji once more appeared as though he wanted to bolt, to avoid all the sudden attention, and Rajesh put up his hand to stay our questions. It seemed he meant to keep them from breaking into a flood and drowning the poor young man in his own inability to answer them.

"There is no explanation that I have discovered," Rajesh replied for him. "It has been a gift and a curse on his family from the first I encountered them. I do not know if it is that he truly hears what others think, or if it is that he somehow sees the gist of a situation through another's mind's eye. But he has never used it in a deceptive or destructive manner, nor had any of those before him, so I have never denied him the use of it, not that I could."

The last he had said with a short laugh and another smile directed at Manji to strengthen the young man's resolve to stay put. Manji had appeared calm enough by this time so I risked addressing him again.

"Do you see anything that we do not, pertaining to our current dilemma?" I asked, looking directly at Manji again.

He had nodded slowly in the negative and pointed to me, then his own temple; again he pointed at me and then again at his temple, finally smiling shyly at me. I was confused, I did not know if he was telling me that I had seen the one we were searching for or if he was saying I knew him. I could not tell if he meant merely that he saw nothing I did not, or even simply that he knew nothing more than I. He too seemed confused now, looking at me, and I realized I must have lost him if he had been trying to follow my thoughts.

"It is all right, Manji," I said at last. "I tell you, from here on, please feel free to nod and smile as often as you feel you agree with our summations of situations. Sometimes, just as when we are speaking with Rajesh and he takes notice of things we had not, it is merely that some things are clearer when viewed by someone further from them."

I smiled again to show him just how much I meant my next words.

"You are welcome to jump into a conversation with us whenever you like," I reiterated. "In any manner you can. As long as Rajesh holds to no specific rules which prohibit that and does not object. I know none of us have held traditional rules of conduct to any high regard in a very long time."

I had glanced around the room to see all of my longtime friends had obviously agreed wholeheartedly with my appraisal of the situation and the benefit of Manji feeling free to be himself with us. They were all giving him smiles and nods to reassure him, but it was Rajesh he seemed the most interested in, looking steadily at our host for confirmation. Rajesh too had smiled at him and it seemed to me they were more friends than master and servant as they both smiled their understanding of the other. Manji finally bowed to all of us, showing he had accepted our open invitation, and then began to refill each of our cups as though no breach of the natural order of things had ever occurred.

I will tell you here that our conversations took on an almost comedic air thereafter, with one or the other of us looking to Manji after we stated something we had just thought, wondering at his opinion. Though he would smile occasionally when he would catch our eye, it only became even more confusing because we were forced to wonder whether it was a smile of agreement or simply his naturally shy response to being focused upon so frequently by his master's guests.

Eventually things seemed to take on a pattern, whether it be some new dream, of which I had quite a few of during our time in Egypt, or some new theory that would draw us all together, something would see us arguing our points politely for hours and hours. Time began to creep past us as our days were spent sleeping to avoid the heat and our nights in random discussions that tried very hard to lead to acceptable conclusions to our problems.

We eventually began to travel about the area and see what sights it had to offer to take our minds off of the more disturbing things and allow us small moments of rest. I would go out late of a night, taking Adreal or Baylor, sometimes both, with me and we would just walk and wonder aloud at all we saw. We told tales in the garden and haunted the Nile late at night and in essence allowed the years to fly while we came no closer to an answer for it all.

I would go out quite often by myself and roam near and far in the spirit, searching harder and harder, for any sign of my Master in the flesh. I still could not believe he had not returned, and the other explanations for how he could be felt so strongly were too outrageous for me to consider overly long. I became increasingly desperate for his wisdom, as I found each evening of talk with those I'd brought with me to be of no use, for they gave no true resolution, only more unproven theory. I would sit for hours before the Sphinx, quite nearly praying to it, so often did I ask questions of it only to hear no answer. It would have seemed to have become an idol to me.

Full moons came and went and Rajesh, obviously having heard of Baylor's strange curse from either Kynan or Lachlan on one of their prior visits, watched with concerned fascination as he walked out into the distance dunes those nights to be alone. Manji, now that I look back on his reactions, had probably had much the same insight as you yourself, at probably much the same time, but had no more a way to tell us at that time than you did.

So it was that we found ourselves three years later, seated as had become custom in the indoor garden, drinking our coffee and searching for new ideas, when another presence politely made itself know in its approach. Then came the expected pull of energy, as it proclaimed itself a Changeling by pulling to it enough energy to give it a form. We were all instantly on our feet, hoping beyond hope it was one come to tell us one of the missing had been found.

I know we all thought many of the same things in those few seconds, praying our Angel had healed and that was the cause of this one's visit, not that it would give us the news that another had gone missing. Rajesh went to the door almost calmly to show a woman in, telling me, by the mere fact he went rather than having one of his servants go, that he had known, even respected, her. Obviously he had recognized who she was, mayhap having known her long enough to have discerned by the feel of her soul who she was, even when her soul had still been quite far off.

~10~

The Council

Rajesh and this new guest hugged as old friends will, and I was sure then they had known each other for quite some time. They then dropped easily into quiet conversation, instantly beginning to share what was on their minds, as he led her to join the rest of us. He walked slowly at her side, head dipped to hers and hand cupping her elbow, in gestures of familiar kinship, listening diligently as they made their way back toward us. He offered her refreshments, pouring her a glass of wine with his own hands and setting her in his own seat, the one he had just been occupying before her arrival.

Soon he was patting her hand reassuringly and turning to all of us, making our introductions, telling us her name was Mikaili and that she had been the one to stand behind him in the shadows and take him into her soul when he had turned his back to the light. Thus we were introduced to the one that had made our friend Rajesh and brought to reconsider many things about him.

Suddenly it all made much more sense. I had been under the wrong assumption, as I was finding to be the case a lot lately. Rajesh had been 'blessed' by vote of the Council, since he was only four hundred years one of us and the Council had seemed in complete control by the time of his change. I had thought that he had merely learned over time to disregard certain aspects of their Code, having resided so far from their influence. Yet now I was rethinking the entire situation and realizing that it was most likely this newcomer, Mikaili, who had influenced him, and quite well. She had to be exceptional, to say the least, to have survived the great purging of our race by the Council when it had arisen, and then to have escaped their anger when she had changed him, for the Council had obviously accepted Rajesh though she had been the one to make him.

Mikaili appeared to be a young woman, perhaps in her middle twenties, with dark cocoa skin and long black hair, done up in more braids than I could have counted with any quickness. These braids were held toward the top of her head not only by the way in which they had been done, being woven closely to her scalp in an ascending pattern, but also by a yellow silken scarf that was wrapped tightly around them. Each braid seemed to have some hidden meaning to me, perhaps due to the fact I knew there was reason for each of Baylor's but mostly because each ended in a bunching of gold or silver beads in varying numbers, with the occasional colored one here or there, seeming to signify something only she would know with certainty.

I suddenly wanted badly to discuss many things with this woman, for she had presented quite a few new mysteries to me in just as few short moments. But then it is not Mikaili's looks or the way in which she wore her hair or even how she had come to save Rajesh which causes me to mention her here, it is what news she brought to us and what that news brought us to do. You see, she made us to realize we had been sitting idly by for nearly three full years, having endless useless discussions and conducting many fruitless searches for my Master, while something or someone had played a bit of unprecedented havoc with a small village in Scotland.

But then you probably know this part of the story even better than I do, Angel.

Yet I will tell you from our point of view. When this amazing woman showed up she brought with her an even more amazing story. This story she got from another, who got it from another, and so on until it had grown well beyond itself, but the end point was still the same. Some creature, be it devil or witch or even worse, had destroyed a whole village; apparently killing men, women, children and priests alike. Nothing and no one had been safe from it, be they Christian or Pagan, and it was not likely to stop any time soon. You can imagine what terrible things we thought then.

Mikaili told us how she had come to hear the tale and been compelled to go in search of the Council, knowing such a story was quite likely about an unworthy Changeling gone on a mad rampage and would be something they had dealt with before. Only she had found the Council all but destroyed, with only three remaining members left to tell the tale to. More strange than this fact to her was that they had asked her to go to Egypt with the news and inform another group of Changelings that they said had gone there searching out the old one. The Council had made an unlikely suggestion to her that it might be something called a Werewolf, a cursed being and a concept which had eluded her. They had thought it possible that one of these creatures had done this damage to the village, in which case another Werewolf they had called by the name of Baylor, which traveled with this group of Changelings in Egypt, should be made aware of the situation.

Mikaili seemed to have a real difficult time, not only with the Council delegating itself appointed protective responsibilities to another group, but also with the fact they had asked her to find and tell this new group, rather than handling at least that much of the situation for themselves.

The concept of a being that had somehow been cursed to a single form and lacked control over the change also seemed a challenge to her understanding. She made some comment under her breath about dark magics, making a strange sign over herself, and staring intently at Baylor as we tried to explain the things the Council had told her and why they had then sent her to us.

Baylor took her intense perusal with the kind of proud nonchalance that I had come to admire in him, making no move to defend or explain himself beyond what facts she was hearing from the rest of us.

Within hours we had all come to the same unavoidable conclusion: that if nothing else we had remained in Egypt long enough to know that no real good was coming of it, and that in the meantime things were sprouting in our own gardens that quite likely needed plucked up quickly before they took terrible root and spread. Baylor had remained quieter than I would have expected, during this short discussion, considering what few things we knew for sure. Something had done serious damage to his people in his absence and I knew this had to be upsetting him more than he was showing at present. I fully expected that at any moment he was going to burst out, in a determined and somewhat motherly tone, demanding that we cease our endless discussions and return to his homeland at once so that he might protect his own, but he did not.

The decision to return at once had been made at any rate, and such a demand would have been unnecessary, but it surprised me nonetheless that he seemed to have become far more intent on saving you than his people. It seemed to me then, that if any of us had thought remaining in Egypt even longer would have furthered the cause of recovering you, that he would have quietly stayed with us and left his Scotland to deal with this new problem on their own. I was made to realize all over again that surly he loved you as much as I did and would never give up on recovering you any more than I would.

We parted company with Rajesh and Manji sadly, for we had all grown quite close over the last few years, and it was with some regret that we could not convince them to travel with us for a time. Mikaili was another we had to regretfully leave behind, yet another mystery we hadn't the time to unravel while still entangled in our current one.

So it was that Baylor and Adreal walked out ahead of Piper and Adonia, who took slightly longer with their goodbyes, and I stayed behind the longest, having more I wanted to say but not sure how. Finally I had simply told Rajesh that once all of this had been resolved, as soon as we had found you and perhaps the others as well, we would have to gather again and spend our time in happier remembrances. It was a sad moment for all of us, but in a way I think I felt it more than the others, for it seemed to me I was saying goodbye to my Master as well, for the second time.

We left Egypt, our new friends and the ever present feel of my Master behind, traveling at a rate that showed our own lack of joy in the act of moving at all. It was almost as though we felt that the quicker we were gone from there the quicker the wounds of parting would cease to pain us. I think there was also a sense of urgency imbued in the return trip that had been lacking when we had come. For now we knew for sure there would be something waiting when we arrived, we just had no idea what exactly that would be.

We had searched the entire route there as ever, for sign of you or any of those evil Changelings we had thought might be able to reveal to us what had done such damage. We had scanned for sign of you within Egypt itself, only to be overwhelmed by the confusion and mystery of feeling my Master's presence so keenly there and the whole while found no solid clues to grasp onto.

Not once had we come any closer to recovering you than the near miss we hadn't even known of at the time which had occurred in Calis. Now it seemed we were being confronted with yet another difficulty when we had still not yet found any respite from all the others already confounding us.

Now I will tell you that the first thing we did upon arriving in Rome was return to the twins' villa and gather the remaining Council together with us. We then proceeded to gather all the facts we could from them of the incident in Scotland, and what we heard did at first encourage us. For now that they had engaged the help of their network of the blessed, it seemed the story had become a little more solidly founded in some actual facts, and at least it seemed that it had nothing to do with a Werewolf.

It appeared to have been a witch that had been destined for the stake that had done the deeds, and she had not destroyed the entire village, only a priest and two other men of the church. It seemed more a matter of witchcraft now than a Werewolf, and this new knowledge seemed to bring Baylor a slight bit of comfort. This also gave the rest of us the excuse to pause long enough to bring the Council members up to date on all we had found, instead of rushing off to hunt.

We began to inform them of all the new theories we had formulated with Rajesh and Manji. It seemed having found we were not desperately needing to go destroy a new crop of Werewolves, we felt instead the necessity to rest and share our new ideas to see what the Council might have to add. It was a very excited conversation to say the least, and came dangerously near to pure havoc more than once, especially when the topic of the great presence they had all sought out in Egypt over the years suddenly came up.

I remember the moment quite clearly. It was getting late and we were all sitting around the large old wooden table that had graced the dining hall for longer than I could know. I was picking at a scar on the old planking of the table's surface, and gazing into the candle that sat lit before me, saying whatever came to mind the moment that it did. We had all been doing that same form of random topic changing, rambling on for quite some time, trying to fill Kynan and the others in on the full three years in one long night. I had just gotten a small splinter caught under my nail and was not thinking of breaking anything to them gently, only of getting the small sliver of wood out with my teeth, so I had blurted my next piece of news out without thinking of a better way to do so.

"The old one you sought in Egypt was my Master," I said, spitting the splinter into my palm.

"What?" Cathmore and Lachlan both nearly shouted in unison.

"Aye!" I replied, trying not to laugh at their shock. "I recognized the feel of him as soon as we came to the place. His presence was everywhere and it was unmistakably him."

"Did you find him, then?" Cathmore said, as close to respectful awe as I had ever seen him.

"Did you speak with him of what is befalling us?" Lachlan asked, and though he seemed more intent on finding salvation than who provided it, I could not begrudge them their quick questions.

"No," I replied, sucking at my injured fingertip, adding, "I never found him, but I found things about him I had never known."

"Such as?" Cathmore asked excitedly.

"Like that he frequently took the various forms attributed to the gods of that place, such as Amun Re," I said thoughtlessly, still preoccupied with my wound. "And that the Sphinx wears his face."

"What?" they demanded in unison.

Again I was hard pressed not to laugh, for they seemed so staunchly disapproving. It seemed I would be forever bringing havoc into the ordered lifestyles the Council tried so desperately to create for us all. I found I suddenly desperately missed the open minded Rajesh and the quietly non-judgmental Manji. Cathmore and Lachlan were now heatedly arguing back and forth, and Kynan seemed lost just trying to follow the path of their argument for the moment. I presumed he was trying to decide if he should become angry as well.

"It does not matter now, does it?" I said more harshly than necessary as I felt the old disappointment in Kynan return. "He has ascended and will not be splitting forms or gathering new worshipers to do his bidding, any time soon. So it is a moot point if it was wrong for him to take the forms those people thought belonged to their gods, now isn't it?"

It was Kynan's turn then to shock all of us, by deciding to rise to my defense and speak out against them, reminding me of the hope I had held out for him three years ago of returning to being a man of his own. I became immediately contrite for having thought Kynan had relapsed and not having given him the credit he was obviously trying to deserve. Yet it was the case in point he used to do it, which delivered the real blow.

"Demosthenes is correct," Kynan had said. "The witch in Scotland turned herself into a half-cat beast, if that part of the rumor is correct, to kill those priests, and you do not sit and squabble over the right of half-forms in her case. You happily call it practicing witchcraft and have done with it. So the one who blessed him chose to practice godliness or whatever you would call it, have done with that as well, 'twas eons ago at any rate."

"WHAT?"

Now it was our turn to nearly shout. Baylor and I exchanged looks I could not describe for you then, for it seemed we had the same powerfully hopeful thoughts at the same time. Adonia and Adreal locked eyes and seemed to have an entire conversation in the space of a heartbeat, which was quickly followed by Adonia swatting Piper to get him to face her, so that she could see if he thought the same as her and her twin. It was clear, though, that we all had, as one after another we caught each other's eyes, we all knew.

It had to be you!

You had to have returned and something had to have gone terribly wrong when you did. I don't believe we said a word to Kynan or Lachlan and Cathmore. Baylor was out the front door and running down the street quicker than such a large man should be able to move. I was ahead of him only because I changed into a hawk and went out the window just before the twins. We were soon swooping and squawking back and forth in happy flight, soaring over Rome for home.

It occurred to me some moments later that Baylor would never keep up in such a manner, on foot, and I turned in mid-flight and flew back over the open streets. When I spotted him, he was still running at full speed and I swooped down, coming behind him and squawking. He did not look back or break stride, but I knew he had understood my intent as I flew in under him. In one smooth movement, of which I am still extremely proud, I became a huge and, this time, well-gaited horse. I lifted him up onto my wide back as I grew the form smoothly beneath him, and neither of us broke forward motion as we continued our mad dash for you.

I think at some point he had caught his breath and thanked me, mayhap even making a comment of appreciation that I had made myself a smoother riding beast this time, but to be honest the majority of the trip is lost in a haze of mental exhaustion. Though I constantly renewed my body and frequently allowed my instincts to control it, my mind was not allowed sleep until we had boarded the boat for Dover. How Baylor managed to keep his seat on my ever-moving back is another of those mysteries we've never solved, but I tell you the man never ceases to astound me. When I did fall asleep, it was like falling into a wonderful welcoming abyss of much needed mental oblivion and I can tell you it was a virtual coma. I awoke to find

Baylor, red-eyed and pale, standing over me with his hand raised as though he were about to slap me.

"Thank the gods, man," Baylor said, his deep voice rougher than usual due to his own exhaustion. "I thought I was going to have to smack you again. We're coming into port, fix your face."

I slowly realized he had smacked me, and quite likely more than once, as pain slowly made itself known to me as it flared in my jaw when my brain began to work again. I rubbed my cheek, taking the pain out of it as I focused on those around me. Adonia and Adreal were almost prancing, ready to be away from all the people and fly again. Piper, though, outwardly appearing much more calm, seemed just as prepared to jump overboard to be off the ship and on his way again as they did. It took me some moments to notice Baylor still looked worried and somewhat sad.

"What is it?" I asked him, confused that he should appear so sad when we were so close now.

"All apologies," he replied tiredly.

"For what?" I was even more confused now.

"For slowing you down," he said softly. "I know how much she means to you, and you could have thrown off your form completely and been at her side long before now if not for me."

"Not so," I said, meaning it wholeheartedly. "Without you I probably would not have survived the loss of her in the first place. You have done naught but help me and I would not leave you behind in any case. We will find her, a day or two more will not matter then."

He had smiled a little then, but not the smile I missed, more one that said he was tired and hungry and did not wish to argue the point. I knew he had hardly eaten in many, many days and that he was going to drop soon if he didn't get food and rest, and I wasn't about to loss another friend over a few hours spared for a good meal. I led us all to an inn. I could tell the others were anxious to be looking, so I told them that if they wanted to go scout about for a while that Baylor and I would eat and then get a room there and wait for them. It only seemed right then, I was still in desperate need of a little more sleep and I knew Baylor had to be in far worse shape.

I think we slept that whole day and night clear through, and had awoken only to relieve ourselves in the small pot that stood in the corner. We had stumbled downstairs sometime the next morning and ordered some stew that tasted far better than it had a right to, only because it was stew in the first place and not random fruits grabbed along the roadside. We were sitting there, in the inn's smoke-filled main chamber, just starting on our second mug of very bad ale, when Piper burst in the front door. If the flood of light intruding into the smoky darkness had not surprised us to full wakefulness, his frantic waving for us to follow him outside did.

We were on our feet instantly and I was tossing coins I hadn't bothered to count over my shoulder at a bar maid who had just entered from the kitchen and stopped in her tracks, giving me the strangest look I'd ever received. I had thought, as I ran out to see what had Piper so excited, that I must have given her far too many coins. However, I was far too hopeful Piper was about to lead us to you to care why she had stared so. I think now it might have been the very same woman you had spoken with of your search for me, your twin as it were, and seeing me had given her quite an understandable pause.

"You won't believe this," Piper said excitedly, the moment we were in the street and out of earshot of the inn. "Angel was most definitely here."

He was walking quickly, apparently leading us somewhere, and we followed silently, listening intently. Suddenly I felt a very familiar feeling and I knew you had been here, you had changed form somewhere around here. It had been a long time ago because the feel of you was very faint, but it was there nonetheless. What was stranger to me than feeling you there at all was that it was your soul I felt, not simply a Changeling's abandoned energies. I heard children laughing up ahead, and tried to concentrate on that rather than being sidetracked with my own amazement, but their words were drowned out by Piper's.

"The twins had turned into wolfhounds and ran sniffing about," he was saying. "I was just walking as I am now when these two children spotted them and said the strangest thing. One of them; the young boy said, 'Look, she is back and she's brought her mate this time.' Then he'd yelled at Adonia that she had better quit leaving her master or someone might keep her. He'd nudged his little sister to see she'd understood the jest and she had piped up then, saying she, meaning Adonia, had probably come back for more of 'Gennie's' milk. Then they had caught sight of me and apologized profusely, swearing they had only been jesting and would never steal my dogs. I told them it was all right, I had not thought them serious. Then they had asked to play with my dogs for awhile, so I have agreed."

I had stopped in my tracks and Piper had stopped too, staring at me. I was absorbed then, not by his words, but the feel of you. I had found it, what there was left of it, right beneath my feet. Piper mistook my blank look for a total lack of understanding behind why he was telling me the tale.

"Don't you see, man?" he said, "Wolfhounds don't just roam freely about these parts, it had to have been her. She took the form when we had gone to Rome, she must have taken it again. These children played with her, fed her, they remembered her. They might know something more."

"I know," I said.

I think he suddenly understood my look had nothing to do with lack of insight then, for he had looked at my feet, as I was doing, and sighed. Then he'd signaled Baylor away, continuing the tale for him, as he led him to the spot about fifty yards away, where two children ran and played laughingly with two huge wolfhounds I knew to be a rambunctious pair of twins.

It was the first I had felt of you in over forty years and you cannot imagine what it did to me. I felt so many things then, I cannot begin to recount them all to you, but it was good. Very good! Good to feel you close to me in any way I could get it, and it strengthened me profoundly. I knew without a doubt then that I would find you somehow.

I knew then with complete certainty that you had indeed survived whatever had befallen you, and that you were here in Scotland. I knew it was only a matter of time before I would have you in my arms and the world would be right once more. I took all of the energy from there, every part that felt of you I made it a part of me then, taking you with me as I went to join the others at play under a tree in the distance. Baylor had looked up at me as I approached, a look quite close to desperation was written plainly on his face, as he seemed to ask that I confirm all the hope Piper's story had given him.

"Aye," I said simply, and I finally got that smile I had missed before.

From there we managed to get the children to tell us in which direction you, or to their minds Adonia, their wandering wolfhound friend, had started out in when heading home, without causing them to wonder why we wouldn't know the direction already. They had pointed toward our home in the Highlands. Though I'm sure they thought they were directing us to some manor just over the next hill, I knew you had continued past those nearer holdings and headed to our home.

For the moment all thoughts of witches escaped us, as we were given back the old hope you would be home when next we arrived. As soon as we were safely out of the children's view, we changed once more into our favored forms for quick traveling. Baylor rode upon my back as I took the favored form of convenience. I had been that large gaited beast so much lately, I was beginning to resent the smell of horse sweat, but not the need for it.

You can imagine the hell-bent ride we went on then, steeple-chasing had never dreamed of being so hair raising and Baylor would have won every award possible had it dared try. I swear I don't know how the man never had a heart attack after being with me so long and on so many heart-pounding adventures. At any rate, we both survived it, and arrived on the plateau without a scratch to find the others impatiently awaiting Baylor to show them how to get in past the ingeniously constructed door.

The mere fact they had even been standing in front of it was amazing to me, considering how well it blended into the face of the mountain. If nothing else I would have thought they would have simply bypassed it, by becoming incorporeal as you had done, and slipping in under it. I think, though, that in some regard they must have felt this was mine and Baylor's moment to go first.

Baylor launched himself from his seat upon my back, at the very moment I was changing into myself and would have disappeared from beneath him anyway. We raced across the distance to the door, once again acting the happy overgrown children. Baylor slid into the door first, hitting it in just the right manner, so that it swung wide on silent, hidden hinges. Both of us fell into the interior of the cavern, nearly landing atop of each other in our haste.

I could feel you everywhere but you weren't there.

The place was dark and you were gone. I didn't loose hope though, by no means. I felt your presence strongly and I knew you had been there recently and for some time. I went about lighting the place, hoping to find some letter or note, telling us you had gone to a nearby village and would return soon. I found none but what I did find was so amazing and unexplainable to me I was speechless.

All of the furnishings I had destroyed had been repaired in such a manner I could not be sure they had ever been broken. Every overturned table and broken dish Baylor and I had left and lived with after I had broken down had been put to rights. One could not have told that any of it had ever been out of place, broken apart or left in a state of disrepair.

Piper and the twins did not at first understand why it was that Baylor and I were lifting chairs and turning them upside down, looking so closely at their legs and backs, for sign of how this had been done. Adonia began to giggle and watch curiously when Baylor went to his cupboard and began to remove and inspect the dishes I had once broken, wondering at the fact they now sat in their place as though they had never been used, let alone abused so harshly.

"What on the gods' great green earth has gotten into you two?" she asked finally.

"Look at this!" I said.

I had come up before her with a small decorative vase I remembered I had once slammed to the floor of the room. It had been from China, as had been so many of the small things of beauty I had taken my anger out on years ago. It had also been left in dozens of small pieces, under an overturned table, beside my chaise lounge, and I had just found it on the now upright table, whole and delicately perfect, as it had been before it had suffered my rage.

"What?" Adonia asked, bemused even more now. "It's beautiful, but..."

"It should be broken like all the other things should be," I said, cutting her off. "It should be destroyed like I destroyed her room at your villa."

"I don't understand..,"she said, looking back and forth from it to me, still very confused.

"It should be broken," I repeated stupidly.

"All right!" she said unhappily.

Still looking very confused, but trying desperately to understand and be helpful, she took it from my hand and threw it to the floor. I stared in disbelief and it seemed that time slowed as it got closer and closer to the floor. Then suddenly it shattered and the noise rang in my ears in proper time.

"No!" I yelled.

"No?" she repeated, now looking at me like I'd completely lost my mind, then down at the shards by her feet. "You said..."

"I know what I said, but..," I began, but I couldn't help it, I started to laugh and it was a moment before I could speak again. "What I meant was that I had broken it, just like I had broken all the things in her room at your villa. I meant it should be broken, in the sense that it had been before, and now it isn't. Well, now it is...."

Adreal and Piper, who had also been watching with as much amused confusion as she had been, looked at me as she was now; as though I had indeed, finally, lost my mind.

"He's right," Baylor said, coming up behind me and trying to make better sense of the situation. "He destroyed this entire place when she never came back, just like he did yours when she first disappeared."

I bent down then, scooping up all the pretty shards at Adonia's feet, feeling you all over them. It was as though you had suffused them with your very essence somehow, and I could not understand that at all. I stared at these small pieces for quite some time, quietly trying to figure how any of it was possible. The others gathered closer to me, and other than Baylor were probably trying to figure the motivation behind my actions, as well as their cause. I just couldn't help them at that point, for I myself could not explain it any better than I had just tried.

"It feels like her," I whispered, but I didn't know what else to say.

"What?" Baylor asked, leaning over to hear me better.

"I said, it feels like her," I repeated a little louder. "The whole vase, or what's left of it, feels like her,"

"How can that be?" Adreal asked.

Adonia reached out quickly and put her hands over mine where they held the broken pieces, and started to apologize profusely. "I am so..," she said again, trailing off then. "I didn't know! Why would she become a vase?" she said then to those pieces in my hand, "Fix yourself, Angel! I didn't mean it!"

"No, she is not the vase, dearest," Piper said, grinning at her and trying hard not to laugh. "I think he means it merely feels like her." He looked toward me then, still fighting hard not to laugh out loud, adding, "Perhaps she held it for some long period of time? Items sometimes retain something of their owners..."

He had added that last part in effort to help me, but I had no answer. I merely looked admiringly at him for a moment, as he put his arm around Adonia, consoling her, somehow managing to avoid any tell-tale laughter that might belie his consolations. He told her once more she had not destroyed you and no she should not feel too silly for having thought such a thing.

I was torn by my own amusement with the entire situation, Piper's apt handling of it, and the sheer inexplicability of it all. I didn't know whether I should be laughing hysterically or sitting down in the middle of the floor, with my head in my hands, wracking my brain for some explanation.

Once more you had provided us a mystery that would not be easily solved.

~11~

Witches

So we had come home to an empty house once again. Only this time we knew for certain you had survived whatever it was that had befallen you and the others some forty years before, and had definitely returned there at some point. We still had no idea how you had done this miraculous fixing of everything in our home, but since every repaired item had definitely felt of you, we were fairly sure it was you who had done it. Though we were uncomprehending of how such a thing would have been possible, we knew you had done quite a few things previously thought impossible, and it was no surprise that you had yet again stumped the lot of us.

It was some time during the inevitable discussion of such things, that we came back to the 'how' of all the other incredible things you had done. I forget whether it was Adreal or Adonia who had posed the question, but it was one of them that had asked if it could be that you were truly a witch. Wondering aloud if you had possibly been taught some of the hidden arts by your mother and these abilities were somehow made stronger or more pronounced by your having become a Changeling. This in turn led us to remembering and discussing, in a new light, the story that had originally sent us on our mad dash to Scotland.

We began to wonder what parts of the story were truths. We began thinking perhaps you hadn't been seen changing forms, as we'd assumed, and been condemned as a witch, but rather been seen doing something more truly a witch's craft, and then been sentenced to die by burning at the stake, only to kill your executioners. It just didn't sound at all right to us. We couldn't see you killing them for their judgment of you, we could see you disappearing in such a manner as to have convinced them completely you were a witch but the other things just didn't fit. Some part of the story had to have been lost in the multiple times of telling and we realized we needed to find out what.

So we left you a letter in the center of the dining room table, where you could not miss it, asking you to wait for our return should you beat us back and set off to begin the arduous task of tracking down the truths within the myth. We started by searching out the actual village where the incident had taken place, which in and of itself was quite the task. We found that most we talked to claimed it had happened to distant kinsmen, or that they had some personal knowledge of one of those that had been killed but none seemed to know where to send us to speak with those that had survived and seen it first hand.

The story itself seemed to swell or shrink, depending upon whom was doing the telling, yet all in all certain facts remained. A witch had been condemned to die. At least the three that had condemned her had been murdered instead. The murders themselves, though they proved the hardest part in which to pinpoint actual facts, seemed to have by all accounts to have been carried out by an unexplainable beast in a horrific chain of events.

It was mayhap a good week and a half before we were at last entering the right village, in the early morning hours, when its inhabitants were gathering in the marketplace. It was small compared to those markets we had so recently been able to visit in the cities traveling between Egypt and Rome, but strangely they all had the same smells to one extent or other. There was to each of them the harsh smells of freshly slaughtered livestock, and live animal excrement and the underlying, slightly sweeter smells of fresh produce, herbs and flowers.

This particular market was unusually loud and there was about the

150

place an almost rowdy, angry feel. The sounds of a fisticuff match being held and the subsequent bets being placed were at war with the raised voices of those trying to hawk their varied wares. All of it would have seemed as any other market at morning but there was an anxiety and underlying fear that permeated it and somehow made it different.

To me, though, unlike the others with me, there was also a familiarity of feeling I could not escape. I knew deep down that I had been to this area of the lowlands before, I just couldn't recall when. I felt suddenly dizzy, abruptly reminded by a wash of feelings of flying over this very area. In my search of your soul, when you had sung out for salvation some forty odd years before, my soul had moved quickly and incorporeal through this very space. Though the experience had been quite a shock, I regained my composure quickly enough, trying to focus and look around for any clues as to your involvement with this place closer to the here and now.

We had at last been directed here by a man who claimed to be a servant of one of the men who had died at the witch's hands. He had told us he had been the one to discover his master, mauled in his bedchamber, as if the devil himself had come to tear him limb from limb. His had seemed the most accurate telling we had received up to that point, saying that he had been there when the priest had sent for his master to sit in council with him in the trial of another witch.

Though we pressed him further for anything that might add to our hopes of finding what had become of you and where you were now, he had not actually seen the young woman that had been condemned by his master's assistance. He had, however, seen and heard the raven, which had followed all of them that had sentenced her to death thereafter and had known his master was doomed. The rampantly obvious superstition of one who had been the servant to a man of the cloth was an intriguing thing to me, so I pressed him further.

He had told us that his master, and one other that had sat with the priest in this condemnation, had been followed by a raven, and each in turn had met with an awful death. He had said he did not see what had mauled his master or the other man but he had seen a beast both cat and woman, dragging the priest himself to the stake. Binding him with dark magic to the post that had been erected for the burning of the witch, this creature had burned the priest there in the witch's stead. Not once had he laid his eyes on the witch herself, but he was sure she had been one, for why else would the devil himself have come to save her from those that had condemned her to die?

We had taken his directions and words of caution with the hope we were at last on the right path. We carefully considering all of it, trying to separate the blander truths from the spices added to flavor the tale, and figure out just what had caused you to wreak such havoc and start the tale in the first place.

Now the very air around us seemed to speak of the terrible things it had witnessed of late. Between that, and my recent inexplicable recollections and dizziness, I was sure then that we had found the right place. We were where you had been seen in your hellcat form and for whatever your reasons had killed at least three men.

We walked about slowly, as though we were actually shopping for our week's supplies, and hoping something would become clearer to us in the process, until Piper waved us over to an empty area of the market square. If it had not been peculiar that such a prime space was empty, when the rest was so crowded, then the large blacked spot in its center was.

We had all gathered around this spot, staring at it as though it would grow a mouth and answer our questions. I could feel your energies all about it, as though it had existed only because of you, and this too was another question for me. Piper had draped his arm protectively around Adonia's shoulder when she had come up beside him, and she held Adreal's hand in much the same protective fashion, as we all just stood there encircling the spot in stunned silence. Baylor had come up and stood beside me, his huge form casting a shadow over the whole of the scene that seemed to some corner of my mind somehow very appropriate.

We were shocked from our silent staring by an old man stumbling into our midst. He bounced himself off of Baylor's unmovable mass and quickly began trying to right himself, as he seemed to suddenly realize where he had come to in his drunken wandering. He did not even look to see who or what he had just walked into, but rather tried desperately to focus upon the large blackened spot of ground he was frantically trying not to step on. Fear was clearly written upon his face. There was something more than his fear which made me want to talk to him, though. I felt as though I should know him.

The man was dirty, unshaven, and appeared to have been lost in a bottle for far too long, but something about him reminded me once more of the day I had come for you by the stream. Suddenly I had another dizzying flash of remembrance, like a light flickering into existence in a dark corner of my mind, hurting my mind's eye with its sudden brilliance.

I saw again, but as if for the first time, a group of girls running away from the stream where I had found you dying. They were giggling and laughing nervously, pushing each other playfully back and forth as they ran. One had been covered in mud and had blood trickling from her lip, but the others had seemed to hail this as a good thing, praising it like a badge of honor. They had been surprised when a young man had been spotted coming down the path toward them, and the one with the bloodied lip had called out to him, saying, 'Colin.'

I pulled my mind back to the present, wondering where I had kept this memory, for surely that is the only thing it could have been. I had not even realized I had it. I looked over as Baylor reached out one of his large hands to steady the man, who seemed on the verge of falling over in his drunken haste, eager to be away from the spot and the strange group that seemed too comfortable being near to it.

I shook my head again, trying to clear it faster, and repeated the name out loud as if to dispel it.

"Colin," I had whispered.

The man, now caught in Baylor's steadying grasp, jerked sharply. His eyes widened in a look nearing the fear they had shown on having seen the spot of blackened ground, so near to his own feet, and I realized that this old man was that young boy in my memory. I realized too that somehow his presence had been what had triggered the vision I had not known I had kept.

"You are called Colin?" I asked him bluntly.

"Am I to know you?" he had slurred.

I knew he was then, but I did not want to raise his fear and suspicion to a new level, by charging at him with a barrage of questions outright. My mind began working quickly, trying to remember what little you had told me of your mortal life and how I might use any of it to begin to talk with him. I was suddenly mortified to realize just how little I knew of your childhood. In all the times we had sat and told our stories, so little of it had been you doing the talking. You had coaxed Baylor and me to tell you so much about ourselves and yet we had heard so little of you.

I realized I would have to try a new tack, if I was going to get him to speak with me, without having him suspect me to be learned of some dark arts as well. I simply disregarded my prior statement and relied on his alcohol-sodden mind to forget I had ever made it.

"What was burned here, that it is avoided so by those at market?" I asked, feigning complete ignorance.

"Shhh...," he said, putting his grimy finger to his lips as he made the sound. "We do not speak of her, so she will not return."

"Who?" I said, again playing at having no knowledge at all of any of it, that I had not yet heard any of the tales.

"Angelica, she was a witch too, you know, just like her mother," he said, looking down at the patch of blackened ground again as if it cleared his mind a little. "She came back from hell, you know, they were wrong, they had not gotten rid of her, they just made her angry. I tried to tell them."

My heart leapt into my throat, and grew hard there, at the mention of your name. He had trailed off swaying again, not noticing our reactions to his words, and Baylor steadied him once more, perhaps more roughly than was truly necessary. He seemed to suddenly take notice that someone held his arm then, and jerked to throw off the hand that held him up. This only seemed to serve to make him dizzy, so he stopped and began to try to focus upon the owner of the hand. He had not noticed the astonished looks that came to all of our faces just moments before, and I was thankful for it, as I tried desperately to think of what I might ask next.

"You're a strong one, but strength won't save you," he slurred, still looking at Baylor's hand. "She is the devil's own mate, you know, and she brings the ravens with her."

"You knew this Angelica?" I tried to keep the hope for quick answers from my voice.

"I only talked with her once, at the stream, when I was very young," he said, throwing his free arm out in the direction I knew already that it lay in. "When I saw her asking about her grandmother that day, I knew who she was in truth and knew she was lying. I knew it was her, the witch had not aged a day since the girls said they had killed her."

He seemed to be on the defense now, trying to convince us he had had no part of her or her craft. I played on this fear in him; of being labeled in league with her, knowing it was my best course for receiving the knowledge I sought.

"So you never spoke with her again?" I asked, as though I had not believed him.

"Nay, I went and got the priest as soon as I recognized her," he said, trying now to focus on me. "They had taken care of her mother so I thought they could take care of her. I told them what she was." He became defensive then, adding, "I tried to warn them she would not die easily. I didn't know she would be so much stronger in her evil than her mother, they didn't have a chance."

I knew by 'taking care of her mother' that he had meant they had condemned and then had her killed as a witch. Suddenly it all began to come clear why you would have killed three men of the church: they had murdered your mother. Quite likely you had come home, found the house empty and in disarray. You had fixed it somehow, and mayhap waited for us for some time, but we had been away in Egypt and not returned to you soon enough.

So you had then gone searching for your mother when you could not find us, likely looking for any connection to your life, only to have found your last mortal link had been severed. I could not fathom what had gone on in your mind at that point, having found your mother murdered, neither could I judge you harshly for what you had done.

The old man was staring at the blackened earth once more and I wanted suddenly to smack him hard across the face for having been the cause of such useless trauma. I was fairly sure your mother had not been anything more than a good healer, whatever the arts she used, and you no more than a Changeling with a few exceptional powers, but then all that is unexplainable has been labeled or condemned by those who cannot fathom it at some point in man's long history.

Even the twins, as well versed in the unusual as they were, had wondered aloud at one point whether it was that your mother had been a witch, that had given you the added abilities of stealing the Yelm of another, and fixing those broken items. I began to think mayhap there were simply some things we would never know about the universe and how it worked, but that we could not fear and condemn them any more than we had Manji and his gift when we found them to exist.

"Well, you could not have known," I said to Colin at last.

I knew he would never fathom the double meaning behind my words to him and would simply feel I was forgiving him for the men that had perished trying to rid the world of a witch he had pointed out to them. I nodded to Baylor that he should let him go, thinking he would stumble back to whatever hole was providing him with his alcohol to hide in, and be away from this spot as soon as he could. Yet he stood there weaving still, even after Baylor released him, staring at the ground as though it had hypnotized him. Suddenly he jerked his head away from it and stumbled backwards as if it had just slapped him, as I had just thought not to.

"Go now and offer my Mem your apologies, for you have sorely wronged her...," he whispered, his mind was in a far away place, replaying a memory that obviously haunted him. Then he turned and ran away from us and the area we surrounded.

We stood in horrified silence as his words sunk in and we all knew they had to have been yours. He was repeating what he had surely heard, because he had used the endearment for your mother you always had. We knew he had to have been one of those who had bore witness to you in your hellcat form, when you had killed the priest at this very spot. He had been one of those who had told the original story that had mutated and grown before it had come to us. Piper shivered and squeezed Adonia's shoulder once more. Adreal just sighed and looked toward me sadly. Baylor stared a moment more at the departing man's back and then looked toward me as well.

"I'd have killed that one too, I think," Baylor said. "Seems he's caused more than one man's share of trouble, in her life, and in this place."

"Aye, but he knew no better," I said slowly, "and quite likely she never knew of his part in it."

We began then to walk slowly around the area, for having traced where you had gone and discovered why you had done what we had heard you had, we were still left needing to find where you had gone afterwards. Somehow we found ourselves once more on the outskirts of the village, facing homeward again. I felt your soul again strongly there and knew you had thrown off the majority of your energies somewhere close, likely becoming something significantly smaller in mass. We realized sadly that we had no more leads than that and all we could do now was to return home once more and do as we had been before.

So we did, we went home, and used the letter we'd left in case you returned in our absence to rekindle the hearth fire. We proceeded to continue our endless discussions and formulations of new theories. At first we thought that any day you would return, but then the days turned into months and the months into years, and from there to one hundred and from one hundred to two, then three and four.

At some point we had begun again to travel from one place to the next, making a trip a year between Rome and the Highlands. Each time Piper

157

or I would stay behind in case of your return, fearing a letter might not be good enough. We still scanned all the time for you, or any for that matter that might give us any further leads as to where you might have gone, but nothing ever came of it.

Yet none of us ever thought to check your bed, neither Baylor nor myself ever brought ourselves to even open the doors of that enclosed space in which you used to sleep. We never found your note you said in your journal that you had placed under your pillow, telling us you had gone to America, or even knew enough of your mortal life to have known that the New World would have called to you. The thought of coming here in search of you never crossed any of our minds, not once.

We were never attacked again and neither were the three remaining Council members, whom we still checked in on regularly, in Rome. So we had no further course to consider for the finding of those that had been involved in that part of our mystery. We went back to Egypt a few more times, each time with the small hope that either you or my Master would make yourselves known to us, but that too never happened.

The sad fact was that we had run completely out of ideas, my Master was not to be found any more than Piper's. Piper did not know how, or even where, to begin to find the one that had made him, for he did indeed search for her as Santon had suggested before he too had disappeared.

Eventually all we could do was just take hope in the fact that we knew beyond a doubt you had survived what had been done to you, and though you might have gone completely mad upon finding your mother dead, someday you might come back not only to yourself but to us as well.

I could not imagine what the whole thing had done to you, or even guess at your current state of mind, but I could not believe you had been irreparably damaged. Someday you would wander in the front door of our home in the Highlands, and it would all be made right.

We began to go about our daily lives under this mildly comforting assumption, allowing the time to pass, because we had no better ideas. We did much as you did, for a very long time, and just watched from our hideaway in the Highlands as the world around us began to change. Of course we interacted far more than you, but then we hadn't the fear of discovery haunting us. We were well versed in not making the mistakes which would cause us and what we were to be noticed by the course of humanity moving constantly around us.

Baylor was the one with the most difficulty over the years, for his fear of discovery was firmly seated in the fact he could not stop his change, or even control it. We had to be sure he was well away from all eyes and ears during each and every full moon, and that grew harder and harder as the years and population progressed. We did at least have the advantage in one thing, though at the time we had not realized why. Other Werewolves eventually became rarer and their sightings fewer and farther between.

We know now that it was the serious lack of belief, within those being bitten, that was what they would become. This was due not only to the changes in the tales but also the general 'enlightenment' of humanity throughout the years. The cause of this drop in the Werewolf population was not so much on our minds, though, back then, we were just thankful for it and thought little more of it.

Time moved forward as it always will and we all eventually came to adore a lot of the same things you spoke of falling in love with in your writing. Piper, Adonia and Adreal began to spend a great deal of their time in England and France, her undying love for poetry and all the arts leading them to be as near to its blossoming centers as possible, and their undying love for her saw them following along.

They would often return with tales of some new play, especially those written by William Shakespeare, which had either broken her heart or given her a whole new hope for humanity, changing for the millionth time her whole outlook on life and the reason for it.

They began to bring back with them some random piece of art, playbill or book, that had struck her as wonderful, and then leave them lying about for Baylor and myself. Eventually their scheme worked and Baylor and I had begun to take our turn going out into the world for short periods of time, not just leaving home in search of you but, eventually, in search of some small measure of joy. Slowly we returned to the small amount of normalcy we had maintained before the unexpected finding and then losing of you.

Adreal spent the most time out and about in the world of all of us, for not only would he go with Piper and Adonia when they would travel, but he would most times go with Baylor and me as well. The fact his sister and he had managed to age in truth in their appearance to match their experience became a blessing of itself, for had they still appeared, when in their natural state, as the children I had met at the baths of Rome, they would have been very out of place in many of the situations and conversations they ended up in throughout their endless travels.

It is these endless travels, though, that in the end led us to finally finding you. You see, Piper and the twins had once again gone 'sight seeing,' if you will, making a tour around the world to visit all the museums. Adonia is in love with museums, you know. All the art, from all the artist she herself had followed throughout all of her time, in one place, makes her so nostalgic. I think it is the tortured poet in her, but she can never get enough of reviewing little bits of her past, so readily displayed in such places.

I myself am one to avoid such floods of memory, but not our Adonia, she will write for days on end after seeing such reminders of things gone; as though it is the ultimate in inspiration, rather than the cause of a great depression, as it would be for me.

I digress again, though. At any rate, a new museum had opened in America, right here in Springfield, Missouri. It was not the kind of museum they were actually touring, but it was close enough to one in St. Louis that they were intending to stop at, that they went ahead and put it on the list anyway. This museum was called a wildlife museum, and the name itself was enough to eventually cause them to visit it.

This visit I'll thank not only God for but Adreal as well, because he is the one that first heard of it and insisted they see it, not just because they were so close anyway, but also because of what we all are. He set forth convincing arguments, such as they might see something they had never seen before, something extinct, very rare, or just hadn't seen in awhile. All in all, being the creatures we are and capable of doing what we do, it hadn't actually taken all that much before they had decided it would, at the very least, be fun.

Once they had viewed the various displays, and committed to memory those they might someday wish to use, they had gone about finding something else to amuse themselves while still in Springfield. They drove around the town for a time, stopping to get something to eat at one of the multiple places near the town's square, then decided to walk for a time. They were thinking to simply walk off their feelings of over-fullness and then be on their way, driving to the next town and next museum, but that is not what happened. They had found themselves walking down Elm Street, being drawn toward something very familiar.

They were almost to your house before they put their finger on what was so familiar about the area. They had been thrown off because they had never been here, hence nothing should have been familiar about it, and yet it was. Then Adonia had suddenly yelled your name out of nowhere and they had all realized that it was you they were feeling. It had come to all of them they were being drawn toward you, and they had taken off running down the street, laughing happily like a bunch of half-day students racing each other home.

They had stopped short on the front lawn of a house, where they knew this feeling of you had been exuding from, stunned and heartbroken by the 'for sale' sign in front of them. They had moved from one extreme emotion to the next, happy to know you were still around and no longer disguising who and what you were and living in fear. They began thinking how now we might find you more easily, since all of us would be able to sense you as a Changeling presence, not just myself who felt you many times they had not. They consoled themselves that at least now they knew the searching needed to be extended to America, but were still very upset they had obviously not missed you by much, since they felt you so strongly.

That is when they had decided to get a hotel room and called me.

They knew I would want to see this house and what clues it might offer of where you had gone to now. My first response upon hearing the news was to want to hang up on them immediately, meaning to disperse my energy and fly off to America right that second, but I calmed myself long enough to think it through.

I asked Piper to get the phone number of the realtor, and meet with him. I told him he had to convince the realtor to let them walk through the house and be sure. If it was your home, I would buy it. I realized if we were to begin searching for you in America, we would need a closer base of operation than Scotland, and why not your own discarded home.

Piper had gone and met with the realtor that afternoon, while I waited half a world away pacing impatiently, and the twins had fluttered around the outside of your house as a couple of birds. They had begun trying to feel what they could of where you might have gone. What they felt had caused them to worry that you had again met the same fate as you had five hundred years before, for they felt you had dispersed within the house, and could feel no path of your exiting in a smaller form. They had said as much to Piper, but he had assured them that what you had left behind of yourself was in an ordered space in the dining room and not the random explosion of energies we had found in your room at their villa.

I spent an agonizing three hours waiting for them to call me back, to tell me whether or not I was buying a home in the heart of America. As soon as they did, verifying it was indeed your house, I told them to call again and assure the realtor I would be contacting him in the morning to purchase it. Then I told them we had to trade places.

At first they were reluctant to leave, until I explained that I would need them to come and close the house up, and get Baylor on a plane to America, while I bought the place and went through it for clues. Then with whatever clues I had managed to come across, we would begin again together searching, only from there. I think more than anything they recognized my need to be there as soon as possible, at war with my desire to be sure Baylor was completely safe, and had agreed only to save me the pain of making such unacceptable choices, when selecting between my heart's two greatest desires.

So they had done as I asked, telling the realtor I would call him in the morning to purchase the place, and then thrown off their own forms to come back home. We had traded places then and I had left immediately for America, while they put Baylor on an airplane, and proceeded to close up the house. I suppose they are still unfinished with that business, since they have not yet arrived. Life these days is very complicated you know, but they are coming.

So I arrived in America and got into one piece. I called the realtor and arranged a meeting, then thought twice about meeting him as I was, dressed in an old kilt and even older sandals. Such attire does not readily instill faith in those you are convincing you can afford to buy something as expensive as a house outright. So I rented a nice car and clothed myself well, so he would not think me some insane drifter with a bad check, and proceeded to the address Piper had given me. I waited for only a few minutes, but they seemed like hours, and when the man finally showed up in his little white car I was near to bursting with impatience.

He had seemed nervous, taking forever to even make it up the last steps onto the front porch and fumbling his keys, and I was having even more difficulty than him, for I was fighting this terrible urge to just yell 'sold'. From the moment I had turned onto the street, I had felt you so strongly I was near to bursting, and now I was so close to you or at least more clues to where you'd gone, I was wanting to jump out of my own skin with excitement. Right when the door came open it was like you were there before me, I saw a spot on the wall were a large picture had obviously hung for quite some time, shielding the paper behind it from being faded by the sun.

I knew instantly you had stood before it many times, quite likely even touching it, for I felt you very strongly. I could contain myself no longer and I wanted the man gone from there, to leave me alone with you. So I had asked him right then if he would take a check, making him even more nervous than he already was. I had assured him he didn't need to turn over the deed until after the check had cleared, but that had not been the cause of his nervousness. I then realized my own mistake, when he'd asked if I wanted to see the rest of the house first. Suddenly I found I didn't care what he thought of me or my actions, I just wanted the house and the feel of you, so I told him the truth, that there was no need.

He had stared at me as if I were insane, as people often have, like I had grown horns or something, as I wrote out the check. I have actually grown accustomed to being looked at like that, and made no more comment than he did, as he handed me the keys and quickly drove away, presumably headed straight for the bank to be sure to get his funds before I changed my mind.

~12~

Amun Ra

As soon as the realtor was gone, I went through the entire house and kept coming to the same conclusion as Piper. Though I could feel your soul everywhere throughout it, as though your very essence had somehow seeped into its every surface, I was repeatedly drawn to a spot in the dining room where it seemed you had thrown off all of your energies in an orderly pile. I stood there for quite a while, just shifting my weight from one foot to the other, while standing above what was left of your form, and happily absorbing the feeling of you.

Then suddenly my foot had gone right through the aging floor boards and I became inexplicably upset, that I had done harm to the very floor that felt so much of you, to the very house that so remembered you. I had bent over to get the pieces of wood that had fallen through with my foot, thinking that I might somehow be able to fix the floor. That is, of course, when I had found your journal, just as you had always meant for one of us to do. You had thrown off your energy here, hoping it would someday draw us to that very spot, and the journal you had purposefully left behind.

I had sat down right then and there, forgetting completely about the floor or fixing it, forgetting the house altogether. I read every word you wrote, sucking it in like a drowning man would take in air when suddenly washed ashore. You cannot know what it meant to me, to finally learn all the things I had never thought to ask about your mortal life, and had regretted not learning for so long. The beginning of your writing was an unraveling marvel to me and made me long to sweep you up in a rib-crushing hug.

Then I began to see hints of deeper things, I was soon reading of your feelings for me, and how I had hurt you by not being willing to show you mine in return. I was heartbroken. I wanted to hurl the wonderful book away from me then. Yet a hundred times, I clutched it closer instead, white-knuckled and full of fresh regret. It was only to get worse for me when I would read of all the near misses we had in finding each other, but I couldn't help but read on. I kept thinking that, by the end, you would say where you'd gone, and then I could go and finally find you. I kept hoping it was only a matter of time before I would be told how and where I might turn to begin to make it right.

I came to the part where you told us of how you had come to yourself and had not at first realized it had been forty years, how you had been afraid we had all been destroyed by the same thing that had nearly destroyed you. Suddenly, reading your words, so much of what had been a mystery to all of us began to make perfect sense. You explained how you had repaired all the things in the house by merely willing them to fix themselves, as though the energy that made them up was yours to will. You then told how so many things were only made impossible by our own disbelief in their possibility, that it was we who placed limits upon ourselves. You explained that the belief itself was what accomplished so many incomprehensible things. Then the most amazing thing of all: you explained Baylor himself, you had figured out the enigma that was my best friend.

I felt your words propelling me forward, as if I had stepped onto a rollercoaster of emotions the moment I had opened your journal. I felt so many things, in the short space of a few hours, it should not have been possible to condense such breadth of emotion into so short a span of time. Then the ride crested to a terrifying peak, from which, I somehow knew, I was destined to fall.

You had started writing oddly and I had started getting scared. I came to the end where you stated your intent to ascend and I lost my mind. I knew then why the spot on the floor of the dining room, not one foot from me, was so orderly, you had left all of you behind to mark the spot for us.

You were gone.

You had survived what was most likely an attempted forced ascension five hundred years before, only to choose to ascend now. I threw your journal away from me and started raging again, I turned and put my fist through the wall, and had there been furnishings I would have mangled them all. As it was, only my heart had really suffered.

Then Baylor arrived, having rented a car at the airport, stopping only long enough to buy some take-out food, knowing I would not have thought to eat, and had come straight here. At first he thought I was upset that Piper might have had me buy the wrong house, but then I had explained to him you had ascended, and he too had begun to sink into the despair that was fast catching me up. Then quite unexpectedly he had asked me if one could come back from ascension, inadvertently reminding me we had once questioned the possibility when we had felt the presence of my Master so strongly in Egypt.

That is when it came to me that maybe all I had to do was believe it was possible and then it would be. I had looked at your book where it lay on the floor where I'd thrown it and remembered all the seemingly impossible things you had written of doing, that you said you had been able to do simply because you had never thought to think them impossible. I knew then that I had to try it. I had to ascend and bring both of us back. There was nothing to say it couldn't be done except for my own doubt, and I suddenly refused to have any.

So I told Baylor to read everything you had written while I was gone, hoping to find you had been right and he would believe it too and fix himself, becoming a Changeling in full before I returned. For if it all boiled down to our belief, then he needed to believe you were right, and I needed to believe I would be back, and with you. I had left him then, swearing to myself and to him that not only would I be the first ever known to come back from the

Empyrean, but you would be the second. Then I gathered all my faith close about me and threw off my form.

I ascended.

Now that I had discovered where you were, after all those years of searching, I was determined to have you back at any cost. I had no other thought than that as I flew up and up, leaving the earth behind me. It became to me only an awareness of a great mass of energy somewhere below me. I had within me a great driving need to find you. You had been so many things to me, my pupil, my friend, my love waiting to be discovered, and it was that force of will that drove me upward. Far away from all I knew and all of the security of its being, from all I was sure of, into all I could only dream, I ascended.

So it was that I drove my soul like a blade deep into the soul of another. I had not even been aware that I had come near to it, I had been so lost in my desire to find you. I had gone howling blindly upward as my soul screamed its want of you and then I was suddenly deeply submerged within a soul as familiar to me as my own, and I could find no thought or word to describe the feeling of it.

Except, "Master?"

Then all of the demons born of anger and loneliness, seeded by his having abandoned me so very long ago, bared their vicious blades for me again. Gone was my determination to be beyond the depression such thoughts could bring me to. Every half remembered pain or hurt delivered to me, by every question he had ever left me without an answer for, poured fresh salt on now reopened, ages-old wounds. From deep within me, it all reawakened and came at me. Torturous ghosts, floating up unbidden out of their graves, deeply buried memories, come back now to haunt me, and move my tongue to angry condemnation.

I said to him, "Why did you abandon me, when so many times I have needed you?"

His soul, so much greater than mine, surrounding me like a father's arms, seemed to be greatly amused by my angry question. This only furthered my wrath and I tried to withdraw into it, only to find I could not escape his apparently all encompassing, peaceful and loving presence.

He said, "I did not abandon you. I merely removed myself to this place. You could have sought me out here at any time, had you need of my company or my wisdom. You were always welcome." It seemed to me he had laughed then, adding, "You better than any should know things are never merely black or white, that often they are grey."

I was stunned, blind and speechless; no thought could form itself completely within my whirling mind. Hearing my own words given back to me just then was like a stinging salve spread over a wound. The old wounds created by the abandonment and loss of him began to close of their own accord, as if realizing they had no right to have ever been wounds in the first place. For what seemed a small eternity, I remained where I was, deep within the comforting confines of my Master's soul, working at absorbing the irony of it all.

Then I came to realize I had many new thoughts and questions that had congealed themselves in my healing mind. I had absorbed from him a new level of peace for my soul, but with it came an unbidden onslaught of confusion about other things. I now remembered I had longed for ages to ask of him, and never thought to have the chance.

"Master," I said. "I went down into Egypt to find an old Changeling. Nearly five hundred years ago, someone I knew said they had felt the presence of a very old one there and I was seeking wisdom from one of greater age. I had within me a need that one might impart some knowledge to me, as you had always done, for I was in a great state of confusion about many things."

"I had even held out hope it would be you that I would find," I added. "For I had felt a great presence of you there when I had drawn close, and I had hoped that maybe you had returned. I had hoped you could unravel the terrible mystery and misery that had and has so completely ensnared me."

"Once there I had found on the walls of its temples and the insides of its tombs a great residual presence of you," I continued. "I even found that the Sphinx itself wore your own beloved face. I thought then surely you had been there, but more importantly I thought you had returned, but I never found you. Where were you that I did not find you and yet I felt you everywhere? Why did you not come to me when I called out to you, or allow at least that I might find you?"

"Here. I have been here," he replied. "As I have been since I left the earth and your company, those many ages ago."

"But how is it that I felt your presence, still so strongly, even then?" I asked, still greatly confused by all of it.

"Because those walls and roads are mine, they were built for me, of me, and will remember me forever," he replied. "Those temples were built to honor me. Those tombs were built in man's attempt to please and commune with me. All of it at some time was mayhap even a part of me in one form or another. I was then, and still am, Amun Ra. Though that was not always my name, it is the one I best recall."

"But I do not understand," I cried. "You *are* a God?"

"No," he said gently and with great amusement. "I merely became as one in an effort to induce my Creator to turn His countenance upon me again, even if it only be in anger."

"I do not understand," I told him again. "Either you are a God or you are a Changeling."

"Oh, Demosthenes, you are ever a source of joy to me," he said. "You should remember that even in this, there is never simply black or white, yes or no."

"But," I told him, still very much confused, "you told me more times than I could count to never split forms and yet I dreamed you made of yourself a model for the Sphinx and allowed all to know. I even went to it to see with my own eyes that the dream had shown me truth. You took such split forms to appear as those they worshiped and allowed them to worship you."

"I know," he said, still seeming to be smile on me as an errant child. "I walked with you in the first of those dreams but found you could not accept my soul's presence as an actuality enough to be able to speak with me. Yet I showed you what I could through them. And those forms were mine to take, and the effects they had on my people were mine to live with. I simply wished to spare you the same burden I bear, by seeing you never did the same."

"So are you Amun Ra, or are you a Changeling who took the forms and pretended to be?" I said, still not understanding him completely.

"Come, be easy within yourself," he sighed, "and I will tell you all I think you must needs now know and did not comprehend before."

So it was that he, whom I had called Master and Teacher, gave to me his name, and began again to teach. Telling me as I am telling you:

"'When in the beginning, my father and mother had first lived in the garden that is sometimes called Eden,' Ra said, 'They pleased the Creator very much and He came to them often. He was to them also a Father and a Mother, talking with them, teaching them and guiding them always. They were happy as none other has ever been happy, for He blessed them with three children, and we, those first offspring, were also happy as none other will ever be.

"'The Creator was a kind and generous grandfather, always showing my siblings and me some new enjoyment to be had of the home He had created for us. We were all then in a constant state of bliss and nothing was ever denied us, but that we should never eat of this one tree. Now I believe our Creator did this that we would choose to obey or not, that we be different from his previous creations, in that we were created with a free will to choose or not to love Him and express that love through our *willing* adherence to this simple command.

"'But that is, as they say, ancient history, for every walk of humanity remembers and tells its offspring those small details. All know what course my mother chose. And my father, in his love of her, not wishing to lose her, followed her in that choice. Such is love. Our Creator was greatly pleased

His creation would love so well and deeply, but saddened then, for He too had great love for them, but found now He had to discipline His children as He had said He would. He took from them many of the gifts that had been bestowed on them. The main of which was that they had been created in His image, which was many, and now they were limited to just the one fragile state.

"'They were cast out of our home and into the wild earth, made to sweat and toil and age and die. Cursed to be human only, with a knowledge of all they had lost to haunt them. My brother and my sister and myself watched all of these happenings, knowing not the full extent of this curse for many, many years. Until the time came when our parents were delivered of more children and our mother's pain in this had been greatly increased, as the Creator in His punishment of her said that it would. Our mother was made to writhe and scream in the bearing of her new sons and they too had only the one form, having been born in our parents' image only and not the Creator's. They too were cut off from our Creator as our parents had been.

"'Yet our Creator remained caring and kind, ever the Eternal Father to them. He then began to set up ways in which they could redeem themselves and commune with him. Wanting to give them a second chance at choosing Him in loving obedience, He began providing for them ways to return to His grace after death.

"'And death came.

"'As we watched, our mortal brother killed our other mortal brother. The emotion that caused him to do this was as yet still foreign to us. Then we observed, still silently, as the brunt of the punishment was brought down, this seeming greater even still than our parents or their new offspring had thus far suffered. For ages death came, but the living for ages with the knowledge they were being denied far greater things seemed to be the worse of the two states. Knowledge, knowledge became a worse punishment in and of itself, the knowledge they themselves had disobeyed to attain.

"'For ages we were simply the silent observers of all of the punishments that the Creator had set down, the quite watchers, noting also all of the chances at redemption He provided. Soon our human brothers and sisters were bearing children of their own, so on and so forth, and all were as our parents had become, fragile and aging, dying from birth. Yet we were forever noticing that even as they chose to turn away from Him, the Creator would provide yet another choice. We too had become absorbed by all of these happenings, just as our Creator seemed to have, and for ages we did not think to wonder at ourselves or our place in the new way of things.

"'One day we did wonder, however, and we called out to Him, asking Him where our place in this new scheme of things was to be. He did not answer, having, I suppose, been preoccupied with some new prophet, another one that He would send out to help these human descendants of our parents.

"'Hence I learned why one of my brothers had killed the other, for I came to feel this as well. Jealousy, to be jealous, I learned this emotion first, for I too felt it over all the attention humanity received. Yet still I watched only, trying to think how I might fit into this new way of things. I thought then that if these humans were so pleasing to Him now, that I would become one of them, I would be the best among them, then in His pleasure He would look on me again.

"'So I took the form of one of these humans and walked among them. I prayed as they did, sacrificed as they did. I studied in their great centers of learning, wishing to join them in their 'enlightenment' thinking to learn my place. Yet it all failed, they as well as I, and throughout it all, still He did not answer me. Still He did not take notice of me or commune with me as He had in the garden. Smaller civilizations came and went, entire branches of my human kin moved to the far reaches of the world or died out all together.

"'Those who remained in greater concentration under my watchful eye still could teach me nothing of how to return to His grace. They too seemed ever unable to do so, no matter how intelligent they appeared to become or how many temples they built to ever increasing heights to reach Him. Their knowledge, as ever, failed them, kept them seperate. The face of the entire world eventually changed, waters rose and fell, religions came and went, much learning was lost, and my people, those I had remained closest to, once more became dispersed, but nothing was ever learned that could have gotten me into my Creator's view.

"'Eventually none that I had known knew me any longer, including, it seemed, my own Creator. I became angry then. I too took to wandering, and it came to me in my anger, as I saw in my wanderings yet another prophet given the Commandments, that if God would not answer me, I would do something to make Him.

"'I saw a temple destroyed by Him in wrath, for He too was jealous, and it had been built up for a false god. This worship of others than Him, He had so recently commanded humanity not to do, so thus it came to me. If my Creator would not turn His countenance upon me in pleasure, not take notice when I called to Him, or even when I had prayed as He had told them they should do, then I would make Him turn to me by setting myself up as a false god. Surely He would take notice of me then, even if it was to turn to me in anger and destroy me. Any notice from Him was to my thinking better than the total lack of any I had existed with for so long.

"'This too did not cause Him to turn to me, even as so many of His people began to worship me, turning from Him. Other false gods he destroyed, other temples raised in their honor He demolished. Yet He took no notice of me nor of all those choosing me then over Him. No punishment came down from Him upon my head.

"'His people were soon calling me by many names, in many different places, spreading word of me throughout the land, building temples for me, sacrificing to me. The inadequacies of language, as it had become, notwithstanding, my worship spread. My name changed more times than I can tell you, and those powers attributed to me grew beyond any concept of truths I had shown them. My brother and my sister, because they had been with me in some of this, also began to be attributed with godly natures and be given other names, their worship like mine spreading throughout the world like a plague.

"'Soon there were temples throughout creation devoted to us three, wherever one would look, masculine and feminine gods of every manner one could imagine were designed in our images. Whatever form we chose in which to appear to them, they accepted and revered, and none of these temples was destroyed, none of these worshipers brought low by the true Creator. Nothing we did drew His wrath or His pleasure. Of course there were always some who recalled the truth of it, who recalled some teaching passed down through time, those who worshiped the one true God and led others to. These did He seem to find His pleasure in, this did I try hardest to understand.

"'Still for ages it spread, this worship of others than Himself, and though He commanded it not be so, still He did not turn, not even His wrath, toward me or my siblings, and we began to tire of it all. Only then, when I became again a silent observer and men began to boast of godliness in my absence, did He turn his wrath upon my Egypt.

My sister grew angry with me, telling me that we were causing humanity much confusion and many wars, that we were leading them from the peace of communion to be found only with Him, and that that could not be our purpose. She was right, it had not accomplished my goal and was never my siblings' goal at all. To be truthful, I think it had always disgusted my sister and bored my brother, but they had stayed with me for lack of better ideas or means.

"'Eventually they did leave me, though, to find their own way, telling me that nothing would ever be changed by this course. So I had become again a silent watcher for a time. Only now I looked out from Egypt, and was alone. Still worshiped and adored, I had become known as Amun Ra, at least in their language, the Almighty Deity, and all other gods were become merely lesser forms representing my supreme power's many facets. This too would change eventually, as you well know from history. Facets became offspring, as stories mutated with each retelling.

Sometimes I would do something to heighten the level of my worship, thinking perhaps to incite some higher level of outrage within my Creator that would draw His attention, but nothing, nothing worked. No feat was amazing enough, no atrocity worthy of turning his visage.

"'I grew unbearably lonely after some time, another of those emotions which so plague creation and drive humans to do such strange, and oft terrible, deeds. I began again to show myself, but only to some small few, not wishing to increase the loneliness that came increasingly closer when these more fragile kin lost their anchors here. I began to show the people things their forefathers had once known, demanding they use that knowledge to do more things for me in my name. Soon I had them change the entire face of Egypt for me. I demanded great tributes, not only to my Creator but to my siblings. Chief among these tributes were three tombs that we would never use because it seemed we would never die, pointing straight to Him, and were a wonder like never before seen. Then I called my siblings back to me that they might see that I had changed things, but that had not been what they had meant when they had told me nothing would ever be changed, and it would be eons more before I would understand that.

"'Once more I was left alone with my desires and no notion of how I would bring them to fruition. How could I bring myself back into my Creator's view, and cause Him to gaze again upon me with the love and adoration I so missed? So it was that a new idea grew in me. I had set myself up as a false god, but I was not truly a god. Was not the true God the Creator? I began thinking that should I find a way to become this, then maybe He would take notice.

"'I had begun to pay attention, more fully to those humans around me, and the events of daily life, wondering how I would accomplish this. The ironic truth, that I had already created something so profound it was beyond my own understanding, would elude me until long after I had met you.

"'It would be a small eternity of witnessing religious wars, one of which led to the discovery of you, before I would realize I had created an entire race of gods, whether real or imagined. I was already a creator and it had done me nothing to draw the true God's attention. When this truth had finally come to me is when I had begun to demand of you that you never split forms. I essentially began to assure myself that you would never use your gifts, as I had mine, or cause humanity the terrible trouble I had caused them.

"'I had felt the full import of this, when I had seen the very son of the Creator, who had been sent down among us. Once and for all, he was to not only right the wrongs of my parents but my own as well, and I knew I had failed my Creator miserably. I had been making a terrible mess of all things and I could not blame Him that He would not look on me. So many wars and confusion, death without recognition or acceptance of the true God's love at every turn, and I had been responsible for so much of it. I could not live with it any longer, which is much of why I had ascended.

"'But as I was saying before, long before this realization, I had thought I had done it wrong and merely had to do it right to gain His attention. I saw there had been new things, inanimate objects, minor inventions, made every day, but they had no soul. Woman brought forth new living beings all of the time, but the soul came to them from the Creator. The soul then was the key I felt I lacked, for I had not the ability to create that divine spark. That was truly the Creator's gift and it was beyond my grasp. Only He had been able to put a soul into the dust and make of it the being that had been my sire.

"'I thought I would have to create something or mayhap reshape it as the Creator had done of the dust to make my father, but the soul was still beyond me. It would then be my own new creation, but in a manner would always be his, this I could not circumvent, unless I was to figure out how to create a soul.

"'I did not know what it was I truly meant to do, I just knew I meant to try something new. It was in this time I came to notice one man in particular who seemed worthy of what I had been thinking to try, even as I was still not completely sure what it was. This was one Phillip of Macedonia. He had come to great power, conquering all of the areas around him, including my Egypt, capturing my complete interest as well. I then left my Egypt to follow him and his progress.

"'I began thinking that this was a man that could I alter and recreate in my own fashion, could not fail to capture the Creators attention, as this man had a will that would conquer even heaven, given such opportunity. How could the Creator not turn His divine head toward me if I accomplished this? But when in time death came to him, I had still found no opportunity to do so, nor had I any notion of how I would do it.

"'I turned then to his son, as great and fearless if not more so, than his father before him. This one, Alexander he was called, went also to his death, without my having a clear course of action or any idea as to how to effect this change. It was in a growing state of despondency caused by these two deaths, while I was still searching my mind for some new path to my Creator's eye, that I came upon you.

"'Your screams, your tormented screams, they drew me like a giant moth to the blaze that was your will. Your will was a beauty that amazed me. It was so much akin to mine, a kinship I was barely capable of recognizing but could not at the same time miss. You would have changed all of heaven and earth and how they worked, to bring your love back to you, just as I meant to do for much the same reasons.

"'I watched you as you screamed your rage at heaven, that it would steal her from you. I recognized my own rage, which I had not yet named such. I saw in you what I had felt, as my parents were taken from me out into the wild world. I saw you as you cradled your lover's lifeless body in your arms. You were doing, as I realized only then, what I had longed to do when I had witnessed my young mortal brother's lifeless body, yet had not thought to do. I had not known then my own emotions, still did not in full, nor did I know how to express them as you did then, so eloquently.

"'Suddenly I wanted to be with you. There was something in your screams I fully understood, that spoke directly to my very soul. I wanted to commune with you, in voice, in spirit, in whatever way necessary that I might understand all of this. I needed you, for you to teach me how you expressed these things, what names you called them by, why they felt the way they did. I thought I would somehow come to you and ask you to be a teacher of sorts to me. I found that, while watching you, an incomprehensible and beautiful appreciation of the humanity I had been so long jealous of had grown inside me. It was an instantaneous and almost painful realization and I wanted more of it, I did not want these realizations to end.

"'Then I saw you raise the knife above your head.

"'I had not seen this in your hand, and suddenly a numbing fear of losing you too, as I had lost everything else, surged up within me. A fear of missing all the new opportunities I had suddenly realized were possible, had only just glimpsed, nearly paralyzed me. I could not lose you. I would not let this be lost to me, as all else had been lost.

"'Suddenly you were screaming that you would tear her back from Hades with your own two hands. You had sent this blade plunging toward your heart. I flew at you to stop you. I knew full well that you could not bring her back, no matter your will. Once a soul returned to the Hall and the Creator, only the Creator could let it return, and then only if it had not finished learning and choosing here. I wanted you to live, needed you to live, so that I might better understand myself through understanding you. I think I was even hoping that I might somehow better understand my Creator through better understanding his favored creation.

"'So it was that I created, or rather recreated, you in my own image, without my knowing I would do it. Holding you within myself, as I am now, not wanting to let you go. I had somehow changed you and then you changed me, but some things never change. Still in you there is the same will you had then, to change whatever you must, flying hell-bent in the face of all you know, fighting to bring your love back into your arms, a living, breathing thing, to be loved in return.

"But," I told him softly, "a different love."

"'No,' he told me, 'only a different body for the same soul. The opportunities provided by the Creator are only as limited as His creation makes them. His desire for humans is that all would learn to love, truly love, and then choose to love Him. If I learned nothing more of Him, I at least learned that, and if learning to love and therefore being able to chose to love

Him require a soul to return to earth, then that is what He allows. The choices humans make from first to last are theirs, that is the beauty of that free will and he created in all of us.'

Again I was speechless, as my mind whirled relentlessly. I remembered how many times I had fought back the urge to be with you, to kiss you. How so often in your writing you had spoke of my soul like a familiar thing, imagined yourself so often as Seraphim in my painting, as your subconscious mind seemed to be repeatedly trying to tell you whom you had been. I wondered why it was that I had not known it was so. Why had I not seen this? Why, in my blindness, had I allowed my loyalty to a lover's memory to deny that same lover my love?

The scope and irony of it astounded me, and again my purpose called to me. I had to find you, make you understand and forgive me. I had to get you back, to tell you I loved you now as I loved you then, as then before when you were Seraphim, as ever, even now. I had to tell you that you had been right in what you wrote, you had indeed been born for me just as I had for you.

"Is she here?" I had begged him, completely forgetting any other questions I might have asked.

"Yes," came his simple reply, "as are others, those who rest."

"Can I take her from this place back into the world?" I asked him then.

"As I have told you," he said, "yours is the will to change the way things work."

"Come with me then. Be with me in the flesh and talk and laugh with me again," I pleaded.

"I have no heart for it any longer," he told me. "In naming my emotions for me, you also made me feel them all the more. As I said in changing you, you changed me; you were as much the teacher as I and I can bear no more now."

I felt his soul contract and I knew this was a kind of hug goodbye. He would not be swayed now, just as I had not been able to sway him so many ages ago.

I had turned my attention then, as I could be kept from you no longer. I was calmer now, knowing that I would find you. Knowing that indeed my search would soon be over, I swept my awareness in a great wide arc, scanning slowly and softly, and there, I had known you. I knew all my Teacher had said was true. Without the trappings of life, and the confusion of all the world's energies swirling about us, I recognized Ra's truth.

Seraphim or Angelica, you were there.

And now we are here.

Part 2

~13~

Shopping

"Yes, we are here," Angel said, turning her head and yawning loudly, "but we, are quite nearly all that is."

Angel had said this while pointedly looking around the still nearly empty living room, which contained only the couch we were lying on and one other thing, an over-stuffed recliner. I laughed then, upon noticing it, thinking surely it had been Baylor's first purchase. Angel jumped up, suddenly full of inexplicable energy, considering she had only moments before been more like a contented sloth, lying on my shoulder, listening to me tell my tale.

"What is the date? What year is it?" she said, surprising me yet again.

"March 7, 2004," I said slowly, wondering how this would affect her.

"Damn!" she said finally. "Well, too bad I closed my bank account, I could have built some healthy interest."

I had to laugh again then, because I had expected that she might be shocked at how long she had been waiting in the Empyrean, or bemoan the eight plus lost years, and instead she had bemoaned the loss of her bank account. Angel turned then, pouting at me, seeming to think I was laughing because she had lost her bank account and interest, and not understanding it had merely been her lack of reflection on the lost time in general which had made me laugh. She never ceases to amaze me, this woman.

"What do you need a bank account for?" I asked, trying to straighten my face. "To buy clothes?"

I failed miserably to achieve the straight face, beginning to laugh again as she looked down at herself, standing in the middle of the living room, naked as a fairy gift, and seemed to notice this state for the first time. Rather than the embarrassment I might have expected from the Angel I had known five hundred years ago, I was pleasantly surprised when she looked me slowly up and down where I lay prone and still nude myself, and merely raised her eyebrow and smiled crookedly at me.

"And you are talking, why?" she said sarcastically.

"Shutting up now," I replied, still unable to lose the stupid grin plastered to my face.

She ran back to me laughing, jumping on top of me. She straddled me, with her hands on my chest. Looking me deep in the eyes, she feigned innocence. She began batting her long black lashes at me playfully and I knew I was doomed to agree to whatever it was she obviously had planned.

"I want to go shopping," she said. "I can make myself clothes but I want to furnish this house again and get it ready before everyone gets here."

"Um hum," I replied. I heard her but I wasn't really registering any of it, my mind had moved on to other things.

"You have a bank account, don't you?" she coaxed.

"Um hum," I said again, putting my hands on her hips.

"Plenty of money in it?" she added, still smiling innocently.

"Um hum," I grinned.

"Then let's go shopping," she said, feigning as though she meant to jump up immediately.

"Later," I said, gripping her hips tight to stay her.

"Um hum," she laughed, leaning over and kissing me.

So, later, the following morning, we went and bought one of those new trucks that can be turned into a multi-passenger vehicle, returning my rental car and paying the fees I had incurred while in the Empyrean. We had

184

decided it would be the best choice in transportation, considering how many of us there were bound to be soon, and that we meant to purchase a few larger items that day, some of which could not be delivered.

We had then proceeded to stop at every store on the planet, not literally, but my gods the woman does not tire of such things. She ran me all over town, sometimes for one item per store and sometimes to other stores for apparently absolutely nothing at all, except to convince herself she had gotten a good deal at the one before. I know the only thing that saved me from it a second day in a row was the fact we had to wait for all our other purchases to be delivered to us, for she in no way appeared to have had enough of it.

She had even busied herself mentally shopping in between the deliveries the following day, composing various lists on little pieces of paper under different stores' names. Yet I could see some method to her madness, as throughout that second day different rooms began to come together a little more with each delivery, and any time I would mention an item as missing or necessary, she would say something like, yes, we will get that at such and such tomorrow, it's on my list.

I thanked the gods I had been smart enough in my great long life to have amassed plenty of money in various places for easy access, because she certainly had plenty of things she meant to spend it on. I didn't mind, though, by any means, it was so wonderful to be with her again, and I loved watching her at work. The putting up of curtains and making of beds became a very beautiful thing to watch. Of course I was frequently made to assist, but this too I didn't mind, it just gave me another excuse to be even closer to her.

The next two days passed in a flurry of shopping, decorating, installing and the overall preparation for the rest of the family to arrive. I say 'family' because that is exactly what we all were. The twins might have been the only ones that actually shared blood, but we all shared something even deeper and far harder to explain. We were Changelings, we lived and loved longer and stronger than most mortals could grasp, and that love bound us more tightly than any right of blood could come close to.

The end of that week saw Angel and myself walking through our newly decorated home, enjoying the fruits of our labor. The first floor which contained the living and dining rooms, the kitchen, a utility room and bathroom, and a den, which we had set up as our own indoor garden, had come together more quickly than the upper floors. Angel had been far more selective with the upper floors because these contained the bedrooms and she wanted each of us to have a space we could call our own, and find comfort in.

The top most floor was made up of only our room, a bathroom and a deck which overlooked the garden at the rear of the house. This we were still working on, but Angel did not seem in such a hurry with its decor as long as the other rooms were prepared. She had seen to it that there was a room readied for Adonia and Piper, even going so far as to pick out a little writing desk for Adonia to write her poetry at. Baylor's room contained a huge, sturdy bed fit for him and his Edana when they returned, and two matched dressers. Adreal's room and the other two which made up the much larger middle floor received just as much attention to detail. In this respect it had been shown me, quite clearly, just how much our family had meant to her and how lost she had been without all of us.

When I had questioned her as to whom the other rooms were for, that she had put equal heart into them as those of which I already knew, she had surprised me yet again.

"Gray will come eventually," she had said, smiling, "even if only for a short visit before wandering again. As will others. Don't think I didn't notice your avoidance of the subject of safety when I first said nothing else mattered because we were together and we were safe and you said yes, we are together. Our mystery remains unsolved and will not simply go away because we have found each other. It has become more so a thing to be solved now, so that we never become separated again."

I had stared at her with admiration then, realizing just how brave and strong she truly was. Angel had noted with quiet reserve the fact that we had never found out what it was that had nearly destroyed her, that we had lost another to it, that we did not indeed feel completely safe from it, and she had gone about the business of making others comfortable, making no mention of it until now. I knew it had to frighten her that whatever or whomever had done that terrible damage to her was still out there somewhere, possibly waiting to do it again, and I was in awe of her composure. This Angel was truly not the Angel I had expected to bring back when ascending into the Empyrean, yet I was pleased. I put my arms around her then and drew her close to me.

"We will figure this out, Angel," I whispered, kissing her on the top of her sweet smelling head. "We will find out who is doing this to us and how to stop them."

"We know who is doing it," she said, looking up at me as though I had lost my mind that I should act as though I didn't know too. "We just need to find and stop..."

"Who?" I cut in, befuddled not only by her look but the fact she seemed to really think I did know.

"One of the others in the dream you had," she said. The dawning realization I truly hadn't put it together the way that she had caused her to draw slightly back from my arms to better look at me. "Manji had told you..."

"Manji never told me anything," I said, cutting her off and feeling very stupid I had missed something she obviously felt I shouldn't have. "He couldn't talk."

"You said," she continued as though I had never rudely interrupted, "you were thinking about the dream and who could be old enough and powerful enough to have done us that damage. You asked him if there was any thing you weren't seeing that he had noticed about who could be responsible, and he shook his head in the negative and pointed at you, then his temple. He was telling you that you knew." She looked hard at me. "He was telling you that you were seeing it right then."

I stared at her dumbfounded, wondering if she could be right, if it could have been that simple. I had thought back then that he might have meant that he only saw what I myself saw, or that we were on the right path with all of our deductions. I had never once considered that he had meant that the very thoughts I had been thinking before I had asked him, had been the ones in which I was literally seeing my own answers.

"You mean to tell me you think one of Ra's siblings is responsible for this?" I was astounded.

"His siblings?" It was her turn to sound astounded.

"Yes, he told me it was his brother and sister he called back to him in Egypt," I said, thinking at least I was not the only one still missing the obvious. "Remember I told you everything he told me. It was they he had grown lonely for, and for them he had changed the face of Egypt to lure."

"Okay, well, yes," Angel said then, barely missing a beat. "Then I guess I am saying it was one of Ra's siblings. What other Changeling would have enough respect for his power to have left you in relative peace and be of an age to have the accumulated wisdom and power to have pulled all of this off?"

"I do not know, but surely not one of them," I said defensively. "They are my Master's own kin, and he is good, they are not like other men, they do not do evil. They never sinned as their parents did, that is how they remained what they were. They never fell from grace. Weren't you listening?"

"Yes, I was listening," she retorted, pulling completely from my arms and staring up at me. "The question is, were you? You are thinking like a human, like everything is fair and good and just, unless evil steps in to change it, but it's not. Bad things happen to good people, good things happen to bad; good people do bad things and bad people sometimes do good. Besides all that, we are not talking about people at all. The First Born are not bound to any human concept of right and wrong, black or white. Ra himself spoke of that to you. It is never that simple! You say it, but you do not see it! Why do you think our human emotions so confused your Master?"

My eyes grew wide as she seemed to swell and shrink in her consternation. Seeming to have to work hard at keeping control of her features.

"They never fell from grace, they never ate of the tree and the tree was *the knowledge*." Angel continued, stomping her bare foot on the newly carpeted floor of the dining room. "They have no knowledge of good and evil, other than what they view of humanity and our labeling of it, therefore they are not bound to being one or the other by a choice or action one might call right or wrong. Ra himself did things that humanity would label evil incarnate. Literally, he was the incarnation of more evils than one can fathom, if you really break it down. He made himself into false a god, *he invented the gods of old*! Humans would call that a mortal sin. Besides, in doing so he started more wars in the history of humankind than any other thing in our world. He is probably the very seed of religious warfare!" Her hair seemed to shimmer more a raven wing blue-black than its normal blood red-black, as her voice rose, "We would call that evil, pure evil! Hitler looks a saint in comparison, but the Creator allowed it because they can do no wrong in His eyes, they are the favored sons and daughter, they never fell from grace. They are not held by Him to the same standards we as humans are."

"But....,' I began.

"No buts, Demon," she said irritability, sounding slightly English suddenly, shaking me more than a little. "Think like a Changeling! Use all the years of having viewed the earth and all its changes to some advantage. There is no such thing as fair. There is no such thing as just. You know this, I know you do, you have told me so yourself. There is only humanity's drive to make it so, to fight to return to some semblance of Eden. We, as Changelings, have been blessed beyond most to fight this reality. The free will we were all born with, which demands we strive for better, because we did fall from grace and we know deep down inside we are being denied a far better reality, is given strength by our ability to change. Yet change is exactly what it has to be, because it is not fair naturally, changing it is the only way to make it even resemble that utopian idea of reality."

I was stunned beyond words, even frightened. I had heard this all in some form or other at many points and from many people. I had said much the same to her when first we had met and she lay dying. Yet my beautiful

Angel, standing angry and hurt before me, hands on hips, demanding that I recognize the truth of it, and not just the words, broke my heart. Broke my heart because she was right, because life wasn't fair, as proven when she had been stolen from me twice. I had surely known life's lack of true fairness then, and so had she.

Had I not screamed to the heavens more than once, about that very lack of fairness that she now required I face again? At some point in our lives I think we all have cried out. I *know we* all have, it is the very will to change it which makes us what we are. Yet it was the raw openness of those wounds, apparent in Angel's voice, and the total acceptance of the fact they were there, which broke my heart the most. I wanted to move on, pretend all was well for a moment, leave those caskets to collect their dust, but her pain demanded I not.

I think it was the fact that I knew we weren't just talking about the First Born too, that this wasn't solely regarding whether or not one of Ra's siblings might have been responsible for what had been done to all of us so long ago. I was seeing just how much my Angel had suffered and what that suffering had done to her in the very way she spoke. The mere fact Angel had suffered so much to have come to these conclusions on her own, that I myself had been a part of that suffering, that she had been made to face it by herself, the very fact that the world would even allow that to happen to such as her, these things broke my heart more than anything.

I know we have all been made to see the ugliness of it. I know we all have been made to feel and taste and deal with it at some point, but I also know we all try to forget it. If we don't, we do not survive. We all have to try to change it and when we can't, well, those are the kinds of things I keep in my caskets, at the very rear of my soul's vault, the things that remind me, so I bury them. Yet here she was demanding I face them, that I drag them out and accept them, that I do as she had been forced to do and learn from them what I could.

My heart was broken all over again because I did not know what to do with this change that had been effected in my Angel. I wanted to live the fairy tale and use that very free will I had been blessed with to make the very best of each new day with her. It was a part of me, that I know it didn't have to be just, that the universe didn't conform to any human rules of fair conduct, but I chose not to visit it on a daily basis, lest I be drawn into the despair I had spent so long avoiding. Yet it seemed to me now that it had become a part of her that she could not help but acknowledge. My Angel had been broken, and I was crushed to find myself unable to instruct her how to repair it and then simply tell her 'now, walk with me,' as I had so long ago.

I reached out then and drew her back into my arms, wanting desperately to make it better somehow even though I knew I could not. She came into my arms then and started crying, and I knew with a certainty that I had been right. We had not been merely speaking of my Master and his kin or their ability to do such to us, be it right or wrong from a human standpoint. We hadn't even really been talking about our mutual dilemma as an endangered species. We had indeed been inadvertently addressing her inability to collate all she had been made to face. I held her for quite awhile saying nothing at all, just running one of my hands repeatedly down through her hair, and holding her tightly to me with the other.

Finally I bent down and lifted her into my arms, carrying her across the room to one of the new chairs she had so happily picked out not two days before. I sat down with her in my arms there and just let her cry it out, because I really didn't know what else to do.

"I'm sorry," I whispered finally.

"Not your fault," she sniveled at last.

"Not entirely," I said, "but I am sorry I can't shield you from it or at least show you how to put it away. You're right, it is easier to ignore humanity's fatally flawed concepts of fair, but it must be our way to find a mean by which we may overcome that fact..."

I trailed off then because I didn't know what else to say or how to word it. I couldn't tell her how I dealt with it because my way wasn't necessarily right. I could only be there, loving her, and hope that was enough to help her through. I knew she had been to the edge of sanity more than once and she was still not completely right with all that had happened, and the changes it had effected in her, but I would be there for her, it was all I could do.

"So who do you think is responsible?" she asked suddenly, as though she too had decided to put the pain away for the moment and get back to thinking of things she knew better how to deal with.

"Responsible?" I asked, momentarily lost.

"His brother or his sister?" she said, peering up at me through her long, teardrop-laden lashes. "Which do you think would be doing this?"

"Well, for one, I am still not convinced it would be either," I said carefully. "And for two, I wouldn't know how to decide. I mean I see where you are coming from about the age and wisdom necessary, and yes, both of them would be the ones to most easily fit that description, but there is still much to consider."

"Like?" she asked.

"Motive?" I said. "Can you think of one?"

She grew quiet again and I was a little afraid she would turn pensive or angry, or worse, begin to cry again. I understood her confusion and her determination to find an answer that would rid her of it, but I was not so willing to pin the blame on the first old Changeling we came upon.

"Okay, so if not one of them, not that I am conceding there even needs to be one in their case," she said finally, "who else could it be? There are not that many of us left."

"That we know of," I interjected.

"Why do you say that?" Angel asked then.

"Well, remember the woman from Africa, Mikaili, the one who changed Rajesh?" I asked. "She was obviously quite old and wise, and yet none of us had heard of her and obviously even the Elders dared not take her on or they'd have done something about her blessing Rajesh. So there may be others we have yet to meet, those that escaped the Council's notice, and hence ours, as she had."

"And remember," I added. "What of those souls hovering about his siblings in the same dream?"

"But they could be anyone," Angel said desperately, "any Changeling then, and that is no help at all."

It seemed possible she would fall into tears again and I wasn't sure I could handle seeing her hurt so visibly again so I was very happy when she looked up at me with quiet determination planted firmly on her face.

"Okay, so we need to try and locate all of us," she replied. "We need to try and compile a list, especially of the ones that would be old enough or wise enough to have formulated a respect for your Master, which would be the reason you have remained safe. If any of your summations in Egypt are correct it would indeed be a very select few to choose from. At least it would be something, a place to start."

"Well, I don't know, I suppose we could begin with composing a list of all of us we know about," I tried, knowing she was desperate to relieve her mind, if only by attacking a different problem. "But remember, there will still be those we do not know about, and we can not just pick the oldest on this list and place the blame at their feet."

"Well, either way, knowing who and where all the others are will be useful," Angel said, appearing to have accepted my warning. "So that we can all be made aware of what is going on. You don't suppose the remaining Elders would give up their histories of us?"

"Well, they might have," I replied slowly. "But they burned all of those things upon our return from Egypt, realizing, as we had, they could be being used against us."

"Will they never get anything right?" she grumbled, but it didn't seem to stir her anger at least.

I patted her head then, thankful that she seemed to have redirected her anger and hurt. I was proud of her strength, I would have expected any other being, Changeling or otherwise, to have broken already. Strangely enough, it occurred to me then that she had broken, I just hadn't seen it that way because I had only seen it in her writing and a few angry tears. I think I was even prouder then, that she had broken and still managed to put herself back together into this beautiful creature cuddled up in my lap.

"We need a piece of paper, then," Angel said, sitting up then and wiping her eyes on the back of her hand. "Better yet we need a computer and...."

And we were off again. Angel had redirected her anger all right and was taking it out on my credit cards. We ended up on the road for yet another long afternoon, hitting at least three stores before she found the right computer at the right price, and still disparaging the quality of these readymade versions we were looking at.

I was momentarily surprised by her knowledge of such things, as I listened to her endless stream of questions, which sounded to me like strings of numbers and letters thrown together with a word or two, but obviously impressed the sales clerk. It took me a moment to remember she had mentioned having fallen in love with her computer and the internet for its ability to let her communicate with others all over the world without ever having to meet them in person.

When she finally made her choice, I happily paid the bill and helped the young man to load it into the back of our vehicle, thinking we were at last going to head home, but I was not to be so lucky. We still had to stop and buy a desk for the computer to sit on and a chair for her to sit in while using it. Then pens and ledgers for keeping other notes and recording of any relevant information, a grocery store for some items she had forgotten the last two times we had been in as many days. Then she directed me to stop at a wine seller, for I don't even remember what, before she was satisfied with that day's outing. I honestly became convinced then that shopping had become her bandaid, her means of forgetting what had been done to her and that the one who had done it still roamed freely. I wasn't about to tell her this at that particular juncture, though, not when we were almost home.

Pulling up the drive to the house, I almost forgot these thoughts as I felt the familiar presence of Piper and the twins, and was relived they had finally arrived. Not because I had not enjoyed my time alone with Angel by any means, but because maybe they could help me to placate her need for answers and keep her mind on the search rather than on the old hurts that had attacked her so harshly today. Not to mention it would be so much easier for me if I could simply hand her my check book or credit cards and send her off with Adonia. I know that might sound awful, but a man can only stand to shop so much.

"They're here," Angel said, just before I could.

"Yes, they finally made it," I said.

"What, have I shopped you to death?" she said with a grin, as though reading my mind. "Are you ready to put me off on Adonia?"

"Well...," I began sheepishly.

"It's quite all right," She said then, surprising me for the millionth time. "I think I hide in it sometimes. You know, the little pleasures and things to think about, the inconsequential delight of where to hang a new picture or place a new figurine. You can almost forget the bigger things for a moment, then." She smiled up at me, also sheepishly.

"Yes, I know, I think I used to do it too," I said, "before I met you. How do you think our home in the Highlands ended up as nice as it was?"

I put the car in park and the conversation ended abruptly as Piper and Adonia both raced out of the house and embraced her before she was even fully out of the vehicle. Adreal came out only slightly after them and held back until his sister, who took far longer to let her go, had finally stepped away to look her up and down. He had waited patiently, exchanging a knowing smile with me that said he was incredibly happy for me, that I had found her at last. He then stepped forward and wrapped her up in a hug I would not have expected, given how short a time they had known each other and how little he seemed to think of love itself. As he gave her a finale squeeze, he whispered something in her ear which made her blush and made me curious, to say the least, as to what he had said. I didn't have the opportunity to ask either of them, though, because a flurry of questions had overtaken all of us and we were soon sweeping into the house with arms full of the day's purchases.

Angel and Adonia ended up in the kitchen putting the groceries away and inevitably began making a late lunch for all of us, as they came across things which awoke their appetites in the process, all the while gossiping happily. Piper and I moved the new desk into a corner of the indoor garden room and Adreal, who displayed knowledge to match Angel's, began to set up the computer on it. Soon we were all gathered in that room with plates of delicious sandwiches on our laps, cans of soda clasped between our knees, and a bag of chips to share between us, as though we had not just spent a very pretty penny on a huge dining room table that would have easily sat eight, let alone us five.

The conversation quickly degenerated into a delightfully rude scene as each of us proceeded to answer each other's questions, whether they were asked specifically of us or not, around mouthfuls of delicious food. Now that I look back, I have to be honest and say I'm not really sure if it was the food itself which was so wonderful, or the company of those I loved to share it with, and the happy jabbering going on around it. Soon we were explaining Baylor's absence, the fact that he was no longer a Werewolf and had ascended to retrieve Edana. Eventually Angel and I were laughing, telling the others they would probably be far better off reading her journal as he had, because these explanations seemed to have came out better in her writing than they were just then in all the excitement.

Adreal and Adonia asked for the journal immediately, their voices blending in their haste for every new bit of knowledge, and again we were laughing. It seemed so right then, at that moment, with the lot of us laughing and poking fun back and forth. Suddenly it occurred to me that the only thing missing was Baylor and I sobered instantly, worriedly wondering just what was taking him so very long. I tried to tell myself it was only that he was having difficulty locating Edana, but somehow I couldn't get it out of my head that I had spent so much time conversing with my Master before finally finding Angel, and still had been in the Empyrean for only three days. Yet all in all, I was left with only the reassurance that he had sworn. 'Until we swear again,' he had promised, and he would not break that oath to me.

Angel noticed my shift in mood almost instantly, placing her hand on my thigh where it rested up against hers, rubbing softly back and forth but saying nothing. I looked down at her hand, my heart swelling with pride that she was mine and that she knew me so well. I covered her hand with my own then, and looked into her eyes. I felt all the peaceful comfort of her soul come to me then, not just from her hand and nearness but through those beautiful eyes.

I knew she understood because she seemed to silently tell me once again that Baylor would be fine. I leaned over then, kissing her brow softly, and thanking her for being her, in the same manner she had just spoken to me. Slowly I pushed my fears aside to listen to the conversation that had continued to go on without us, as though we had stepped outside of time for a moment and not been missed.

As the conversation then turned to the new computer in the corner of the room, and our reasons for having gone to purchase it that afternoon, the oddity of the moment Angel and I had just shared soon got lost within it. Piper, Adonia and Adreal had all agreed with this new plan of action we had come up with, immediately popping off with all the names of those they had met in their various travels. Beginning with those we all knew separately seemed the obvious place to start, since Angel or myself might not know one that Piper or the twins had met on some separate travel, and those would be the ones most easily left off the list. Adreal got up and quickly sat down at the computer to input all these names and what information whoever was speaking could relay about that Changeling.

As we were each spouting off names, he would ask the occasional question about each of these Changelings, assuring us that such things as who had changed them, or where they were from, were entered in his new database.

~14~

Baylor

"What do you mean, you didn't ask?" Piper was yelling.

"I assumed you had and I didn't want to bother her with the same questions twice," I replied, with only slightly less volume in quick self-defense.

"Well, that proves what they say about assumption, doesn't it?" he had retorted angrily.

This was not going well. At first the names Changelings we knew, had flowed out of all off us, along with an abundance of information about them. We are a curious breed, gathering all manner of information wherever we can, and this had thus far served us well. Now, though, we had begun encountering problems, problems that never should have existed in the first place, and more problems were not what we needed right now. We had begun this endeavor on a high, hopeful note, thinking to find solutions. But we had swiftly descended into the basement of angry despair on the staircase of our own stupidity and oversights, and it was fast wearing on me that Piper kept pointing mine out.

"And just why should it be left to me to ask Mikaili who changed her?" I asked, trying hard to lower my voice. "You had the same opportunities that I did. In fact, you had more, since you and Adonia took so long in saying your farewells to her."

"I was asking her about her hair," Adonia spoke up, defending Piper's equal lack of foresight.

"Of course you were," I replied, raising an eyebrow in consternation, "because that's important."

I was now torn between anger and an almost overpowering need to laugh. The fact that one of us would have thought to engage Mikaili in a conversation about her hair style, but never ask who had blessed her, blew my mind, the fact it had been Adonia, however, did not. We were a curious breed indeed just perhaps not always about the right things. My lip must have twitched, as it will when I am amused but not willing to be, because Piper seemed suddenly even angrier.

"It is not funny, Demon," Piper huffed then. "We had just spent months bemoaning the stupidity of the Council's Elders for not gleaning such information of the old one they had met, and then for us to turn around and do the same ourselves! It just isn't funny."

"Actually it is." Angel surprised me, speaking up from her previously quite place at my side. "Think about it, really."

All of us had turned to look at her, thinking she was on the verge of imparting some wisdom to us, that perhaps, yet again, she had picked up some clue we had overlooked while listening quietly to us as we argued. But instead she locked eyes with Adonia and they had both burst out laughing.

"She really did have the most gorgeous hair," Adonia finally managed through her laughter.

Adreal and I started laughing the moment Adonia had half of her sentence out and eventually Piper could not resist either. Between the contagious laughter and subsequent release of tension, I think we had all decided there was nothing to be done about another missed opportunity. With the mood a little lighter now, it wasn't but a few moments before we all made an unspoken agreement to leave it that way. It was the kind of decision that makes itself known through the excuses being given for exiting the room and consequently the discontinuing of all talk that might lead to another argument.

Soon we were all heading in the direction of our appointed bedrooms and bidding each other a good night's rest. I noted with a bit more amusement that Adonia had swiped Angel's journal from off the desk. It had been on the desk where Adreal had found it when he had begun his typing. He had tried to cover it with a sheet of paper when he'd found it there, but obviously Adonia had seen him. Adreal had yet to notice its absence but I was sure he would miss it when he got to his room. I knew he had wanted to begin to read it before falling asleep and felt a little sorry for him that his sister would forever be his equal, if not his better, when it came to being sneaky. I said nothing, though, figuring that would be an argument better left between the two of them. I was for bed myself and other things besides reading before going to sleep that night.

I got to my feet and leaned over to offer a hand to Angel, whose smile told me she had also witnessed Adonia's swift thievery and had been equally amused by it. She placed her hand in mine and came up to her feet, falling against me in a manner completely unnecessary and just as completely welcome, whispering in my ear.

"You know I love you," she stated quietly.

"Aye, and I you," I whispered back.

Suddenly having whispered in her ear, I recalled Adreal having done the same earlier and my aforementioned curiosity got the better of me.

"What did Adreal whisper to you when we got home?" I asked.

"That he was happy to see me again and happier to see me so happy, but warned I should go easy on you," she said grinning up at me. "He said you're an old man."

"Old man, is it?" I said, feigning hurt. "Well, so much for feeling sorry for him that he lost his reading material for the evening."

We were in our room but a few minutes when the expected ruckus erupted downstairs. First we heard what we assumed was Adreal descending to the first floor to retrieve the journal he had forgotten, then his much more hurried ascent as he had realized it was not where he had left it, and finally his frustrated knocking upon his sister's door, which I might add she admirably managed to ignore completely. He eventually gave up, recognizing the futility of the situation and resigning himself to wait until she was finished with the journal before he would have his turn. Thus Angel and I had been adequately forewarned that breakfast would be an exercise in hiding our amused smiles while being forced to observe a pouting Adreal pushing his food around.

Indeed, the next morning went much as we had thought it would, with Adonia sleepy-eyed from reading all night, smirking her now superior knowledge across the table at her twin. Adreal handled it better than we expected, though, merely ignoring her and eating his pancakes in silence. If he put butter on the same cake twice or over-poured his syrup we were meant to surmise he was merely not yet fully awake, and not that her looks were actually doing their job of disturbing him. Breakfast was otherwise uneventful and passed with the occasional request for a refill of milk and compliments to Angel on her skills at the griddle, at which point I refused to cast a shadow over her glory by telling anyone the delicious flavor had come from a box and all she had added to it was a dash of vanilla.

Soon we were all gathered in the indoor garden again, and this time it was Angel sitting before her new computer and asking questions. We quickly fell into a rhythm with the whole process, spouting off first the name of the Changeling, then his or her either known or presumed age. Next we would tell Angel from what area they had come, whether they had been born there or changed there, to the best of our knowledge. We would then give her what other tidbits of information we felt might somehow, at some point, prove to be relevant, telling her things like what had been their favored forms or what they might have said at some juncture that had perhaps given us pause to think.

The list was indeed very small, even after we decided to add those we knew to have ascended already, along with the proper notation as to whether we thought it to be by choice or not. We all seemed to know intuitively that our list should be much larger. This began to bother us deeply, but not so badly as my own thoughts of the things I had overlooked. For instance, I was very upset that I had never found out for sure who had been standing in the shadows behind my friend Kynan when the light had come for him, and all the who's, when's and why's of the beautiful-haired Mikaili. I began berating myself for not only those oversights themselves, but for the fact they were no doubt going to lead to another berating from Piper.

I was jerked from these troubled musings by the sudden recognition of a Changeling pulling form together within the house somewhere to my left. All of us became aware of it at the same time and we were all on our feet instantly. I glanced around at the others, noting quickly that Adreal was not present, and for a fraction of a second I thought it could be him returning from somewhere he had neglected to tell us he was going. Yet I quickly discarded this thought as I realized that, this soul did not feel like our Adreal. This soul was wounded, and its pain exuded from it in waves.

We were all out the door of our indoor garden room before most of these thoughts were even fully formed, chasing this feeling down the hall, around the corner and into the dining room. I stopped short, stunned, the others, unable to stop as quickly, knocking me into that room and a situation I was in no way prepared to meet. My heart turned over and tried to stop as I frantically digested what I was seeing.

"Baylor?" I whispered finally.

I knew it was him; my words weren't really a question. It was more that I wanted him to tell me he was still the same Baylor that had left me some week and a half ago, because this Baylor felt different. The huge man before me, that I had always known as the purest exemplification a warrior in strength of both mind and body, was now laying in the middle of the foyer, like a broken thing.

I took a tentative step toward his prostrate mass, watching closely for any movement from him which might tell me he knew of my presence, or even was aware of where he was, but all I saw was the soft jerky movement that comes in the chest of one who still cries but barely has the strength to breathe.

"Baylor?" I whispered again.

The others were frozen where they had regained their footing in the old archway, staring. I looked back over my shoulder, wishing for any of them to tell me what I should do. I noticed Adreal slowly descending the stairs with Angel's journal in his white-knuckled hands, and Angel herself on the verge of taking a slow step forward, but none of them seemed to know better than I what should be done. Still the disheveled mass of red hair did not move, the ragtag kilted legs made not a motion. So I took another hesitant step.

"Baylor?" How many times had I whispered his name now?

I had come to stand directly over his head and still, in all the time this had taken me, he had made no motion to indicate he knew of my presence. Slowly I bent my knees, bringing myself down to a level at which I could put out my hand and brush his hair from his eyes, but here again I faltered. Afraid, I think, of what I might see, afraid his deep blue eyes would be open yet unseeing, depthless and unable to know me even then.

"Baylor?" I repeated, frightened and hollow sounding even in my own ears.

I looked over my shoulder once more for strength and saw the others had also moved closer. Adreal was on the last stair and Angel had her hand on the back of the chair closest to us, the one at the foot of the table, for support. Piper and Adonia had each other in a death grip about the waists, appearing to be the only things holding the other up. Finally, gathering all my courage about me, I lowered my hand and moved the random strands of wet red hair from my old friend's eyes.

Suddenly his arm shot out, grabbing me about my waist and pulling my lower body under his head, his vice-like grip unavoidable, and next thing I knew he had me in a great bear-hug with his cheek pressed into my hip. He started sobbing loudly then, hugging me even tighter and saying my name over and over again. It was like I was a rock found in the middle of an open and stormy sea, and not only was he beyond grateful to have found me but he was never going to let me go.

His sudden outburst seemed to break a spell the others had fallen under, and Angel broke lose her grip from the back of the chair and flew the rest of the distance to us. She fell to her knees beside me and threw her arms around Baylor, pressing her face into his chest, and began to cry.

"Angel?" Baylor whispered, seeming instantly more coherent when he heard her weep. "Don't cry, sweetling."

"I'm so sorry, Baylor," Angel sobbed compassionately.

"You couldn't have known, Lass," he whispered, removing one arm from my waist and placing it on her head where it rested against his chest. "It'll be okay."

With that he sat up, pushing up from the floor and away from me, pushing his inner turmoil away just as surely. He patted my shoulder and came to a sitting position beside me as though nothing out of the ordinary had just occurred, and yet I could not escape the feeling, that something had, something far beyond my ability to understand. He then patted Angel's cheek and smiled at her, seeming to set aside his own inner agonies in preference to making her feel better.

"But what happened?" she asked, wiping her hand across her eyes and looking desperately up at him. "Why wouldn't she come back for you?"

I could see this stabbed him afresh straight through the heart, a wound he had only just pulled closed. I know she saw it too, for both of us wished instantly that we could reach into the air and pull back the words before they reached his ears.

"I'm sorry, Baylor, please forget I said anything," she said regretfully. "I'm horrible. Come on, let me feed you. You can talk to us about what you want to talk about, the rest is yours."

She got up quickly then, obviously in a hurry to be about mending the situation and forgetting how thoughtless she felt she had been in creating it. Baylor and I got up more slowly, not looking directly at each other. Remembering vividly the very unmanly situation that had directly preceded Angel's hasty words, I suddenly felt like laughing, that it would made us feel so awkward now was very amusing for some odd reason. We had known each other so long and been through so much that it was just another one of those things. I'll blame my reaction on stress.

"Queer," I laughed, pushing him back over as he tried to stand.

"Your momma," he replied with a half-hearted laugh.

And that was that; as with so many other things, we would most likely never speak of it again. Though hollow and short, it was a laugh at least, and I hoped it signaled Baylor's swift return to his normal, stable self. We followed Angel back toward the kitchen and I observed his mildly approving looks as he surveyed all the changes that had taken place in his absence. He didn't ask how long he had been gone, as I had done; he seemed to still be somewhat withdrawn.

Baylor appeared to me to be merely viewing pleasant changes at a mental distance from which they bore no actual relevance to him or his present state of mind. I think a lot of things had yet to settle in his mind and he was just back, neither happy to be here nor wishing to be elsewhere, just back and it would take him some time to actually return. So it was with some surprise to me that as we were all sitting down to our second meal of the day, Baylor was the first to speak.

"I'm going to tell you all of it, Angel," he announced unexpectedly. "And you are going to write it all down just like you did the other things."

"You don't have to, Baylor," she protested, but he cut her off.

"Yes, I do," he said. "And you have to get it out to all of them. We are going to publish it all: your journal, your coming back, my experience, all of it. Every one of us needs to know all of it."

She stared at him in awe, disbelief as plain on her face as I'm sure it was on all of ours. Her face went through many changes then, as she seemed to have a dozen statements or possible arguments run through her head in mere instants before finally settling on something to say.

"You are serious?" she asked him incredulously.

"Absolutely," Baylor replied.

"Who would publish such a thing?" she tried. "We would be laughed out of every publishing house in the world. No one believes we exist and it is probably better that way."

"So we'll publish it ourselves, as a work of fiction," he said, still very determined. "The ones that it will matter to, will know it's not fiction. They will be able to figure it all out and learn what they need to from it. The rest of the world can just enjoy it as a dammed ingenious idea for a tale or use it to start their fireplaces."

"But....," Angel began again.

"No buts now, Angel," Baylor said. "I don't care about the Council anymore than they care about me, and I know you don't care about the Code any more than I. The parts of it that matter are more about having common sense than needing to be told it anyway, as you yourself have said. The point here is that all Changelings need to be made aware of what they are. There is no sense, common or otherwise, in letting them believe they are Werewolves or Druids or God only knows what else.

"I am sick to death of guilt. I have hunted those I felt I had spawned in my own homeland for ages, trying desperately to keep safe my own, and for ages they have hunted in turn, simply spreading far beyond those boundaries I protected. Humanity's disbelief may have slowed them, but even twenty years ago there was one spotted in Germany, by security guards no less, not some wandering tale-about. So such beasts born of ignorance are not going to be completely stopped, unless we do more than I can do alone. We must teach them; they must learn they can be more."

"Okay," Adreal said after a moment, grudgingly conceding Baylor's well-made point, as the rest of us just sat absorbed by his words. "But what about those who aren't Changelings?" he continued. "What if others recognize the truth in it? We will have another epidemic, of those both worthy and otherwise, all denying the light. There will be countless hauntings, unnatural numbers of lost souls. People will win their battle against the light only to find themselves without form, when and if none of us hears them. In their surety and stubbornness they will be left behind by the light yet disadvantaged and without form, forced to continue the existence they fought so hard for in that unacceptable way. That breeds uncommon rage in some of them, we know this; my gods, we invite a whole new level of chaos if we tread that path." He paused, sighing thoughtfully, then adding, "Also, consider all the unworthy that will suddenly be making themselves available to our enemies to be changed and then come against us as well."

"Doubtful," Baylor said. "No one believes in anything anymore, that point is made clear by the fact of just how rare finding a Werewolf has been these last few hundred years, even in my Scotland. Now whether the story of such creatures came to us from elsewhere or we propagated it ourselves doesn't really matter, what matters is that my people used to believe it wholeheartedly and therefore would become it, but it doesn't really happen anymore, people just don't believe in such things like they used to. I was probably the only one to hear the tale the security guards told of a 'wolf-like-man-beast' leaping a seven-and-a-half-foot-tall fence and know it for more than the bored production of a sleepy mind."

"Let the world believe it is just that once more, a great delusion, cooked up by a very bored mind, and it will be to our advantage once again. Because what we need to do is get the word out there to all those who will know it is true because they already believe," he added vehemently. "They will already know they are different, they just have yet to be told to what extent, and that it is a thing that can be controlled. The rest can call it a good fantasy or even rubbish for all I care."

"And that which Angel has done?" Adonia asked, apparently weakened by Baylor's arguments but still worried. "Do we want others to know what she has found to be possible? With knowledge like that, we could turn what was at one point a small coven of witches or Druids or whatever they call themselves these days- those that feel they had some small measure of control over the universe, passed on to them by their ancestors with the help of spells- into a very powerful group that could rise against us."

"That is the chance we take," Baylor said, unwavering. "We are a formidable group, we can force ascensions as the Council did to restore order if we find we need to, but we cannot withhold such important information from others like me. What about all those other Werewolves that I would otherwise have to hunt down and kill? I can no longer only extend my protection to my own homeland and excuse my total lack of involvement otherwise as preoccupation with recovering Angel. She is back now and she has given me, us, a better way to solve the problem. What about Vampires? They kill, or at the very least interfere in the lives of, countless humans each year. What if they too are just Changelings like I was, walking around by night believing they are cursed, and thinking they must kill or wound to survive because they know no better and we refuse to tell them?"

"Good gods, I had not seen the scope of it," I said, finally breaking my contemplative silence. "Baylor is right. Werewolves, Vampires, witches." I looked at Angel then remembering her pulling the cork from our wine by sheer force of her will. "Even those with such powers as telekinesis or what have you, they could all just be Changelings, having had unknowing contact between their soul and one that was changed, and neither of them the wiser. They are just wandering about in the dark and we are sitting here with matches debating on how much harm it might cause if we were to light a candle and let them see."

"I mean, really," I continued. "We know that my Teacher probably began all of the myths of the gods and goddesses with his allowing others to live in the dark. Look what havoc that wreaked on the world! Now for thousands of years other such myths have sprung up, for whatever reasons some Changeling chose to leave another in the dark, and done nothing but cause confusion. We can put a stop to it once and for all. If nothing else, we might tell them to be wary of such random contact of souls."

"Vampires...?" Angel said slowly, as though she just heard the word for the first time. "Yes, it follows. What Baylor said has merit beyond even what I had seen. I mean, I had thought but I had not *thought*." She smiled sheepishly at all of us, adding, "I had a lot on my mind. But just like with Werewolves, though, if stories of such half-wolf and half-man beasts had already circulated, then it was only a matter of time before the stories mutated once more after Baylor disappeared under such strange circumstances. Things were added or changed over time. Take silver, for instance. Those were poor people facing a frightening task, killing a beast they didn't understand."

"There had to be another way to destroy it than beheading it," Angel continued quickly. "Beheading took a strength most did not possess, and that left them feeling hopeless. So it is eventually suggested it might be done with a blade made of silver, although of course obtaining one would be just as difficult, it had to be, to be in keeping with the problem itself, but it became a possibility for a greater number of people to feel safe. You might not be of a stature or strength to behead a Werewolf, but if you could somehow obtain enough silver you could save yourself. Of course the stories of the area are what its residents believe, and when one of those residents becomes a Werewolf they become the Werewolf they believed in. We know this. I told all of you because I had thought it through."

"The same would hold true about Vampires, though, and explain how different versions of them and their traits, strengths and weaknesses have circulated throughout the centuries and continents. Some stories of Vampires say that they too change their shape. Wow, do I feel stupid." Angel continued excitedly, despite her brief blush, "If one grew up hearing tales of horribly disfigured creatures of the night that drank the blood of the unwary and slept in coffins, then met such a thing, or rather, a Changeling that resembled what they had envisioned, they would become that creature from the tales they had been told. If they grew up with tales of beautiful seductive immortals, filled with endless guilt about their means of survival and constant torment over the status of their souls, then that would be what they then became."

"Anyhow, the end point is still that the souls make contact at the point of drawing the blood, or being bitten by the Werewolf, or even merely being conceived." Angel continued as she looked over at Baylor, smiling, "At the point when the soul would either be entering or leaving the flesh, it makes contact with the changed soul. So what would have been human is irrevocably changed and it becomes only a matter of the new Changeling soul's beliefs that dictates what they become. This is proven time and again by the fact there are so many different types and tales sprung from the things we now know are merely misguided attempts at understanding what we are and what we are capable of."

"The original cause of it all was a Changeling," she added. "one somewhere buried deep in our own shadowed past who had been given bad information or mayhap even one who passed on bad information for whatever purpose. But those still walking this earth blindly believing their own myth will never know unless we tell them. Such problems will only continue to mutate with the tales themselves unless we let others know."

"I mean, think,' Angel continued, narrowing her eyes thoughtfully. "The whole Vampire breed could have started with something as simple as one being changed and then told not to go about in the daylight. If for no other reason than the one who made it didn't want it to be seen, and thought it best this new Changeling only go out at night, even if only for a time. This could have been misconstrued; the one who changed it could have even disappeared before taking the time to better explain itself. Then, left to its own devices the new Changeling invents repercussions for disobeying this last order. The mutations of the tale, its repercussions for future generations spawned by that one Changeling, become an endless web of half truths from there." She looked at all of us then, as determined now as Baylor had been, adding, "We have within us the ability to put a stop to all of it. We have the obligation to!"

"But what of what happened to Baylor?" Adonia interjected yet another argument. "Say others read your journal, others who know they are different. Say they fix themselves, and we have no more Werewolves or Vampires, or what have you. That would undoubtedly be wonderful. But," she paused here, obviously searching for the right words, "what if, let us say, others begin to ascend into the Empyrean as Baylor did to retrieve lost ancestors or lovers or friends? I myself even thought to go in search of Edsel and Santon and probably would have, had I not just seen with my own eyes the damage done Baylor," Adonia admitted. "What if they don't make it back?"

"So?" Adreal asked her, "just means Darwin was on to something."

"Okay. Mean! But okay," Adonia conceded, then asked, "And what of those who succeed? The world could be overrun with Changelings, from the ancient to otherwise; both good and evil, brought back by those that might succeed as Angel and Demon. Once again you ultimately have chaos: too many Changelings, in too small a world!"

Piper, I noticed, remained consciously silent, and for that I could not fault him. I knew him to be intelligent enough to make the right decision when the time came, but silent enough not to make the decision making process any harder than it already was. Adonia and Adreal would voice their fears readily, and I loved them for it, but Piper would merely digest these fears and see how they sat in his stomach.

"No, it won't happen that way," Baylor replied, his tone sad but sure. "We will just have to write a second book heading off all such nonsense. We will tell them just how impossible it really is, and warn them of all the peril involved in even trying. How it was that Demon and Angel managed to find each other and return so quickly is beyond me, but I know I would strongly warn others not to take such a risk."

"We will write as many books as it takes, Baylor," Angel said sympathetically. "I agree that all of us deserve to know everything. What I don't understand, though, is what it was that was so difficult for you up there. It all seemed so easy for Demon and me."

"And that is exactly why I am going to explain it to all of you," Baylor replied. "Not only you five here, but all of them. I would not wish such an experience on my worst enemies, and we will not risk others suffering it simply because once more no one bothers to tell them."

Baylor's flat statements and bleak outlook disturbed me greatly. I mean, I fully understood and agreed with his conviction that all should be made aware of the full truth of what they were. I thought it was only his lack of sprit, his flat, downtrodden tone while expressing these convictions, which disturbed me, but I was wrong. I had yet to be made to fully appreciate the way in which they came to be convictions, instead of just passing thoughts, prudent ideas, and there would be more to disturb me than just his tone.

As we all settled in to hear what he meant to share with us, and for us to share with all of you, it quickly became apparent it went far deeper than what I had yet seen or thought. The why of it, however, was much shyer about making itself known.

~15~

The Empyrean

"I threw off my form as I had read in your journal that I could do," Baylor explained. "I was so excited that I might finally get the chance to be with Edana again that I never thought to ask you what it would be like, so that I might be better prepared. The initial feeling of being without my flesh or any semblance of form was at first very exciting. I reveled in the fact it really was true, I really was a Changeling in every way and I could do any and all of the things you had written were possible for us. I was light and full of purpose heading, up and up and up."

"Then suddenly I felt things, not actual objects whole or real, but feelings I guess you could say, near to me," he said, lowering his voice a little more in his sadness. "It was as if random bits of thought had taken up parts of space around me even though they were, shapeless and without form. I thought these must be the souls of the others. I was overjoyed that I had made it, I was in the Empyrean."

"I thought they must be like I was," he continued. "Present in spirit, only lacking form, but not thought. I felt I had become a thought. So I called out to these others with my soul and suddenly they were flying away from me in every direction, as though I had dropped like a stone into the middle of the calm lake that was them and they were repelled from me in rippling fear."

"I called out again, telling them that I meant them no harm," he said then. "I tried to tell them I only sought to bring the happiest of news to one of their number. I asked if any of them might know where my Edana was, but none stopped their flight from me, none answered me."

"I was suddenly alone," he said. "For as far as I could feel there was nothing, and that nothingness seemed to settle into me. It seemed to become a part of me. I began to forget what it was to feel something. I began to forget what it was to feel at all."

"I called out then, frightened of my own forgetfulness." Baylor looked up at Angel as though of all of us she would understand. "I spoke just to hear my own thoughts, yet I wasn't even speaking in truth, and this saddened me. None heard my calls, which soon became cries, as I resorted to the simple repetition of her name and mine. They seemed the only things I could remember. I was Baylor and I searched for Edana. I repeated this to myself over and over. It was all I had."

"The nothingness descended upon me, seeped deeper within me, and it seemed I no longer cared why I was there," he continued. "Yet I was sad, very sad, and for a moment I couldn't remember why I was so desperately unhappy. Then it occurred to me to wonder who was *I* that *I* should be so sad. Maybe if I could know that, then I would understand why I was sad and I could combat this nearly overwhelming depression I was falling into."

"My name came back to me like a swift blade to the heart: Baylor, his mother's vengeance; Baylor, his father's doom; Baylor the cursed beast spreading a plague throughout his homeland and among his own people. Suddenly I knew not only who I was, but also why I was so sad. I had done it, I had remembered what I had sought to remember, but this had only made me sadder."

"Yet there seemed to be more, a glimmer somewhere within my consciousness, and I fought to grasp it. It seemed that had all happened long ago," Baylor said, now looking at me. "I remembered then, in an instant brilliant flash, that I had once been something more. I recalled that once I had met those that had seen more within me, called me more. I had been Baylor the friend; Baylor the brother; Baylor the storyteller. Then finally remembering being a storyteller I also recalled having once been told a story too. That tale had made me Baylor, the Changeling. That meant I could change it. I had to change it, because something else began to echo in my consciousness, my own voice again mixed with another, saying, 'Until we swear again'."

"After that," Baylor said, "it was a matter of trying to remember how to get home, and I ended up descending slowly, not even sure I was going the right way but hoping the universe was obeying me when I had bid it take me there. I felt the energy of the earth as I drew near to it and I was relieved beyond words that I had come back to it. Then I demanded my own form be returned to me and there I was, but I didn't feel completely right, I still don't."

"There was also the awful onslaught of all the other feelings would have been far easier not to have to face," Baylor said quietly. "Everything I had ever learned over time to forget or ignore came back too, just as much a part of me as this body. The sudden maelstrom of recollections and the swift drowning in every remembrance, both cherished and suppressed, seemed more than I could take. Every single memory I had collected in over two thousand years of living is still congealing within me. They are as equal a part of me as my flesh, and were recalled to me just as surely as I recalled my form."

"What I mean to say is, it was amazing to feel again, physically, and I latched onto anything that could be touched." Baylor smiled apologetically at me as he continued, "it's just that it all seems more, mentally, than I know now what to do with. I seem to be forced to remember everything except for the thing I really need to; I can't recall how it was that I had managed to leave such things behind. How is it I made it all just the path behind me, and kept the what ifs from constantly torturing and tormenting me?"

I was not quite sure what to say. I suddenly thought of what my Master had said about escaping memories and being afraid to come back to them, and I wondered if I could have spared my old friend this pain if I had only understood what he had meant.

"My Master said something to that effect," I said at last guiltily. "I just didn't realize how that might be something to warn you of before you left."

"I didn't exactly give you a lot of time to come up with any words of advice," Baylor said, taking my apology in stride.

"I never noticed time," Angel added thoughtfully then. "I guess, looking back, I didn't notice much of anything, I think I pretty much ceased to exist. I don't know how to explain why it was different for us, all I know is I was completely unaware of anything, and then I was suddenly aware of Demon. I *knew* his presence and I wanted to be near to it, it was that simple. I had no idea you were heading into such an awful experience or I swear I never would have let you go."

"I doubt you could have stopped me, Angel," Baylor replied. "We are a stubborn clan."

He added this last while looking pointedly at the twins, who had offered such stubborn resistance to the idea of publishing all we had come to know lately, and I felt them begin to surrender. He had made many valid points but so had they. In many ways I too was unsure we should do it. The thought of empowering our enemies even further by telling them all we had discovered frightened me, but I told myself Baylor was right and we were a strong enough group to handle it. I figured we could cross that bridge when we came to it.

"Are we agreed, then?" I asked all of those present.

I figured now was as good a time as any to take a vote. Nothing more needed to be said. We all knew what the risks were, we also knew what the benefits could be. It was now just a matter of which weighed the heaviest upon our hearts.

I was surer the twins would give their assent than I was that Piper would, so it was him I looked to first. Adreal and Adonia, when it all boiled down, still trusted completely in me, and for this I have been eternally humbled. I knew deep down they would agree eventually. They might be stubborn, a trait that had served them well by making them capable of aging naturally so many years before, but they were also still very much my adoring siblings at heart and would follow my lead in time. The only possible reason they would not, would be if Piper still opposed the idea, at which point I would lose Adonia and hence most likely her twin as well. So it was Piper we all waited for.

"You better write the whole truth," Piper said finally, grinning at me. "Everyone needs to know I'm better-looking than the rest of you."

That was pretty much the end of that part of the discussion, as Piper swung his long auburn hair and began to pretend to primp, leaving the rest of us laughing hysterically at his ultra-feminine antics. I say hysterically because I don't think it was anything like our normal laughter, it was more relief than joy, but that was okay. The only problem was that Baylor did not laugh with us, he merely gave a small pinched smile. Piper's antics had provided the rest of us much needed relief from the gloom that had settled while Baylor had told of his ordeal, as I think Piper had known they would. He had broken through the pall and made it possible for all of us to eventually ease back into more pleasant conversation, but he had also made me worry for Baylor even more.

Soon the conversation turned to who would do the writing and where to begin the tale. It was Angel who finally suggested that we begin with her journal as it was, since it was already written. She suggested that I could simply write an introduction for it, and possibly an afterward. She added that we could get at least that much of it out, and then worry where to begin a second book to complete our sharing of knowledge among us, giving ourselves time to figure out how to do so. I was thus elected as storyteller yet again and consequently set about taking random notes. As things transpired that might be relevant to the writing of our second book, I would write them down. You can figure out the rest, I am sure, but I am getting side-tracked again.

The discussion and my subsequent hurried note-taking it had brought on were soon all but forgotten by the others. They quickly went back to reviewing the list we had been compiling on the computer before

Baylor had arrived, and of course filling Baylor in on all that had transpired in his absence. There was not really that much we needed to tell Baylor that he could not see for himself as evidenced in the transformation of the house around him, so they were soon simply naming names again.

The list was quickly narrowing down to those that all of us had known, as I've said, those members of the Council that any or all of us could relate any number of details about. For a while the information flowed out in torrents and contained more details than we knew what to do with, but once more I became the focus of Piper's angry questions, just as I had expected, as I was suddenly unable to relate what he felt I should know.

"You don't know who blessed Kynan?" Piper asked again, aghast. "He was your best friend!"

"Yes, and I meant to ask him," I retorted defensively. "But at the time I realized I was not entirely sure who it had been and that my assumptions it had been Lachlan might not be correct, we were already nearly to Egypt."

I looked then at Adreal, hoping at least he would remember the conversation wherein he had led me to that realization, and understand my mistake and from whence it had stemmed. I will admit now that there was no good reason that in nearly two thousand years I had not found the time nor even the desire to discuss with my oldest friend the details of our blessings, but I was unwilling to engage in this discussion, while being put so abruptly on the spot by my hot-tempered Irish companion. Seeing Adreal smiling sympathetically in my direction, I took heart in that at least one of them was listening fairly as I attempted to excuse my oversight, and rushed on in my own defense.

"And by the time we were back in Rome," I said hurriedly, "where I might have rectified my oversight and asked him outright. You know damn well we were all preoccupied with the rumors surrounding the killings in Scotland. We rushed off like our tails were ablaze."

I trailed off, looking at Angel as once more she put her hand on my thigh in a reassuring gesture, and I realized there was no defense for it. It was all just the path behind us now, as Baylor used to say, and all we could do now was strive to rectify such problems as we came to them. Piper simply threw his hands up and looked exasperatedly at Adonia, whom I noticed had placed her hand on his shoulder in an effort to calm him. It seemed once more we had reached a place in our searching were we would find nothing but confusion, and anger us at ourselves for not having known to look ahead and prevent it.

"Well, I could have asked him just as well myself," Piper admitted. sighing heavily. "I spent far more time in his company than you since he was changed."

"I will call him in the morning," I said, quietly accepting his apology for his second outburst as nonchalantly as it had been presented. "Besides, I should let them all know we have finally found Angel." I paused here, thinking for a moment before I added, "For now the fact that she was in the Empyrean and I went there to retrieve her, that we both came back from an ascension, I think that revelation should wait until we have figured out just what warnings should be given with the knowledge such a thing has been accomplished."

I looked at Baylor as he grunted his assent. I wondered again at my friend's state of mind, for he still seemed distant in a manner I could not quite affix a name to. Normally in conversation he was either the storyteller incarnate, full of vigor and descriptive energy, or the quiet listener, interjecting only when it was of the utmost import, and then his input was generally full of insight.

I knew that grunt had been his agreement, and I am not saying I disapproved at all that he had agreed with me. His agreement was not the issue. It was the manner of presentation, the grunt itself, which disturbed me. There was something terribly wrong with my friend. Something beyond mere memories was eating him from the inside, and I was very afraid it would hollow him out. I tried desperately to push this fear away.

When he pushed away from the table and headed toward the kitchen, asking, only as if in afterthought, if anyone wanted something to drink, I knew this was just an excuse to get away. I watched Angel looking sadly at his departing back and then share a silent look with Adonia. I supposed then that women must share some otherworldly kind of understanding of such things as heartache and how to help others through it, they always seem to band together and pull each other through, but I myself was at a loss as to what to do for Baylor. As the others tried to pick up the thread of some conversation or other to fill the silence, I found myself contemplating my friend as I had not in many, many years.

When he did not return from the kitchen in the time I thought it should had taken him, I began to think that maybe I should go to him, try to talk to him. I had no idea what to say but I found myself on my feet and headed in that direction, knowing only that I had to do something. He had always been there for me, offering words of wisdom or revitalizing my faith with his unfailing hope, and I needed not only for his own good but also for mine to do whatever I might to return that kindness to him.

I found him sitting on the steps of the porch that led from the kitchen into the side-yard, taking a long draught off a long-neck bottle of beer. Obviously Piper had stocked a few things in the fridge as well. I took a beer for myself, making a mental note to thank Piper later for the both of us, and sat down on the step next to my oldest friend. I didn't say anything as he looked up at me, and he didn't say anything either.

Baylor's deep blue eyes seemed far deeper than usual, almost as if the light had been stolen from their depth. This had been undeniably apparent, in his brief glance, before he turned back to his silent contemplation of the moon. Once more the fear he was being hollowed out slithered into my heart.

His massive shoulders, which had always epitomized to me the strength of his legendary forebears, drooped as if they bore a weight heavier even than his curse had been. I knew with absolute certainty he had quietly tried his best to ignore his own pain in an effort to stave off our Angel's tears, but I feared that some deeper, more terrible, and possibly irreparable damage had been done to my friend's soul. I feared he wouldn't remember how in time. Even if the weight of such an onslaught as two thousand years worth of memories and regret, being recalled all at once, could be stowed sufficiently to survive their weight, I wasn't sure he'd be the same after such a task. I could not imagine what might come of me were I suddenly forced to recall and re-bury all those coffins which rested within my vault.

I was frightened suddenly that when he had been denied in so agonizing a manner, his heart's most desperate desire for the second time, that whatever it was that enabled him to trudge unflinchingly through the centuries bearing grudgeless every blow dealt him by a very harsh world, had been ripped from him as well. To have survived such a heart-wrenching denial twice in one terribly long life time I could not fathom. In essence, I feared he was loosing his will. And a Changeling without will is nothing.

What would I have done had I not found Angel and been able to bring her back with me? My heart constricting, I thanked God that Baylor was not howling, that the Werewolf was not out this night telling his pain to the moon. I had heard his tormented howls before and I knew that tonight they would be so filled with suffering that they would break us both.

Eventually he stopped gazing at the moon, as though whatever answers she offered him, if any, had been unacceptable. Looking down, he began to pluck blades of grass, staring at each one. I saw my old friend's bright red head bowed down in despair, and caught myself counting my own blessings and at the same time feeling dreadfully guilty for them. I determined then that we would make it through, we had to. We would make it as we had always made it, together.

"Don't." Baylor's deep voice surprised me from behind the curtain of his hair as it fell around his face and shielded his expression from me.

"Don't what?" I asked, confused and unable to garner any clues from an expression I could not see.

"Don't pity me," he said, swinging his hair away from his eyes as he turned those now dead blue eyes to face me. "I will not deal with that too."

"I...," I stammered.

I didn't know what to say or how to be, or what I might do to begin to change what was happening.

"Don't," Baylor said again. "I will find my way through this as I have everything else, just do for me as you have always done and be my friend and that will be enough. But do not pity me."

We lapsed back into silence as we finished our beers and I wondered whether I had done more harm than good in coming out on the steps to be with him. I did not want him to feel pitied. I just wanted him to understand that he was not alone and would never be. I knew that there were things I could never repair for him any more than I could fix them for Angel, things that every conscious being ever to exist had to accept. I could not simply tell them how that I had handled those things, for I was a different person than they. I had hoped reverently that I had helped Adreal some five hundred years ago by sharing my experience but, ultimately, it was up to each individual. All I could do was what Baylor asked: be there, be their friends, love them and pray to the heavens that this might be enough.

Suddenly I wanted desperately to make him laugh. I cannot explain it, it was simply one of those things about me. When Angel cried I wanted to hold her and absorb all of her pain. When the twins were down, I wanted to teach them something new to occupy their minds and distract them from whatever had made them upset. When Baylor was hurt- well, Baylor was so rarely the one hurting or at least showing it, I didn't know what to do. I wanted it to go away. I wanted my old Baylor back. I wanted him upbeat and full of energetic hope. I needed to hear him laughing, and the best I had managed to that end had been the short excuse for a laugh I had gotten by poking fun at him about the attack-hug he'd given me upon his return.

"You're going to screw the whole world up this time," I said, before I had thought better of it. "Not just your own homelands."

"How so?" he asked, in a tone that said he hadn't decided yet whether to take offence.

"You know all those people who get out of the shower and think their dog is staring at them just a little too intently?" I asked. "Or just can't comfortably change their clothes in front of their cat because it just seems too intelligent?" I smiled at Baylor as I continued amused now by my own thoughts. "Those poor people are going to be so suspicious after you get done with them. After you tell them this great fiction story of ours, they will all turn into a bunch of paranoid neurotics. House pets world-wide will hate you!"

I started to chuckle, envisioning people locking their dogs or cats in the other room before having sex or closing their bathroom doors before showering. Baylor must have seen much the same scenario playing out in his mind, for I succeeded in making him laugh at last. Soon we were ribbing each other and laughing all the more as one or the other of us shared some new thought that had just occurred to us.

"They may not believe it," Baylor said at last. "But it will sure mess with their minds."

"Who may not believe what?" Angel asked, coming up quietly behind us. "What are you two laughing about?"

"The world, Lass," Baylor said, pushing up to his feet and patting her shoulder as she turned her bemused gaze from me to him.

"What about it?" she asked me, as he headed back inside, leaving me to answer her.

"We are going to turn it upside down," I said, smiling at her as I caught her under my arm and led her with me after Baylor's large form.

Angel continued to stare up at me expectantly as we walked into the room where the others all awaited us, and I knew I would have to expand my answer or risk a thrashing from a magically appearing brush. So I spared myself the bruises and told her, as well as the twins and Piper, what I had just related to Baylor out on the steps. Piper merely raised an eyebrow and looked sidelong at Adonia, I think in some manner fearing her reaction. The twins stared at me with shock and disappointment registering quickly on their faces, then immediately faced each other as though they had just shared a most marvelous thought.

"Why didn't we think of that?" Adonia said, still facing her twin.

"That will be the fun part!" Adreal grinned back at her.

223

Well, I was relieved that the disappointment I had read in their faces had not been in me; was not in the fact I had found the prospect of disturbing so many people in such a manner amusing. Yet I wondered what new brand of mischief they had in mind as they continued to smile conspiratorially at one another. As my eyes went back and forth between the two of them, trying to divine their thoughts, I caught a glimpse of Piper's indulgent smile just before he spoke.

"Just had to tell them, didn't you?" Piper asked me, "Like they don't find enough mischief on their own."

"Sorry?" I said.

I was not quite sure I meant it but I felt I ought to say it anyway, given he was looking at me as my father would have if he caught me snatching a tasty morsel from the cook before she was ready to serve us our dinner. Piper cocked an eyebrow at me and his smile turned almost superior but not quite, he was far too amused himself to have pulled that look off completely.

"Not yet," he said. "But I'm sure you will be."

After that comment we gave up compiling our lists. Instead, we ended up listening raptly as Piper related tale after tale of the twins and their endless mischief. The late evening hours witnessed the lot of us laughing loudly as Piper related these stories with a comedic flair none could have resist. I was heartened repeatedly as Baylor's laughter came more and more to sound as it used to, and it was as good a sound to my ears as Angel's laughter. Time after time Adonia would feign hurt betrayal and smack Piper playfully as her twin repeatedly denied each incident had not been 'quite as bad as all that.'

"Poor old Miss O'Leary had naught to do with it," Adreal insisted during one tale. "And neither did we. We have been officially exonerated of that one, and you know it."

"You know darn well it was those men from the pub," Adonia put in. "The one who fell asleep, there in the barn, with a pipe in his hand. He was already drunk and forgot he had come to steal milk for mixing drinks with his comrades that night."

Piper continued anyway, ignoring their constant protests, determined to get their goats. He looked disbelieving at Adonia, pretending he was still skeptical of her and Adreal's avowals of innocence. This was obviously an old argument between the three of them, one Piper found immense enjoyment in bringing up every once and awhile. I myself had heard it before but Angel was a new audience and Piper a true performer at heart. As Adonia huffed her irritation, Piper looked sidelong at me and smirked proudly. Upon catching sight of his look and seeing how well he had played her, Adonia back-handed his upper arm in disgust.

"Ugh you, you...!" Adonia tried and failed to find a word she felt was appropriate.

"Cow?" Piper supplied sarcastically with much amusement.

"No," she answered indignantly. "Pig!"

We all dissolved into laughter once again. The evening had passed quickly in this happy manner. We all found ourselves making our excuses one after another and heading off to sleep in an elevated mood. Much like the night before, we all ascended the stairs on our way to our respective bedchambers. It wasn't until Angel and I directed Baylor to the room we had prepared for him that a dark pall seemed to descend once more. He entered without a word, making no comment about the dual cherry wood dressers or the king-sized bed, but I could feel how they hurt him.

Piper and Adonia slipped down the hall to their room, and Adreal too closed his door behind us, leaving Angel and me to do what we might. I didn't know whether I should say or do anything. I was afraid I would only make it worse if I did, and yet afraid too that Baylor would again feel pitied if I said nothing and remained quiet as I had on the steps. Angel came to my rescue in this dilemma, finding something to say where I could not.

"Baylor," Angel whispered. "It *will* be okay."

There was something in the way she said it that made me think she knew, I mean really knew, it would be. Baylor, however, said nothing, so I couldn't have told you if he had found any reassurance in her words. He merely turned and kissed her forehead, then, squeezing my shoulder briefly, he stepped into his room and closed the door.

Angel and I ascended the final flight of stairs to our own room. I didn't ask her why she had said what she did, or question the manner in which she had said it. I refused to. I wanted to believe it, and I didn't want her response to make that impossible. I think I thought if she told me a reason for her words, those reasons would have proven to be somehow too mundane and hence broken the spell. So I left it at that, deriving what hope for my friend as I could from her strangely confident words.

~16~

Family

I awoke the next morning to find I was alone in the bed. I could smell bacon wafting all the way up from the kitchen and it made that not such a bad thing. I rolled out from under the blankets with a sense of purpose, knowing I was to call Kynan and ask him a long overdue question: who had blessed him. As I brushed my teeth I contemplated just how I would do this, realizing how odd it would seem for me to call him out of the blue with a question I had so thoughtlessly forgotten to ask long ago. It was kind of awkward-sounding in my own head no matter how well I tried to word it, like I was about to ask my own mother what her name was because I had never before thought to find out. But then how long had I known my Master before I'd learned he was called Re?

Finally I decided there was no right or wrong way to do it, it would just have to be done. I descended the staircase, busily convincing myself I was making more of it than necessary, and that Kynan would in no way take it amiss. As I came to the second floor landing, Baylor stepped out of his room, closing the door behind him, and I was suddenly full of other things to think about.

"Back to the kilt then, are you?" I asked, looking at his choice of clothing.

"Well, somehow it only seemed right this morning," he replied, with a weak grin, "After all, it's how the universe made me when I told her to make me 'me' yesterday."

"Are you sure she just couldn't think of any other thing to drape over your sluggish mass?" I said, grinning mischievously. "And didn't want to harm the rest of us and our delicate sensitivities by forcing us to view you naked?"

"If anything, she was just being kind," Baylor grinned, a little more believably this time. "I'm sure she didn't want to destroy your ample egos by providing proof she has always, shall we say, loved me more?"

"Like there would be any proving that!" I laughed outright as I pushed passed him to be the first to descend the stairs.

"Only because you're a Changeling," Baylor replied, near to laughing himself now as he came quickly after me down the stairs.

As we reached the foot of the stairs and began speed-walking and elbowing each other for position to be first to the kitchen, he finally started laughing outright as well, apparently thinking he had the last word. He thought wrong.

"And you are what?" I asked.

I elbowed him again as we came around the corner, and he paused in thought just long enough for me to move into first.

"Uh huh...that's what I thought," I laughed, sliding into the kitchen ahead of him. "Full of it!"

No sooner had I raised my hands above my head in triumph, about to yell I'd won, and claim a piece of bacon for my prize, than Adonia and Angel both cut me off. Turning in unison as though they were the twins in the family, one with a spatula in her hand and the other a stack of plates, they proceeded to spoil all the fun.

"Out!" they said in unison.

"Breakfast will be served in the dining room in a moment," Angel began.

"And there will be no thieving of bacon before then," Adonia finished.

Angel pointed with her spatula in a queenly manner, indicating that two steaming coffee cups on the edge of the kitchen's island would be all we would get for now. Baylor and I both hung our heads and proceeded with our coffee, in a now more subdued manner, to the dining room where the women were so determined we would break our fast like civilized people. There we found Adreal and Piper waiting impatiently.

"Shooed you out, too?" Piper grinned.

"Aye," Baylor and I both replied as we pulled out our seats and sat down with them to wait.

Adreal didn't seem the least upset. He sat with Angel's journal open before him, obviously nearing the end and raptly focused. Yet I could tell from his grin that he had heard every word of our complaining and found it very amusing. I was feeling oddly mischievous still, and just when I had begun seriously debating whether or not to steal the journal from him, thereby obtaining my own amusement for the morning, he was saved by the girls. They came in just in time and began swiftly laying out a veritable feast for us.

As our breakfast of bacon, eggs, biscuits and gravy, and something Angel called grits, progressed and bellies got fuller, conversation began to trickle back and forth across the table. It probably would have begun sooner, had the food not been so delicious that we kept our mouths full for quite some time. Adreal was the first to speak. He had been reading just as quickly as he ate, and when he had finished both his meal and the journal, he slammed the book closed.

"Damn good read, Angel," he announced. "It just amazes me that we never figured all of it out for ourselves."

"Thank you," Angel said slowly. "Honestly I think it was merely a matter of the forest for the trees. I probably wouldn't have seen it either had I not been forced away from the situation."

"I would like to try what you thought about with that bar wench," Adonia added, obviously happy she could now discuss what she had learned before her twin without ruining any surprises.

"Yes," Adreal said immediately, remembering the incident Adonia was talking about. "I wonder if we really could do that kind of thing for others."

"Dentistry would never be the same," Adonia laughed. "Imagine it, going to see a Changeling about your teeth instead of a dentist. Imagine them just putting their hand on your cheek and commanding the universe to fix your teeth for you and it working just because it was energy in contact with them."

"We'd be assassinated!" Adreal said, laughing too.

"Economic threat number one!" Adonia agreed.

"Don't you two start," Piper said, trying to hide his own amusement. "You have caused enough havoc for humanity as it is."

"Spoilsport!" Adonia pouted.

"I thought I was a Pig," Piper laughed, unfazed by her showy lower lip and barely succeeding in containing his laughter.

"Well, I am going to see if I can't figure out a program which might allow the computer to do much the same for us," Adreal said, quickly changing the subject before they really got started. "I mean see past the trees, I want to see if I can track some sort of pattern. Maybe find that these occurrences have followed one Changeling in particular, or happened where and when we know a certain one was at a certain time. Something, anything, at least set it up to track such things for us." Adreal then turned to me, adding, "Have you called Kynan yet, Demon?"

"Not yet," I admitted.

"Better hurry," Adreal prompted. "They'll all be going to bed soon."

Unable to put it off any longer, by pushing what remained of my food around on my plate as though I actually had any more room in my stomach and intended to eat it, I stood up from the table. I went swiftly to the table in the foyer and grabbed up the little hand-held phone before I could change my mind and put it off for another hundred years. I still couldn't say exactly why I didn't want to ask him, other than I think I was just embarrassed I hadn't done it already. I dialed the number direct and walked into the living room, pacing nervously as it began to ring.

"Hello?" Kynan's voice came over the phone.

"Kynan," I said slowly. "Did I wake you?"

"No," he replied quickly. "Is something wrong? Is everyone okay?"

Instantly I felt even guiltier. I called this man my friend, and yet I called him so rarely he thought it must be an emergency of some sort for me to be calling now. I felt dreadful.

"No, no, everyone is fine," I said quickly. "Actually, I have really wonderful news. We have found Angel."

"That *is* wonderful!" Kynan replied. "Where was she?"

"Here, here in America," I told him, relaxing a little with the idle chatter. "Springfield, to be precise, just where they thought. Piper was right after all, he had found where she lived."

I didn't bother to go any further into the details. As we had discussed, we would leave all the deeper revelations of our finding her until we had figured out what warnings should be given. We needed to find out why Baylor's experience was so different from mine and Angel's and which of our experiences was the more likely to occur with others. It wasn't something I had spoken with Baylor about as yet, but I felt there had to be a specific reason it had gone so differently for him. It was yet another little mystery we would have to solve, but until then I didn't think it was anything the Elders needed to hear about.

There was an uncomfortable silence growing and I searched my mind for something to interject into it. Finally I found myself lamely relying on the old faithful of polite conversation, asking about the weather back in Rome, and the state of things with him and the other two remaining Elders of the Council.

"And you?" Kynan asked. "What are you all up to?"

He had finally provided me with what would most likely be my best opportunity to ask him what I needed to know, without making him feel it was the only reason I had called. Once more I felt dreadfully guilty that I had even thought in such terms. I was appalled by my own inability to carry on an extended comfortable conversation with someone I had known so long. Was I so ready to take the opportunity he had provided because there was nothing more of him I wanted to know? Had we grown so far apart it was now irreversible?

"Well, actually, we had begun recreating a kind of genealogy chart for all Changelings," I said, hating myself for doing it. "We are trying to trace down where we all come from."

It wasn't entirely true and yet, even as I said it, I saw the value of doing exactly that. Suddenly I knew the kind of program Adreal should follow. I wasn't sure if he might have better results with what he meant to do, but I still wanted to try my idea anyway. Kynan was silent for some time and for a moment I almost forgot he was on the phone as my mind ran ahead.

"Have you managed to find out anything that might shed light on who or what attacked Angel and the others?" he asked then, jerking me back to the present.

"Not yet," I admitted. "Actually, we have not even gotten down all of the who-blessed-who's of everyone. Obviously we know Edsel blessed the twins, and they were able to tell us he had been blessed by a woman he had told them was called Philana. They are not positive whether she is still around or not, but said he spoke of her as though she had ascended,"

"Yes," Kynan said helpfully, "I believe he had told me once that she had."

"I knew already that Santon was blessed by one named Thomas that had most definitely ascended long ago," I continued. "Piper also was able to tell us that Cathmore was blessed by one named Favian that had come from Alexandria, and Cathmore himself had been the one to bless Lachlan a short time later. I think also that this Favian had returned to Alexandria and Cathmore had lost all contact with him before the Council was even formed, but that is all we really know of that one."

"Well, I know no more than you about that one," Kynan said after a brief pause. "Cathmore doesn't talk much about the past. I think it wounds him too much. I can tell you all you need to know of myself, though."

I was relieved then that he had made this offer without seeming offended that I had yet to ask. I was sure that in some manner he had to have known this was, at least to some extent, the reason I had called, but he didn't seem to feel there was anything amiss. I began to think at that point that maybe I had merely blown it all out of proportion and should have taken it as nonchalantly as he obviously was.

"I don't have much more than a name for the one who blessed me," Kynan said without preamble, shocking me to rapt silence. "After you had left me I had wandered in my drunken state down the darkening streets looking for you. I think I meant to somehow convince you to stay there with me. Rather than finding you, though, I found a small band of thieves exiting over the curtain wall of one of the villas I passed. They turned on me then, noticing me just as I noticed them, and I think meaning to rob me as well. I was very drunk I thought I could fight them all off, but of course I was outnumbered. I was stabbed, robbed, and left for dead. I didn't even care..."

"A Blessed One came upon me then and claimed me before the light could," Kynan continued softly. "He didn't stay long with me, though, just long enough to direct me where to find another to teach me of what I had become. He said he had not intended to bless anyone at that time, that he was unprepared to be a teacher to me. He said he could not then be dedicated to me or offer me the time it would take for him to train me further."

"I was not in any position or state of mind to question him further on this and merely did as I was told," Kynan continued, a little quieter now and it seemed to me this was an old wound in him. "He directed me to find one that he said he knew, one that would teach me all I needed to know, and I went to find that one. That is how I came to find Lachlan, ending up frightened and still unlearned before his door. I told Lachlan of being blessed and then being directed to find him."

"Lachlan seemed flattered, I think, that another Blessed One had not only heard of him, but obviously held him in high regard and felt him a proper teacher for their newly created pupil. Lachlan took me in and questioned me as to the extent of my knowledge, seeing that I was told everything I could possibly need to know. This was of course before the Council had need of being formed, you understand, or the introductions might have gone quite differently. That and, of course, the name the one who blessed me gave me to give him, Arwin, seemed to make Lachlan more than happy to be a teacher to me where that one hadn't the time."

"He never withheld any information from me," Kynan added then with a small laugh, trying hard to sound unfazed or hurt by the memories. "So I guess, my unwitting creator had made a good choice in a substitute for himself. I never saw him again or learned any more of him, though. It seemed to me he had been very occupied with other matters and in a hurry to be about them. Having stumbled upon me, he'd wanted to save me, but was otherwise incapable of setting those pressing matters aside to take on a pupil who would be in great need of his time and energies.

"You pretty much know the rest. When the Council was being formed, nearly three hundred years later, Lachlan did not yet feel I was ready to sit on it. Yet as the dust settled after its initial conception, and the other Elders began to ascend, or possibly, as you feared, were forced to, he decided I was mayhap not so much ready as needed."

"Wow," I said at last. "I had no idea, Kynan."

"Well, it never came up," he replied nonchalantly. "But has it helped you at all to know it now?"

"Well, maybe not like I had hoped, but 'tis good to have another name for our list," I admitted. "Have you ever tried to locate the one that blessed you again?"

"Never to any avail," Kynan said derisively.

"So Lachlan could give you no information about this Arwin that helped to locate him?" I prodded, wanted to be sure that all avenues had been explored this time.

"Only that Lachlan had heard the name spoken with awe by Favian before that one had returned to Alexandria. It was obviously an old and well thought of name, but he knew nothing more," Kynan paused a moment then added, "They were quite a different lot back then weren't they, not very insightful? So, no, I've had no more luck than you did in Egypt, finding an old one that doesn't wish to be found is a useless endeavor..."

He trailed off and, not wishing to wound him further, I let it go. I too knew what it was like to feel abandoned by a mentor, but at least mine had not been so willing to just leave me to another and the great wide world.

"It has been good to talk with you again," I said at last, sounding a bit lame even to my own ears.

"And you, my friend," Kynan replied.

"I will call you again if we find out any more," I said.

"Until then," Kynan said.

"Until then," I replied.

As I hung up the phone, I was struck suddenly with the sadness and injustice of all of it. Not only had I lost Seraphim to thieves but I had nearly lost him to them as well, and never known it. Yet it wasn't so much that thought which struck me as being so wrong. It was the fact my friend had lost Seraphim too, in more than one way, and then been abandoned by me. Then in the same awful day he had nearly lost his own life, only to be given it back by yet another that simply abandoned him. It seemed life didn't care what you truly deserved after all. It was not until some time much later that I would think I should have told him that Seraphim had been returned to us, that my Angel *was* our Seraphim.

I wandered back into the dining room, still contemplating all I had just learned, and was immediately struck by the faces of all those dear friends that surrounded the table awaiting my return. I was very thankful then, realizing I had indeed been blessed beyond most. Here I had before me a wonderful group of friends, a family better than most could hope for, and I never had to feel abandoned by them. I was also blessed enough to have been made to realize that even my Master, Re, the only one I had ever felt abandoned by, had never truly meant to leave me. He had simply thought that, had I need of him, I would come to him in the Empyrean.

Angel looked up and smiled upon seeing me reenter the room, and suddenly I felt unworthy, as if I had never in my life done anything to have earned the gifts I had received. And yet had I not just been contemplating how life held no regard for what one deserved? Once more I was made to realize that there was no such thing as fair, you only got what you got, and it was up to you what you did with it. Kynan had obviously done well with it, and I felt proud of him, something I had not felt with regards to that particular old friend for a very long time. I was soon jerked back to the present and away from these thoughts, though, as Adreal too turned and took notice of me.

"Well?" he asked without preamble. "Who was it?"

"Someone who gave their name but not much else," I replied. "It was Arwin, and that's about all he knew."

"What?" Adonia asked, sounding more than just a bit confused. "How could Kynan not know any more than that about the one that made him? The Elders are beginning to seem more and more incompetent, the more I learn of what they never bother to."

So I sat back down beside Angel and proceeded to tell them of the entire conversation. Adonia quickly recanted her earlier comment, at least with regards to Kynan himself and that particular situation, listening compassionately as I explained the manner in which he had been blessed and then promptly left behind. Angel listened silently, absorbing every word much as the others were, but after I had finished telling them everything Kynan had just told me, I found she had been thinking of more than just what I had been saying.

"Arwin?" she said thoughtfully, not long after I had gone silent. "Isn't that the name of a god?"

"I believe so," I replied, now curious as to where her mind had wandered.

"Yes, yes it is. A god of music and poetry, I believe," she answered herself thoughtfully, as though I had not.

"And?" I questioned then, as she just seemed to lose herself again in her own thoughts, thus losing the rest of us as well.

"I have it!" she said excitedly.

"Have what?" Piper asked first.

"The motive," she said triumphantly.

"Motive?" Baylor asked.

"Okay, look," she said, seeming gather her thoughts and trying to calm down so as to be able to present them properly to the rest of us. "We know Demon's Master started all these god myths, right?"

"You think Re was also Arwin and made Kynan too?" Adreal asked.

"No, just listen," she said.

Angel seemed to be concentrating very hard and didn't want to be sidetracked. I didn't think she had intended to sound as rude as she had and I was pretty sure the others recognized this, for no one seemed to have taken it amiss.

"I'm sorry," she said immediately. "No, I don't think Re ever made any others. I mean, think about it. We know he made Demon and taught him right, he put a lot of time and effort into assuring himself Demon was well learned. Re made sure to tell him not to do a lot of the things he himself had done, warning Demon in essence not to make the same mistakes he had. He was at the very least an exceptional teacher. From what he said of his own lack of knowledge as to how he had even accomplished the blessing, I think Demon was by some standards an accident that was not repeated. All his time and energies were directed to Demon until he chose to ascend."

Angel looked at all of us as though we should be following her easily, but I, for one, wasn't sure where she was going. She appeared to think we would have been prompted by what she had just told us to come up with the same conclusions she had. Only none of us seemed to have the slightest idea where she was trying to lead us or what she was trying to say. Obviously we were making that very clear with our blank looks and failure to say anything, because finally she sighed and went on.

"No, as I said, I don't think Re ever made any other Changelings," she continued. "I think from all Demon has said that Demon was his only recreation, an accident, that he was determined would never inflict the same damage on humanity he had. He took no chances that Demon could repeat the same mistakes he had made."

"But," she added, "we also know 'Re', as he liked to be called, was one of the First Born and hence had been around since 'before time was time,' as he'd said. *One*, there were others though; two others with the capability to create such as us. Two others that obviously had, because we know Demon was by far not the only Changeling around even back then."

"If you remember Demon's dreams in Egypt, he had one in which he was a soul somehow attached to Re," she said, looking to all of us to be sure she had not lost us completely. "I think this was a showing of their link. I believe dreams tell us hidden things, things we know already on a deeper level than we might be incapable of accessing easily when we are otherwise aware and awake."

She had looked at me while stating that last, and I began to feel I was going to feel very stupid once again for not seeing some obvious fact for myself, something she was about to tell all of us.

"Don't you see?" she asked then, still looking at me. "You also dreamed of the other two First Born and one of them had a great many souls attached or linked to it, the female of the two. You said of all those souls you got the feeling only a few of them had any real power, that the rest of them only seemed to amount to anything because they existed in mass. I think the power each exuded was derived from their knowledge of themselves. I think those lacking in the appearance of power are those who were not taught right by her, those who didn't or don't know the full extent of the gift she had given them, those like Baylor had been."

"But what has that to do with Re beginning all the god myths and a motive to destroy us?" I asked.

"Not all the god myths, he said himself that his brother and sister had also been likened to gods," Angel said with a wide grin.

"Re's sister began other myths then, in her own way, if those lesser souls represented such creatures as Werewolves," Piper said slowly.

"Exactly," Angel said excitedly. "If we find the roots, the very first Werewolf myth or initial Vampire legend, even the first Druid with the gift of shape-shifting, we will most likely have found her first recreations and perhaps even one who can lead us to her. She was creating the ill-taught among us."

"Then she can tell us why she would withhold such knowledge from others in the first place," Adreal added excitedly, looking at his sister once again. "Why she should want to leave them so ignorant."

"Perhaps why she wants Changelings to know less than they should?" Adonia said, seeming to follow his thoughts. "What good it served to have made weakened creations?'

"And perhaps also how she managed to kill off those that saw to it that Changelings were taught better." Angel ended her thoughts with a proud grin directed at me.

It was obvious she felt as if she had just won the debate we had left off the week before by proving me wrong with the answer she had just provided. Before, she had been unable to push her point with me further, incapable of doing as she had done just now, providing a motive, and yet I still had trouble believing it would be that simple.

"And what of the others?" I asked her. "Those I saw in the dream that were powerful? She obviously didn't keep all of her recreations in ignorance."

"Of course not," Angel said, nonplussed. "She would need some powerful ones to help her achieve her goal."

"And what goal is that?" I said.

Angel grew quiet again, and I found myself feeling guilty for pointing out those roadblocks we kept encountering in our path.

"What about the brother, though?" Baylor asked. "You said the one attached to his brother had appeared tortured or wounded. Why have we not considered that one? Could it be that it is mad, driven insane over time, and then becoming our hunter?"

"No, this one was powerful, I could tell that much," I answered, thinking back. "But I don't think it was evil. Then again I sensed no evil about any of them. Honestly though, there was only an aura of great sadness about it, much as there was in you when you returned from the Empyrean."

"You said it didn't seem to know it was attached to Re's brother," Baylor said then. "Might this not imply the brother could have left one in ignorance of itself, as Angel has suggested about the sister, only this one was powerful even in that ignorance?"

"I don't know," I answered honestly. "But I wouldn't think that possible. How can one not know the full extent of their power and yet make use of enough of it to be seen as powerful? My best guess is that the reason it did not know it was attached to Re's brother was that it was not as yet. Remember, I had thought in the dream as time moved forward that I had to be born in order to be alive, to even be remade? I was self-aware because I knew my place in the dream. I was already a Changeling. Perhaps at the time of the dream this one had not yet been made and therefore did not understand its place. Maybe it was even at the time of my dream experiencing some great torture or trauma which would explain the feelings I got from it, and ultimately lead to its nearing death and calling out for change."

"True," Baylor said thoughtfully, "I suppose that could be so. It was your dream, you would know best what it felt of and what impressions it left you with."

"So we will stick to searching for the one we know created those she never taught properly," Angel said.

"One other thing," Adreal said. "We must be prepared for disappointment. We won't likely find any of those less powerful creations still alive to tell us where she might be. Most will have aged and died like humans because they will have believed that is what would occur."

"But we can try to track the various myths to their origins," Adonia said then, still hopeful. "At least we might sort of begin to figure a general location in a certain period of time, maybe narrow it down where to search for her. And most Vampire myths say they are immortal, so we could get lucky." She looked over at Adreal, excitedly adding, "Okay, I need the computer, Adreal."

"But I was going to try to...," he began to protest.

"I think we simply need to buy a few more computers," I intervened quickly. "I was actually considering getting some sort of genealogy software anyway and seeing what I can come up with using that kind of tracking. Not only that, but I will also need one to type out Angel's journal and add to so it will be ready for publication."

"I think it would definitly be best if we had a few more computers available," Angel said in agreement, "if we plan on doing any or all of these things with any semblance of timely order."

"Well, let's go then," Adonia said, pushing to her feet and beginning to gather up the dishes.

"You'll want to get a better internet connection too," Adreal added, looking at Angel. "I can actually handle that part if you don't need me along. You know everything you'll need, right? Router, cable..."

"I'm sure I can figure it out," Angel laughed.

"Yes," Adreal conceded. "I suppose you could, you obviously know your way around a computer, yours is certainly a nice one."

"I'm glad you like it," Angel said, still grinning.

"Yes, I do," Adreal agreed.

"I'll be sure to pick up another one just like it, then," she added, laughing.

"That would be ideal," Adreal said, now grinning too.

"Baylor," Angel asked, "are you coming or staying here?"

"I'll stay with Adreal," he replied.

We all began to help Adonia gather the remaining dishes and quickly had them all rinsed and stacked beside the sink to be washed more thoroughly when we returned. Soon we were all loading up the vehicle and backing down the drive toward another day of shopping, which I had the distinct feeling was going to somehow end up far longer than necessary. After all, we had two women with us now, and I had come to fully believe it was an absolute impossibility for those wonderful creatures to go into a single specific place and purchase a specific desired item sought no matter how well planned the trip. Women truly seemed incapable of returning directly home once they had embarked on a purchasing expedition.

Piper and Adonia walked ahead of Angel and me as we entered the store, and moved immediately in the direction of the movies and music. I assumed this meant Angel was the one to be trusted to pick out the computers. I followed along dutifully with my wallet, as she approached the same clerk who had helped us before. They spoke briefly and I noted the young man's smile brightening as she gave him her verbal shopping list. He headed happily for the storage room and Angel turned back to me, also smiling.

"It will only be a moment," she said, grinning. "I ordered you a laptop as well."

"Oh, did you now?" I laughed. "Well, thank you."

"You're welcome," she replied, tiptoeing to plant a kiss on my cheek.

Piper and Adonia rejoined us as we were having our bill totaled up, and Adonia placed a few items on the counter. I noticed these were some software packages, those things I had actually known I wanted when coming here and had almost forgotten.

"Thank you," I said, turning to look at her.

"No, no, thank you," she grinned, placing a stack of compact disks beside the software to add to my total.

I noticed Angel glancing about and felt the fateful moment was imminent; any second now she would think of something we had missed and therefore desperately needed to go elsewhere to purchase before returning home. So when she turned back to me excitedly, eyes round with a sudden realization, I prepared to be told where we had to go next.

"We left Adreal and Baylor alone!" Angel declared.

"And?" I said, "They are grown men."

"But they are not you or Piper," she cried, cutting me off. "You and Piper are both here!"

"Baylor traveled alone on a plane here and was fine," I answered, trying not to panic. "He even awaited our return from the Empyrean for three days and nothing attacked him."

"He was not a Changeling then, at least not that he knew of so he could broadcast it," she said, gritting her teeth in fear. "And Adreal has never been left alone."

Before she even finished her sentence, I realized my own stupidity. The sales clerk gasped as I threw the credit card receipt I had just been signing at her and yelled at the man with me.

"Keep them safe, Piper," I hollered, running out the front entrance.

I stopped at the truck only long enough to leave my form and the keys in the front seat. I saw Piper herding our two frantic women, and some very frightened porters with all of our purchases, hurriedly toward me just before I left all my energy and flew like a demon for home.

~17~

Help...

God, how could I be so stupid? What had I been thinking? Rather, why had I not been thinking? How could I have left them alone? Not since the loss of Angel had Piper or I left any of the rest of our family unattended, especially since realizing that there was something about the two of us which kept the others safe. Always it had been like second nature, Adonia and Adreal were nearly inseparable and Piper never left her side. It had been Baylor and me forever, and if and when Adreal had pried himself away from his twin it was only to be with us. Even when it had not been intentional, before we had ever thought it was our own presence which had kept them safe, we had never made such a mistake as this.

I arrived home within minutes of throwing off my form and was drawing together a new one in the foyer when Baylor came rushing down the steps toward me, his precious sword Bane raised over head. I appeared before him just in time to stop him abruptly in mid-swing. Suddenly I was forced to remember our first meeting some two thousand years before; he had nearly beheaded me then as well, only with an ax. Though I was relieved beyond words to see him, no matter the reception, I had yet to see Adreal and something felt wrong.

"That's twice," he laughed, obviously recalling the same incident I just had.

"Where's Adreal?" I demanded.

Baylor's laughter died in his throat as he registered the worried look on my face and realized it had nothing to do with my having just narrowly avoided a beheading. His face showed first confusion, then fear.

"In the garden room?" he replied, sounding very unsure.

I was barely able to keep ahead of Baylor and out of his way, as we both raced for that end of the house. Sliding down the last few feet of the hard wood corridor, we jammed the entry way only to view an empty room. The computer chair was empty and suddenly my chest was too.

"Adreal!" I yelled.

We split up then, racing through the entire house. We had quickly covered all three floors, both of us calling Adreal's name repeatedly, before we began to look outside. I checked the garden while Baylor looked in the side yards, then we met back in the foyer.

"Where was he when last you saw him?" I said, turning to Baylor as he approached me.

"Putting the phone back on the charger here in the foyer," Baylor answered. "I was going up the stairs to take a nap, he told me proudly that when I woke we would have super fast internet. Then he wished me a pleasant rest. I assumed he would go back to his programming or whatever it was he was doing with that list you were all working on." He looked at his feet, then added in a desperate tone, "This is my fault, isn't it?"

"No," I nearly yelled. "If it is any one's fault it is mine for leaving you guys. It could have just as well been you. I know better, what was I thinking?"

I was so full of self-loathing then I couldn't think straight. I was wondering if I could bring Adreal back or if my experience in the Empyrean had been a once-in-a-lifetime thing. If the only reason I had managed it with Angel had been that I had run first into my Master and had his words to keep me anchored in my purpose and thinking straight. Or if it was the fact of Angel's and my strange connection, and her soul having been so different, having lived two lives and holding two Yelms, that had allowed us to not only recognize and not fear or flee each other, but also to combine our wills to return so easily.

"Did you feel anything?" I asked Baylor at last.

"Something in the kitchen, I think," Baylor replied sadly.

"What do you mean?" I asked him.

"What do *you* mean?" Baylor looked perplexed.

"I mean did you feel any strange presences or forces," I answered slowly now, a bit perplexed myself.

"No," Baylor answered thoughtfully. "I was asleep. Next thing I knew was this pulling feeling. I wasn't sure at first who or what it was, it was just a pull of energy from all around me, what gravity might feel like if it were being reversed, but then I remembered Angel talking about that feeling and I knew it was another Changeling. I wasn't sure who, though, if they would be good, or bad, so I came running down here prepared." He sighed, adding, "I thought you meant had I felt anything of Adreal's presence."

"Did you?" I asked, trying to restart my heart.

"Yes." He looked quizzically at me again. "In the kitchen, I think."

Baylor had to run after me to finish what he was saying because I was already running off in that direction as he continued, "When I went through to check the side yards, I thought I felt something that was like being around him. I'm still new at all of this though. I don't know..."

I stopped dead as I reached the center of that chamber and felt it too. Baylor stared at me as I stared in the direction of the kitchen's two sinks and began to slowly step toward them as though they were a poisonous thing.

"I was right, wasn't I?" Baylor asked despondently and with something nearing anger I couldn't name.

I was unable to answer him but I knew he already knew my answer. Both of us seemed to sink into a liquid and tangible sadness as I began my approach to the matt that lay on the polished wood of the floor before the sinks. I could feel all that had been Adreal was all over it and I didn't know what to think or say. Then suddenly I froze, as I heard the screech of brakes and thumping of feet, as the others arrived and came racing through the house.

Adonia came upon us in the kitchen. Seeing our faces, feeling what we felt, she went immediately white. Piper raced up and threw his arms around her waist as she started to fall, fainting dead away, and Angel just stood frozen.

Angel seemed the only one of us who could think, as she began to slowly move through the room with her head cocked, with some apparent purpose that I myself could not fathom. The kitchen seemed deathly silent; none of us seemed to even have the know-how to cry. We were all in shock and Angel's behavior made even less sense than ours. She just kept cocking her head this way and that, moving purposefully toward one surface or another, ducking and tiptoeing as though the kitchen itself was telling her something.

Adonia opened her eyes and jerked from Pipers arms, suddenly spinning to face me, and I thought for sure I was about to suffer the brunt of some awful outburst I cannot say I didn't feel I dissevered. Instead she had focused her eyes beyond my spellbound and heartbroken form, walking slowly toward the sink just as Angel was. They both came to stand upon the matt and then Adonia too was cocking her head as Angel had been. They both just stood there staring out the window with their heads cocked to one side. I took a step closer to them, trying desperately to figure what could be going through their minds.

Then I heard it too. It seemed far away and very small, but I heard it. I heard Adreal's voice. I stepped up as close behind Angel as I could, placing my hands on her shoulders and leaning forward to better hear it, but I just couldn't figure out what he was saying.

"Help me," I heard finally as I adjusted my hearing, making it like that of some keener creature, I don't remember what.

"Help me," Adreal's small voice came again, but from where I didn't know.

Then Angel pointed out the window, or so I thought until I went to look out of it and saw I was looking through a spider's web. There spanning the open window was a large web and in it a tiny little fly with a very odd looking head.

"Help me," Adreal said again, then started laughing.

"You little ass!" I yelled, reaching up and ripping the web down just as he flew off.

He pulled his form back together and began laughing again behind Baylor, who just happened to be furthest from me and appeared would make an effective shield. Adreal was wrong, though, and didn't get to laugh for long, as Baylor turned around swinging and knocked him out cold.

I finished filling the bucket with water, then walked over to Adreal's prostrate form and threw it on him. His eyes fluttered open to behold a circle of very irate Changelings standing over him. Even Adonia was of no mind to excuse him this time and offered him no assistance as he struggled to rise, rubbing gingerly at his offended jaw. I had suffered the brunt of such a blow from Baylor on more than one occasion, and knew exactly how badly it hurt, but I was taking no time for pity now, any more than the others were.

"What the hell is wrong with all of you?" Adreal demanded. "Did I miss the mass recall on sense of humors today?"

"What is wrong with us?" I demanded right back.

"You call that humor?" Baylor fairly yelled.

"We thought you were destroyed!" Adonia cried.

"Why would you think that?" Adreal yelled right back.

"We realized we had left you and Baylor alone," Angel said. "That Piper and Demon were both with us."

Angel sounded a little calmer than the rest of us, I think she was the first to realize that Adreal had not frightened us on purpose, and truly didn't understand why it had been so frightening to begin with. His face seemed to register some measure of that understanding as well, with the answer she had given him, and he slowly got back to his feet.

"Well, I was fine," Adreal said rubbing his jaw again and facing Baylor. "'Was, being the operative word."

"We searched everywhere for you," I said, still angry. "We called for you in every room in the house."

"You had us scared to death," Baylor added. "I thought I had failed again to protect one of my own."

"Well, I am sorry, I didn't hear you," Adreal said, appearing genuinely sorry he had made Baylor feel like that. "I didn't exactly have the greatest hearing capacity in that tiny little version of a head I had there. I was just going to wait till Adonia came home and started doing the dishes, then make her laugh. Really, I meant no harm. I am sorry I worried all of you."

Adonia reached out then and pulled him into her arms, squeezing him tightly. I think we all felt bad then because it had been just a big misunderstanding and quite probably could have been one of his better pranks, it had just gone awry somewhere along the line. Baylor grabbed Adreal just as Adonia set him back from her, and spun him so that they were facing, looking him hard in the eye.

"I am sorry I hit you, Lad," Baylor said slowly. "I just, I can't lose another..."

Adreal just hugged him and said nothing, and I saw in him the seeds of me then. The ways in which he handled things were the very ways he had learned from me. He said nothing more of it, and when he turned to face me I think I might have had some proud moisture in my eyes fighting with a desperate need to laugh, if only as a tension reliever.

"Good prank," I said, tousling his hair fondly, "terrible timing."

I hugged him tightly for a moment, then pushed him back as Piper and Adonia both reached forward to pull him toward them and proceeded to sandwich him into another long hug. I noted then that Piper had remained strangely silent, and I wondered what was going through his head. I knew he was an incredibly strong individual but I wondered how those fears had been digested and just how well they had sat in his stomach as he had driven the girls home.

Angel had offered to do the dishes then, leaving the rest of us to bring in the day's purchases and find places to set them up. Indeed it was I then, who realized we had forgotten to buy some things today, only I had made it home first. We would defiantly need more desks. I went back into the kitchen to bring this up to Angel along with the idea of using the screened-in back porch that looked out on the garden for a kind of office. I found her drying the last of the dishes and still staring out the window with a distant, almost lost look on her face.

"What is it?" I asked her.

"I knew," she said softly. "Somehow I knew."

"Knew what?" I asked, now a little lost myself.

"Somehow I knew he was not destroyed," she whispered. "The Fear wasn't here. I didn't feel it when we got in the house."

"*The Fear,* you mean?" I questioned her. "The one you felt when you were destroyed?"

"Yes," she replied, still nearly whispering. "When I realized we had left them, I was scared to death. I felt it for a brief second and I remembered, I recognized the Fear. It is Fear, the fear of death. Then I thought that was what had drawn it to me in the first place, so I pushed it away. Yet I remembered and that is the point, isn't it? It will start to hunt us again now, won't it?"

"No, Angel," I whispered, taking her head in my hands and looking into her big brown eyes. "I don't think so. I think you feel this fear when you feel *it*. Something about it is recognizable to you, and creates that fear. I don't think you draw it, though. This is not and has never been your fault."

"But," she began.

"No, we know how we feel about the 'buts'," I said, coming back to my normal tone. "Remember, Edsel disappeared before you, and Santon long after. You were nowhere around then to have drawn it anywhere near either of them. If anything it was probably closer to us, when we were in that store, than here, and you did not draw it, it simply came. If you drew it with your thoughts of it, then it would have followed you here."

"What if it did?" she asked, still very worried.

"Do you feel it now?" I asked.

"Well, no, but," She began.

"You with the 'buts' again," I said. "If it is not here, it is not here, and if it comes we will find a way to fight it, but it will not be because of you."

"I love you," she said, dropping her head to my chest and wrapping her arms around my waist.

"And I, you, Angel," I said, kissing the top of her head.

We stood like that for some time until it seemed she was ready to move past her fears once again and attack them head on. Angel's method of doing this seemed to have become either shopping for hours or actively looking for an answer as to who or what it was that was doing this. Knowing this, I chose this time to present her with the opportunity to do both.

"We forgot to buy more desks," I told her, "and I would like to set us all up on the back porch so we can all work together. We can have some actual windows put in to replace the screen."

I took a deep breath, preparing to continue describing my plans for the back porch, thinking that I would have to convince her that my idea would make better use of the space than the small pieces of lawn furniture and plants she had placed there, but I was shocked I did not need to.

"Of course," Angel agreed without pause. "We'll just move the furniture out into the garden and the plants can be placed wherever. Do you want to go now?"

"Go now?" I asked.

Considering her easy agreement with my plan, since I had known she had enjoyed the creation of the atmosphere on that porch that I meant to change, I was momentarily thrown. I had not thought it would be so simple a thing to convince her of the need to do so, and once again I had nearly forgotten about the desks.

"Go buy desks," she said leadingly.

"Oh!" I laughed. "Yes."

So it was that by nightfall we were all diligently at work on the back porch, the cool night air and sounds of the city keeping us company. I sat in a comfortable lounge-type chair; my feet on its matching ottoman and my laptop open, busily writing an introduction for her journal.

Adreal sat in front of his desktop computer, still trying to create a program that would make sense of all the information we had gathered about all the others of our kind we knew.

Piper had begun working quietly on my idea of trying to make some sort of family tree on the software Adonia had remembered to purchase. Adonia herself was setting up an e-mail address, saying it would be useful in keeping contact with the remaining Elders, and searching online for the best route toward publishing our 'work of fiction.'

Angel and Baylor both leaned over her computer, trying to track down the roots of any myths resembling the Werewolf. The evening began to slip by quickly, with random questions the only things to occasionally break the comfortable, near silence of clicking keyboards and the occasional frustrated sigh or triumphant "aha!"

"I think I'm going to write some of what Re said as a prologue," I said, at one point.

"It would add an interesting flair, I think, especially if you can remember his actual wording," Angel said. "But, a prologue and an introduction?" she questioned me over her shoulder.

"Yes," I said, grinning and adding sarcastically, "This is my project now, unless you want it?"

"No," Angel had laughed then. "I'm sure you'll do fine."

"Did you know there have been stories resembling those of Werewolves," Baylor said to no one in particular a moment later, "whether closely mimicking the type I had been, or otherwise, stretching as far back as recorded history can recall."

"Yes, we are finding them on every continent," Angel added. "Those that change their shape, due to some factor other than a recognized volition to do so in their own psyche, but there is more. There is also quite a bit of myth surrounding not only half-beasts with canine heads but full canine type transformations. I wonder if this was a single myth at the beginning, which split somewhere down the line?"

"Of course, there are also tales of those who meant to change and were capable of it at any time," Baylor added. "Those that had the ability for one reason or another to change, and it had naught to do with the moon. Some, it would seem, had this ability passed on to them, while with others it was viewed as a gift from the gods."

"Well, at least that tells us why and how the people of his village came up with their wild ideas about Baylor's disappearance," Adreal said.

"And part of how Baylor ended up screwing himself up so bad," Adonia added, then suddenly she turned to Baylor and amended, "No offense."

"None taken," Baylor replied.

"But we still have to track down where those ideas started," Angel said, with a frustrated sigh. "What I can't understand, is how these same half-beast, or all-beast transformation myths exist about other creatures than canines, without nearly the same terrible outcome. I wonder why."

Angel and Baylor trailed off into silence again, presumably pursuing an answer to Angel's latest question. It was hard to know which lead to follow first. We never knew if we were just going to be wasting time trying to answer a question to which the answer would prove to be irrelevant, or if we were going to accidentally stumble upon a very relevant answer to a question we had never thought to ask. I think they spent a lot of their time chasing geese, but there were some interesting points made, if not more interesting conversations started.

"Someone should order pizza," Adreal suggested some time later, and someone did.

That night signaled the beginning of a trend to be followed almost every night thereafter. For nearly two weeks, each night was passed in much the same way. Until, come the middle of the month, when I had finished preparing our first novel for publication, then we were all brainstorming as to what to say about the author, even what the author's name would be, and suddenly the long spaces of silence were gone.

The ideas and the volume at which they were presented only seemed to be getting wilder, as it became apparent that there would be no easy meeting of the minds on the last count. So in the end it had actually taken longer to agree upon a name and author bio than to type the tale out.

As the end of April approached, we were all beginning to show signs of wear, becoming rough around the edges from working too long cooped up in our impromptu study. The windows had been installed promptly following the computers and we had to close them more and more frequently due to rain. This had contributed to our feelings of being closed in. Hence we were beginning to find ourselves answering peevishly even the most innocent of questions, and laughing less and less.

We had been hard at work for far too long on our various self-appointed tasks, had not as yet received any answers from our research, and the disappointment was showing. I often joined Angel and Baylor in their search for the roots of myths and occasionally tried to assist Piper in the filling in of the leaves on a Changeling family tree. More often than not, though, we would all end up in a heated disagreement rather than helping each other.

Since our little family seemed to thrive on laughter, this worsening condition became a cause for concern. I had a brief flash of understanding then, of the Council, and how it had become what I had known of it. Beginning as a small group of friends trying to solve a problem it had discovered over drinks in a tavern, and ending up a select group of foul-tempered, uppity Elders.

I was desperate that we not become like the Council, but could not for the life of me think how to prevent it. I tried to think of some other thing we might all focus on, anything that would not be such a cause for stress. I thought if we might be able to accomplish some smaller task, we would be revitalized in spirit, rather than suffering this constant downward pull we all felt because we seemed to be getting nowhere. It was actually Angel who came up with the saving idea, though.

"Have any of you ever been on a pub crawl?" Angel asked, out of nowhere.

"I have crawled out of a pub," Piper answered in unlikely good humor.

"Well, they have these things here, called pub crawls," Angel said, grinning at him then looking around at the rest of us. "One cover charge will get you into all the down town bars. Everyone turns out, it has always been quite amusing to watch. We should go, relax for a night."

"When?" I asked, thankful for her help.

"May fifth," she said.

Angel grinned happily to have come up with a plan that we all seemed pleased with. She seemed to have found nothing odd about the date when this celebration was to be held.

"The Mexican Day of Independence?" I asked, slightly confused.

"These kids around here will use any excuse they can get to party." Angel laughed then, waving her hand dismissively, apparently feeling that was enough of an explanation.

Angel came over to me and removed my laptop from its place, so she could sit down where it had been, laying her head on my shoulder. Though Angel and I tried to spare each other snippy answers, we had argued more and cuddled less, and it felt good now to simply hold her.

Just the thought of a reprieve, even if it were still two days off, seemed to lighten the mood, at least enough so that we all stayed our failing tempers when speaking to one another for the rest of the night.

Then, unexpectedly, another reprieve came the following afternoon when Baylor brought in the mail. It was mostly the usual random junk such as any new resident would receive, and we paid little heed as he tossed it on the table. We all simply began to eat our lunch and might have missed altogether the small packet that lay mixed in with all the rest, but luckily Adreal is a curious creature, even about such trivialities as junk mail.

"Here's something from one of the publishers we found on the internet," Adreal said, giving us all pause, as he tore at the envelope.

"What's it say?" Adonia said, swallowing first.

Adreal tore open the envelope and displayed its contents, saying,

"It's a brochure and paper samples. There is all kinds of information. They've given a website and e-mail address, apparently all they want is for us to upload our novel,"

"So it begins," Baylor said with a grin.

The mood was wonderful then, as we set about the small, pleasurable business of checking out our prospective publisher's web site and figuring out how to upload our fantasy novel. There was a small game of keep-away between the twins, over the brochure, which was fun to watch.

Eventually, we all stood around in a circle with our hands on my laptop giving a proper send-off to our first work of fiction, each of us touching it as though to imbue it with good energy in a very Wiccan way. It's kind of funny now, looking back, because I am forced to wonder just how much good energy we did actually put into it.

We managed to retain this upward momentum, even when the evening hours found us all back in the study, going about our usual tasks. There was renewed purpose in our work, and I found myself wanting to begin outlining the second book. Knowing we still had much to discuss, as to what some of its content should be, I steered clear of those questionable parts for the time being. Yet I felt I could at least safely begin with a few things that would not need as much careful consideration, and soon I was happily typing away.

Angel and Baylor seemed to be finding more and more things of interest in the search for the roots of myth, or if not, they were not showing their disappointment. They leaned contentedly over the computer and as usual printed the occasional page or jotted a note to themselves. Piper and the twins' mood seemed much the same and that was a start. All in all, the room, though not full of laughter, was at least devoid of frustrated or angry responses. I meant to keep it that way, so I left my questions about the next book for a better time, and wrote what I knew I could.

Soon I just found myself telling the story and not really worrying so much about other things. When Angel approached me and put out her hand, to invite me to come up to bed with her, I realized I had felt nothing of the passing hours. It was a surprise to me, to find I had written till dawn, and her tired eyes told me she had stayed up just as long. As I followed her up the stairs I found myself agreeing with the kids of this town. I would take any excuse I could, to go get drunk and just relax for a night. I was very thankful then that Mexico had its own Independence Day and I was also very ready to celebrate it that night.

~18~

Crawling

I awoke that evening to the sound of Angel humming happily as she moved about the room. The bedchamber, indeed the entire house, was filled with the happy excitement that I heard in her voice. We were all to be freed of stress this evening and this knowledge had changed everyone's mood. No sooner had I opened my eyes than Angel was looming over me, a beautiful smile lighting her whole face.

"You ready to play?" Angel asked, beguilingly.

"Every time you are, Love," I smiled.

Later, when we joined the others downstairs, they were all just as ready as we were to be on our way. We chose to walk to the downtown area, saving ourselves the hassle of finding parking, and taking the opportunity to laugh and joke among ourselves. There was much happy joking about the short walk there, and the long crawl home.

"Not going to make me carry you as I had to through Rome, are you?" Baylor said, grinning and looking toward me at one point. "I think you're heavier when you're drunk."

"I have more than made up for that," I replied, laughing. "As I recall, I've carried you too. And I know damn well you're heavier period, drunk or sober having nothing to do with it."

"Are you saying I need to go on a diet?" he asked, trying to look hurt and failing miserably, thanks to a tell-tale twitch at the corner of his mouth.

"Only if they've invented one to help you loose fat from between your ears," I answered, not even trying not to laugh.

We arrived earlier than most of the party seekers and ate at the same restaurant Piper and the twins had the day they accidentally come across Angel's house. They suggested it not only to revisit the place that had started it all, but because they said the food was dangerously good. By the time our meal was finished, small groups of college kids had begun passing by outside the restaurant's windows, and the girls were more than ready to be moving on with them.

"Where to first?" Angel asked, as we gathered on the sidewalk.

"We picked the place to eat, you pick the place to drink," Piper said, getting himself neatly off the hook.

"This is your idea, your town," I answered, hoping to do the same, I didn't want to be held responsible for choosing poorly any more than Piper had. "You choose."

I'm still not sure whether this had been a mistake, leaving it to the women to take the lead for the rest of the evening. Instantly I thought to recant, unable to see how I could have made any worse a choice. They took off walking arm in arm before the rest of us, proceeding to lead us to the loudest door with the longest line. Granted it was still early and later I would wish that all of the lines had been as short as the first had been, but it didn't stop me from bemoaning with Piper as we trailed along behind.

It was a good thing the line was there, though, as we saw those ahead of us being asked to show proper identification. Baylor was the only one of us who had such a thing, as Piper had gone to quite some trouble a few years back to procure a passport for him. However, Baylor had left his passport at home and the rest of us had not bothered with such things *ever*. Angel was once again the one to come up with the solution. She turned from the entry way to all of us, pulling us into a circle and putting her hand forward, palm up. Angel then looked pointedly at all of us.

"Give it to me," she whispered, closing her eyes.

As we watched, an identification card appeared in her outstretched palm. I had created clothing for my form for thousands of years, without having ever thought to do this kind of thing. I had always been told I could create a covering for myself, that it was energy in contact with me and hence in some way merely an extension of my form. Yet I had never even considered creating other things, demanding auxiliary items from the universe, until Angel had written of having done so in her journal.

Now, we had actually seen, with our own eyes, her doing what she had told us she could. Only then did it become not so much a thing probable, because Angel had wrote about it, but a thing possible because we had witnessed and now believed. I couldn't really put my finger on the difference this made to us, but there definitely was one. We were crowding now, all leaning over and looking more closely at her creation.

"Funny, you don't look twenty eight," I laughed.

"Yeah, you look young for your age," Adreal added, taking the card and looking thoughtfully from it to her.

"Well, she better look younger than her age," Adonia giggled, "a *lot* younger."

"I'd hate to think what she'd look like otherwise," Piper agreed, wrinkling his nose in mock distaste.

Baylor gave an exaggerated shiver at the thought, making a grim face while looking at Angel. Then he started laughing and bouncing backwards, covering his upper arm as she took a swing at it.

"You're too old to be out partying grandma," Baylor teased her once he was safely behind me.

"You're about four times my age," she said, too amused to pull off the angry tone she tried for. "And besides, I lived here eight years ago, and was supposed to be around twenty then, just another kid claiming my inheritance and going to college, so I may as well stick with it for a while."

The line moved forward and we moved with it. I noticed Adreal and Adonia eyeing each other as if in some private debate that she obviously won, because he sighed resignedly as they clasped hands briefly, coming apart with cards of their own held in their hands. I glanced at Adreal's to see that she had wanted them to be twenty three, at least for tonight, and chose not to remind him he had lost the debate by asking him how old he had wanted them to be. Besides, I was still basking in the pleasure that was seeing my old friend Baylor laughing and joking. I hoped it wasn't just for our Angels sake but truly meant he was coming to better terms with everything he had been through recently.

The line moved again and Baylor reached over my shoulder, putting his new form of identification before my eyes for inspection. It looked just as perfect as the others had, and I noted with some amusement he had made his age the same as Angel's. I laughed out loud then.

"You never learn, do you?" I asked.

"Hope not." Baylor laughed too, sounding the closest to genuine I had heard since his return from the Empyrean. "That would take all the fun out of it, then what would we do?"

Piper and I were suddenly facing the man at the door and he was asking for our IDs and a cover charge. I had no time then to consider Baylor's words more fully as I was instantly preoccupied with reaching my hand into my pocket to 'find' mine and explain I was also paying for the woman and the giant behind me. Piper produced his ID in much the same hurried manner and was soon following us into the bar with a very happy Adonia and an only slightly less happy Adreal in tow.

When we had finally cleared the entryway, it fell to us men, to lead the way. We began making a path to the bar through sheer virtue of Baylor's enormous size. It was not so much that the building itself was very crowded at this point, but more that most were still gathered around the source of their liquid courage, and had not yet spread out to the more available space of the dance floor.

I finally got one of the two bartenders' attention and placed our drink orders. Laying a bill on the bar sufficient to cover the cost, I proceeded to look around the place as he filled the order. It wasn't a very large place and I was surprised that Angel no longer seemed the least bit frightened by either the crowd or the noise, beautifully poised with Piper and the twins and apparently unbothered by the jostling humanity surrounding her.

"Were you wanting shots too?" The bartender's voice cut through my musings.

I realized later that it was a thinly veiled suggestion that I leave with my drinks and make way for others to place their orders, but at that point, not yet fully aware of what I had gotten myself into that night, I had merely thought he was suggesting I *should* order shots.

"Sure," I had replied, happy for the guidance. "Any in particular, you would suggest?"

He sighed then, looking at me with the discouraging realization he obviously had a 'newbie' on his hands, and a determined-to-make-it-through-a-very-long-night look came to his face. Stilling himself to train me right, he poured six drinks quickly, mixing from a small can and a chilled bottle at the same time. He took the required amount from the stack of change he had placed before me just moments before, then, sliding the new drinks toward me he looked over my shoulder.

"Next," he called.

With that I realized that, at least on a pub crawl, the age of the friendly confidant slash therapist found behind a bar for the price of a drink was gone. This town kept their bartenders far too busy on those nights to be able to stand and waste time with idle chatter.

Realizing this was only the beginning of a hard night's work for him, a night everyone was out to relax and probably not conscious of his plight, I left him the change. Handing the drinks to the others, I quickly removed myself. It was quite likely the biggest tip he got that night but not nearly the last untrained customer he would meet by the time he was done. I moved with the others further from the bar, very aware of the fact that most would soon be too drunk to even notice his attempts at training them, and silently wished him luck.

"Two drinks?" Angel questioned, as I handed hers to her.

"These ones are shots," I said, as I too looked at mine.

"A bit large, aren't they?" Adonia said, somewhat nervous.

"Well, its not *all* alcohol, it's mixed with something," I said, trying to encourage everyone, including myself. "It should be fine."

"To *relaxing!*" Piper said, suddenly raising his shot and emphasizing the word while looking pointedly back at both of the girls.

T point was well taken. We all promptly raised our glasses and drank our shots down. Angel and Adonia soon had all of us on the dance floor, pointedly citing *our* need to *relax* as well. After a few minutes it didn't seem to matter much that we had gone out onto the floor pretty much alone. Others quickly followed, and soon I was more concerned with holding my drink high enough it didn't get spilled by someone bumping me, and no longer thinking so much about the fact I wasn't at all sure about some of these new dances.

I was enjoying myself despite the fact that the small floor was soon very overcrowded. Angel was amazing me more than ever, and as the crowd closed in I found I liked some of the new dancing such proximity afforded us. All in all, I think we were all having a wonderful time. More than once I caught Baylor blushing or Adreal smiling stupidly as a very pretty, if under-dressed, young woman also took advantage of the proximity on the dance floor to get a little closer to them.

I'm not sure how long we remained there, but when our glasses were empty, rather than try to make it back to the bar, as that area had grown significantly more crowded, we used it as the motivation to move on to another location. We began a kind of pattern then. We would enter each bar, purchase a shot and a drink, make a toast, then dance until the drink was finished. I will admit that my accounting of the night becomes rather sketchy sometime around midnight, but I never expected the shots to hit us the way they did. I certainly had not foreseen any unwanted outcome from a night which seemed to be going so well, nor did I know I would spend half the next day putting it back together.

At some point we gave up the dancing and managed the near impossible feat of finding a table in a bar that provided live music. A waitress approached us as we sat laughing over Baylor's apparent inability to handle his recent popularity without turning red. Adreal ordered us all another round of those same shots we had been enjoying all night, saying we would salute Baylor's outstanding blood pressure.

As the shots were being delivered, all we males were suddenly and inexplicably spellbound. Now I am not saying, by any means, that either Angel or Adonia are lacking in any manner, but rather that if you were male you couldn't have helped but look as this redhead, with the largest, well, chest I had ever seen, that any of us had ever seen, went, quite literally bouncing by our table.

"Holy-bouncing- baby-feeders, Batman!" Adreal said, in an overly loud whisper. Leaning into my ear, but not lowering his voice, he added, "God is good!"

"No way," Piper said, shaking his head and laughing too, even as his eyes remained pivoted. "Those were made for a man, not a baby!"

Baylor just looked from me to the redhead repeatedly, as though I would some how make use of my open mouth, and explain to him what he was seeing. I could come up with nothing good.

"I think those were made by man, for man, but babies could become involved," I managed finally, laughing as well.

"That's just not natural," Baylor stammered finally.

"Then to better bodies through science," Adreal replied, raising the shot that had been set before him. "I knew something good would come of it."

As I swallowed my shot and slammed down the glass with the rest of the boys, I remembered myself suddenly. I glanced over at Angel to see just how much trouble I was in, trying to think up a quick defense. I found none was necessary apparently, as the girls were laughing and slamming down there own shots, seeming focused on the band when our little masculine exchange had occurred.

I didn't know if it was the amount they'd had to drink by that time making the little things begin to escape them, or if I had just been blessed, but I was grateful no matter which was the case. The girls soon excused themselves for a bathroom break and we men took the opportunity to expel our sighs of relief.

The night seemed to slip away after that, with shot after shot delivered to the table, and much laughing and joking was soon all that was on our minds. I think at some point I made a short speech about remembering how we felt right then, saying we were never again to get to a point where we resembled more closely the old-stick-in-the-mud Elders than the loving family that we were. I wanted for all of us to recall the happy camaraderie we felt right then. If ever we began to catch ourselves becoming snippy, or felt ever again that we had been cooped up for too long, we were to do exactly this.

I began to doubt those statements, however, the moment I became conscious the next morning. My head felt as though in had been squeezed in a vice until my temples caved in and was thumping its protests loudly. It thumped so loudly, in fact, I thought for a moment it had expanded beyond the confines of my skull. I looked at the ceiling where I could have sworn I had just heard a responding thump. I shook my head soundly, repairing my damaged form, and immediately realized there was indeed a thumping on the roof.

I changed my form for the second time in as many seconds and flew out the window, in the form of a parakeet, wanting to see just what strangeness was going on atop my house. I found Adreal there, looking very much the worse for wear, and regaining his feet for what was apparently not the first time. When he just continued to weave, nearly falling over again, I couldn't resist taking my own form and laughing so hard I too nearly lost my balance.

"What in the world are you doing?" I managed finally.

"My wings won't work," he muttered in disgust.

"That's because you don't have any, freak," I laughed again.

He rubbed at his temples and I felt his pain, I just wondered how long it would take him to remember he could fix it. He tried to focus on me then, obviously trying to make sense of my words. When it seemed he was somewhat focused on me, or at least facing the right direction to be, I couldn't help but tease him a little bit more.

"Well, good morning, Mr. Sunshine," I said with unnecessary volume and exuberance.

"Is that what that is?" he asked, rubbing his eyes with his left hand and while covering them with his right forearm. It was quite fun to watch, as he tried once more to focus on me with that bright enemy at my back, adding, "Tell them to turn it down."

I started laughing again, and it was at least another full minute before I finally reminded him he could simply change his form and be done with it. I added that he should come back in with me through the window, before the rest of the world woke up and spotted us. Once back in my room with him as normal as he could be, standing at my side, it occurred to me Angel was already awake and gone. I glanced around a moment, then Adreal and I proceeded downstairs, wondering what was for breakfast and how the others had fared with their recoveries.

As we reached the middle floor we were met by the strangest scene. Piper was backing out of his room, trying desperately to remain very quiet and looking very, very nervous about the whole matter of closing the door. He looked first down the hall where Adreal should have been sleeping then spun, putting his back to his own door and staring across the hall at Baylor's. When he turned to check the final available direction, where he could exit, he spotted us. Adreal and I had observed him up to that point in silence, but when a completely terrified look crossed his face we could remain silent no longer.

"What is wrong with you?" I asked bemusedly.

Piper just slammed a single finger to his lip and gave us both a desperately pleading look I could not help but heed. Adreal and I were terribly curious now, and could not fathom his reasoning. Inexplicably we found ourselves tiptoeing down the hall toward him.

"What the...?" I began again, only in a whisper this time.

He cut me off, looking desperately at Adreal as if apologizing for some great sin, a sin he didn't know how to confess.

"I'm sorry," Piper whispered at last. "I am so, unbelievably, screwed."

"What are you talking about?" Adreal asked him, looking from Piper to the door he blocked. "Did you hurt my sister?"

He shoved Piper out of the way, with little resistance from that one; Piper merely allowed himself to be tossed aside and stared at me, silently begging forgiveness. I was still incapable of grasping any possible reason for his actions so far, and so I too found myself pushing past him to see into the room. Adreal was frozen in the doorway and it took me a moment to find a view over his shoulder. When I did, however, I too was frozen, and understood Piper's behavior completely.

"Oh! You *are* screwed," I announced quietly.

"I'm going to kill you," Adreal announced a little louder, through clenched teeth, "Over and over and over again."

"How could you?" I managed finally. "Where is Adonia?"

"I don't know," Piper whispered. "I woke up with that..."

"Did you..." Adreal couldn't finish, he was so mad.

"I think so," Piper admitted slowly. "I remember..."

Piper just trailed off and stared at his feet, saying nothing more. It seemed he was just going to stand there and allow Adreal to torture him, when we all heard footsteps on the stairs. I honestly don't know whether it was Adonia or Piper we meant to protect, but suddenly we were closing the door, and trying hard to pretend nothing out of the ordinary had just been going on.

"Why is Adonia asleep on the couch?" Baylor asked, as his head came into view and he saw all of us. "What is going on?" he added, as his face registered the suspicion our various poses warranted.

Baylor stalked down the hall toward us, obviously noting our protective stance around Piper's door. Piper flinched involuntarily, when Baylor's progression down the hall took him over a creaking board. Baylor looked at his feet and, grinning wickedly, he raised his foot as if threatening to set it down again on the same board.

"What is going on?" he repeated, demanding to be let in on what he admitted later he had thought was an elaborate prank in the making.

Piper's finger again went to his lips begging for silence. Had the situation not been as serious as it was, I would have laughed out loud at the sight of Baylor with a childlike grin, exaggeratingly tip-toeing the rest of the way toward us, obviously thinking to join some humorous new conspiracy. Piper didn't say a word as Baylor came up to us, he just silently swung the door wide once more.

As Piper stepped back, indicating Baylor should look inside, I almost felt sorry for Piper. He was completely dejected, he couldn't even look us in the eye. Baylor jumped back as he saw what we had all seen: a very, very busty redhead snuggled up in Piper and Adonia's bed, fast asleep.

"I thought you were planning a prank," Baylor said, all humor gone from his face he turned angrily on Piper, closing the door behind him in one motion. "This... this is not funny."

Soon we were all not only staring angrily at Piper but trying desperately to figure out a way to salvage the situation. In a way, we felt he'd made his bed, he could sleep in it. Only it was Adonia's bed too and it made things so much less cut and dried. It was obvious none of us wanted to see Adonia hurt by this, but at the same time in no way did we feel inclined to help Piper out of this mess. So we were all feeling quite confused and very upset. You might add 'wishing to be dead' to Piper's list of emotions, but as long as you end all of our lists with 'frantically casting about for an acceptable solution' you would probably be quite close to summing the lot of us up right then.

Then the dread of dreads, we heard more foot steps on the stairs and it had to be one of the women. Suddenly we were more than frantic, we were downright desperate. I turned to Baylor, thinking fast.

"Stall her?" I whispered quickly.

"Me?" Baylor asked incredulously. "You!"

"We have to get rid of this girl," I said in desperation, motioning toward Piper's closed door.

He narrowed his eyes at me, promising retribution with his look, and then, planting a smile firmly on his face, he spun around just as Angel's head came into view. All of us were instantly mimicking Baylor's sudden false good mood, plastering overly large smiles to our faces and hoping they passed inspection.

"Good morning, Lass,' Baylor said, rather too happily. "What are we making for breakfast? I'm starving. Eggs! Eggs sound good. Scrambled eggs, yes, let's go make eggs..."

Baylor continued rambling as he walked toward Angel, hoping to intercept her and lead her back downstairs. Angel just looked up at Baylor in amused confusion, as he dropped his arm around her, stopping her progress toward me. Then we all heard Adonia and our hearts fell. Adonia's voice came floating happily up the stairs.

"Hey, you guys," Adonia was calling up to us as she came. "I fell asleep on the couch, can you believe it? How come no one woke me? My back was killing me!" Then, as her head too came into view and she saw all of us, she added, laughing, "What's going on? Did I sleep through roll call too?"

"Apparently we are deciding what to have for breakfast," Angel said, still looking quizzically up at Baylor. "Apparently Baylor has awakened with quite the craving for eggs."

"Eggs?" Adonia said, sliding smoothly past a horrified Baylor and heading toward her brother, Piper and myself. "Sounds wonderful, I'll brush my hair and come down to help."

All of us, with the exception of Angel, stared on in horror. It seemed time was trying to stop, as Adonia's hand went toward the door knob in slow motion. Piper was just as frozen as I, and I know his heart had to have quit beating, because mine had, and it was not my woman about to discover another woman in my bed. Suddenly Adreal's hand shot out covering hers and stalling her entry. Looking down at her brother's hand, Adonia never saw the many levels of hell Piper was being promised a tour of just then from Adreal's very angry, dark eyes.

"Just fix your hair," Adreal suggested with an amazingly steady tone. "Like you obviously did your back and hangover."

He turned his eyes to her just as she looked up at him, and amazingly his eyes had become all happy amusement just in time. She stared at him for a long moment, trying to read him, and I thought I was about to die. I couldn't breathe, the air was too thick to take in and it certainly didn't taste good. For one second I thought she might listen to him, but it was only the one second, because I knew damn well he never won when they locked eyes like that. Finally the moment of truth came and I was almost glad of it, no matter the outcome, because I simply needed to breathe.

"You know I always brush it," she smiled, twisting the knob beneath his hand and opening the door to slip inside.

We were all still holding our breaths, though. No swift relief came with her mere entry into the room. No scream came from behind the door to end our torment. I tried to think whether it was possible she just might not see the woman in her bed. I tried to remember how the room was laid out because suddenly I could picture nothing but the horrible outcome we all awaited. Most of all I simply tried to remember how to breathe.

"You can breathe now, boys," Adonia said, popping out from behind the door with a huge grin on her face.

We all just kept staring, unable to understand her reaction, until Angel giggled and they exchanged smug grins. Piper just dropped to his knees beside me and started chuckling hysterically, but it took me a little longer as I just kept looking from one to the other of the girls. When I realized this had all been some sort of elaborate prank after all, only on their part and not ours, I couldn't decide whether or not I should be upset. I think the joke had been almost too much for poor Piper's nerves, though, because he couldn't seem to stop his relieved cackling.

"You planned this?" I said, looking askance at Angel.

"Well," Adonia answered for her, "you men couldn't tear your eyes from her form last night. I thought we should show at least one of you what it would have been like to take her home."

"You saw that?" I asked, cringing a little myself; remembering how I had been unable to stop staring.

"And heard it," Angel agreed. "You all completely forgot the shots had been ordered for another toast altogether. So while you forgot all about us and began busily toasting 'better beauty through chemistry' or whatever it was Adreal said, we decided to lift our glasses too, only we were toasting the ultimate proof that Darwin had most definitely been wrong."

"But how...I mean," Adreal began, then, catching his sister's eye, he swallowed and tried again. "I just didn't want to see you hurt...," he whispered.

I thought back to the moment in which Adreal had tried to keep his sister from entering the room and felt sorrier for him than myself. I turned to Piper, a little worried the episode had permanently damaged him because he was still cackling, but I was also disgusted. Somehow I was blaming him for getting us into this mess by not recognizing his own woman had been the one in the bed beside him.

"How did you not know it was Adonia?" I asked him. "She's been your woman for how long now?"

"Because," Angel said, the unlikely one to take up his defense. "I taught her what I taught all of you, had you paid attention when reading my journal: how to *feel* only like what you appear. And this little scene is by no means his fault alone, Demon."

"And when did you plan this?" I asked quickly.

I suddenly wanted to change the subject because not only was I more than a little annoyed at myself for having forgotten the lesson that had made this particular lesson possible, but I had somehow managed to shine the spotlight on myself again and wanted it off. Of course I was not about to be voicing any upset feelings concerning 'forgetfulness' just then, since it appeared that merely opening my mouth was getting me into a lot of trouble lately. Instead I chose to stay silent and listen to how and when they had planned this. They seemed to take great pride in their plan and that was better than them being upset any day.

"When we went to the bathroom," Adonia answered smugly. "I'm sure all of you were busy sighing your relief to have gotten away with it, but we were planning your punishment."

"Yes," Angel agreed. "When we got to the bathroom I had commented to Adonia, in disgust, how breasts seemed to be nature's ultimate male IQ reducer."

"I told her," Adonia added, still grinning, and watching Piper as he tried getting slowly back to his feet, "that you would all get yours. She told me she'd like to be a fly on the wall when you did."

"Then Adonia said," Angel took up the story, as Adonia took pity on Piper and helped him to his feet, putting her arms around him, "'I was hoping you'd say that.' So we concocted this plan to keep ordering those shots, only quit taking them ourselves. We would see to it that you were all drunk enough you wouldn't know for sure just what you'd done or not done."

"From there it was merely a matter of timing," Adonia said, smiling up at Piper, who had finally quit his insane cackling but still looked like he was a lost dog, in a very big park, without any people to claim. "Angel would slip out of bed, and take her place on the couch looking like me, once Demon passed out. I would simply change into the redhead and wait for you to wake up." She kissed Piper's chin before saying, "When you were waking up and started to snuggle me, the moment you let go of me, I knew you had felt the size of your mistake, literally. So when you slipped oh-so-quietly out of bed, I flew out the window and made sure Angel was awake too, so she could witness it all just she had wished."

"How and when did I end up on the roof?" Adreal asked. "How did that fit into the plan?"

His voice was still somewhat shaky, attesting to the fact he too was still as unsure as I, whether he could safely speak.

"You were on the roof?" Angel laughed.

"Yes," he said sheepishly. "That wasn't part of this?"

"No," Adonia said, trying not to laugh too. "You must have had a plan all your own."

"You didn't put me there?" he asked, as though he didn't believe her.

Adreal was still looking very confused and quite embarrassed now that he had even brought it up. Adonia gave up trying to hold it back and began to laugh with Angel.

"Nope," Adonia barely managed the word a moment later. "Last I saw of you, you had taken a good long look at Baylor in his tartan as he headed upstairs to bed. Then you went running through the dining room and out into the garden, hollering 'freedom!'"

Adreal's face went redder than Baylor's had ever hoped to the night before, and he lowered his eyes a moment before finally shrugging his shoulders and starting to chuckle.

Their prank didn't really seem all that fair to us, considering their 'lesson,' as they had dubbed it, had nearly given us all heart attacks and made us feel quite stupid. I guess that had been the point, though. There really wasn't much we could do, for now at any rate, but accept it. I certainly wasn't about to open my mouth to dispute, or protest, anything at that moment. I was, actually, just very glad it hadn't been me because, looking back, I couldn't even remember the crawl home, let alone getting into bed. None of us men seemed to know what to say.

Angel's was suddenly distracted, and no longer felt inclined to point out our short comings, by someone coming to the front door. I will chalk it up to the relief that unexpected visitor provided, that would cause us to miss the significance of Baylor's next statement.

"So you ladies were quite miffed then, yeah?" he said as an aside to Angel as they descended the stairs. "I thought I picked up the scent of a lust for blood...," he trailed off, as her face brightened dramatically and we were all forgotten.

~19~

Grey

"Eggs is it, then?" Adonia had asked Baylor at the same time, helping his comment get lost.

"Yes, egg's please," Piper had said, with an exaggerated sigh.

"Grey?" Angel asked.

"Grey eggs?" I questioned her. "I thought it was green eggs."

"No," Angel replied, excitedly pointing to the front door. "Grey!"

Angel was running for the front door before it registered she had been saying the name of the young Indian boy she had changed hundreds of years ago. The knob of the front door was already twisting when she slid into the foyer on her sock-clad feet, and when the young man poked his head around the edge of the door, he found himself being swept into a crushing hug before he knew what hit him.

"Grey," Angel was giggling happily as he raised his arms and hugged her back, "I have not seen you in ages. How are you, my friend?"

The young man's handsome face, now registered a deep sadness. Where mere seconds before, his dark eyes had shown with happiness to have been reunited with his friend and teacher, they now betrayed an obvious pain and perhaps a little fear. Angel stepped back, holding him at arm's length to better look him in those expressive eyes, and I knew she saw this too.

"What is it?" Angel asked, instantly concerned.

"I do not know," Grey answered her slowly, confusion lacing his voice. "That is what I have come to ask you."

Angel's eyes flew wide as she feared she had grasped his meaning, and quickly she turned to look at the rest of us still on the stairs, to see if we suspected the same. We had, and she saw it clearly. She pushed the door closed behind them and put her arm around Grey, turning and stepping out of the way so that we might all see this young man better. Thus, facing the rest of us, she preformed a quick introduction.

"And this is Grey, everyone," Angel said at last.

Angel knew we were familiar with Grey from having read her journal. She asked him if he had eaten, commenting he looked much the worse for wear, and led him into the kitchen, leaving the rest of us to follow as we would. We all stood frozen on the steps, each thinking much the same thing: that whatever evil had hunted us on the other side of the world had found its way here and it had somehow made itself known to this frightened young Indian who looked no more than seventeen or eighteen years old. He must have lost someone too. What else could have him so scared and confused?

"Do you think....," Adonia began, but trailed off when she could think of no words to express our fear.

"We will know soon enough." Piper answered her grimly.

As Piper and Adonia started in the direction of the kitchen, followed closely by Adreal, I glanced at Baylor to see if he were coming too, and was surprised to see a grim smile forming on his face. I could not fathom what about the recent events could possible bring such a look to his face and was forced to ask him, simply to relieve my own curiosity.

"What are you thinking?" I asked him.

"That I am a Changeling this time," Baylor replied. "And I will not be hunted or caught unaware ever again. If I can find Werewolves when others can't, then I can find it, it will just be a matter of getting the scent."

"I hope you are right, my friend," I whispered, as we too headed for the kitchen.

The preparation of breakfast had become a much less joyous thing than it had promised to be before Grey's unexpected arrival, but none held him to blame for this. We simply worked in silent contemplation, ordering our thoughts and stowing our questions, until Grey had been fed and was ready to talk. I noticed Angel seemed distant as she poured coffee for each of us and began mixing it the way she knew each liked. Normally this was the highlight of the morning, standing around with our coffee cups sending their wonderful aroma into the air around us, and discussing the day's agenda while the food was prepared.

Sometimes Angel and Adonia reserved the kitchen, first thing in the morning for just the two of them, allowing the rest of us our coffee but nothing more, shooing us into the dining room as they worked. But most mornings the kitchen was haven for all of us. We would sit on the stools set to the side of the kitchen's island, drinking our coffee and talking idly or helping them prepare the food. Baylor had even, on a few occasions, when he had been first to awaken, sent them away, and took care of the food preparations himself. The kitchen in the morning was the best place to be. This morning, however, seemed to have taken a turn down a dark path, and all our moods had gone with it, leaving us little enjoyment where we usually found a lot.

Eventually the food was ready and we all moved into the dining room and took our seats. You could have cut the tension with a butter knife, as our thoughts had been stewing and congealing throughout the morning and everyone seemed ready to burst with them. I did not know if Grey simply didn't know where to begin or if he was just unsure when he could. Everyone seemed reluctant to open the conversation too soon and appear rude or insensitive. I didn't know whether I should just come out and ask him to tell us what had happened or let him decide to speak of it when he felt comfortable enough. Angel apparently felt none of our qualms.

"Now, Grey," she said when we were about halfway through our meal, "did something happen to you or someone else?"

"Another," Grey replied slowly, as if ashamed. "I could not protect her, I did not know it would come for her."

"It?" Angel questioned.

"Death," Grey replied.

Suddenly we were all hopeful that we had misunderstood what the situation was. Maybe it had been that a mortal woman he had meant to change had simply gone into the light. Maybe he had been too far away to have arrived in time to offer her the change, and he just could not understand why he had not been given the opportunity to pass his gift along to her. Perhaps we had indeed escaped our antagonist's attention here in America, as we had at first assumed, and could continue to do so until we knew better what we were up against, and chose to go in search of it.

"Death came for one you meant to change?" Angel asked him, obviously thinking as we were. "And you found no opportunity to change her? That can sometimes happen, not all deny the light..."

"No," Grey replied, cutting her off and appearing upset. "I had changed her, and Death came for her anyway."

"You are sure you changed her," I asked.

I was hoping against hope that he had merely thought he had changed her, but that had left out the essential contact between their souls, that somehow he had been mistaken and so she had been unable to refuse the light successfully as a Changeling could have.

"Demon, is it?" Grey said, turning to me. "You are the one who taught Angel?"

"Yes," I replied slowly, curious as to where he was going now.

"Well, Angel taught me," Grey said. "And I am therefore no more ignorant in that regard than either you or she. I had given her the gift of change and Death was still able to claim her."

My heart fell. Not only did I now know exactly where he had been going with his questions, but I had been led to answers I didn't want, just as Angel might have led me. Even as I absorbed these things, Grey began giving us even more to think about.

"The one I speak of had been with me in the change for many years,"

Grey continued. "We had never thought to separate and had lived together on her reservation from the time of her change. I had come to think of her people as my own and never thought it would or could change. She was very strong and intelligent. I had taught her everything Angel had taught me, *everything*. So I also never thought any harm could come to her during the short times I left her alone."

"I had left her many a time with no harm coming to her," Grey continued. "Sometimes I would be gone for weeks at a time, in some city or other trying to further our cause, or get some new law passed. I had taught her what Angel had me, the art of thinking of other things or projecting the thoughts of other beings other than what we are, should she have need to avoid some evil. But she had never once spoken to me of any occasion such action had been warranted. I had left on another trip feeling she would be safe as always."

"Then the day I was to return to our home," Grey said, lowering his voice, "I had a bad feeling that Death was coming again. I did not know for whom it was coming, but I wanted to be on the reservation when it did, in case it was coming for one deserving a better choice. I rushed home, but to no avail. At first I thought all was well, but it was not. None of my people were called home that day, but strangely she had been gone when I arrived. At first I thought she had merely thrown off all of her energies, to become some small creature, for whatever reason, and would return very soon. But she never came back."

"After a few days I began to consider things more thoughtfully," Grey continued. "Things I had thought odd before but had not taken much interest in when I had expected her back at any time. I had been more than happy that none of my people had been visited by Death, this had filled my mind and I began to realize I had overlooked things I might not have otherwise."

"For one, she had not left for me a note or any other indication as to where she had gone," Grey said, sounding more than a little upset once again. "I had no idea when or if she planned to return, and that was not like her. I realized I had no indication she had intended to leave in the first place, she had made no mention of any plans for the time I would be gone, and this too was not like her. Had some emergency arisen, which she felt compelled to leave and deal with, she would have told someone. I could not believe she would have left me or her people without a word, and the fact she had not come back worried me."

"Another thing I began to reconsider was why she had dispersed her energies throughout the room so randomly." Grey continued looking at us for answers. "It was as if she had swallowed a small bomb. I began to worry then whether I had been right about my feelings that day, and Death had indeed come among our people, only it had been for her. I could come up with no good reason for her disappearance, so I feared the worst. I have searched desperately for her, but to no avail. I have been unable to find any sign of her other than what remains in our home. Now I have come to you to see how it is that Death was even able to claim her. "

"We don't know," Angel admitted. "That is a mystery we are trying even now to uncover."

I was considering Grey's reference to Death as if it were an actual entity and wondering if it could be the same presence Angel had felt and referred to as The Fear before her own near destruction. I was thinking if the two of them had sensed it, and it was indeed the same being doing us the damage, then we might find a way to hunt it as Baylor had suggested. We might have at least two among who knew how it felt, and could recognize it, if not teach us to as well. I had yet to consider the other possible connections, but soon would find them unavoidable.

I said as much to everyone, finding that Angel and Grey had come to the conclusion already that it was the same being, exchanging grim looks over their coffee mugs. They too realized that whatever had nearly destroyed Angel had done the same or worse to Grey's charge. Yet neither knew of a way to explain to us how we might recognize our enemy by its feel. When asked to better explain it, they appeared at a loss. It was as hard a concept to grasp as the fact Baylor hunted Werewolves by the smell of their rage. They merely knew it when they felt it, and the sad fact was the rest of us could not.

"You are safe here, though," Angel was telling Grey while the rest of us, lost in thought, silently cleared our dishes. "We have found that when we remain in a group, and either Demon or Piper is present, we are safe."

"Why?" Grey asked, following all of us back to the kitchen with his dishes as we all began the clean up.

"Why did this happen to your lady friend?" Angel asked, rinsing her plate and stacking it with the others. "Or why is it safe in our group?"

"Both," Grey whispered in response, walking toward the back door and looking out its window.

She had joined him gazing out onto the side yard and I knew we had a lot more explaining to do than he even realized. I left her with her pupil then, refilling our coffees, as she explained our thoughts on why any Changeling that had been properly trained was a target. I handed their coffee back to them quietly, then Baylor and I followed Piper and the twins toward the indoor garden, leaving Grey and Angel to come when they would. It seemed the right place to be for all the talking we would do this day. Grey would need to be informed of all that had transpired or been uncovered. This young man definitely deserved all our answers and we would see he got them.

Angel opened the door and motioned for Grey to take a seat on the step beside her. I discovered later that those steps seemed destined to become a place of sad revelations as she later told me of their conversation. Angel was aware there was a deeper sadness rooted in him than had been planted by what we knew of this most recent of disappearances, and she meant to find out from whence the seeds had come. Grey had been a much needed friend to her in a time she had not even known she could use one, and she meant to return the favor now by helping him to express and expel his pain.

"Did you love her?" Angel had questioned, when the rest of us had gone.

"Yes, but not as you do the one called Demon," Grey had answered, with much insight. "More as you do me. I have never found for myself a life mate, though once I had hoped..."

"And she?" Angel prodded gently.

"She would have destroyed the world as we know it," Grey had replied slowly. "And I could not keep her with me, with peace as the price. She would have never given up her war, not even for me."

"And something about this recent disappearance of the other has forced you to remember her," Angel had said, understanding how such things worked for us. "I watched a movie once, it destroyed me with the memories it brought back to me, I let it drive me mad. But I did not have anyone to talk with about it, to help me work through those memories and put them back to rest."

"I would not know where to begin," Grey had whispered. "So much time has passed."

"Not enough, though," Angel said gently. "There is never enough time between us and our memories."

"But there is no changing it," Grey said, still thinking it futile to discuss it. "I let her go."

"Let who go?" Angel prodded again. "Tell me, Grey, put it to rest."

"The day Two Leaves, that was her name, disappeared," Grey had begun slowly, letting her pull it from him. "I told you I had felt Death would visit that day. I remembered that felling, that is how I knewn. I had felt it before, the day Lozen died."

"You knew Lozen?" Angel said, surprised at his mention of the great Indian heroine.

"Yes," Grey replied sadly. "I was her spirit guide. I never told her the truth of what or even who I was, but I was there for her, I could not resist her. In the days she sat on the mountain top, left in solitude and taking no food, to commune with the spirits, I had been drawn to her. She had been very young then, not yet known to the world, but her spirit was the same. As her body had weakened, from lack of food and sleep, her spirit had only grown stronger. She had thrived in the face of such adversities and would continue to throughout her life. I was drawn to her, by the beauty of that will, beyond my own good reason."

"I had gone to her but only in the spirit," Grey whispered. "I became her guide and hence the guide of her tribe. With my help they managed to avoid a harsh death, or worse, capture, and loss of their freedom, for many years. I never allowed her to see me in the flesh or to know I was not of her tribe, and I was always careful that my soul never made contact with hers when I led her. I knew she was not ready yet for what I could give her. I was content to simply be near her in the spirit and wait until she was ready. I was confident that day would come."

"I fell in love with her. I could not remain away from her for any length of time without feeling a great void growing in me. But her determination to survive, for her people to thrive once more, grew into anger," Grey continued. "Though her soul was a beauty to me I cannot describe, it was also growing full on this anger. Anger became rage and spawned acts of vengeance I could not fully accept. Oh, I could understand those feelings and her reaction to them, please understand, but I could not condone some of what she did. In her thirst for revenge she lost some of herself, and I began to worry that she would never be able to let the past go. I began to think the world of the future, the world I saw coming, would hold no place for one that could not move peacefully through it."

"I remained with her, though," Grey went on. "I could not resist or abandon her. I loved her, you see. I continued to guide her and sometimes found my guidance helped her to do things I felt were wrong. I became burdened down with sadness, but it seemed to fade when in time her tribe decided to move down into Mexico, abandoning their fight with those that took over their lands. I was suddenly hopeful for her and the new life they could begin, when she would put her vengefulness to rest. I wanted to see a return of the old determination in her, in the formation of new homes and rebuilding of the tribe. I wanted for her to give up her war and move into the future, to live. I did not want her to die, you see, not then, not so full of the thirst for revenge. I was afraid what I might do if she did."

"I went with her as they began this journey," Grey continued. "happily finding for them a path free of those who might attack, thereby feeding the thirst in her I hoped would dissipate in time, in their new home. But among her people was one heavy with child and this became a double edged blade. We both watched over her, as she carried within her the next generation, a generation that would be offered a better life at our destination, but it was not to be."

"This woman began to feel the child coming before we had made it to safety," Grey whispered. "Lozen chose to remain with her throughout the birth, hence I remained with her too, and a hope grew strong in me in those moments, that Lozen would find herself again, in the caring for this woman. But the tribe, as it moved on without us, met a terrible ambush attack, and my hope was shattered then. Lozen and her people, or what remained of them after this attack, were gathered and put on a train for Florida, but not before they were posed and photographed.

"Lozen had finally been captured and sent away from the home she had meant to make, but this had not affected her nearly as badly as having her picture taken. I think she still held to the old fear that the light from the box drew her soul from her and stored it on the paper. I wished there was some way I could make her see, as I had, that the light which draws one's soul home, is so much greater than could have been contained in that fearful box, but I could not. I was only a spirit guide and could not bring myself to be more, even then. I was forced to watch in silence as she became more and more like a raging wounded she-bear, more deadly than ever as she awaited any opportunity to have her way with they those who had wounded her and killed her cubs.

"Still I remained with her, though. I remained hopeful. To the very end, I held out hope those final days before Florida would not be the irrevocable last straw: the murder of her brother even as he retired the field, the stealing of her soul for their photograph as surely as they stole her freedom to follow it. I hoped beyond reason she would reveal to me some spark of understanding or forgiveness, even just some foresight into the future, anything that meant she would be able to move with me into that future, as it was becoming, and not thirst forever, fighting it to the bitter end."

"But that was her, I realize now," Grey continued sadly. "That was part of her beauty, part of what made me unable to resist being near her, made her so unstoppable and made her soul appeal to me so strongly. I felt Death come for her one day as I hovered near her and I let him have her." His voice broke as he forced himself to continue. "When she was dying, she called out to me, Angel. Not just her soul, that beautiful soul, but by name. She called me by name, a name I had always answered to for her. But I let Death have her."

"I was afraid you see?" A silent tear slid down his bronze cheek and he swiped at it halfheartedly, continuing, "I knew that given my power she would be a force of rage none could stop. I knew her vengeance would know no bounds and the war which had once been all but finished would begin again. I knew she would have never been able to let it go." Grey stopped, looking up with tears in his eyes, begging for another to understand his decision.

"I understand," Angel had stated softly. "I think you did the right thing, if that helps you at all."

"She would have gathered her people and begun again to fight," Grey continued, as if still needing to defend his actions of so long ago. "Any that fell in battle, she would have simply changed and it would have never ended. Not until they were all that remained."

"You did as you knew you had to, Grey," Angel said, putting her arm around his shoulder.

"Did I?" Grey demanded angrily, trying to push his pain back. "When I left the reservation to come and find you, I followed the old trails. I came up the way of Lozen and it is naught but empty, unused space. Not a glimpse of humanity as far as the eye can see, a harsh span of land that none want now, and yet, at one time, it is all she had ever wanted."

"I know, Grey," Angel whispered compassionately.

"And I think if I had stood up to Death when first I met him," Grey said, wiping angrily at his eyes, "maybe he'd have not been so brazen as to come into my own home and take Two Leaves from me too."

"The same presence you felt at Lozen's death is the one that you think came for Two Leaves?" Angel asked, confused.

"Yes," Grey answered, confused then as well and still wiping at his eyes. "Death is Death, no matter who it comes for."

"We must tell the others," Angel had said, squeezing his shoulder and jumping up suddenly.

"Tell them what?" Grey had asked, following her as she hurried to the indoor garden and to us.

"What I have just figured out." Angel threw back over her shoulder.

"What have you figured out?" I asked as she came through the door with Grey close on her heels.

"Why I felt Fear, why it is Fear, to me," Angel said excitedly. "It is more than just Death to us Changelings, it is Death to all."

"Why? What?" All of us were more than curious.

"We are being hunted by Death, and I called it Fear because I feared it," Angel announced. "Because I knew it, I recognized it. I had met it before, when I died as Seraphim."

We all stared at her dumbfounded. None of us had anything we could condense into a single coherent thought and present as a comment or question. We just stared open mouthed and eventually she filled the silence, trying to make us understand.

"Don't you see?" Angel said. "I died once. I was murdered. Death must have been there, and because I was afraid when I died, I associated that fear with Death. So I called the feeling of Death being near, The Fear. Fear is what I feel when it is close. I have even thought that my fear is what drew it, but no, now I know it is merely a subconscious response to some deeper recognition that knows it, when it is close. I must have recognized the feel of it when it came snooping around the Highlands, and that is what had made me so afraid."

"But we are changed, beyond Death's reach," I said, very confused. "At least as mortals think of it."

"Are we?" Angel asked. "It nearly destroyed me, as you well know. I had two Yelms to anchor me, and even still it took some forty years to recover from its attack. It is the same feeling, the presence I felt when dying as a mortal and the presence I felt when I was nearly destroyed. The same feeling Grey felt at the death of his mortal friend is the same as was felt before his changed pupil disappeared."

"We are being hunted by Death?" Adonia repeated fearfully.

"One thing you are forgetting is something we should have all learned well by now," Baylor cut in, following Angel's line of reasoning. "Death, as an actual entity, has always been a myth."

"But this myth is true," Adonia cried.

"So are a lot of others," Baylor said, unfazed and apparently unafraid. "I am proof of that."

"What are you saying?" I demanded.

"I am saying that if we are being hunted by Death," Baylor answered, "and Death is an actual entity, who is present when one dies, hence acquiring his name, then Death is most likely just another such as we. Death is just another Changeling that started another myth. Now granted he would be a Changeling with some sick fascination with death instead of life, but a Changeling none the less. One with a myth going back so far, would most definitely be exceedingly old and powerful, but still only a Changeling. He would still just be one of us, that is the important part to remember, because we know now that Changelings can die if you steal their Yelm, or even be forced to ascend." He grinned cynically at his own thoughts, adding, "Obviously not all can come back from ascension, and its doubtful from all Angel says that, once ascended, one recalls a 'want to' of their own accord, so that might be enough."

"But if Death is a Changeling, trying to keep other Changelings ignorant of their own power," Adreal asked, "which is what we have concluded is the motive, then why is it killing mortals too? Mortals think we are all myth, they know nothing of us. It would seem pointless to bother with them. I don't understand."

"It's not supposed to make sense to you, Lad," Baylor said, cutting Adreal off. "The damn thing is mad, rabid, obsessed with death, maybe it likes death so much it matters not whether it's a mortal dying or a Changeling, so long as something is dying and it gets to watch. If you understood its reasoning, I'd be worried about you."

"My gods!" Angel declared then, realizing something more. "Remember how I said it was nothing like other evil Changelings, that it was frighteningly unfamiliar and almost inhuman? Well, it was unfamiliar to my consciousness, but not my subconscious. My subconscious recognition of it triggered the sudden fear I felt when it passed near me. It was, however, still unfamiliar. Later, when I had reference, having met an evil Changeling, I knew it was not like them either. It was nothing like a Changeling at all. It may not know what it is, just as Baylor wasn't recognizable as a Changeling when he didn't know he was, it may not be recognizable as one either."

"Or it knows damn well and is just as good as you at disguising itself to appear as whatever it wants to," Adonia interjected. "Either case makes it very dangerous."

"It would have to know what it is," Baylor said. "Because we know it had to have done the same thing when approaching the Council, to set it up how it wanted. It disguised itself as a normal, well-meaning Changeling, with a lot of abnormal but good ideas. It is just a very old and powerful Changeling with a Hitler-esque agenda for all of us. It obviously has a lot of issues, and I, for one, am going to see to it those issues are dealt with."

"That would definitely explain its fascination with me, then," Angel said slowly. "I was a threat to continued ignorance because of my discoveries. That is, if we are indeed still assuming it wanted to keep Changelings ignorant and helped with the formation of the Council to that end. Also, if it recognized my soul too, having stood by and watched me die once, it would have been fascinated all the more to find my soul had returned and lived again, only now as a Changeling. Still more fascinating to it, might have been that I now had a soul with two Yelms."

"That would also explain it following Grey," Adreal said slowly.

287

"Your soul contacted Grey to make him a Changeling, his in turn contacted Two Leaves, to change her. After failing to destroy you it might have feared trying again, hence it left you alone all those years. It may have even feared angering you by killing your first direct descendant, Grey. That is, of course, depends upon whether or not this whole 'descending from a certain one protects you theory' is valid. But it might hold a kind of morbid fascination with, or liking for, the feel of your soul, a soul it never touched to change when first it met you, and yet somehow found later to have returned and been changed anyway. It may have gotten some perverse joy in forcing Two Leaves, someone with a small part of you about her, to ascend."

"The main point to focus on is that we have nothing more to fear than we did before, Adonia," Baylor cut in, trying to relieve the fear which still showed on her face. "We are still only tracking down a very old and powerful Changeling, just as we were before. It is become no more and no less a thing to fear merely because we have put a name to it. We are still simply looking for one of the very oldest of us, be it Ra's sister or one she made early and taught well." Baylor grinned reassuringly, adding, "We simply know a little more now and actually can feel a little safer."

"A little safer how?" Adonia asked incredulously.

"Well, we know it fears or respects Ra enough to leave Demon and those around him alone," Baylor answered. "We also know it must hold Piper's mother in much the same regard, because all those around him have remained safe. Now we can assume that since it failed to destroy Angel, it has either formed the same kind of respect for her or now fears her, since her first descendant has remained safe and it has made no further attempts on her. So we have three among us that it obviously steers clear of. We will be okay for now."

"But I was not my Mother's first or only descendant," Piper said.

"Well, then, maybe it fears her enough not to bother with any of her *direct* descendants," Baylor said, furrowing his brow. "But my point is the same. We are safe as we have ever been, all here and together, and we now have more clues."

"More clues?" Adreal questioned.

"Yes," Baylor replied. "We are looking for one as old as the first myth that refers to Death as a being. We track that, we track it. When we do find it, we combine our will as the Council did when it began. We force it to ascend or we help Angel kill it, as we will any other that threatens us. It may be old enough and powerful enough to be forcing ascensions on its own, but we are a powerful enough force as a group to return the favor."

"I think Baylor may be right, Demon," Adreal spoke up.

"About what part?" I asked.

"That it could be Ra's brother's descendent." He put his hand up, staying any response, and added quickly, "Hear me out. If it was made early on, long before Ra even figured out how to make you over and it was trained well, it could be powerful enough to disguise its aura, even insofar as to how you perceived it in the dream. Or," he added thoughtfully, "it is simply quite mad, never feeling of or exuding the same discernable things for any given length of time. Think about it."

"I don't know," I said slowly, thinking too many things at once, "I cannot say that I don't agree it would have to be one of the first reborn of one of my master's siblings, for I cannot believe it would be one of them directly. Yet I didn't feel anything bad about any of those attached to them. You'd think I'd have felt something."

I trailed off into silent contemplation, remembering all that Angel had demanded I not forget about fairness and other such purely human concepts. I recalled my Master's teachings about things not always being black and white. It seemed the others were lost in thought too, as the silence grew and thickened while we sat motionless.

"We have narrowed down our research, anyway, that is indeed a start," Angel said at last, breaking the silence. "We can focus on finding the Death myth's origin, instead of all of them."

So we all headed for the study knowing only a little better what we were doing. Grey sat silently before the same computer as Angel and Baylor, but I often noticed him staring off into the distance out the window, lost in his own memories. I thought I would have to ask Angel what she had learned from him while they were alone, not only to better understand what had led her to her earlier revelation, but to better understand this sad young man. I put those questions off till later when we would be alone and got back to my writing, knowing I would insert his part of the tale where it was needed, when I had heard it from her.

~20~

All Good Things...

Soon we had settled into a new groove, working hard through the long night hours, but somehow we managed to remember what we had promised ourselves after many a round of shots in early May. We made a conscious effort to remain kind and patient to each other and to remain joyful in our quest. We went on picnics or short day-trips occasionally to alleviate the boredom. We even visited some theme parks which were not too long a drive away, and always found ways to make each other laugh.

Baylor slowly came back to resembling his old self. How he had managed to restore his many hurts and memories to their proper places and put his solid, stoic self back together was a mystery to me still, but I was glad for it nonetheless. I prayed it had all truly become the path behind him once more and that this was not a temporary recovery destined to fail. I still recalled with dread the empty blue depths of his eyes when he'd turned them on me the night he came back and told me not to pity him.

He was grim on the hunt, but that was not unusual, some people go shopping to ease themselves, Baylor goes hunting. I told myself it would all be okay in time. Baylor questioned Angel and Grey both about the way they scented Death, but seemed either unable to make them understand what he needed to know or they were incapable of telling him. Once he even made mention of catching a scent of something like rage, only more of a blood lust, here in Springfield. He said he'd caught it more than once and the first time mistaken it for the girls' anger the night of the pub crawl. He had asked both Grey and Angel if that might be it, but neither of them could say for sure. In Grey's case I don't think he fully understood the concept Baylor was trying to convey about Werewolves smelling like rage and needing to catch Death's scent.

Grey, who chose to remain with us, offering to assist in any way he possibly could, also seemed to return a little to being the person I had read about. Slowly he regained some measure of readiness to smile and join in our constant laughter. After having heard of what had occurred in his life since he had left Angel's company, I could understand his sadness and was very happy to see this change in him too when it finally came.

Adonia became our communicator. She kept up contact with Kynan, Cathmore and Lachlan, exchanging e-mails to keep us all up to date. Adonia made and kept contact with Rajesh and eventually she even managed to get him to buy a computer, forcing him to move forward in time with the rest of us, by convincing him that he might be able to help or at the very least better keep in touch.

After many a long phone conversation, she finally had Rajesh using the computer, and began a correspondence with him via the internet, discovering a few things in the process. Not long after Adonia informed him of Angel's safe return, Rajesh told her something we should have learned long ago: Mikaili had been blessed by one named Jendayi. Though this didn't really help us, we were at least glad one of us had finally asked. What did help, however, was when he made mention he was not the only one Mikaili had blessed, telling Adonia he knew of at least one other.

Apparently, long before Mikaili blessed Rajesh, she had blessed one named Philana. So the family tree came together a little more, and so did something else. We now knew why the usually fanatical Council had not tried to destroy Mikaili when it had all the others that blessed without their consent; she had been Edsel's grandmother in a manner of speaking. Now if we could only find out where Mikaili's creator, Jendayi, fit in our family tree, we might be a little closer to our roots. Yet it still seemed the longest unbroken line we had uncovered thus far, moving from Jendayi all the way down to the twins, and did much to keep our spirits high.

Because of the fact that we knew Ra had made only me and I had made only Angel, and we knew Angel had made only Grey, we knew this was an unbroken line back to our beginning. Yet we were making much slower progress with the others. We knew Ra had two siblings, and assuming my dream had been a showing of hidden truths, the female of the two had either created a great many or created another one that had. So we assumed it would be she that we would eventually work our way back to, as we traced the majority of Changeling's lineage.

Working with the same dream in mind, we thought it possible that the one that had been seen as linked to Ra's brother had been another much like me. I, personally, felt it had been a single offspring, most likely made sometime after the year 1563 when I had the dream, but we all agreed that, most likely, Ra's brother had made no others.

We did, however, all concede that much of that could be a large and possibly dangerous misconception. We discussed the possibility that since I had not noticed any others linked with me to Ra, which I should have, given the fact I had already made Angel; that this one linked to his brother might also have started a line much like my own. It might have appeared a single soul, as it did, due to the fact all that sprung from it had been properly trained, as had all that sprang from Ra through me.

There was another very possible explanation and thought-provoking idea we began to consider. If Ra had made only one and his brother had made only one, then we had to reconsider the grouping I had seen linked with his sister. It might not be that I had seen an entire lineage coming from her, as I had at first thought, but rather a large group of direct offspring. It was likely all of the souls, both weak and powerful, had then been directly linked, just not all properly trained.

It was a lot to assume but it was all we could do, all we had been able to do all along, and it did indeed seem to fit in with other conclusions we came to later. We had no names to put to Ra's siblings and, until we tracked them down by other means, could not ask them for ourselves. I saw how it was that Angel had come to her conclusion that it would be Ra's sister at the heart of our dilemma, it was indeed the likely choice. Yet I still wanted to believe it would only be an early offspring of hers and not herself. Furthermore, I was still thoroughly confused by my feelings, or rather lack of feelings, that might hint at such evil in my dream.

I didn't want to believe my own Master's sister could do such a thing to us, especially when it appeared she was the greatest grandmother of most of us in the first place, even if she had left some of us in the dark. Ra had made mistakes too and I did not think worse of him for it. It seemed just as likely to me that any early offspring of hers would still be old enough and powerful enough to be doing this to us. It would indeed still hold her and her two brothers' other changed ones in a high regard, if for no other reason than to stay their wrath, and thus leave those direct offspring alone.

I said as much to the others, and at last even Angel conceded it was just as likely as any other theory we had as yet come up with. It would also provide another motive I had yet to consider. One of her offspring could have grown jealous and tried to rid the world of the others. This could indeed have given rise to the Death myth. We were able to find one in nearly every culture back to the earliest of times, and began to think we were onto something. Especially when Angel had an epiphany one especially warm and sticky August night, as she leaned over her computer reading yet another web page dedicated to Death as an entity/deity. I had just walked up and put my hands on her shoulders to rub the tension out of them, and she had shrugged them off.

"Ugh!" Angel said, looking up at me apologetically. "You don't want to touch me. I'm hot and sticky and gross."

"Hot and sticky, maybe," I had laughed, "but never gross."

"Touch!" She had nearly yelled. "That's it!"

"What's it?" Baylor had asked, appearing to have just been jerked back from some mental wandering but happy to be back if it meant she might give him a lead on his prey.

"Death's touch," Angel announced. "Almost all myths regarding Death speak of his touch! It could be that he steals the Yelm from mortals as well as Changelings, bringing death to both by removing their anchor to this life. He may not merely be present at mortals' deaths, he may be causing them outright. He may not be forcing ascensions alone, he may be actually killing us. Only the fact I had two Yelms at the time may have confused him and saved me, he had done me massive damage but been unable to kill me." She smiled sardonically. "A lot also looked at death as not just an ending but a new beginning as well, reinforcing the fact he is merely a Changeling capable of giving or leading one to a new life."

"Then Edsel and Santon are truly beyond recovery," Adreal said. "Even were we to figure out a safe way to move between earth and the Empyrean, retrieving the ascended without losing ourselves, they may actually be dead?"

"Possibly," Angel said sadly. "If I am right, I am sorry."

We sat silently for a time, digesting all that Angel had said and trying to see if we could accept it. Piper sat back in his chair, once again appearing to silently digest it all, it seemed to sit, if not exactly well. None of us liked it, it was bitter, but it was a thing we had to accept if Angel was right and she had an eerie knack for being right. Then suddenly Grey spoke up, giving us something else to think about than the fact our losses might indeed be permanent.

"So Ra's sister creates a Changeling sometime early in man's history," Grey said. "Then she moves on and makes others and it grows jealous of them for some reason. It then either figures out it can steal the Yelm of others, or she had told it sometime before, and it begins to kill these others off. So what, it just started to like it or something? It started killing mortals after that?"

"Maybe that is why she quit teaching others so well, and why those others, even directly attached, seem weaker?" Adreal said. "Maybe she began leaving little gaps in their education because she realized she had told that one something it was using to do evil."

"So it could have been she who was responsible for the formation of the Council and hence their lesser instruction of others, but perhaps not the deaths to those early Elders," Adonia added. "She may have meant to prevent harm rather than cause it."

"And the gaps just grow bigger from generation to generation," Adreal continued. "As do most things, it seems, with the passing down of information."

"Yes!" Piper said excitedly. "I think we are onto something. I think it more likely to be Death who helped form the Council though, he would have had the most to gain by keeping us easy prey. If she wanted to prevent harm it is unlikely she would have pulled a force together and taught it how to force ascensions and kill others for any reason."

I was surprised by Piper's sudden input because so often of late he had been silent, merely listening and digesting, and rarely speaking up. I didn't think about it for too long, though, because there were other things coming up to take our minds in new directions. Adonia's computer sounded in the thoughtful silence, announcing she had a new piece of mail in her virtual mail box. She spun in her chair to see who had sent it and we all waited impatiently for her to relay what news she had received. We had all been awaiting any further information or names Rajesh might uncover in his searching, and were hoping this would be yet another link in our long chain, but it wasn't. Instead it was a note from Kynan, but it still provoked some thought.

"Well?" Adreal asked, when his twin had still said nothing after some time had passed.

"Nothing really," Adonia replied. "He's just checking in. You know, the usual, he asks how we are all doing and if we have come up with any further answers or need anything from him or the others. He says they are all well and good, but otherwise have had no luck on their end, etcetera."

"Sure they have," Grey laughed, grimly, "They're alive, aren't they? If that isn't luck, what is?"

"What do you mean?" Adonia asked, obviously wondering at his odd sense of humor.

"Well, Piper and Demon are both here," Grey announced, as though she should have seen it. "And you guys say they are the ones that keep the rest of us safe. So it is lucky they are all well and good, right?"

"Damn the forest for the trees!" Angel gasped. "Why have we never questioned that? I mean, whoever is hunting us has quit picking off the Council. He has not killed any of them in more than five hundred years."

"Yes, but it took it fifteen hundred years to pick off the other four," I said, suddenly worried for Kynan. "Maybe he is merely biding he time."

I was suddenly trying to figure out how to either be in two places at once or get the remaining Elders to here, but Angel put a halt to my whirling thoughts almost as quickly as they began to spin.

"Or maybe it had destroyed all of them it wishes to?" Angel questioned thoughtfully. "It took out three of the original seven very quickly, right?"

"Yes?" I said, wondering where she was going this time.

"Those three may have been more intent on letting certain learning continue. Kynan was elected to take one's place but the other two spots were left empty," Angel said thoughtfully. "But from what you have said, Kynan was not the type to be changing any policies unless Lachlan told him to. So the Council was safe until Edsel found out the twins had been taught more, and not only didn't try to stop it but also began to consider the validity of allowing better learning to take place. Same goes for Santon and explains why both of them were destroyed. But I think it also explains why the other three are still okay: they have no intentions of changing anything, they are just as happy as Death is to leave the rest in the dark."

"Angel is right, I mean it isn't as if they are going about making others and then teaching them things this one doesn't want others to know," Adreal added sarcastically. "I haven't heard of them voting favorably on a blessing in ages. I think the only reason Adonia and I are here at all is Edsel and Santon."

"Maybe it is done with them for now." Adonia finished for him. "Could be the Council, as it stands in its weakened state, is safe now if only for its record keeping. Certainly makes it easier to locate all of the new ones that get reported to it, and us for that matter, possibly for some master plan we have yet to uncover."

"They destroyed those records," I said hastily, still very fearful.

"They still receive and gather the information, though," Adonia responded. "Whether they record it on paper or merely speak of it aloud amongst themselves, seems irrelevant if a powerful Changeling wanted to know something. It could simply disguise its presence and listen in."

"I will not argue the possibility he has followers gathered for some master plot," Angel said, "because I was one of those attacked by evil Changelings on the way to Rome. But I think the actual killing has all been done by him. He wouldn't share such knowledge with even his own followers. If we have been right in any of this, then he would jealously guard his power. He would want that knowledge and ability over them, over all of us, he wants to be the only one of any learning among us. The last man standing, so to speak, so that his creator, Ra's sister, will notice him again, just as Ra himself strove to draw God's attention by doing what he did. Maybe my accidental uncovering of his greatest secret was just the final nudge in his prior obsession with me and my soul, and why he came after me."

"I agree," Baylor said. "So we are assuming, that an offspring of Ra's sister had been given her full attention and all the knowledge she could possibly give it, that explains how he had it to give, in part, to the Elders. She then makes another and another and so on and he is no longer the beneficiary of her full attention. So this Changeling grows jealous. He decides to be rid of all the others to regain her full attention. So he joins a conversation the Elders are having and gives them just enough information to enable them yo get rid of half the Changeling population for him. He then destroys the ones he sees may make others just as powerful as themselves. He leaves just the three, too few to force an ascension, which was the most potent idea he gave them, but just enough to continue keeping track of such information he feels he can still use when the time is right."

"Then that would be why she stopped telling her offspring everything," I agreed. "She wouldn't have changed them if she hadn't wanted them to live, and she wouldn't want them able to kill each other. This may be where she began teaching others less. I saw many attached to her but only a few were powerful. It makes sense this way."

"Then we will really make him mad now," Adonia announced. "Baylor is right, we are definitly going to call it out."

"We publish your journal, Angel, and *all* will have *all* the knowledge he has sought to hoard," Adreal said, following his twin's thoughts. "We probably won't need to search for him then, he'll come find us."

"Good!" Baylor said. "Then two good things will come of this. Let him come and he will be taught something as well. I will explain pain so fully, he will sing for its end."

We all grew silent again after that and listened to the haunting echoes of what Baylor and the others had said. I couldn't help but wonder at Adonia and Baylor's mention of the concept of this group we had labeled the Anti-Council moving into position for something worse. Such questions as, 'position for what?' and 'what could be worse?' kept running unchecked through my head, nauseating me.

So that night, as well as many more to come, was spent in a redoubled effort to track down either Death or the one who made him. We needed to find either Ra's sister or one of the old ones that had been among her first creations, one that would be either Death himself or know of him and where we might find him. Keyboards and mice, is that right, mice, were heard clicking long into the nights as August turned into September, and September into October.

We would go over what we had found frequently, sharing it with the Elders and Rajesh as well, via electronic mail to be sure there would be none of the forest for the trees kind of mistakes we had so often found to be at the root our shortcomings. We tracked a good many myths, in one form or other, back to the area of Egypt and found ourselves unsurprised due to what we already knew. The jump back in time from such half-creatures as Werewolves we knew now, to paintings and carvings of the god Anubis, seemed not so far a leap once Rajesh pointed it out. The ways in which we had found certain things to have come about were beginning to make many other things, like how my own teacher had begun many of these myths with his own taking of half-forms, and why he had insisted so vehemently I not do the same, make a lot more sense.

With different colored markers, we drew lines across the continents of a large map pinned up in the indoor garden. We began tracing the spread of each tale and labeling each with small pieces of paper and stick pins. We made notes as to when we thought a tale had grown or diminished with the retelling, and hence how that had affected the Changelings hearing the tales if they had believed them. One particular pin in the map intrigued us and had us conversing for quite some time. We'd all heard the tales in some form or other of a prince who'd been damned for eternity to drink blood and hide in the shadows. Not the first vampire myth nor the last, but knowing he had merely been changed it was shocking to review this particular myth in this new way. It had us wondering what kind of Changeling would have given that prince such a gift.

The full scope of what we were, what we were capable of, and what that had done to shape and change humanity was astounding to us. We who thought we had remained apart, shielding the world at large from our existence, were made to see we were the minority. Quite a few hadn't remained nearly so well hidden. This was clearly illustrated by just how many lines and stick pins were crisscrossing and studding our map.

We soon began to see a trend in healers too, those attributed with healing powers, and considering our thoughts on dentistry after reading Angel's journal, we began to wonder if this wasn't somehow also a link to our roots through those such as the Druids.

One evening, we found ourselves in the indoor garden room, watching as Angel painted a large tree trunk on one wall. She began with three roots and painted the word "Ra" beneath one of them. Then she went up the trunk and branched off in three directions. The one branch she filled in completely, writing first my full name then her own, followed by Grey's. She had done her best with the main, middle, branch which was Ra's sister's, though it lacked a name as yet. She'd filled in quite a bit, but I could tell when she sighed at the last that what had begun as a project meant to make her feel she was getting somewhere was only making her more frustrated.

I had a feeling that though we had all held out far longer this time, when it came to allowing our tempers to fail, that we were all growing close to snapping again. It was indeed discouraging, I have to admit, because all in all it was just a lot of lines of color on a very big map of a very big world, and a tree with a lot of leaves we still didn't know where to place. In essence, though we did all we could think to, to find either a powerful ally or our enemy, in the end, each night we were forced to simply retired our brains to our pillows without any luck.

We kept at it, though, each day trying our best to find something new to encourage ourselves, and toward the end of October it seemed the fates were smiling on us. We had ordered pizza again, for a late lunch we had nearly forgotten. When Baylor returned from the front of the house with our pizzas, it seemed one of the boxes didn't quite match and this held his interest far more than his usual meat-lovers.

"What's that one?" I asked, indicating the slightly smaller parcel.

"From that publisher we used," he replied, all grin.

"Oh, this is wonderful," Adonia announced, swiping it.

We all instantly piled up around her, forcing her to shoulder and shoo us back as she tried to open the box. Finally, triumphantly, she withdrew and held up a very plain-looking novel. It was properly bound and well-made, but somehow very plain, in a way I could explain. It reminded me very much of the 'Changing for Dummies' Baylor had suggested. Although darker than those books were, it seemed to me it should have been more bright and wonderful looking considering what it was.

This was apparently called a 'proof,' an initial copy we were to look over and approve before it would become what was to be presented to the world. I liked it, 'proof,' it made me smile.

Adonia then withdrew from the box a contract.

The contract was very important-looking and some of it was difficult to understand, so that soon we were all asking what certain parts of it were supposed to mean.

"I have a lawyer, or used to anyway," Angel announced suddenly, pointing out yet another odd-sounding statement on the paper before us. "Let me call him and we'll have him explain this part."

"You had a lawyer?" I asked, "For what?"

"When I decided to ascend, I put all of my assets under his control," Angel answered. "I told him I was moving to some commune in Asia or some such thing and that he was to auction off everything and donate all of the proceeds to charities. That's when my bank account was closed, by the way. He was to pay his own expenses from it and then give the rest away wherever it was needed."

"Oh," I said.

I was a bit taken aback that I hadn't already known this about her. Of course, I should have known it would have been something like that, because I had known the house was hers and then had gone to auction. I knew from what the realtor had said that he had owned it for some time, buying it too soon after her ascension for her just to have disappeared and it have been declared abandoned or her declared legally dead. I was still thinking these things when Angel hung up the phone, telling me we had an appointment with the lawyer in one hour.

So Angel and I left the others with Piper and went to meet with her lawyer. She held the contract in trembling fingers as we drove the short distance to his office, and I wondered what frightened her more. The fact she was about to tell all Changelings what exactly it was they were? Or the fact that the imminent publication might draw the wrath of the one that had nearly destroyed her already once. Considering all the possible repercussions, those we had discussed and otherwise, that could come of it, I could not blame her in either case.

"Are you going to be okay?" I asked, taking her hands in my free one to steady them as I drove.

"Yes," she said, surprised by my worry. "I'm just excited, Demon. This is it." She raised the contract and looked at it, adding, "We sign this and it begins. Whether we find any of the old ones or not, after this, one of them may find us."

"Does that frighten you?" I asked, trying to read her.

"A little," she replied, looking steadily at me. "But I am more excited, I think. I never have liked being afraid, running away and hiding from problems, and it is all I have ever done. I am ready for a change. I think I would rather face this fear and die then spend the rest of my life afraid. We live too long for that."

"You will not die," I said sternly. "Never again will we be parted!"

We pulled up in front of the lawyer's office and I went around and helped her from the truck, putting my hand up to her still trembling fingers and pulling her down into my arms. I held her like that for a moment, giving her back some of the comfort she offered me by simply being near. She was a very brave woman, more so than any of us because she knew first hand what she invited. Angel had suffered our enemy's wrath before, and it had taken her forty odd years to recover, and yet she was willing to risk it again, not just for Baylor and all the others like him, but in hopes of drawing our enemy out. Here she stood before the bull, proudly putting on a red sweater.

"Ready?" I whispered.

"Ready," she answered, raising her chin and smiling up at me.

We entered the building and were promptly shown into a well-appointed office, with a distinguished-looking older man sitting behind a solid oak desk. I know it was a nice desk, and had probably cost him quite a bit, because I had bought so many in the last year. I soon realized a lot of what had first impressed me had probably came from that desk and not the lawyer himself. This first impression only lasted a moment, as I soon found myself reminded more of a retired hippy than how I thought a lawyer would be.

"Angel, you haven't aged a day," he exclaimed, coming out from behind his desk and shaking her hand briskly. "How was Thailand? Treated you good, I see, you look wonderful. I need to try that. And who is this good-looking young man? You're not here for a pre-nuptial agreement, are you? You know, I swear they ruin more marriages than they protect, starts them off all wrong."

Angel started giggling at his excited reception and unexpected wave of questions. I too was forced to smile as he gripped my hand, shaking it vigorously.

"You're a lucky man," he said. "Angelica is the sweetest creature on the planet, a true Angel."

"I quite agree," I answered.

"So what is it then?" he asked again. "Not a pre-nup, please."

"No," Angel answered, finally gaining control of her facial muscles. "I have written a book and," she held out the contract, smiling, "we would like for you to go over the publishing contract."

"Absolutely,' he said, happily taking it from her and returning to his side of the desk. "What is it about, your time in Asia?" He grinned then, adding, "No, a romance, right?"

Angel started giggling again and he looked up over the rim of the spectacles he had just put on. He smiled, obviously knowing how he sounded and why he was amusing her. I think he did it on purpose, he must have learned long ago how to put people instantly at ease, and I could see why she had chosen him. He was quite proud to have made her laugh, and looked at the contract as she began to tell him briefly what her 'fantasy novel' was about.

He was quiet while she spoke, and I wondered if he was really listening or just pretending to, whether he was actually reviewing the contract or just looking at it, and which I preferred. Angel finished with her description just as he flipped the last page and looked up at her.

"Sounds very interesting," he said at last. "I don't generally read such things, but I think I might just have to now. The contract is very precise and I see nothing in it to worry over. It actually appears it will be a very lucrative deal for both parties, all very fair. Now, you said you tell people where Werewolves come from, fantastic idea. Amazing! Yes, I think I will have to read this."

Angel and he began to chatter idly and I realized he could not only do two things at once, such as read a contract and listen to a story, but also appeared to have more than one line of thought running simultaneously at all times. They jumped from topic to topic so erratically, I often found myself wondering how one comment related to the previous one, only to realize they had no relation at all. How Angel followed him, I have no idea, but she appeared to be doing better than I so I just let her do the talking and sat back, pretending to keep up.

It was quite a while later that Angel finally stood and told him we had to be going. He glanced at his watch and hastily agreed, saying he should have picked up his mother for dinner a half hour ago. Then he grabbed her hand again, as though he meant to shake it in farewell, and his eyes widened with something he had just remembered he wanted to tell her. I steadied myself for another round of endless random chatter, but I was to be saved.

"You remember that painting you had?" he had asked then. "The one from the foyer?"

"Yes?" Angel said, suddenly very interested.

"I kept that one," he admitted, somewhat sheepishly. "Just couldn't make myself sell it. It's at my mother's house right now. That's what made me think of it. I couldn't bring myself to auction it off to someone who didn't even know you. I thought if you ever changed your mind and came back it would be the only thing you couldn't replace. You want it back?"

"Absolutely," Angel said hastily. "If you wouldn't mind. It was truly one of my favorite things."

"I don't mind. Not at all, it's yours," he replied, just as hastily. "I will get it back from Mother tonight and have it cleaned. I'll call you as soon as it is ready."

"That would be wonderful," Angel said.

He led us out of his office and through the reception area. I realized his secretary had left sometime during our long conversation with him, as we all exited together and he turned to lock up behind us.

"Good luck!" he called, as we parted ways in the parking lot. "Hope it's a bestseller."

I handed Angel up into the cab and she smiled down at me, obviously happy with the day's events. I walked around to the other side and drove us home, happy because she was. We were met on the driveway by a mixture of worried and excited faces and quickly found out they hadn't expected us to take as long as we had, but were glad to see us back and anxious to hear what we had found out. We quickly informed them all was well, with both ourselves and the contract, and moved into the house to sign and post it.

None of us seemed in the mood to return to the study on such a high note and we all ended up wandering into the indoor garden room to settle in for a night of easy conversation. That is when another wonderful bit of news came up. We were sitting around, comfortably sipping coffee and discussing the swiftly cooling weather, when Adreal brought it up.

"Halloween is in a few days," Adreal announced with a huge grin.

"My favorite holiday!" Adonia said with a matching smile.

"Yes, I know," Piper said, smiling indulgently.

"I've always thought Halloween was the best one too," Angel agreed. "I love looking at all the costumes."

"Well, since you told the twins about your hellcat form," Piper interjected, "they have enjoyed *being* all the costumes. It really isn't fair to everyone else."

"We have never entered any contests," Adonia explained. "That would be unfair."

"There will be a pub crawl for Halloween too," Angel said, trying to change the subject before the conversation turned into another verbal 'get the goat' contest.

"No!" Piper said suddenly, feigning terror. "Adonia will want to go as a busty redhead then!"

"I'll be nice," she said, turning an overly sweet smile on him and batting her lashes. "Can we go?" Then, kissing him repeatedly all over his face, she began with, "Please, oh please, please, please..."

"Stop! Sugar shock! I'm feeling suddenly diabetic," Piper laughed. "We'll go, just quit before you put me into a sweetness-induced coma!"

"Yes!"

Adreal and Adonia both raised their hands over their heads and clapped, celebrating their victory. Angel looked at me, smiling happily too, and it seemed all would go well, one way or another. Talk quickly turned to what each of us would be for the happy event. The twins began modeling their different ideas and soon had us all in stitches with their antics. The atmosphere of the room was that of rowdy fun as the mood grew light and the laughter ran wild along with the ideas.

I think we all knew in some way that this was only the beginning of something very big, and we were giddy with anticipation. We were not just going to be going on a pub crawl to celebrate Halloween. We were not even just going out to celebrate the publishing of our first book, either. It was more than that. We were celebrating *our* independence from fear, not just for Angel but all of us. We were sending out an open invitation to all: to those who believed, who wanted change for the better, we offered them a way. We were inviting them to learn to be more. We were striking our match and lighting that candle. For those that sought our deaths, we were telling them to come and get it, that we were no longer willing to hide in the shadows or let shadows be cast over the rest of our kind.

The next few days flew by, even the late nights seemed no bother, as this elevated mood stayed with us. We were not to be brought down, because we knew that, in essence, we were about to go out, get really drunk, and tell the bad guys to 'bring it.'

~21~

The Wizard

I awoke with a start. Something was breathing on my neck and it didn't feel like Angel's soft breath. It was stronger, almost gusting from its nostrils. I opened my eyes and slid my vision to the side to see what it was. There was a hellcat leaning over me!

"Happy All Hallows Eve," Angel purred.

"Um hum," I agreed, grabbing her and rolling with her until I had her pinned beneath me.

"Thou shalt not mate with beasts...," she started playfully.

She had meant to intone this in her best imitation of the Elders when quoting that most dreadfully silly portion the Code, but I cut her off. I had always felt that was the most unnecessary portion of it, if one had a brain in their skull, and quickly had her too busy giggling to even try and finish. Besides, I was in no mood for such recitals now, I had much more entertaining things in mind.

"So what have you decided to be?" she asked me sometime later.

"I don't know." I answered. "What do you think?"

"Don Juan?" Angel grinned. "Or Casanova?"

"Whatever," I laughed, crawling out of bed. "Why can't I just go as myself then?"

"That's it!" Angel said, jumping out of bed and happily dancing over to me where we both stood before the mirror. "You go as a demon and I'll go as an angel. It'll be like old times," she added, laughing, "and we'll make such a perfect couple!"

I laughed with her then as she sprouted little white wings and clad herself in a short white toga. Angel looked herself over in the mirror, spinning before it and me. She examined the wings for a moment and obviously approved, because she then turned her excitement on me again.

"Okay, where are those horns?" she asked, examining my forehead. "I know they're in there somewhere," she giggled.

I couldn't quit laughing as I tried to concentrate, I had never done such a thing as this before. The closest I had come was when I had taken a Werewolf's form close to five hundred years ago, and that had ended badly. I had altered my eye sight or vision on occasions where such seemed warranted and even mimicked the Sphinx when none was looking, but here I was about to grow horns for real and wear them out in public. There just seemed something wrong with the whole idea of letting myself be seen using my abilities.

"It's okay," Angel said, noticing my nervousness. "No one is going to know. They will all just think you've done an awesome job with your makeup. No one believes anything anymore, remember?"

"Well, we shall see," I said, growing horns from both sides of my forehead. "Now what?"

"Make them a little bigger," she laughed. "Don't be shy now. Okay, now make your skin grey or something."

As she continued her instructions, I stood before the mirror and watched as I became less and less Demon and more and more demon. She soon had me clad in something resembling what a gladiator of my own time would have worn, and looking quite the warrior servant of Lucifer himself. She stood back, looking me up and down approvingly, and then, taking me by the shoulder, she spun me around to look at me from behind.

"Nice, very nice," she said after a moment.

"My costume or my butt?" I asked sarcastically.

"Wouldn't you like to know?" she giggled, sashaying from the room.

We joined Baylor and Grey in the kitchen where they were both already enjoying their coffee and awaiting those of us who had slept late after the long night before. I was surprised at the apparent normalcy of Grey and Baylor's dress. Grey was dressed as an Indian and Baylor as a Highlander. When I commented sarcastically on their choices I was surprised by their answers.

"How original of you guys," I said. "Did it take you long to figure those costumes out?"

"No, but it is defiantly good to wear them again," Grey answered for them both.

"Yes, it's not exactly a thing we can wear everyday anymore without getting stares," Baylor added, rubbing his worn tartan of green and blue shot through with yellow, and glancing toward his shoulder where Bane was strapped securely, just like in the old days.

I was suddenly nostalgic, as I looked at them in a new way, realizing they were right and how that must feel. I had stopped wearing the traditional garb of my people long ago, and were I to do so now, I would be laughed out of every place I went. I had even given up wearing the traditional tartans, such as Baylor wore now, that I had once adopted when living with him ages ago. I could see how it would be good to revisit my own past in that way for a single night, as they were, without it being considered incredibly odd. Yet I knew Angel was far too pleased with the costumes we had created to let me change my mind now.

When Piper, Adonia and Adreal descended the stairs and joined the rest of us, I was more than surprised, I was shocked. Their choices were simple but spoke volumes as to our recent state of minds. Piper was clad as a traditional media-style Vampire, complete with fangs and black cape with red satin lining. Adonia was done up as a typical media Witch, all the way down to the pointed hat, striped stockings and a broom. Adreal was, most astonishingly, a darn good Werewolf. I suppose if we were going to call them all out soon, and change their lives, we may as well walk a mile in their shoes first. Even though it was all in fun, it had us thinking, as we left out just after dark, walking toward downtown.

We received lots of stares and compliments as we walked down the streets, and at first I was very nervous about both, until Angel reminded me that everyone thought it was all just good makeup and effects. I realized half of the compliments stated those exact sentiments, and slowly calmed myself about Adreal, Angel and myself and the fact our costumes were indeed *too* good. We were even approached more than once by people who wanted to know how Adreal walked on those fake legs or how Angel had attached her wings so perfectly. Both times Adonia had taken over answering for us, as my tongue lodged itself in my throat.

"Oh, he can't tell you,' Adonia giggled when someone asked about Adreal's exceptional costume. "It took them hours to get him in that get-up and now he can't even brag about it. Which is cool," she added playfully, "he talks too much when he's drunk."

She had ribbed Adreal, playfully reminding all of us of the last time we'd gone crawling and gotten ourselves into trouble by following Adreal's toast. She waved back as the one who had asked the question accepted her answer at face value, and waved over his shoulder, running off to catch up with his friends. I began to calm down after that, realizing just how right Baylor and Angel had been, no one did believe anything anymore, even their own eyes.

We stopped at a quaint little restaurant and ate our fill, while laughing and making our own comments about the costumed passers-by, which were steadily growing in numbers outside the window. We got quite a laugh out of Adreal having to pass up the meal in favor of tilting his head back and dumping his drink down his throat, so as to give it all a touch of fake.

Later on, as we stood in our first line of the evening, someone bumped Angel's wings and she had yelped 'ouch' before she could think. The young man had been surprised it would actually hurt to bump someone's fake wings, and began apologizing. Once again Adonia saved the day, informing the young man they had super-glued Angel's wings on her and he should be more careful before he tore the skin from her back.

Angel and Adonia collapsed into a fit of laughter as the young man wandered away muttering his disbelief, saying that only a woman would superglue something to herself for a Halloween costume. The point that no one would question us was well made, though, and for the rest of the night I didn't worry anymore. Adonia quickly covered anything that could have led to our discovery and I assumed her quick wit was due to many years of practice. Yet I was beginning to think all excuses were completely unnecessary, at least for this night.

The night began much as the first time we had done this, with us having a drink and a shot at each bar we entered, and then moving on. Only this time we chose to avoid those oversized shots we males blamed for our prior behavior. Instead I found myself taking yet another bartender's advice and purchasing for all of us smaller glasses, of a clear, thick, cinnamon-flavored liquid, with thin gold flakes floating in it.

The bartender smiled, invitingly pursing her lips, and complimenting my costume as I put the change in her tip jar. I wasn't sure exactly what her costume was meant be, other than just ultra sexy and very tip-able. I also think she was actually complimenting my bare chest more than my costume, but I wisely chose not to find out about either her costume or her comment by saying anything more. I was not of the mind to risk further trouble from the women, so, turning quickly, I moved to rejoin my group before I became the blushing one in it.

Baylor and Adreal once more found themselves the center of attention on many a dance floor, only this time they received a lot of competition from Grey, and Adreal got a lot of attention for far different reasons than the last time. No longer was Adreal the only one with sleek, long black hair, and beautiful skin tone drawing many a feminine eye, however, his skill at dancing on his supposed stilts became the subject of much envy, and in a few cases, heightened desire. I'm not sure exactly how such things worked in some of those more intoxicated women's minds, but apparently they felt if he displayed such dexterous skill in that area he might also in others. I think we were all very thankful, at times such as these, that Adreal was unable to join them in conversation due to that same most amazing costume.

Time and again we were nearly brought to our knees with side-splitting laughter caused by some outrageous comment or costume. At one point, a woman dressed as a pregnant nun was just dying to know whether or not our Scotsman friend was a true Scotsman. She went so far in her intoxicated curiosity as to try lifting his tartan to see for herself, and I was sure Baylor was about to do more than just turn another darker shade of red; I thought he was going to faint. He had been saved from this revealing experience just in the nick of time, by a man wearing a thong, quite literally. Baylor's savior was dressed in a skin-colored body suit with a giant flip-flop strapped to his back. Baylor brought us to tears with laughter as he swore he'd have never thought he would be grateful to see a man in a thong, but this time he was thanking God for it.

Toward the end of the evening, upon entering yet another bar, the first thing we heard was the blaring beginnings of a very energetic song. 'Calling all freaks', it said, and I couldn't help but agree. I found it all extraordinarily funny. We all did. All of us were laughing heartily about it, knowing that was exactly what we were celebrating doing, but finding it funnier than we might have had we not had so much alcohol in our systems. I think a lot of our reactions to things that evening were due to the fact our shots were proving far more potent than their size warranted, and tasting so good we had long since quit caring.

We danced and laughed and somehow eventually forgot to move on, remaining the last hour or so in a bar that offered up its patrons and heavy techno beats to the gods of sweat and lust. There was a mood about the place that was simply too appealing to resist, bodies glimpsed briefly under flashing lights, writhing about as if caught up in some pagan sacrificial ritual. Too soon we too had sacrificed enough of ourselves out on the dance floor. We realized we desperately needed water, if we were to continue to pay homage.

Angel and I then headed for the bar, eager to purchase a few bottles of that life-saving liquid for everyone, panting and laughing as we were bumped and bounced, pin-balling our way to the bar.

"My gods!" Angel said, slapping my arm harder than necessary to get my attention. "Look at that!"

"What?" I asked.

I tried to focus where she was pointing. Angel had flung her arm out in the direction of a very tall man dressed up as Big Foot. The costume was good but I couldn't see how it had warranted slapping me. It wasn't, after all, a pregnant nun saying Hale Mary to a man in a giant thong offering her a drink.

"What?" I asked again.

"Big Foot, Yeti, Sasquatch," Angel started rambling excitedly. "Hell, even the Abominable Snow Man, they're all the same. Do you see? Do you see?"

I squinted at her, trying to figure out what had her so excited. I wondered if she had drunk far too much and was just rambling madly, or if I was the one too drunk to have seen her point.

"Yeah, I see it," I said. "What?"

"Look at it," she said, bouncing happily. "There is our answer. Hey, sober up a little and pay attention. Get the water, I'm going to get the others."

I turned to the bartender, who was asking me tiredly what I wanted for probably not the first time, and for a moment I didn't know what to tell him. I want to understand that woman, was my first thought, but when I opened my mouth, "water" is what came croaking out, followed a little more swiftly by "seven" and "bottles."

The others walked toward me with confused looks plastered to all but Adreal's face. His expression was unreadable but somehow reminded me of a lost dog, and I wanted to laugh again. The bartender took the money from my hand as Angel came into view herding the lot of them, and steered us all toward the front door. As we passed the man in the Big Foot get-up,

Angel pointed him out again and still I could not see why. All I seemed to be able to grasp was we were heading for the exit and I really didn't want to, until we got out on the street and she began talking excitedly again.

"What do we know about Big Foot or the Yeti or any of their other various names?" Angel asked.

"The myth or the reality as *we* know it?" Baylor asked, suddenly sounding far more sober than I knew he was and giving her a quite believably serious look.

"Both," Angel answered.

"Well, the myth is pretty much of a large hairy creature that lives in heavily wooded areas." Baylor studiously took a deep breath, adding, "Of course there is the snow version as well, but... Anyway, it tries to stay far removed from humanity, avoiding settlements of all sizes. It is assumed to be a lost link in human evolution, I think, and though sightings are widespread and some footprints or pictures have been acquired, no solid proof, such as bones, has ever been found."

Baylor grinned proudly at me for having pulled the answer off so well and slapped me on the back as if challenging me to do better, before he hiccupped loudly and gave the whole act away by giggling.

"It was, in actuality, a highly evolved creature, closely related to but far more intelligent than the common ape," I said, sobering a little, though reluctantly, and taking over simply because I was eager to know where her mind was going this time and wasn't about to be outdone by Baylor. "It was as widespread as humans were, only earlier. Though it became extinct very early in man's history, the form was remembered and passed down from Changeling to Changeling. Just as I learned it from my Master and you learned it from me, others have learned it from their teachers throughout time."

"And that is why there have always been sightings," Adonia said happy, to add her little bit and impressively outdoing both Baylor and me. "Footprints, but never bones."

"Exactly, because we don't die," Angel announced.

315

"Where are you going with this?" I asked, still confused.

"I think I know where Ra's sister is," Angel said, stunning us all.

"How?" I asked, "What are you thinking?"

"What form is older than even that of a Yeti?" she said, teasing us and enjoying our perplexed looks. "But has never been taught to any of us?"

"I hate riddles," Baylor griped, "Don't make me think anymore, just tell me."

"A dinosaur," Angel said happily.

"A dinosaur?' I asked, more perplexed now than before.

"Where's a dinosaur?" Grey said, looking around quickly and causing all but Piper and Adreal to laugh hysterically for quite some time while he figured out he had missed something and looked to Angel for answers.

"So we need to find a dinosaur then?" he asked at last, bemused.

"Yes." Angel stomped her foot in a mixture of amusement and impatience that this was taking us so long to grasp. "A dinosaur is the oldest known creature to have walked the earth," she added, "or swim in its oceans or other large bodies of water. But they are forms that have never been taught to any of us and still there have been sightings of at least one, even very recently. I think it is Ra's sister."

"Nessie," Piper whispered, "the creature in Loch Ness? You think it is real *and* it is Ra's sister?"

"Yes!" Angel jumped up and down in excitement. "I mean, it fits. Yes, most of the myths we tracked down began around the area of Egypt, but many of them at one point or other passed through Britannia. England, Scotland and Ireland heard them all. And the newest and most long-standing remains there to this very day. The Loch Ness Monster is quite probably the oldest form, being taken by the oldest Changeling still around."

"But that is impossible," I interrupted, once more the one to block her path. "One cannot gather and hold that much energy, not for any length of time."

"Oh, really?" Angel replied sarcastically. "What have I said repeatedly about our own disbelief being our only limitation? How many times must I prove it? I myself became a full-grown orca, and me only some forty years in the change." She smiled then, adding, "The universe bends to us, but its waters bow. And the one I speak of has been around *far* longer than a mere forty years."

I shut my mouth then and just listened with the rest of them as she told us of her ideas. Behind us, drunken party-goers began filing from the bar, in search of the taxi cabs or after-parties, but none seemed to take note of the strange circle of creatures intently listening to the excited Angel.

"We have already hypothesized that Ra's sister would have chosen to withhold the whole truth from those she made, if one she had made before had used the knowledge she gave it to begin killing others," Angel continued. "So it would make sense that she never passed down those oldest and most likely deadliest forms: dinosaurs. If Nessie is just a plesiosaurus form being taken by Ra's sister, then it would make sense that stories of Druids with the gift of shape-shifting were so predominant in that same general area. She never actually quit making Changelings, she simply began teaching them fewer of the powers that could be used destructively and more of how to use them to love and care for others, bringing them a different kind of gift: 'enlightenment.'"

"Yes, if she made the Druids, spiritual teachers, healers and leaders with just enough knowledge of their supernatural gift so as to make them believed and easily followed, my gods, then it makes perfect sense. We know Ra's sister left Egypt long ago," Adonia said. "So if she spread myth with her as she went, by whatever means, much as Ra, it was only a matter of time before it got ahead of her, taking on a life of its own. What she may have seen as a good thing could have been mutating without her even noticing it at first, becoming the things we see now. Then, when she did notice it, she could have remained in Scotland, taking her oldest form and even older knowledge, into the murky depths of the Loch. Why, though, to rest in her regret or feelings of failure, she didn't try to fix it at all?"

"Tuatha de Danann," Piper said, in another whisper. "Guys, I think

I know why the twins have always been safe with me now."

"Huh?" I asked.

"Well, the thought crossed my mind before now, but I couldn't make it mesh. I didn't want to say it might be my mother, when you were all thinking the woman who started those myths was responsible for what was happening to us," Piper said hastily. "I couldn't believe my mother was responsible for all those attacks, but I also knew she was responsible for others that had not been properly taught." He looked at the ground sheepishly. "You were suggesting preservation of ignorance as a motive, but you were also thinking it was one of Ra's siblings. It was all so confusing."

"After Adonia and I read Angel's journal and I realized that those Druids that changed their shape were but untrained Changelings, I knew my mother had left many of them ignorant. I could not fathom why at first, but what I did know was that she had been a Druid of sorts herself and had created others, others that she never told the whole truth to. At least, she never told them what she told me. I didn't, however, think she was Ra's sister; when she spoke of her brother it was not Ra she seemed to speak of. So even as I was quietly questioning myself, I was unable to believe it had been her and at the same time wondering if it was possible."

Suddenly I remembered how quiet Piper had been. I had thought it due to so many other things, but never even come near to this. I remembered then, that what rare comments he had made, had been short and seemed hard for him to swallow. I also remembered his sudden willingness to jump into the conversations when they had turned into a search for one of Ra's sister's first offspring and not her herself. We all stood dumbfounded on the sidewalk, in front of the bar, as Piper continued explaining.

"When you all were searching out the roots of myth, still so sure that the one responsible for all the other myths was responsible for hunting down others of us, I couldn't believe it," Piper continued apologetically. "Even as we figured out that most of those myths had begun just like the Druids, with ignorance as to our true nature being promoted by someone not teaching everything. I mean, you all thought this same someone was actually killing those that were putting an end to ignorance by teaching others better. I knew my mother hadn't taught others as fully as she had me, but there was not one mean or evil bone in her body."

"She was always so loving and kind," Piper continued softly. "You must understand, I was trying to see my mother as something less than what I had always known, and I could not. She had been a teacher and healer; she loved music, poetry, all things of beauty, and above all, me." He paused, looking pointedly at me, silently asking to be understood as he added, "Not to mention she never spoke of your Master, at least not in such a way I could put the two together until now."

Piper's eyes were pleading that we understand the reason for his silence. He continued quickly, as though afraid we were going to condemn him at any moment, "I mean, it made sense in some ways, because she had known of the Council, which seemed to fit with your reasoning. I remember she had directed me how to find it not long after it had been formed. She said if I ever met any trouble I could not fix on my own, and she could not be found, that I could find help from them in Rome.

"Yet you were all discussing this *evil* one as having had part in the Council's formation. I still could not believe she would kill anyone or anything or teach anyone else to. Though I knew she had known of it, I could not believe she had helped to form it. You must believe I never thought she really could have been the one we sought, or I would have said something sooner. I was just trying to sort it out. I knew there had to be another explanation for everything. Even at that, I, we, had never been able to find her before, so what good would it do to tell you that you might possibly looking for my mother, yet again? I mean I didn't think her *that* old, not old enough to have been Ra's sister. So I just kept thinking and stayed silent."

"I kept trying to see it from your point of view. Then when you realized it could just as likely be one of Ra's sister's first offspring, saying anything still did no good. I still had no clue how to find my mother, haven't since before you guys were even born," he said, glancing at Adonia and Adreal apologetically.

"It's okay," Angel said at last, trying to settle his rambling and let him know we weren't going to condemn him. "Just tell us what you are thinking now."

"I knew she was old, as I had said before, and I knew she had propagated such half-truths and ignorance before, but not until just now did I realize the full extent of relevance of those facts," he said, still apologetic. "Only just now did I realize that Ra's sister could indeed be my mother, and that you are right and she might indeed be found."

"How?" Angel asked quietly. She genuinely didn't appear upset, just curious. "What finally made it mesh?"

"Nessie," Piper replied, still a bit sheepish but no longer appearing afraid we were going to be angered he hadn't said anything before. "She loved the Loch and even after she could not be found, I have always found comfort there." Piper looked up at Angel and then me. "You wrote in your book about the strange level of comfort you drew from Demon's nearness, even if it was only residual, like you found on his chaise lounge. You wondered if it was because he had made you, because your souls had touched once. Well, I believe that it is more than that, in your case, but I do think I was feeling a part of her too, and that is why I felt comfort there. I think that is why I love the place and always feel compelled to swim in it. Maybe it is even why you found yourself drawn to it too. "

"You know this about my feelings for the Loch. I have told you as much before, just not in such detail. If Angel is right and the creature sighted in Loch Ness is Ra's sister, and I too am right and that is my mother I feel there, then we now know why the twins have always been safe with me. I too would then be a direct descendant of one of the First Born, just like Demon."

Piper went silent then and we all just stared at him. I don't think any of us really blamed him. That wasn't what the staring was about. It wasn't like he had come up with any definitive answers we had really needed, and then withheld them from us. He himself had barely noted the relationship of his mother's love of the Loch and the feeling it gave him in relation to an old Changing knowing an old form, and put it all together. I could not blame him for doing as he had always done, silently digesting his fears rather than spilling them out upon the rest of us when it might not be necessary. I don't think any one else could blame him either. I think we were staring because we were shocked he had been *afraid* to share his fears with us.

I probably would have done much the same thing had the roles been reversed. Had I not defended Ra's sister only because of her relation to my Master, felt her incapable of such things merely because of her relation to someone I loved? Knowing the answer to that question was a resounding yes, how then could I think to judge Piper's silence in defense of the one he called Mother? It was just hard to be made to realize that one we had known so long had actually been afraid to share his thoughts with us. Had we grown so mad in our quest for our enemy that we were unknowingly alienating each other?

"What has that to do with the Tuatha De Danann?" Grey asked, obviously unfazed by Piper having said nothing before. "What is that, anyway?"

"The folk of the god whose mother is Dana," Baylor translated softly, as if he had slipped far back in time to retrieve the answer. "They were a legendary people said to have brought us enlightenment. They came bringing knowledge, music and poetry. Piper's mother was one of them. Yes?" Baylor looked to Piper for confirmation.

Piper nodded. "Actually, now I look back, I think she may have led them. You see, she was old by all means but I never thought, well anyway, it doesn't matter what I thought or didn't, now." He looked at us all then. "The point is that when you guys put it the way you did a moment ago, speaking of Ra's sister spreading myth with her as she traveled away from Egypt and sharing just enough of her gift with others so that they could help her to bring enlightenment, that description fit the mother I had always known. That is what made it click, if you will. I was no longer trying to see her as anything more than what I had always known, because you had just described her right and well. Then I remembered something else that made it fit all the better.

321

"My mother spoke once of leaving some area with her brother, which follows could have been Egypt and the other brother besides Ra, and moving through Persia, Greece and Turkey, fleeing the misconception she was a being to be worshiped and trying to spread the appreciation of beauty with a group of those she had trained to help her. This misconception she'd been fleeing would have been the one began by Ra, that they were gods, and that too fits my mother to a tee. She said once that she had been called by different names, one of which was Dana. It meant nothing to me then, just a name she had been given and ran away from at some point in time, but it all makes sense to me now. Maybe it would have sooner, had I not been so afraid I was going to be forced to realize my mother really was the one hunting us, and for this I am sorry."

"Seems Rajesh was right after all," Baylor said, surprising all of us with his recollection and sounding not the least upset with Piper either. "Piper too is the reborn of a goddess of old. Dana."

"Anu," Piper corrected him, "Mother or Anu. She never wanted to be worshiped and never answered to anything more. This is another reason I never put it together, she had only mentioned the name once and would have been very disappointed in me were I to have repeated it. She was always adamant she was no goddess by any name."

We all stood stock still and aghast. His look resembled a trapped animal, much as it had the morning he had woke up with a redhead in his bed. I said as much, while patting him on the back to let him that he had done us no great wrong.

"None of us blame you," I announced. "It's not like you withheld vital information. You just figured it out along with the rest of us."

"I haven't lost your trust?" Piper asked.

"No," Angel answered for me. "You are family. I can only wish we would have been more approachable and that you wouldn't have felt unable to talk to us about your fears, but I feel I must take some blame for that. I get so headstrong when I think I am on the right scent." She looked over at me then, smiling apologetically, adding, "I probably would have done much the same if it had been assumed someone I knew and loved had been responsible."

"You will have to tell us everything now, you know," I added, dropping my arm over his shoulder. "I would like to hear more about your mother before we go to find her."

"I smell another good story here," Angel agreed, laughingly. "At the very least, some significant additions to this one."

"Of course," Piper laughed then, obviously feeling a great weight had been lifted from him. "But can we go home first, I suddenly don't feel like dancing, I've been dancing for months it seems, and I don't want to stand here all night either."

"Sure the bars are closing now anyway," I said. "And you'll want to get plenty of sleep tonight."

"Why?" Piper asked.

"Because tomorrow we drop form and go back to Scotland," I announced. "And you're going to be doing a lot of talking when we get there."

"Good, I was afraid you would suggest flying," Baylor said, not at all surprised by my announcement and taking it in stride. "Planes are made for little people."

"We're going to Scotland, tomorrow?" Grey asked, sounding a little scared.

"Yes," Angel said. "Why? You aren't afraid of dropping your form, are you?"

"No," Grey replied, embarrassed. "I've just never been across the oceans."

"Well now, let me tell you, Lad," Baylor said, dropping into his old Scottish brogue and causing us all to laugh again. "The first time's always the scariest, but once you've done it, you'll find you like it quite well."

We headed home full of even more purpose than we had left with. We had finally caught the scent of a very old one, quite possibly another one of the First Born, but even if we never found Ra's sister in Scotland and it simply turned out to be someone else, it would still have to be old enough to tell us something. Beyond that, the book would be on shelves soon, and all else failing, an old one would find us. We had laid out our bait and it was going to print. Once we laid waste to the ignorance, Death had tried to see kept all of us weak and easy to kill, he would be drawn out. It had begun. The one we sought was going to come to us, and in the meantime we were all on the highest of clouds, only hours away from a good old-fashioned hunt. Only this time we were hunting a Changeling, instead of one hunting us, and we were more than ready.

Or so we hoped.

"Oh, damn!" I said as we turned a corner and headed down Elm Street.

"What?" Angel asked, instantly concerned.

"What will we do about the house?" I asked.

"What about the house?" she asked, missing what I myself had just barely remembered.

"Who will keep it up?" I said, enjoying the rarity of having thought of something before her.

"Oh! Never mind that," she replied, taking winds of pride from my assuming sails. "I was just going to call the lawyer and leave a detailed message for him in the morning. We'll just leave the keys hidden somewhere for him and have him find someone to care for the house. He can handle all our other business here for us while we're gone."

"Are you sure?" I asked, glad then despite myself that she always seemed a step ahead of me. "I mean, yes, he would be a perfect choice, but will he do it?"

"Yes, but he'll need access to your bank account," Angel laughed. "You know, I don't really mind so much now that I closed mine."

"I can see that!" I said, laughing too.

As we walked I noticed that Baylor kept looking over his shoulder, as though he feared we were being followed. Angel apparently noticed it too, because she made a comment before I could.

"What are you looking for?" Angel asked.

"Just making sure I'm not being followed home," Baylor said, cracking a grin and adding, "by some overly large-breasted redhead."

I wasn't so sure that was all it was, though. I got the distinct impression he had been scenting the blood lust again and just didn't want to worry Angel. I thought I would ask him later, but for now I let it go and grinned at Angel as she bought his excuse and poked him for the purchase.

"Have courage, my perpetually red-faced friend," Angel replied.

"Courage?" Piper said, sticking his foot in it again. "Need more than that with you two women around."

I grimaced even before Adonia opened her mouth.

"Well, if you had any brains, when in the presence of boobs...," Adonia began.

"If you had a heart...," Piper cut her off.

Seeing the opportunity laid out so beautifully before me, I simply couldn't help but take it, and I cut all of them off by quickly changing into Dorothy and turning to Adreal.

"Seems we all need to see a Wizard!" I announced, waving Adreal to my side, "Come on, Toto!"

Adreal followed my lead instantly, dropping to all fours and taking on the famed terrier's form. He ran along after me as I skipped down the road, singing "we're off to see the wizard!" The others found they couldn't help but follow me either. Baylor turned into a lion, while Adonia became a scarecrow and Piper a tin-man. They ran to catch up and fall in beside me, skipping and singing along. Angel was left behind with Grey, watching open-mouthed and frustrated she'd been left the least appealing choice.

"I'll get you, my pretty!" Angel finally called after us, accepting what was left and becoming a witch to give chase.

Poor Grey stood a moment longer, probably bemoaning the fact he had gotten himself reborn into the wrong family, and thinking us all quite mad. Eventually he too gave up fighting it and, changing into a winged monkey, came hopping down the street behind Angel. We were all laughing as we reached the porch, hoping any that might have witnessed our antics simply found they were unable to believe their own eyes.

Afterward

There was a heartbreak echoing in the Empyrean. ..

The quite peaceful oblivion, of countless sleeping spirits, was irrevocably shattered as it sounded over and over again. There was no hope of reversal now. The normally calm surface of the pool that was neglected consciousness would not be stilled. It rumbled and rolled through the heavens, in repeating waves of pain. It thrashed itself ruthlessly upon the rocky shores of a million forgetful souls, which chose to try and ignore it, rather than be reminded how to feel.

Yet there was still recognition, moments when one could not help but remember, when one responded thoughtlessly, if only for a moment, because there are some things a soul never forgets. That was the way of things there, these were the tired ones, the ones that no longer wanted to be, let alone feel, and yet, on the crest of an echo, couldn't resist.

As I have said, though, there are some things a soul never forgets. There are also things one always regrets.

Regrets...

When sweeping the fields of their golden dust,
Blown low beneath the marble moon,
And disregarding their touch of rust,
Autumn colors for Winter gloom;
I allowed, just for once, my soul to wander,
From one memory, to that, then another.
Finding one in which I wounded myself,
On the dual-edged tongue of a lover;
It called to me from leaf-strewn vales,
Like words now cracked and yellowed,
Bespeaking tome-less loves and other ails,
Dying whispers of things once bellowed.
As I slipped into the softer warmth of gray,
And whiteness aged to a darker shade,
I allowed the caressing fog to lure me away;
When all purer comforts had decayed;
But I realized tears were the blood of the soul,
On the pale velvet of my cheek,
Cried for all the passing dreams of youth,
And all the words I would never speak.
And the tongue-numbing awe that stung my being,
Begging me, beyond my scope, not to forget,
Shook with the echoes of another's pain.
It demands I escape further regret...

Coming soon

Myth's Requiem

By C. C. Guice

The First Born Saga

Book Three

www.ingramcontent.com/pod-product-compliance
Lightning Source LLC
Chambersburg PA
CBHW022210010726
47493CB00002B/491